MADE MEN VIII

DOMINIC

SARAH BRIANNE

YOUNG INK PRESS

Young Ink Press Publication

YoungInkPress.com

Connect with Sarah:

AuthorSarahBrianne@gmail.com

www.facebook.com/AuthorSarahBrianne

@AuthorSarahBri

DOMINIC

PROLOGUE
O-V-E-R-C-O-M-E

Dominic stood in front of the dark, mahogany desk that he grew up seeing his father sit behind. For twenty-seven years, he had watched his father's black eyes become soulless more and more each day, until not even a thousand bright lights could bring a sparkle to them.

With his rich, hazel eyes, Dominic stared at the old, brown, tufted leather chair until Lucifer "appeared," sitting in the high-back seat, disapprovingly staring back.

"Why did you call a meeting so late?"

He tore his eyes from his father's mirage to look at his middle brother who, if he wasn't covered in tattoos from the neck down, would have been the spitting image of a young Lucifer.

Matthias didn't wait for an answer, continuing to speak with urgency. "If we're making a plan to get Angel back, we should do it in the morning when everyone's well-rest—"

"We're not making a plan to get him back," Dominic broke it to him harshly.

"What the fuck do you mean, *we're not getting Angel back*?"

"You heard the Carusos …" Looking at an angered Matthias, it was clear his brother knew what it meant to leave their brother behind in the Carusos' care. The two had shared everything, including a womb, both not only the spitting image of their father but of each other.

The twins were extraordinary—until they were split apart. What had made them alluring quickly vanished. It was like looking at half of a person when they weren't together, and unfortunately for Matthias it was impossible not to compare the two. One twin was superior; sadly for Matthias, it wasn't him. He needed his twin to be whole and to survive.

"Angel's their insurance till the contract is complete."

"You know Lucca; that could be months … years!" His brother's erratic voice echoed off the concrete floors. "We can't just sit here and do nothing!"

"We're not." For the first time, Dominic didn't look at him like a brother, but a soldier. "We complete the contract."

Even though Matthias's almost-black eyes turned into slits, he saw the betrayal in them. "You've already gone to the Carusos begging for forgiveness, and handing over your own brother without even so much as a fight. Our father would kill you where you stand for what you've managed to do to the Luciano name."

Turning back to the Luciano throne, Lucifer still sat there as stone cold as his pale skin.

"He's why we're here in the first place."

Lucifer Luciano had been as depraved as a person could be, and unknown to Dominic, years ago, his father had left his mark on a fourteen-year-old girl with a knife, promising her that he'd return to claim her at eighteen. The Caruso underboss was also transfixed by the same girl, and while the two men were cut from the same psychopathic cloth, Lucca had not only taken her from Lucifer's grasp, but he'd also taken her heart. Unable to accept defeat after years of waiting for his prize, Lucifer stormed the Caruso family home, shooting Lucca's bodyguard five times before taking the sole thing that could start a war.

Chloe Masters.

Dominic and his brothers were still alive because the girl told Lucca they protected her from Lucifer until the Carusos had shown up. The only reason the two mafia families of Kansas City weren't at war now was because of the contract Dominic had agreed to, which the Carusos ensured by holding Angel's life in their hands.

"Don't worry, I plan to uphold the Luciano name." The oldest Luciano spoke the promise so fiercely into the ether, it almost shook the ground beneath his feet.

The loud creak of the rusty door had both brothers looking at the youngest of the Luciano siblings.

"Everyone's here," Cassius informed them with a little nod of his teenage head.

Putting his back to his father's image, Dominic stood proudly in front of the throne. "Send them in."

The youngest brother held the metal door open as men filed into the abandoned factory that Lucifer claimed years ago. It wasn't an ideal place to run a crime family, but there weren't many options on the shit side of the city.

He remembered the first time his father brought him and his twin brothers here. They had been children at the time, so the space had appeared even larger. Dominic thought Lucifer had fucking lost it when he'd told him they would run the family business out of the factory, while Matthias and Angel thought it was awesome, looking at it as a skateboarding playground. He couldn't even remember how many old T-shirts they'd gone through while dusting the space and the amount of blisters he had gotten on his palms from continually sweeping the concrete floor with the old wooden broom. It wasn't until their father placed the desk and chair—where he sat now—did he see Lucifer's vision hadn't been crazy ... at least, not then.

Like every time before, each man took his place in line, but this time it wasn't to face the devil, but the devil's son.

Dominic's voice was firm as he spoke to the men. "As you all know, I had a meeting with the Carusos, and in order fix the pile of shit Lucifer placed us in, I had to agree to their terms. The first term will hurt all of us. I agreed to hand over 50 percent of our profits."

He heard the angry and exasperated sounds, but no one dared to say a word.

"Secondly," he continued in a harsher tone, "a Luciano woman will be chosen to wed a Caruso, in hopes to mix our blood and cease any future wars between the two families."

It was clear that some of the men were disgusted hearing the new terms; they weren't able to hide their expressions.

"Which woman are you going to choose?" one soldier, whose sole concern was about his dick, asked.

"I am not in the position to choose," Dominic told them the harsh reality.

Having heard enough, an older Luciano spoke up. "And you agreed to this? To not only hand over half our money to those rich fuckers so they can use it as toilet paper to wipe their asses, but you would let them fuck one of our women and have her breed with the enemy?"

"I did"—there was no hesitation in his answer—"right as they took our brother, Angel, as collateral to make sure I held up the contract. That's why you do not see him here." He waved his hand beside him.

The men's eyes went to the two Luciano brothers who stood by his side.

Matthias, who was on his right, looked to the ground at the mention of his twin's name, uncomfortably shifting side to side the longer the meeting went on. On his left, Cassius stood stoically, staring out at the men as if a single thought hadn't crossed his mind.

Thinking back to when he was in Dante's office, he remembered his final promise.

"You may carry the name, but will they accept you?" Vinny, the Caruso *consigliere, asked after Dominic told him that he was going to be taking his father's place.*

"They already have." Dominic stared back arrogantly. "They'll follow me; I'll make sure of it."

There wasn't a soul in the room prepared for what was about to happen next as Dominic reached for the cold metal at his back. The sound in the factory was the scurrying of rats before the ...

Bang.

Bang.

Bang.

Bang.

Bang.

Bang.

... gunshots rang out, piercing the ears of the living and the skulls of the dead.

When the sixth body hit the ground with a *thud*, the remaining noise was the rattling bones of the men who stood perfectly in place as the dead men around them had been taken out with a quickness not even Usain Bolt could have out run.

Hazel eyes stared down at the older Luciano who had made the "breed with the enemy" comment. "Anyone else have a problem with the terms I've agreed to?" Dominic asked, wiping away the droplet of blood that splattered above his brow.

Each man stood quietly, their answers given with their silence.

Looking over at the young soldier concerned about which woman was to be married off, Dominic saw he was now splattered with blood. Dom would bet the inside of his pants were no longer clean, either.

There was a difference between the living soldier and the dead ones on the floor. He had spared the soldier's life because the only thing he could be convicted of was ignorance. The six others, however, were the ones who had been closest to his father and had known about his sick obsession with the Chloe. Cleaning up the last of Lucifer's mess, while simultaneously placing fear in his men's hearts, was a two-for-one special he couldn't pass up.

"Good." Putting his Glock back in its rightful place behind his back, he snapped his fingers, motioning to his brothers. "Move them."

It took a second for Matthias to move. He was trying desperately to hide the fact that he had been startled. He wasn't shocked by his older brother's action; it was the suddenness of it.

Cassius, however, was a different story. Walking up to the dead body at Dom's feet, he picked up the lifeless hands and began sliding the dead man across the factory floor, leaving a trail of blood with every step he took. And even though he was just a teenager, he had his first dead body halfway across the factory before Matthias even began. Every single soul had jumped at the sound of the bullets ... all but one. The only reason he hadn't was because Cassius had been born without one.

Dominic swiftly spun on his heel, turning back to see Lucifer's critical glare as he sat on his throne. Placing his inked fingers on the front of the desk, he slid his fingertips across the mahogany wood, feeling the indentions of the grain.

"I will do what you never could." Giving his father one last defiant look, he whispered his final vow for Lucifer's ears only, "I *will* be king."

As Dominic took a seat on the leather throne, Lucifer's image disappeared into the wind; the ghost of his father vanishing as quickly as he had appeared. Son replacing father, underboss replacing boss, new replacing old.

Never once had he sat in it as a child, to dream about this day. He'd always known if he even touched his father's chair, the punishment wouldn't have been worth the daydream.

"Now"—Dominic sat back as he squeezed the tufted leather arms in the palm of his hands, the dark, gothic-style lettering of his tattoos spelling out the letters O-V-E-R-C-O-M-E across his fingers—"let's begin."

JESSE JAMES WAS A MEAN SON OF A BITCH

DOMINIC, AGE 5

Sitting *crossed-legged on the dusty* wooden floor, a young Dominic stared up at the small TV that was a foot away. A Wild West movie was playing, which looked fuzzy when the signal went out. It wasn't just his favorite thing to watch, it was the only thing he watched. He thought that was all the two-by-two-foot box played. When he'd gone to kindergarten and was around kids for the first time, they had asked him what his favorite cartoon was, and when he said he didn't know, they all looked at him funny.

Dominic quickly learned he was much different than the other kids in school. They wanted to play cops and robbers, and all he wanted to play was cowboys and Indians. The kids spoke of shows like *Bugs Bunny*, *Rugrats*, and something lame called *Thundercats*— that looked like a human fucked a cat—while all he knew was John Wayne, *High Noon*, and Clint Eastwood. When asked what he wanted to be when he grew up, Dominic confidently stood tall, telling the class he wanted to be Jesse James.

Jesse James was a mean son of a bitch who could dual and wield two pistols all while riding a horse. He was the greatest outlaw to ever live, and one day he wanted the name Dominic Luciano to go down in history, right beside Jesse James.

The front door opening had Dominic turning his little head away from the epic draw that was about to play out on the buzzing TV to see his father walking in carrying two baby carriers.

"Where's Carla?" he asked when Lucifer kicked the door closed behind him.

Without hesitation, his father answered, devoid of any emotion, "She's dead."

His little lip curled up, feeling a sudden sadness, but Dominic didn't let himself cry, knowing he'd be punished if he allowed any tears to fall.

Carla had been nice to him and even gave him ice cream a couple of times for breakfast when Lucifer was still sleeping. He thought he was finally going to get a mommy, but even at five years old, he knew he wasn't going to see Carla again. When they left for the hospital, his father had been looking at her the same way that Clint Eastwood did right before he whipped his gun out to shoot someone.

She had cried almost every day, and whenever Dominic asked what was wrong, Lucifer always spat out, "because she's weak," before mumbling under his breath that his sons better not come out weak either.

When he set the carriers down on the living room floor, young Dominic scooted his knees across the hard floor, the head of an exposed nail tearing apart one of his hand-me-down jeans. Peeking over from behind the carriers, he saw the two tiny, sleeping figures.

"Don't you dare fucking wake them up."

"I won't," he promised on a whisper, just wanting to get a good look at them. They were so small and perfect. They looked just like the baby doll a girl in his class always carried around with her. "What are their names?"

Pointing to the one on the right, Lucifer told him, "Angel"— before pointing to the baby on the left—"and Matthias."

"But, how do you know who is who? They look the same."

"You'll see when they wake up. This one doesn't stop crying," Lucifer said, pointing to the one called Matthias. "Like that," he grumbled when the baby woke up right on cue and began crying.

"Go get the bottle out of the bag on the table," Lucifer snapped at him.

Dom quickly got up and ran over to the diaper bag, pulling out the plastic bottle. "I can feed him," he said when he came back with the bottle that was still half full, wanting to help.

"That's all right." Lucifer took it from Dom's little hand and put it in the baby's crying mouth before scrunching up the blanket that had been covering his tiny body so he could drink it without anyone having to hold it.

Baby Matthias's tiny mouth sucked the rubber nipple until it popped out and he began to cry again.

"I can hold it." Dominic went to grab the bottle, but his hand was slapped away.

"He'll learn to drink it just like you did," Lucifer assured him, bottle propping the baby again, this time holding it steady until Matthias got in a rhythm.

Holding his struck hand, Dom used his little knees to scoot himself back to sit in front of the TV, away from his father's grasp.

Dominic watched the fuzzy screen, seeing his favorite part was about to happen. He had seen this part of the movie about a million times and mimicked what was happening on screen as it played out. When the cowboy blew on the end of the barrel, blowing away the smoke coming out of his pistol, Dominic blew on his pretend finger gun, then placed it in his jean pocket right when the cowboy placed his gun in the holster.

"Where's DeeDee?" Lucifer asked, intently staring at him from behind.

He shrugged. He hadn't seen much of her since she had been here watching him. "Asleep upstairs, I think."

"Go get her."

He quickly got up, following the order, going up the creaky steps to find DeeDee passed out in his father's bed. Dom shook her lightly at first, trying to wake the rough, woman who smelled like the yellow piss she liked to drink too much of. When she didn't wake, he shook her harder and harder until she finally managed to open an eye and slur out her words.

"W-What the hell do you w-want, kid?"

"My father's her—"

Without even finishing what he was going to say, DeeDee hopped out of bed the second she found out Lucifer was here.

Running over to the tiny attached bathroom, she threw water over her face and hacked out a thick spitball into the sink after clearing her throat.

Going down the steps, she was just as quick, with only a few missteps from the hangover. If Dominic hadn't been walking down in front of her, she wouldn't have been able to catch herself on his head and would have drunkenly tumbled down the stairs.

DeeDee tried her best to speak like she didn't smoke a pack a cigarettes a day. "Yes, Lucifer?"

"Watch the twins while me and Dominic go out back."

"All right." She smiled, going to get a look at the babies. "They are so cute, just like their fath—"

"Let's go." Lucifer pushed Dom along, paying the woman no mind.

"What are we doing?" Dom asked as they headed out the back door and into the backyard that was a muddy, desolate area where grass mostly refused to grow, only yellowed-green patches here and there.

"You're ready," his father told him, picking up an old, slightly scrunched up soda can that littered the yard. Taking it to a stump a few yards away, he set it down, then came back.

"For what?"

Lucifer pulled the pistol out from behind his back. "To become a man."

Staring at the shiny silver metal, he saw it glisten as the sun bounced off it, practically blinding his eyes, but he couldn't look away. He wanted so badly to reach out and touch it, to finally touch the thing he wanted most in the world that would get him one step closer to becoming a great outlaw like Jesse James.

He'd grown out of the toy gun he'd been given at two, when he realized it was for babies because a bullet never came out. He wanted a real one, always staring at the very gun his father was now holding out to him. But he would never forget what happened when he had reached out to touch it once after Lucifer had set it down on the kitchen table.

Dominic had been three, and his father had covered his tiny hand with his own, stopping him before he could even see how it felt. Lucifer had only said one thing, "That's not a toy for a little boy; it's a weapon for a man," right before he snapped his little wrist, breaking it. Needless to say, he had never reached for it again. Even now, he was sure it was a test.

"Well, take it," Lucifer insisted, pushing it closer to him.

"For real?" Dom looked away from the gun to finally meet Lucifer's eyes, seeing he had been serious. "I won't get in trouble?"

"You will if you don't take it. Now take it!" Lucifer snapped.

Jumping, Dom slowly reached for it, and when the metal fell into his hand, he almost dropped it, not expecting it to be so heavy. It felt different than he thought it would, but strangely right. When he lifted it again, he was prepared for the weight.

"Good, you're strong enough to hold it."

Dom wasted no time pointing it toward the soda can and pulling the trigger, only to hear it *click*.

Lucifer quickly snatched the gun from his hand. "Did I fucking tell you to shoot it?"

"I'm sorry. I didn—"

"You're not ready." His father shook his head and started to walk away.

"I am!" Dominic yelled at his back, promising he was. How was he supposed to know he wasn't allowed to shoot it?

"First lesson you're going to learn the hard way." Lucifer stormed back, snatching Dominic's hand and placing the pistol in it correctly. "When you put your finger on the trigger, you have to be prepared for the consequences, whether you think the gun is loaded or not."

Dominic's hand shook when Lucifer lifted the pistol, making him point it at his father's chest. Staring up at the barrel that pointed right at his father's heart, every death scene he had seen in the Wild West movies played through his mind, but instead of the dead cowboys, he saw his father in a puddle of blood.

"Your finger rests here"—Lucifer touched Dom's pointer finger that was resting along the bottom of the barrel—"until you're ready to shoot, and only until then do you place your finger on the trigger."

Dominic felt tears well up in his eyes as his father forced his finger to the trigger.

"Because you have to be certain of what's on the other side when you pull it."

CLICK.

When his father forced his finger to pull the trigger, wet tears fell to his cheeks and not because he was scared of killing him, but because he liked the thought of it.

"Now." Lucifer made him point the gun back at the soda can, then properly fixed his stance, showing him how to hold the gun while looking through the sight. "You're gonna stand there until I say you can move."

Dominic didn't say a word as his father walked back in the house, and no matter how tired his little body got or how badly his arms shook from holding the heavy weapon, he stayed perfectly in place without his finger on the trigger. Because one good thing actually happened—he finally got to hold the gun he'd been dreaming about.

Staring down the barrel at the scrunched-up aluminum can, he prepared himself for the day it would be loaded.

It wasn't until the last bit of sun was about to fall did his father come back outside to take the gun from him, telling him he could go back inside.

When his arms dropped to his sides, they felt like they had fallen off. He had to make sure when he was running back into the house they were still attached.

Going back in, he watched DeeDee place the twin called Matthias back into the carrier before propping a bottle in his mouth. The only reason he was sure it was him was because when DeeDee got up to meet Lucifer in the kitchen, he saw Angel sitting happily.

Dominic took a peek at the kitchen, making sure Lucifer wasn't coming, before he went to sit between his brothers, then grabbed the bottle to hold it for Matthias.

Sitting there, he fed his baby brother while he rocked the other one to sleep.

He supposed two good things happened today.

He got to hold a gun …

And he was no longer alone.

PATIENCE
DOMINIC. AGE 6

Dominic stood in the same spot he always stood outside, the dirt now slightly dipped from his constant weight. Going through the drills his father had trained him to do, he pulled the gun from his waist, loaded it, racked it, aimed, then pulled the trigger before he placed it back at his waist, then repeated it again and again until the sun went down. The only problem was … there was no gun.

It had been one whole year since he touched the gun, twelve months of Lucifer's gun-less drills and his father telling him to be patient. At first, Dominic thought it would only be a week before he could get the gun back in his hands, and when that didn't happen, he was sure he'd get it in a month. When that still didn't happen, time started to blur, and the only thing that kept him going was that he'd held it in his hands once. Hope was all he had to keep himself going, to be able to touch that precious metal again.

Dominic's six-year-old body had grown a lot in a year. His arms had toned from the motions, even though his hands had been weightless. Not knowing what he was training for, he looked like a dancer with how gracefully precise he moved. It was almost … beautiful.

The thing he hated the most was the stupid scrunched-up soda can he had to look at that his father had nailed into the stump. For twelve months he stared at that thing, wanting to blow it to smithereens, like Jesse James would have. The dirty can was his constant reminder of how he hadn't come any closer to becoming the great outlaw he wanted to be.

Dominic felt Lucifer's presence before he even opened the back door. It was another thing his father had trained him in, even though it wasn't intentional. It was a survival instinct the six-year-old ingrained in himself to keep from getting beaten for the silly reasons Lucifer declared.

He felt sorry for his twin brothers, who were just now starting to walk. The beatings were coming for them, and they were coming soon. Their size was the only thing that had saved them so far. That was another thing Lucifer complained about—how small they were for their age. Dominic might've had something to do with that.

He didn't let his brothers over eat, only giving them just enough milk and baby food to keep them from going hungry. He did everything to try to hold off the inevitable, even if it kept his twin brothers from being hurt—even for a month—then it was worth it.

He hadn't been as lucky as Angel and Matthias. Having been born a hefty baby, he'd looked about "six months old out the womb," as his father liked to brag, proud of his firstborn's stature. So, when Dominic was six months old, he had already been smacked.

Seeing his father standing in front of him, blocking his view of the soda can, he continued his dance, never stopping until his father gave him the order to do so. Lucifer reached behind his back and pulled out the gun.

"You're ready."

This time, Dominic didn't ask why, and didn't hesitate to take the unloaded weapon.

The last thing Lucifer held out to him was the magazine, fully loaded.

Dominic took it in his free hand, but it wasn't until Lucifer moved out of the way, giving him the go-ahead, did he snap in the mag in one swift motion and rack the gun before bullets flew out, each one nailing the soda can until the only thing that remained was the little piece of aluminum attached to the nail. Dominic then released the empty magazine, holding it and the hot gun out for his father to take back. It all happened in under a minute.

That was the first time he had seen a slight smile touch his father's lips, and it almost scared him. Lucifer was a scary-looking man, but his smile made him look terrifying.

"Wait here," Lucifer told him, taking back the gun and magazine before going back inside.

He waited outside for about ten minutes before his father finally returned, this time with a much different gun in his hand. It was a matte black revolver, requiring the five bullets to be loaded one by one, just like the ones they used in the westerns he loved to watch.

Lucifer showed him how to properly use it. He first loaded the five bullets, flicked it shut with the flick of his wrist, then cocked it and shot it, hitting the stump right in the middle. This gun sounded fuller with a heftier boom. Dominic also noticed how his father's hand flew farther back than it had with the Glock, meaning a much bigger recoil.

Lucifer took out the bullets, then handed the empty gun over to his son before giving him the remaining bullets. "I want you to feel it, memorize how it feels in your hands, and load it. I'll give you one hour with it, but I better have four bullets when I get back."

The fear of his father was enough to keep those four bullets from firing.

Dominic did as his father asked, cherishing those sixty minutes like it was the last time he would hold the revolver. He began a new dance all over again, beautifully moving and ingraining the weight and feel into his mind. The hour seemed infinite ... until it wasn't.

"That's all you get," his father said, taking the gun from his hands.

Little did Dominic know that it would feel like forever before his hands would touch that revolver, as the cycle began all over again ... sans gun.

The next day when he went outside to practice, a new soda can had been nailed to the stump. Thankfully he didn't have to look at it for a year, only three months.

When Lucifer gave him the revolver to shoot his first shot, he had blown the remaining bits of the Coca-Cola can back a foot. After that, he was able to practice shooting every day, with a gun.

Over the next few years, he was given different guns, mastering them all, one by one. The targets got harder, farther, and smaller. Dominic had become so proficient that he outshot the cowboys in his favorite movies, and it was all because of patience.

That was the one and only good thing his father taught him.

Coincidentally, those were the last three months of peace for Angel and Matthias, before they were smacked across the room.

A BIG OL' MEANIE
DOMINIC. AGE 7

Making *himself a bowl of* Fruity Pebbles, he accidentally splashed some of the milk on the counter, too excited to get back to the western he heard coming back on TV after the commercial break. It was a Saturday, and his twin brothers were passed out in their room after their lunch, so he could actually watch his show without keeping an eye on Matthias to see if he was about to do something that would get him in trouble.

Plopping himself onto the dingy, green plaid couch, he took a ginormous bite of the sugary candy-like cereal that caused some milk to drip down the corner of his mouth. He wiped it off using the back of his hand before picking up the spoon to take another huge bite.

The front door opening didn't even have him looking away from Clint Eastwood on the fuzzy screen.

"Go to your room," his father ordered after shutting the door behind him.

Dominic looked over to see that his father had brought his new girlfriend over.

Girlfriend was what the kids at school said, but that wasn't what he'd call the women who came over to see his father. You were supposed to like your girlfriends, and Lucifer didn't like anyone. Not even his own children.

Lucifer slightly raised his voice for him to hurry. "Go on."

"It's almost over. Can I please watch the end and finish my cere—"

"I said, get your ass to your room *now.*"

He didn't understand. They always went upstairs to his father's room, and it wasn't like he hadn't been around Lucia the past month. She wasn't the nicest woman who had hung around his father, but she definitely wasn't the worst.

Taking one last, huge, sweet bite, he was about to jump off the couch when Lucifer crossed the room in a flash, snatching him up off the couch and spilling his bowl of cereal everywhere.

"I was just taking one more bite! I was going to get up!" Dominic yelled when his father started dragging him across the floor, first by his hand, then he stopped to grab him by the neck of his oversized T-shirt.

"Lucia, clean this shit up," he told her over his son's wails.

Quickly, a terrified Lucia jumped to pick up the mess.

Seeing her face right before being dragged down the hallway, Dominic realized something was different. He had never seen Lucia like that. He had seen her jump once when Lucifer had raised his voice at her, but she had never looked scared. She had the same look Carla did before she left for the hospital to give birth to his brothers.

He wanted to scream at her to run, but he was scared himself. Not for his sake, but for Angel's and Matthias's. If anything happened to him, he wouldn't be able to protect them.

It clicked for him then. Putting on a brave face, he no longer fought his father as he was dragged into a bedroom, then dropped. Closing his eyes, he waited for his father to hit him. Instead, he heard a door creak open.

Opening his eyes, he saw Lucifer throwing out old, dusty suits from a closet and onto the floor. When he stalked toward him again, Dominic was sure he was going to hit him now, but then he was shocked when Lucifer dragged him into the closet by his shirt.

"By the time you get out of here, boy, you'll be asking me how high when I tell your ass to jump."

When the closet door slammed shut and the darkness enclosed, the sound of the lock pushing into the doorknob surrounded him, echoing off the walls in the tiny space.

He guessed he was supposed to be scared, but he wasn't. Darkness didn't scare him. It was peaceful, a gift that kept you from seeing the horrors of the world. Small spaces didn't scare him, either. It was cozy, and the best part about it was, if he was in here, then that meant his father was out there, unable to touch him.

"A girl!" He heard his father roar so loud it came all the way from the living room.

Quickly, Dom put his ear up to the thin wall, trying to hear better. There was some shuffling, and then Lucia screamed something at him, but he couldn't make out what she said through her tears.

"You either get rid of it, or I'll help get rid of it for you."

Dominic pulled his ear from the wall, knowing what was going to come next, before the gunshot even rang throughout the house. It was quiet for a split-second, and then the fear finally set in for Dominic when he heard the twins crying from their bedroom.

Lucifer hated when they cried. Angel had learned quickly, like Dom had, after having their little legs pinched. Poor Matthias, it only made him cry harder. His boney legs were covered in purple and blue bruises.

Wondering if he would be strong enough to knock the door down, he contemplated if escaping would be the right thing to do, scared it would only anger his father more, or worse, keep him locked up in here longer, unable to protect his brothers. A small amount of hope arrived when Angel stopped crying, and he never heard his father's footsteps travel down the hall.

He didn't know how long he had been in there when he heard the front door open, then DeeDee's loud mouth.

Letting out a sigh of relief, Dom was happy their so-called babysitter was there. At least she would care for the twins and keep Matthias from crying.

Yawning, he lay down on the dusty, cold, wooden floor, rubbing the hand that Lucifer had snatched him up by. It was slightly sore, but it was fine. Dominic found that strange, but before he could figure out what was strange about it, darkness had not only surrounded him but his mind as he fell fast asleep.

The light glaring on his face like a thousand suns had him waking up from his deep sleep.

Lucifer studied him hard for a moment, as if looking for something before he walked away.

"It's Monday; you got school."

Monday? Shakily, Dom stood still, trying to get used to the light after being in complete darkness. He walked out of the room and into the bathroom, quickly relieving himself and cleaning himself up after spending what he couldn't believe was the rest of his weekend in that box.

Getting dressed and grabbing his little backpack from his room, he went back down the hall and into the living room, seeing his brothers playing on the floor with some old blocks.

"Bubba!" they excitedly screamed, jumping up to run and give him a hug.

Angel stumbled over some words. "W-we misses y-you."

"I missed you too." Dominic gave them both a big squeeze. "I have to go to school, but I'll be back later. Now go back to playing with your blocks, okay?"

"Otay." Angel grabbed Matthias's hand, making him go back to playing blocks like his older brother had told them.

Noticing the new, brown leather sofa, Dominic hadn't even thought about what had occurred in here two days ago. Even though he was young, he wondered what that said about him at his age.

He had heard the term "like father, like son," and right now, he didn't give much thought to Lucia and her death, but to how hungry he was.

Going to the kitchen after hearing his stomach roar, his father, who was making himself a cup of coffee, stopped him.

"You're going to be late."

Dom's stomach could be heard rumbling on cue again. "But I'm hungry."

"That's why they feed you at school. Now get going, or I'll have to come up there and tell them to mind their business when they ask me why you're always late."

He hung his head low. That was the last thing he wanted; even the principal looked at him with fear in his eyes. The only adult there who was nice to him was his teacher Mrs. Smith, and if his father visited the school, she might not be nice to him anymore.

Dominic walked out the door sullenly, quietly closing it behind him and beginning his journey to school with not even so much as a sip of water.

He never minded walking to school, not having to spend the time with Lucifer. Even though they lived in the poor part of town they called Blue Park, no one bothered him, mostly because everyone on this side of the train tracks knew who his father was and, just like at school, everyone gave him a wide berth. No one even cared to know Dominic; they got all the information they needed simply from his name.

Passing the gas station that he walked by every morning, he stopped to contemplate going inside and stealing something to eat since he didn't have any money on him, but then his eyes were drawn to a woman who sat outside with her young child. He had seen them around town through the years, always either baking in the sun or freezing in the cold. Today, they were covered in filth, and he never noticed just how skinny they were until his own hunger pains ate away at him.

Looking at her helpless son, who looked a couple of years younger than him, reminded Dominic how hungry he could get.

Dom had only gone a weekend without food; how long had the mother and son gone? He hoped to never know. So he put his head back down and continued to school, unable to steal food or eat for himself knowing they were going hungry too.

Kicking a rock, he watched it skip across the cracked sidewalk, only thinking about the fact that he was starving and not his father's crimes.

Realizing this, he muttered, "Maybe they're right to stay away from me."

The walk seemed to last forever, and by the time he made it to his class and took his seat at his desk, he practically fell down into his chair.

"Dominic, are you feeling all right today?" Mrs. Smith came over before class started and placed her hand on his sweaty forehead to feel if he was running a fever. "Should I call your father to come pick you—"

"No!" He quickly rubbed the sweat off with the back of his hand, trying to think of what to say. "I-I just forgot to eat breakfast this morning before walking to school, is all."

Mrs. Smith studied him for a minute. He was thankful when she didn't question him further. Instead, she went to her bag beside her desk then came back, handing him an unopened bottle of water and a box of candies.

"Sometimes my sugar likes to drop on me if I don't eat a good breakfast. This will help, but don't eat them all at once, okay? Just try to suck on some and tell me if you don't feel any better before lunch. I could go to the cafeteria and see if I can get you something."

"Thank you, Mrs. Smith," Dominic said, as the bell rang and she had to get all the students to their seats.

It took everything he had not to down the water as he opened it and put the liquid to his lips. He made sure to only drink half, not wanting to alarm his teacher. Unwrapping the candy, it was like heaven when he tasted the sugary cherry piece. He let it coat his mouth for minutes, sucking on the flavor until it became tiny and his patience for not eating it had worn thin. He felt better instantly, as if the little candies were medicine to cure starvation.

All morning he ate the candies one by one until there were only a handful left. As the hand on the clock was about to reach lunchtime, he was afraid someone would steal his box of candy—after all the envious looks he got—so he shoved the foiled-covered pieces carefully down his little jean pocket, then threw away the box as they went out the door in single file.

Getting to the lunch room and smelling the food made his stomach growl all over again. He wish he had gotten up fast enough to be in the front of the line instead of the back, but he patiently waited until he got his tray of low-budget food and sat down.

It wasn't his favorite school meal, but it definitely wasn't the worst, and it definitely wasn't DeeDee's nasty cooking. He practically inhaled his chocolate milk and Salisbury steak with gravy mashed potatoes. He even ate his peas, though he thought they tasted like mushed vomit. He saved his little fruit cup for last, savoring it and not inhaling it like the rest, wanting it to wash down the gross food he had just eaten.

When their teacher came to pick them up at the cafeteria, she looked at his empty plate. "Did you get enough to eat, Dominic?"

"Yes, Mrs. Smith. I'm feeling better now."

"Good." She smiled at him sweetly before addressing all the kids. "All right, single file, please. It's time for recess."

Excitedly, all the kids lined up, but Dom didn't care where he was in line this time. At recess, he always had to ask to play any of the fun games, like tag. They always let him play, but it was never fun because they let him win. Even if they were on teams, his team always won.

So, when he got outside today, he did what he usually did and played on the jungle gym by himself. Going up to the huge silver dome, he began climbing the bars to the top, to his favorite spot he liked to sit at. Going over the little curve, he saw a boy already sitting up top. He was about to sit on the bar where he was when the boy's eyes went wide once he saw him. The kid hadn't even given Dominic the chance to tell him he could sit there before he quickly moved, climbing back down the structure.

Maybe it was Dom's fault? He could have tried harder if he wanted, he could have yelled out to him that he could sit with him, but he didn't. Instead, he just kept his mouth shut and took his favorite spot.

At the top of his dome, he looked out at all the kids laughing and running around. *Maybe I'm bad too.*

"It's your fault we lost!"

Hearing a boy yell right underneath him, Dom looked down to see a blond kid bugging Bristol, a girl who was in Mrs. Smith's class with him.

"Nuh-uh! You threw the ball too hard at me! I couldn't catch it!" The girl shook her head so hard her blonde pigtails swung in the wind.

"You're so stupid!"

Bristol gasped like he had just called her a bad word.

"That's right; you're just a"—the boy smirked, clearly glad he had hit a sore spot, and said his next words so harshly that he practically spit all over her cute face—"*dumb ... stupid ... blonde!*"

Something inside of Dominic snapped when he saw Bristol's eyes well with tears.

Grabbing the monkey bar underneath him, he swiftly swung down and let go of the bar. His feet hit the ground with a *thud*, causing a little puff of dust to rise as he dropped right between them.

"If blondes are so stupid, then what does that make you?" Dom asked, standing face-to-face with the bullying boy. "Or are you that freaking stupid you forgot the color of your own hair, Kayne?"

The kids who had gathered around the outside of the jungle gym, all said, "*Ooooo.*"

Kayne's gold eyes that matched his hair turned into slits. "Everyone knows dumb blondes can only be *girls.*"

Dom crossed his arms. "Says who?"

"My dad!"

"Well, your dad is just as stupid as you if you think the color of your hair makes you dumb."

"And your dad is crazy!" Kayne's gold eyes glowed in the sun as he took a step forward, right up to Dom's face, even though Dom was bigger than him. "That's what my dad told me! He said I should stay far away from you!"

Dominic looked down at him, square in the eyes. "I guess he's not as stupid as I thought, then."

The blond kid stared up at him for a minute, clearly deciding on whether or not he wanted to "fight," like the kids surrounding them were yelling. Then Kayne finally walked away with a clear promise in his eyes; next time, he wouldn't be the one to walk away.

With a longing sigh from the students surrounding the dome, they all walked away.

Dom turned to Bristol. "You okay?" he asked.

Bristol sniffled. "Yes."

"Sorry. Kayne picks on girls because he's too afraid to pick on someone his own size."

"It's okay." She wiped the tears off her cheeks with the back of her hand. "Boys only pick on you when they like you."

Dominic's brows drew together as he wondered where the heck she'd heard that. "No, it just means he's a freakin' bully."

"Really? Because that's what my momma told me." Bristol's bottom lip poked out. "So, it doesn't mean Kayne likes me?"

"If he liked you, he wouldn't have called you stupid. You wouldn't call your friends mean names, would you?"

"No, I would never do that."

"See," he told her, wondering if the women around his father thought the exact same thing. However, he knew why Lucifer was mean to them, and it wasn't because he liked them. "You shouldn't let boys be mean to you, even if they do like you."

Finally, with the way he had put it, she realized how stupid her mom's words were. "Wow. So, Kayne really is just a big ol' meanie?"

"Yes." Dom laughed. "If he's ever mean to you again, you just tell me and I'll make sure he never messes with you again."

"Thanks, Dominic." Bristol gave him a big smile, revealing that her two front teeth hadn't come all the way in yet. "Do you want to come play hopscotch with me?"

"Uh …" It was the first time in a long time someone had asked him to play, and if it were last Friday, he would have said *yes* without a second thought, but today, he found himself at a crossroad. He was just about to say yes when he heard Lucia's final scream in his head.

I'm afraid I'll hurt her.

"I don't like hopscotch, but thanks anyway." Dom grabbed the closest bar, running away from her before she offered to climb with him. It made him feel really awful to watch a sad Bristol walk away as he climbed to the top of his dome.

Reaching his spot, he sat down and took a long, deep breath. Then, slamming his eyes shut, he began repeating the words to himself quietly, "I'm not good. I'm not good. I'm not good."

ONE BAD MOTHERFUCKER
DOMINIC. AGE 8

Dom narrowed his eyes at the minuscule target that Lucifer had placed in the knot of a tree. He tightened his grip of the Glock as he prepared to pull the trigger.

"Aren't you afraid he'll shoot his eye out?"

The voice he heard from the back door didn't break his concentration. He waited until the bullet shot out before turning.

Dominic couldn't put a name to the man coming outside to stand next to his father, having only seen him a few times before and always in the dead of night.

The man had never been allowed to come inside, nor had Dom seen him in the day. He looked like a shady character at night, but right now in the light of day, Dom stared at him in awe.

The brown leather jacket he wore looked soft from wear while the inside looked warm, lined in a wool. The ginormous collar of cream sheepskin framed the man's unshaven face and shaggy brown hair. He looked like a character all right, but not your typical, shady one on this side of Blue Park. He reminded Dominic of the men in his westerns. It wasn't only his coat giving him that vibe, but his matching brown leather boots and tight-fitting, washed-out Levi jeans.

Whoa, he looks like one bad motherfucke—

"No," Lucifer answered, staring at the tiny target his son had nailed.

The man reached inside his brown leather coat to take out a long thin box, pulling out cigarillo, he narrowed his eyes on Dominic. "No one will ever be able to say you're father of the year, heh, Lucifer?"

Dom's young eyes widened, amazed at the way the man was speaking to his father.

"What are you doing here, Anthony?" Lucifer wasn't angry at the sarcasm, which continued Dominic's amazement.

The man turned and stared directly down to his hazel eyes as Dom swallowed hard at the tall man towering over him.

"Good shot. Can you do it again?"

It was Lucifer who answered. "Dom can do it every fucking time I tell him to."

Anthony continued to stare him down through the smoke he blew out. "He doesn't take after his old man, does he?" Anthony winked at him as he insulted Lucifer. "Your old man couldn't hit a target unless he put his glasses on. He's nearsighted as fuck."

Dom turned his head back and forth between the two men, waiting for Lucifer to shoot him dead at the insulting way Anthony was talking.

No, he is one bad motherfucker.

Anthony started laughing, turning back toward his father. "The kid looks like he's about to piss himself. Don't worry, kid, Lucifer knows I'm just joking."

"Your jokes will get you buried six feet under one day," his father warned.

"You wouldn't kill me for a harmless joke." Taking another puff of his cigarillo, he asked, "Who can you trust as much as me, and who would do your dirty work for you?"

Lucifer must not have had a good answer, as his face got red in anger. "What are you doing here? You'll be no use to me if we're locked up in prison."

"Chill. I borrowed a car to drive here."

"Whose?"

"Urie."

"He didn't want to pay?" Lucifer's face went a deeper shade of red.

Anthony shrugged under his coat. "No. I told you he wouldn't. He has principles."

"You left him alone in the car?"

Flicking the ashes off the thin cigar, Anthony shrugged again. "Don't worry; he's not in any shape to take off, even if he could manage to get out of the trunk." Reaching inside his pocket to take out a set of car keys, he tossed them to Lucifer. "Figured you might want to give the final pièce de résistance in person. He called you a wannabe Caruso."

Dominic stood perfectly still, making sure not to draw Lucifer's attention to him at the apocalyptic rage that overtook Lucifer's face.

"Stay here with the kids; DeeDee's out at the liquor store," his father hissed.

Dom didn't release a shaky breath until Lucifer stormed out of the backyard.

"So, can you make the shot again?" Anthony asked with a smile, looking back down at him.

He nodded. "Yes."

"Show me."

Dominic turned on his heel to face the target, raised the gun to the tree, and fired off another shot.

Anthony nodded at him approvingly. "Damn. You're good, kid. Better than me, for sure." Dropping the cigarillo to the ground, he crushed what little was left under the heel of his leather boot. "Has your old man taught you the most important lesson about guns?"

He quickly thought back to what Lucifer had taught him, trying to determine what would be considered the most important, when the gun was suddenly ripped out of his hand and his feet swiped out from under him.

Anthony laughed down at him, tucking the Glock into the front of his pants. "Any motherfucker can take it away from you unless you have the muscles to hold onto it."

Dom watched as Anthony bent down, holding out his hand, but he didn't take it.

"Don't worry, kid, I won't punish you when I give a lesson."

Those words still didn't stop him when he rolled to his side, getting to his feet without any help.

"Always expect someone to kick the ground from under you. If you let a motherfucker put you on the ground, you've already lost. Stand like this." Anthony stood with feet braced apart, one foot slightly forward. "That way, you'll be able to keep your balance."

Nodding, Dominic carefully kept his eyes on Anthony's feet, not seeing the slap coming until it was too late. He kept his hand from reaching for his stinging cheek.

"Lucifer might have taught you how to use a gun, but he hasn't taught you shit about protecting yourself, has he?" Anthony said casually, reaching into his coat to pull his cigarillos out to light another one.

"No," Dom admitted after a few moments.

"You know why?" he asked through lips pursed tight, as he blew smoke at him.

He shook his head slowly.

"Then let me educate you. He gave you a weapon that he can take away anytime he fucking wants to. Knowing how to fight, now *that's* something he can't take away from you, and Lucifer can't control how you use it against him. You might want to spare a few minutes from target shooting to strengthen those puny muscles of yours."

"You know how to fight." Dominic found the courage to state

after checking to make sure Lucifer wasn't within hearing range.

Anthony laughed, flicking ashes off his cigarillo. "You asking for my help?"

"Would you?"

Anthony narrowed his gaze down at him, then lifted his gaze to stare off in the distance, as if debating his response.

The man might have talked back to Lucifer, but Dominic saw fear cross Anthony's face before he returned his eyes to his. "Why not? As long as we keep it between us."

"I can do that," he agreed.

"That means you don't tell anyone, not your brothers, and especially not DeeDee. The sorry bitch will break a leg running to tell Lucifer so fast."

"I won't tell anyone," Dominic solemnly promised.

"Then why fucking not?" Anthony gave him a hard pat on his shoulder that nearly sent him back to the ground. "My apartment is across the street from your school. Number 234. I'm usually home on Tuesday and Thursday afternoons. You could stop by for about fifteen or twenty minutes before walking home."

Dom didn't know if it was the cold wind blowing or the cunning way that Anthony was looking at him that sent shivers down his back.

"You better get inside, kid. You look like you're freezing your ass off."

Looking down at his feet, Dominic killed a dead tuft of grass. "I can't go back inside until Lucifer tells me to."

Anthony gave him an eye roll as he took his coat off to place it around his shoulders. The heavy weight swallowed him in layers of warmth. "That will keep you warm. I'm going to make sure the other rugrats aren't about to burn the house down. Go see how many times you can lift that log over there until I come back."

Watching him leave, Dom stared at the thick muscles exposed under Anthony's short-sleeved T-shirt before he went to pick up the log after shrugging his arms into the large holes of the coat. The coat was heavier than the log.

On the doorstep, Anthony stopped to laugh at him, seeing his predicament.

"The coat makes the man," Anthony quoted. "Your muscles are strong enough to either wear the coat or hold the log," he said derisively. "Choose which one is more important—freezing your nuts off or working up a sweat." Going inside, Anthony didn't wait to see which one he chose.

Dominic carefully took off the brown leather coat and placed it on a rusty old lawn chair before picking the log back up. He was still lifting the log up and down when Anthony came back outside when it started getting dark.

Anthony walked over to him to take the log away before putting the coat back on his shoulders. "How many?"

"Two hundred and three."

"Better than I expected. Take a hot bath when Lucifer comes back. Your shoulders are going to hurt like a motherfucker in the morning."

Moving the lawn chair, he placed it behind Dom. "Take a seat. You look like you're about to drop."

"I can't——"

"Let me guess; you'll get in trouble if you sit down."

Dom was nodding his head when Lucifer came back, yelling, "Dom, get your ass inside. DeeDee needs help carrying the groceries from the car."

Heading toward the door, he warily passed Lucifer. Just as he started to walk through the door, Lucifer flung him against the door jamb and jerked Anthony's coat off his shoulders.

"If I wanted him to have a jacket, I would have given him one," Lucifer snarled at Anthony.

Anthony shrugged, taking the coat away from Lucifer and putting it on. "My mistake."

"Don't interfere with the way I raise my son."

"Like I said"——Anthony raised both hands up apologetically—— "my mistake. You get rid of Urie?"

"Yes. Drive his car back to his business and make sure no one sees you getting out of it. I can't have my enforcer getting locked up right now."

Enforcer. The title of the man ricocheted like a bullet through his mind.

"Won't matter if anyone does; they'll keep their mouths shut," Anthony muttered, ignoring Dom as he walked between him and Lucifer.

"Anthony …" Lucifer stopped him before he could leave. "Next time, don't fucking bring anyone to my house for me to finish them off."

"Will do. You're the boss."

"Remember that," the Luciano boss warned threateningly.

"Won't have to. You'll never let me forget it."

Dominic lowered his eyes when his father's glare returned back to him.

"What are you waiting for?"

"Nothing," he quickly mumbled, racing inside, then running outside the front door to bring in two paper bags that DeeDee had left in the back seat. The liquor bottles inside clanked together at the unsteady way he was holding them, the soreness in his arms and shoulders setting in.

"Don't forget to take a hot bath," Anthony informed him as he got in the front seat of the stolen vehicle.

"I won't," Dom whispered, as if Lucifer could hear him from inside the house.

As Dom used his hip to close the car door, Anthony started the car, silently rolling the window down next to him.

"Loose lips sink's ships," the enigmatic character told him ominously.

Dominic pressed his lips together at Anthony's meaning, giving him a silent understanding.

Carrying the so-called groceries inside, an overwhelming feeling hit him for the first time in his life …. He might have just made a friend. But not just any friend, a *secret* friend whom Dom felt would be in his corner. Even if it was only the two of them who knew.

Dominic could deal with that, it was one more than he had ever had before.

THE LITTLE SECRET HELD IN THE BARREL

DOMINIC. AGE 10-11

Dominic sat in the darkness, blindly reaching into his jean pocket. He pulled out one of the pieces of candy he kept on him at all times. Unwrapping the foil, he popped it into his mouth, slowly sucking on the cherry flavor so he could make it last as long as possible.

It was a trick he learned that day so long ago. His old teacher, Mrs. Smith, had called his father right after school, concerned that Dominic might not be eating enough at home. He would never forget when he came through that door to find Lucifer waiting for him. He had dragged him into the closet to sit for another night without food or water.

The candy his teacher had given him had saved him, and since then, he hadn't gone a day without a few in his pocket. Whenever he ran out, he stopped by the gas station and bought them with the change he managed to scrounge up around the house. Change was the one currency his father didn't bother to count, so he never noticed when a few nickels went missing from his pockets.

Sucking on the candy until the last sliver disappeared on his tongue, Dom stood in the tiny confines of the closet, stretching his legs, before he began a set of exercises. He kept it light, careful not to sweat as he did sets of ten jumping jacks, high knees, squats, pushups, sit-ups, and even pull-ups on the wooden pole that once held the old suits.

Letting go of the rail, his feet hit the ground in the darkness, and then he decided to pass the time in the only way that kept him sane. Dominic lay on the cold floor, having to scrunch his legs to his chest more over the years as his legs grew. He felt bad for finding his own sort of peace in here, where he was safe from his father. Where all the responsibilities he placed on himself for caring for his brothers were gone. He hated that about himself, that a little part of him liked it when he was locked away while Angel and Matthias were forced to fend for themselves. And while that had it's allure, he hated it more each time he was forced to visit the closet, when he was forced to look within himself. It might've been black in here, but the mirror on his reflection was visible in the darkness ....

Dominic's tenth birthday wasn't like any other ten-year-old's. There was no cake or celebration, not even a "happy birthday" from his father. Instead, Lucifer saw the day not as a day to celebrate but as a milestone that Dominic was mentally capable for what was next in his training.

"Anyone can shoot a gun," Lucifer told him as he took a seat at the old kitchen table. "And just because you can hit some fucking target a few yards away, that doesn't make you special."

That was a saying he heard almost every day. His father constantly reminded him just how un-special he was, no matter how many times he hit a bullseye or how far out the targets were placed.

"But learning how to care for your weapon, knowing what every piece is for . . . that makes you a master."

Nodding, Dominic listened carefully, prepared to memorize every step he was about to teach, because if he failed, the punishment would be severe.

"Cleaning your gun seems easy, but this is where men make the stupidest mistakes, because it's supposed to be simple. It's also where you'll pay the biggest price if you accidentally fire a gun in your home. So, when you sit down to clean your guns, safety first. You unload it, then check the chamber."

He watched his father release the empty mag, and even though Dominic was certain there hadn't been a bullet in the chamber and knew his father was certain, as well, Lucifer still checked, racking the gun to see no bullet pop out.

Continuing to watch him, Lucifer then broke the gun down slowly, showing him how to do each step until all four pieces were laid out on the table. Four pieces that were nothing but scraps of metal apart, but together, they made a deadly weapon.

Dominic didn't think he'd ever forget it. Something about it was meaningful, even to a ten-year-old boy.

The light touching his face always woke him up when the closet door was opened, unlike when he slept in his own bed; then it was his father's footsteps.

Lucifer stared at him for a hard second like he always did. Dom never understood why he did that or what he was looking for, but he always walked away unsatisfied.

Leaving the closet, it was never his body that betrayed him; it was the light. He hadn't yet found a remedy for that and didn't think he ever would.

His first stop was always the bathroom, using it and cleaning the filth off. The second stop was checking in on his brothers, but when he entered the living room, they weren't there.

"Where are the twins?" Dom asked Lucifer, who was sitting at the table, counting his money while all his guns were laid out in front of the empty seat where he usually sat.

"They laid down for a nap, but you can go wake them up. Dinner's ready." It was DeeDee who answered with her rough voice.

Lucifer shook his head, pointing for Dominic to sit down. "We don't eat until after Dominic cleans the guns."

"Okay then." DeeDee closed the pot, then grabbed her cigarettes and lighter and headed to the sofa. If his mouth could water, it would, even for the gross spaghetti DeeDee liked to make with ketchup. It was like drinking the thick red liquid out of the bottle with a side of noodles. But with his stomach growling, even that sounded good right now.

His dry throat barely let him swallow as he took a seat in front of his father.

Picking up his favorite gun first—the Glock—he felt the weight of it instantly. Instinctively, he knew the little secret held in the barrel.

"How long was I in there?" he asked his father as he dislodged the empty mag.

Lucifer's black orbs coldly stared at him before he looked down to the Glock. "Three days."

His trigger finger, which was safely under the barrel like his father had taught him, made the slightest waiver ... right before he racked the slide, sending the golden bullet that had been hidden in the chamber safely flying out.

It had been a test. He knew it the second he saw his father's smug face, but he went on cleaning the gun, pretending nothing had happened. If he had acknowledged it was a test, then his father would know he had contemplated using it.

Lucifer got a large glass of water from the sink; he set it down in front of Dominic. "Son, I think it's time to know your purpose."

He quickly dropped what he was doing and picked up the glass, drinking down the glorious liquid loudly until there was nothing left. It took him a second to catch his breath.

"My purpose?"

"There's a war coming, and when it comes, we'll be ready."

Dom's little bushy brows furrowed. He didn't know much about war, other than people died, but he knew there were two sides. "Who are we fighting?"

"Another family, like ours," Lucifer told him, barely able to get the name out of his mouth without disdain. "The Carusos."

"Carusos …" he repeated the name, liking the way it sounded against his last name. *The Carusos and the Lucianos.* It was like the Hatfields and the McCoys but even cooler sounding.

"They're like us, but with a lot more money." Lucifer looked down at the stacks of cash he was counting as if it was nothing. "And more men. But I plan for you to have more brothers to help us fight when that day comes."

Dominic, who began cleaning his gun again, looked up at his father. "Is that why you don't want girls?"

"A woman has no place in a war," he told him simply, making the words and the reality of what he did in his past somehow even harsher.

Dominic saw how Lucifer treated women, and while he didn't treat most men with respect, his behavior toward women was worse. Much worse.

Dominic didn't get it. The only person in the world who had been nice to him was Carla, and she was a woman. All the girls at school were nice to him, even though he thought they stared at him a bit too much, while all the boys were told by their parents not to talk to him.

"What are we fighting for?" he asked.

"A long time ago, there was a war, and we lost. The Lucianos who were left agreed to a truce so the name wouldn't get wiped out, but in return, we could only control"—Lucifer looked crazed,

holding up two pinched fingers together with no space in between—
"a very tiny part of the city the Carusos never fucking wanted to
step foot on anyway, in their fancy shoes."

Dom's brows drew together. "So, we're fighting over land?"

"No." His father pounded the wooden table. "We're fighting
for *power*. More land means more money." He picked up a stack of
cash, fanning it out. "And money gives you power."

Dominic nodded.

"One day, everything that I put you and your brothers through
will all be worth it."

Picking up his second favorite gun—the revolver—Dominic
gave the barrel a spin, his voice traveling over the sound making his
words seem as if they didn't come from a ten-year-old. "Like locking
me in a closet for three days?"

"Yes." Lucifer's unrepentant eyes somehow turned even blacker.
"Especially for you, Dominic."

Squeezing the handle of the pistol as hard as he could, his
fingertips turned white. "Why?"

"Because, when we win and I'm gone … it'll all be yours."

Dominic's hazel depths traveled down to his hand, seeing the
tan color of his skin return to his fingers. Flipping the gun over, he
stared at his hand; his father had harshly grabbed it the first time
he'd ever thrown him in the closet. Since that day, he noticed his
father avoided his hands, while not caring if he marked his face or
torso.

It was as if the winds had changed in the house as realization hit. *He needs me.*

His father needed him. He was Lucifer's heir, and if the Luciano name was so precious to him, he was going to make him pay for it. One thing was for sure: the twins were never going to get his approval, because Lucifer saw them as weak, and Dominic intrinsically knew, no matter how much they grew up, their father would never like them. Dom realized why he let them live—he needed them as numbers, even if they would only be casualties.

Lucifer might say Dominic's gunmanship was nothing special, but he seemed to think it was worth protecting.

"Mark my words; I will be king of this city one day." Lucifer snapped a rubber band around a stack of cash. "I won't stop until my dying breath."

It'll all be yours.

Since finally getting to hold the gun in his hand, Dominic hadn't wanted anything. However, if he was going to go down in history as the greatest outlaw to ever live, he needed a city to run.

The only problem was that meant he needed Lucifer too.

AGE 11

The banging on the door started when the final gun had been racked, and when his father didn't make a move, Dominic got up to answer it. He almost missed it at first, seeing no one standing on the other side of the door, but then he saw something squirm at his feet and knew what lay on the porch.

"Dad ..."

"What is it?" Lucifer asked, getting up from the kitchen table. He only looked at the thing for a second before he headed back to his seat. "Get rid of it."

Looking down at the snuggled-up contents, he picked up the pink blanket that was wrapped around a beautiful baby girl. The blonde hair had him wondering why in all the houses in Kansas City had they picked this one, but when his eyes met her black ones, there was no denying it.

Taking her in the warm house, he glanced at his father. "Is she yo—"

"Don't know, don't care."

Dominic had to think for a minute. "I think there's some baby stuff still in the basement."

"I said to get fucking rid of it," Lucifer demanded with his hot tongue.

"But it's dark and cold outside."

The devilish man stood abruptly, going for the baby. "Fine, I will."

"No." The young boy did his best to match his father's tone. "Let her stay for the night, then I will in the morning."

His father stared at him with that crazed look in his eyes before he threatened, "I better not see or hear that thing. Do you understand?"

Nodding, he quickly walked to the basement door to get her out of sight before the devil changed his mind.

The six-year-old twins followed closely behind, wanting to be with their brother instead of alone with their father.

"What is it?" Angel asked when they reached the bottom of the steps in the cold basement.

"Hold out your arms. Strong arms, strong arms," he coached as he placed the chunky baby in his little arms. "It's your baby sister."

Matthias looked at the pink bundle in his twin's arms. "Our sister?"

"Yes." Dominic pulled a wooden cage into the middle of the room, dusting it off as best as he could before going back to his brothers.

He bent over, meeting them eye to eye, getting their full attention. "And we have to protect her. Can you help me with that?"

Angel was the first to bravely nod, then Matthias followed.

Dom picked her up and placed her in the old crib that all the Luciano brothers had used. He figured she was about a year old, remembering how the twins had looked when they were younger.

He'd been trying to keep his brothers alive since he was five years old, and he hoped he could do it again, but something told him this time was going to be different, considering the baby was a girl. Lucifer wanted an army, grooming his boys into men, who would one day control the city. The only women in his life were the many he used to try to fulfill those dreams, throwing them away when they didn't get pregnant or had a girl in their bellies.

There was no place for a girl in Lucifer's world, let alone a baby girl. Just like he had told him a year ago.

Angel looked up at him with almost the same dark eyes that she carried. "What's her name?"

Reaching down when she twisted the blanket open, he touched the chubby baby's onesie that was light pink and covered in cute little cats.

He'd heard a name somewhere before, unsure if it was on TV or in a book, but he had liked it, thinking from time to time of the beautiful name when he had been reminded of it.

"Katarina."

Sometime early in the morning, Dominic groggily went up the basement steps, leaving the twins and their new baby sister sleeping downstairs. When he reached the top and entered the main room, he rubbed his eyes, then saw his father still in the same chair at the kitchen table like he hadn't even left or slept last night.

"What do you think you're doing?"

Squinting, he couldn't make out his father's expression due to the morning sun that was shining through the dusty blinds behind him. He could only make out his silhouette, but his grim voice told him all he needed to know about his expression.

Dom looked down at what he was carrying in his hand. It was the old, light blue bottle he had found in the basement, along with the other baby stuff that Lucifer had saved to raise his army.

Bravely, he stuck his chin out as he squeezed the plastic and headed to the fridge. "I'm making *her* a bottle."

Lucifer took a sip of his coffee. "I told you you're getting rid of her *right now*." He emphasized that morning had come.

Picking up the milk from the fridge, Dom then slammed the door shut. "No, I'm not."

Within moments of the coffee cup hitting the table, Lucifer's grip encircled his son's wrist. "What the fuck did you say?"

"Go on . . ." Dominic's hazel depths traveled to his father's hand that was squeezing his shooting hand's wrist even harder. "Break it."

Lucifer squeezed slightly harder until the pressure eased a bit.

"You can't, can you?" Dominic looked into his father's cold, black eyes. "My wrist is worth more to you than I do, and you know it. When you crushed it the first time, it made my wrist stronger. That's why I can hold the heavy guns perfectly straight." A corner of his lip turned up at his taunt. "*Straighter than you.*"

Lucifer's mouth didn't move but his silent, black eyes did.

"If you break it again, it either won't heal this time, and you'll lose the best shot you got against the Carusos, or it will heal even stronger again, making me that much stronger than *you*." Dom flashed his teeth as the corner of his lip went up higher. "Your choice."

Lucifer released his wrist.

With his hand freed, Dominic began pouring the milk on the counter. "If she leaves"—he kept his face stoic as he made the hardest choice of his life: choosing between his twin brothers who he'd known for five years or his baby sister who had stolen his heart with one look just hours ago—"I leave. If anything, and I mean *anything*, happens to her, I'll walk out that door and won't ever come back. Then, the only army you'll have is Angel and Matthias."

He hoped Lucifer believed him when he didn't even believe himself that he could leave his twin brothers behind.

Lucifer stared at him thoughtfully for several moments before he walked back to the table. "I don't want to see it or hear it. You got me?"

"Katarina."

Lucifer stopped before taking a sip from his coffee. "What did you say?"

"Her name is *Katarina*." Dominic announced not only to the father of the baby but to the world.

Putting the milk back in the fridge, he managed to keep it together as his heart began to shatter.

He was heading back downstairs when he stopped, unable to turn around as a tear rolled down his cheek. He hoped his brave-sounding voice held his secret as he made one last demand. "And you will not lock me in the closet anymore."

When only silence and no violence met his demand, he got his answer.

If only he had turned around, he would have seen the pride in his father's eyes. It was the kind of pride a king saw in his prince—of the promise that one day the prince would uphold the family name.

Going back down the steps, tears streaming down his face, he thought about how he had escaped his father's wrath this time, but Dom knew he was walking a fine line.

Lucifer got off by having control over people; his children being his ultimate victims, seeing them as his property. Dominic needed to subdue his father's dominance somehow.

Unfortunately, when he asked not to be put in the closet, as to not leave Katarina defenseless, it meant he couldn't protect Angel and Matthias any longer.

He'd chosen.

Staring at his sleeping brothers on the blanket spread across the cold, concrete floor, the tears on his cheeks fell in droplets onto his old, ratty T-shirt. The two would only have each other to protect, and he wasn't sure if both would survive Lucifer.

He wiped the tears with the back of his hand and went up to the old crib. Picking up the baby girl who was awake and happily content, he held her in his arms and fed her the bottle.

It was inexplicable the way he felt about her as he looked down upon her. All he knew was he loved her very much already, and she was worth protecting.

He didn't know how yet, but he knew in his gut that Katarina would be more valuable to the Luciano name than he and his brothers would ever be.

Even if it cost them Matthias's life.

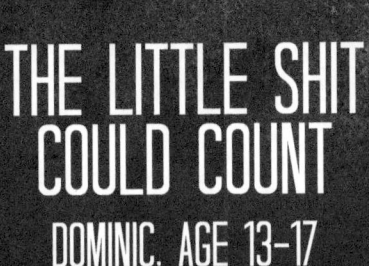

THE LITTLE SHIT
COULD COUNT
DOMINIC. AGE 13-17

Dominic ran down the basement steps from his first day back at school; it used to be his haven, but now his thoughts were about Kat and if she was safe while he was away.

Scrunching up his nose when he reached the bottom, he looked at DeeDee, who was passed out asleep on his sister's tiny bed. Seeing that Kat was fine, playing with her toys, he went over to DeeDee to shake her awake.

"I'm up!" the older woman popped herself up like the rising dead from a crypt.

"I've told you a billion times not to smoke down here around

Kat."

"And how many times have I told you I take orders from your father, not you?" she snapped at him with a bit of a slur in her voice.

Dominic's bushy brows furrowed, giving her a deadly look that had her taken aback.

"And when my father steps down, whose orders do you think you'll have to listen to?"

"Well—" DeeDee swallowed, her dry throat making her sound even more hoarse. "—I didn't smoke in here; you're just smelling me."

"Six."

Both Dominic and DeeDee turned their heads to Katarina, who was playing with her blocks.

"One, two, three, four, five, six!" Little Katarina clapped, proud of herself. "Six sticks!"

Going over to his baby sister, he bent down so she would look up at him. "What did you say?"

"Six *blocks*," DeeDee said with a nervous laughter. Going over to where they were, she began counting the blocks. "Look, one, two, three, four"—when she ran out of blocks, she counted two of the same ones over again—"five, six!"

"That's right, honey. Good job! You're so smart."

Dom rolled his eyes, but little Kat was the one who shook her blonde head.

"No. Four blocks," Kat said, pointing to her blocks. "Six sticks." Kat brought her fingers to her mouth, mimicking the way she had seen DeeDee smoke.

DeeDee's face instantly dropped its fake smile.

Dominic stood back up and folded his arms across his chest.

"I wasn't aware the little shit could count," she said through another fake smile. "Let's be clear. I promised I'd watch her and keep her out of your father's hair, not that I'd turn into Saint Mary while babysitting her."

"DeeDee," Dominic called after her as she walked away and started up the stairs. "If you stop the smoking around her, take care of Kat right from now on, and keep my father away from her, then I promise, when I get power in this family, I'll release you."

"Release me?" she whispered.

Dom pointed to his nose, closing one of his nostrils to breath in quick with the open one. "He gives you just enough, doesn't he? To keep you coming back? That's the only reason you put up with his shit, isn't it?"

She didn't say a word, but the deadly grip she held on the hand rail told him he wasn't wrong.

"Lucifer doesn't give you the high you want, though, does he? He gives you the hit that you need to function, but not enough to fly."

DeeDee rubbed her nose, practically salivating at the thought of her precious white powder.

Dom took a step toward her, promising her the world with his hazel eyes. "You do as I ask, and I promise, one day, you won't need him or his shit for your fix anymore."

It took her only a second to think before nodding, then going up the steps.

Running his hand through his brown hair, Dominic didn't know what was sicker, promising to supply drugs to an lady at the age of thirteen, or that he had to depend on a druggie to help protect Kat. However DeeDee was his only option, and she hadn't killed him or his brothers, so ... *how bad could she be?*

Not wanting to answer his own question, he went back to his sister and sat on the floor next to her. "Do you know what comes after six, Kat?"

"Seven, eight, nine, ten, eleven ...."

"What are you coloring?" Dominic asked, sitting down in the tiny chair at the plastic, colorful little kid table that he had picked up on the side of the road and cleaned up to give Kat.

His little sister proudly showed off her cute stick figures. "That's me, Angle, Matty, and ... you!"

Even though she was three and talked far better for her age, she still had trouble pronouncing her twin brothers' names, but it always made him smile.

"I see. It's so pretty, Kat. Good job."

"I love my brothers." She pointed to Angel's and Matthias's stick figures, then pointed to Dominic's stick figure. "And my daddy!"

Dom's mouth fell open at hearing her call him that. Stammering, it took him a second to get his words out. "N-No, Katarina, I'm your brother, not your father."

"You're not my daddy?"

He shook his head.

Kat's little bottom lip poked out. "Can't we pretend you're my daddy?"

She was starting to break his heart, but he stayed strong. "No, we can't pretend."

"Why not?" She furrowed her brows, getting more upset.

"Because it's important to know who your father is and where you come from, Katarina."

"But the scary man upstairs can't be my daddy." Her eyes started to well with tears. "You take care of me, not him."

Dom reached over, picking her up to place her on his lap. "Just because I'm not your dad, doesn't mean I don't love you just as much, and it doesn't make us any less family," he told her, wiping her tears off her rosy cheeks. "But I'm your brother, Katarina, along with Angel and Matthias. Our father is the scary man upstairs, whether we like it or not. But we have to *know* that. One day, you will understand why it's important to know that, and to know who we came from." Waiting until she slowly stopped crying, he wanted to make sure she understood. "Okay?"

"Okay." Kat nodded her head against his chest, understanding as best as she possibly could at her age. "I still love you, even though you're not my daddy."

Laughing, he gave her a squeeze. "Good."

Holding Kat's hand, he watched her skip beside him, as her tiny pink backpack that looked too big on her flew up with each skip.

"You excited?"

"Yes! I'm so happy I get to leave my room and finally go to school!"

He gave her tiny hand a squeeze. "Me, too."

When they reached the door that he and his brothers had once gone in every morning, he bent down to talk to her. "Okay, this is it, Kat. I'll be right here after school's out."

"Wait … You're not going to kindergarten with me?"

"No." Dom shook his head, wondering why he felt a pain in his chest. It should be no different than when he had taken his brothers to middle school for the first time, just on the way here, but it didn't feel the same. "I already went to kindergarten. My school is just right across the street."

"Oh …." Kat nibbled her lip.

"Going to school means you're a big kid now, and big kids go to school all by themselves."

"But Angel and Matthias go to school together."

"Well, they were born together, remember? We didn't get so lucky, so that means we have to be brave and try new things on our own."

"What if the other kids don't like me?"

"Some might not." He told her the truth, wanting her to be

prepared for what the last name Luciano meant. "But not everyone has to like you." Lifting her chin with his finger, he smiled down at her. "Plus, I know, once they do get to know you, they'll love you."

Katarina smiled big back at him.

"Now, what are we going to be?" he asked.

"Polite to my teacher and kind to my classmates." She nodded but quickly spout off again, "Oh, and now brave without you."

"That's right." Dominic gave her a big hug and had to clear his throat before he continued. "Now go on and have fun, Kat. I'll see you after school."

"Okay. Bye," she told him with a wave of her hand and a smile.

Dom didn't dare let a threatening tear fall. "Bye ..."

A YEAR LATER

Dominic gave Kat the biggest hug when she came running out the school. "So, how was first grade?"

"Wow, you were right. Mrs. Smith is really nice. Way nicer than my old kindergarten teacher."

"I told you. She was my first grade teacher, too."

"And you were right about the baby stuff. No more nap time; thank gosh," Kat continued, as if ready to be shipped off to college.

"Yep." He laughed. "It's all downhill from now—"

"Dominic?"

"Mrs. Smith." He stood up straight, the seventeen-year-old who now towered above his first grade teacher.

"I should have ..." Realization hitting her, Dom could tell she felt dumb when she put two and two together. "I'm sorry. I have so many students and names to remember, I must've not been thinking."

"It's only the first day," he told her. "Give yourself a break."

"So, Katarina is your ...?"

"Sister," he said the word along with her, confirming what she thought. "Yes."

"Listen ... um, I was hoping one of her parents would pick her up, as I would like to talk to them."

Clearing his throat, Dom looked down at his sister. "Hey, Kat, why don't you go sit down on that bench over there and let me talk to your teacher a minute, okay?"

"Is it all right if I go talk to some of my friends over there instead?" she asked, pointing to a group of girls who were waiting for their parents to pick them up.

"Yes, that's fine." Dom let her go, then waited until she was out of earshot before he turned back to Mrs. Smith.

"Kat doesn't have a mother, and her father is the same as mine, and I know it's been a long time since I was in your class, but I'm sure you know that getting my father down here isn't going to happen."

"I was afraid of that."

He continued, "So, whatever it is that you want to say, Mrs. Smith, you might as well tell me, because I'm all she's got."

The teacher thought for several moments before she gave in,

knowing he was right. "Katarina is … gifted."

Dominic just stared at her blankly.

"As in, her intellectual level far exceeds her fellow students. I believe she may be a mathematical prodigy."

"I know," he told her simply, clearly unfazed by the news.

"I-I …" Mrs. Smith had to think about what she wanted to say next, surprised by Dominic's quick response. "I don't think she belongs in the first grade. Hell, I don't think Katarina belongs in this school. There are much better schools out there for he—"

"No, thanks." Dom shook his head before looking for his sister. He should have known Mrs. Smith wouldn't have been like the rest of the staff, who turned a blind eye to a Luciano. "Come on, Kat!"

"Dominic." Mrs. Smith touched his shoulder, stopping him from leaving. "She's sitting in a class where the other students are still learning four plus four, for Christ's sake, and she can already multiply numbers that I have to use a calculator for."

"Like I said, I'm aware."

"Maybe this is something I really should have talked to your father about." Taking a step back, she tried to level with him. "I just think Katarina deserves an environment where she can perform to the best of her abilities, is all."

"If you think my father would give two shits about her solving equations that he has never looked at a day in his life, then by all means, give him a call." Dominic spoke to her quietly but firmly. "I wasn't sure if you knew who my father was back then, but now I'm sure you know exactly who Lucifer is, don't you?" Changing his quiet tone from firm to soft, he relaxed his facial features. "Mrs. Smith, I appreciate that, unlike the other teachers here, you care, I really do, but like me, she was dealt a shit hand on the shit side of the city, and this is the only environment a Luciano is going to get."

Looking to see Kat was still talking to her friends, he was about to yell for her again.

"I tried to help you, you know? Back then. I called everyone I knew, even Social Services, but the second they heard your last name, they all hung up on me." Mrs. Smith looked down at the pavement, her voice sounding as broken as an old record. "I'm sorry I couldn't help you."

"You did," he said, taking a step forward to place a hand on her shoulder. "You gave me a safe haven for eight hours, five days a week … and now that's what I need you to do for Kat."

Mrs. Smith looked up from the ground and managed a smile. "I can do that."

"Wait here," Dom said, when he got to the front door of their house. Walking in and not seeing his father anywhere, he let Kat in. When she booked it to the basement door and flew down the steps, he went after her.

"Are you going to tell me what's wrong?" he asked as Kat ran down the steps with her little legs.

When he had picked her up on her second day of first grade,

she had acted much differently than she had the first day.

"No!" Kat huffed after slamming herself down on her pink bed.

Sitting down on the edge of it next to her, he pretended to beg. "Come on, *please*."

Kat huffed, shaking her head, her pigtails that Dom had put up for her this morning swung adorably.

"I'll tell you what ..." He leaned over to whisper, as if what he was about to tell her was top secret and the most important thing in the world. "If you tell me what happened at school today, I'll go get your baby brother to come play with you."

"*All* night?" She emphasized the only deal she was willing to take.

Dom smiled at the lawyer in the making. "All night."

"Well, I don't really know what happened," Little Katarina began. "Yesterday was fun, just like kindergarten, but today, none of my friends would talk to me. And when Katy passed out her birthday invitations, I didn't get one. I asked her why, but she said her mommy said she couldn't 'cause of my name." Looking up at Dominic, she looked confused. "I don't get what my name has to do with not being my friend anymore."

Dom took a deep breath. He knew this day would come, but he'd hoped that Kat being a girl might have somehow made the Luciano name less threatening to the gender-stereotyping parents. Hell, he even understood why a parent would tell their kids to stay away from Luciano men, even if they were only boys. The whole city knew where their footsteps were bound to follow.

But Katarina was different. She was everything him and his

brothers weren't. She was smart, kind, loving, and funny. If they spent just five minutes with her, they'd want their child to be around her in hopes that she'd rub off on them. No one on this side of the city were upstanding citizens by any means. They all were poor pieces of shits, who either had a drug problem, a drinking one, or were suppliers to those problems. No one here was better than the other, *except Kat.*

"Kat, our father isn't only the scary man upstairs to us ... he's the scary man to everyone else too."

"He is?"

"Yes, he is a bad man out there too." Dom nodded. "And because your last name is Luciano, people are scared of that last name because of our father. But that doesn't mean they are scared of you, okay?"

She thought for a moment. "Did this happen to you?"

"Yes, exactly like you. Kindergarten was fine, because kids don't really listen to their parents at that age, and they don't care about stupid stuff like what you look like or how much money you have. They just want to have fun, no matter who they are playing with. But when they get older and get a better understanding of right and wrong, good and evil, they start listening to their parents, even if their parents are wrong."

"That's stupid."

Shocked at the simple response from a smart six-year-old, he couldn't agree more. "You're right; it is pretty stupid."

"Katy was my friend, even though her daddy smells like DeeDee, and *I still wanted to go to her party*. So she should still want to be my friend, even though the scary man upstairs is mine."

Dominic gave a chuckle. "She should. But you're smart enough to make your own decisions about who you want to be friends with."

"Well, then I don't want to be friends with Katy, or anyone else who doesn't like us because of a stupid name we didn't even get to pick, anyway."

Staring down at her, he didn't know whether he should be worried about the things that came out of her mouth or proud. However, he decided the latter was easier to handle. "Okay, then I guess that's settled. We didn't want you to go to Katy's party, anyway."

"Nope," she sassily agreed. "Now, can you go get my baby brother already?"

"I'll be back."

THE LAST LUCIANO
DOMINIC, AGE 17

Going to the door of the littlest bedroom in the house, he reached up above the doorframe, grabbing the tiny gold key to unlock the door. Opening it, he saw what he always did—DeeDee passed out on the old rug. This was about her naptime every day, and she continued to do what she had done since he'd been a young child—locking them in a safe room and calling it babysitting. Sure it was babysitting, but whether it was actual childcare was up for debate. He figured it was effective, and none of them had gotten seriously injured … *yet.*

Stepping over DeeDee, he went to the small child who hadn't looked up at him or cared that he had entered. The youngest

Luciano was … different. Not in the gifted way that Kat was. No, in a strange way that Dominic hadn't quite yet understood.

The boy didn't cry, didn't smile, didn't laugh, all the things he'd seen from raising his other siblings, except for …

"Cassius," Dom called out to get the four-year-old to look up from the same blocks that he had used to watch Kat play with.

The little boy didn't look up.

"Cassius." Kneeling down, Dominic made his voice firmer. "Look at me when I'm talking to you."

When his baby brother finally looked over at him, a chill went up his spine as he stared at him. It was like looking into a mirror.

None of his siblings looked like him, bearing their father's resemblance, but Cassius didn't look like he was fathered by Lucifer … but from Dominic himself.

Their skin was a beautiful tanned brown with a matching full head of thick brown hair and both of their eyes were hazel ….

Dominic didn't know how early it was when he woke up on the pink, fuzzy carpet in the basement. He and his brothers would take turns sleeping down here with Kat, not wanting to leave her alone. They secretly wished they could be down here all the time with her, because at least, down here, they were away from their father.

To outsiders, Katarina appeared to have it the worst, but he actually worked hard to find her a safe haven in hell.

Not knowing what time it was, he went upstairs to see if he needed to start getting ready for school as his little sister slept peacefully.

Opening the basement door, he quickly found out that morning had yet to break, but it was the two figures in the kitchen that were heading for the back door who had his attention. One was his father, and the other a woman, who he was seeing out. Since he had seen his father with many women over the years, it was unsurprising, but looking at this particular woman had the hair on his arms standing up.

It was the way she looked at him, he supposed—her brown eyes softening as she stared at him—or maybe it was her look that had his attention. She was truly beautiful. Her thick, brown hair went to her hips, shining even under shitty lighting. He had never seen hair that long before. She didn't look like she belonged next to his father. The two looked like complete opposites, and he wondered if that was why she looked so breathtaking—because she looked normal standing next to a monster.

"H-Hello," the woman choked out after several moments with a quick glance at Lucifer, making sure that it was okay before she continued. "I'm Elena."

Dom didn't move. "Hi."

She brought her hand over her heart as she took a step forward. "You're Dominic, right?"

"Yes."

Her brown eyes went glossy. "How old are you now …?"

"Thir …" He trailed off when she seemed to already know the answer.

"Teen." Wiping a tear that had fallen on her cheek, she tried to put on a happy face over her longing one. "My gosh, you're so grown up and handsome now."

"It's getting early," Lucifer interjected. "It's time for you to leave."

Elena stared at Dominic for a moment longer, not hearing his father's words until he touched her arm.

"Yes, it is." She cleared her throat, giving him one last look. "It was nice seeing you, Dominic."

He tried to form the words "you, too," but when she gave him her back, the words wouldn't come out. Instincts told him to run after her. He didn't know why, only that his gut begged him to, yet his feet remained planted, because of the little girl who slept in the basement.

He thought maybe a part of him should warn her, even though he seemed to know this woman didn't need a warning. The real reason why he desperately wanted to run after her, he hadn't known at the time ….

Looking at Cassius, he saw him with new, rose-colored glasses as he watched Kat place one of her pink bows in his hair. It was a good thing for his sister that their baby brother didn't care what anyone did to him, as she used him as her own personal baby doll.

He stared more intensely at the four-year-old child who was looking like him more and more every day.

I'll be damned …

Pulling out the old, wooden chair, he joined his father at the table and cracked his knuckles before picking up the Glock to clean it. He cleaned his father's guns meticulously every night, finding pride in the act of keeping something that only brought pain working in tip-top shape.

Putting the gun back together after cleaning it, he had just set it down and was about to pick up another when he noticed a dark red mark on his fingertip.

He looked at his finger more closely, rubbing the dot with the pad of his thumb. He had expected it to disappear, but the red mark spread. The shiny red speck *smeared*.

Blood.

After all the numerous times he had cleaned his father's guns, not once had he thought about the lives they had taken. Did this mean the blood was not only on his father's hands but his too?

He rubbed the red mark again with the pad of his thumb until it disappeared. "Me and Cassius are brothers, aren't we?"

The band that had been snapped before the words had left his lips was the only thing you could hear as they all went quiet. Even his twin brothers, who were changing the wheels on their skateboards on the floor, didn't make a sound.

Lucifer lifted his black eyes from the green paper. "Of course he's your brother—"

"No," Dominic stopped his bullshit answer. "We have the same mother. We're *full-blooded* brothers, aren't we?"

Picking up another stack of bills, Lucifer licked his pale, skinny finger to begin counting them, blatantly ignoring his son's question.

"Answer me!" Dom pounded the old, wooden table, causing a stack of unsecured cash to fall when his father's lips had yet to move. "You won't tell me because you killed her, just like you killed Carla, huh?" Dominic didn't hesitate to say that, even though Angel and Matthias were in the room. He had told them stories about their kind mother ever since they were babies, and when they got older and asked where she was, he told them the truth. Sugary, cute lies about how their mother had grown wings and flew to heaven was what you told normal children, not those who were born in hell.

"Yes, he's your full brother!" Lucifer roared back. "Is that what you want to hear?"

Dominic glowed back at him. "I want to hear the truth."

"Okay, here's your fucking truth." His father stood up so that all his sons could see him as the harsh words fell from his evil mouth. "Carla was weak, and the only reason I chose her was because I knew twins ran in her family. I thought, since I was the father and would be the one raising them, there was no way they could be weak, but clearly, I was *wrong*." Lucifer looked at Angel when he said the last part. "When she was delivering them, there was a complication, and the doctor made me choose between saving Carla's life or theirs. I didn't hesitate in my decision, as it saved me a bullet, because I had decided her fate before we even left for the hospital. I didn't want her babying *my sons.*" He emphasized his belief that his sons weren't meant to be shared, like they were his property and his alone.

He looked at Dominic. "Yes, Elena was Cassius's mother … and yours. Unlike Carla, she was a strong woman, and when her younger brother joined the family, she asked me to let him go. I told her I would under one condition, and she paid the ultimate price a woman and a future mother could pay. After Carla birthed these sons"—he waved at the twins, who were fiddling with their skateboards, then looked at his oldest—"I wanted another soldier."

When his father finished, Dominic watched him proudly sit back down. If there had been a bullet in one of the guns laid out in front of him, he was certain Lucifer's brains would have been splattered on the wall behind him, while his soul would have been on its way to hell, where it belonged.

Their father had said some sick shit to them over the years, but for him to make his twelve-year-old sons believe they were lesser than their brothers was something Dom wanted to blow him to kingdom come for.

Thankfully, for Katarina's sake, none of the guns were loaded. It gave him a moment of clarity.

"You said *was.*"

"*Was* what?" Lucifer spat back.

"You said, 'she *was* a strong woman.'"

"I told her, if she gave me a second son, that I'd let her see you both. I would have kept her around to give me my army, but she ended up being too strong for my liking. As soon as Cassius popped out of her, she asked to see you, and when she didn't want to hand over *my newborn son*, I knew I had to get rid of her."

Dominic bunched his hand into a fist, squeezing tightly, his tanned knuckles going pale white. Every pore in his body steamed as the world around him went red. The only thing that remained in color was the revolver.

He picked the heavy weapon up by the muzzle and bashed the butt over his father's head, as if it were a club. Dominic wanted the last Luciano he created to be his true and final one, not wanting another woman to lay with the devil or have a child born by the creature ever again.

The liquid that spewed from Lucifer's helpless head dripped down onto the pile of money with a *thud*, matching the coloring of his new world ....

And then the imagery was gone and he returned to the real world where his father sat counting his money, perfectly healthy before him. Dominic stared at the muzzle of the gun for a moment longer ... and then he started cleaning it.

YOU DON'T WANT TO
MEET ME IN THE PIT
DOMINIC. AGE 18

"**D**o *you want to be* partners?" Bristol asked with a smile when the history teacher asked them to pair up.

Dominic was caught off guard, but he finally answered, "Yeah."

Bristol scooted her desk closer to him, causing screeching noises when the rusty legs scraped across the dirty, tiled floor.

The once cute, little blonde girl had turned into a pretty teenager who all the boys in high school wanted to either kiss, date, or fuck. Ever since that day on the playground, they had stayed friends. She was actually one of the only friends he had besides Anthony. The boys at school kept their distance from him for obvious reasons, but the girls only kept theirs when he never paid them attention.

"Why are you acting all surprised that I asked to be your partner?"

"I don't know." He laughed at her lighthearted question. "I just thought you'd ask one of your friends."

She playfully hit his arm. "You are one of my friends, silly."

"You know what I mean; your *popular* friends." He had wanted to use a different word to describe them but thought better of it.

"Well, you would be one of those, too, if you actually talked to people."

What she said was mostly true. He was sure he could squirm his way to the top of the high school totem pole, like Matthias and Angel had done in middle school with their looks and charm. But Dominic didn't want any of it.

"I'll pass." It wasn't like he was unpopular, per say. Everyone just stayed the fuck away and gave the large senior a wide berth.

Bristol looked at him through her lashes. "You know, *we* could be more than friends ..."

"We've talked about this, Bristol." Dom's gut sank, feeling bad for having to let her down for the hundredth time.

"I know." She gave him a big, cheesy smile. "I just like making you feel bad."

He had a smile of his own. *I should have known.* Bristol wouldn't be Bristol if she didn't tease him or give him a hard time. It was why he was able to keep her as a friend.

"Now, are we going to get started on whatever the hell this is?" she asked, looking at the project rules she didn't understand when the teacher had gone over them. "Or, are we going to fail this one like the last one we did?"

"I shoulda told your ass no when you asked to be my partner, huh?"

"Well, Dom"—she gave him the side eye—"it wouldn't have been the first time you turned me down …."

The silence between them was only slightly awkward until they both busted out laughing and began the project, seriously this time.

On the outside, Dominic looked like his brain was focused on the project, but on the inside, his mind swirled with thoughts of what she had jokingly said. He knew they were jokes, but he also knew they were jokes with truth behind them. Funny jokes were all created the same, with a little trauma.

He should have stopped being friends with her in the sixth grade when she had asked him to be her boyfriend the first time. He'd known when they made it to freshmen year in high school and Bristol asked again, in hopes that he'd grown over the summer or changed his mind, he shouldn't have continued talking to her. Dominic, however, couldn't resist since she was his only friend in school. She helped make his life bearable, and every time she asked to go out, he hated himself a little more for not having the decency to let her go.

It wasn't that he didn't like Bristol. He did. But she deserved a hell of a lot better than a Luciano.

Dominic knew the path he walked led him to hell; whereas,

Bristol's path led to a white picket fence. He wouldn't let his life of murder and guns ruin the future she should have. The future she deserved. So, no matter how much he liked her, he had promised himself they'd never be more than friends.

When the last bell rang for the day, Dominic and Bristol exited the classroom together, laughing their way into the hall.

"We're going to fail that project, aren't we?"

"Probably." Dom shrugged. "But at least it's the last one we could possibly fail since school's almost out."

Bristol looked down at her feet, clearly saddened by his words. He knew why. She could probably see it in his eyes that he planned to cut her out of his life the second they graduated high school.

He was about to be an official made man, and he didn't want Bristol to be anywhere near him. It was time to cut ties and go their separate directions.

Her mouth formed a word, but she hesitated, and before it could came out, Bristol was suddenly grabbed and pulled into a locker.

"You're really just gonna walk past me like that, Bristol?"

Dominic stopped in his tracks at seeing Bristol get pushed up against a locker by the guy she had recently started dating. She'd had little flings throughout high school, since he continuously turned her down. And Bristol had shitty taste in men, though it wasn't like Blue Park High had the cream of the crop. Still, she managed to get involved with the worst ones here. However, she had really scraped the bottom of the barrel with this one who had his hands all over her.

"Sorry, I didn't see you." She tried to laugh it off, clearly embarrassed by her boyfriend's behavior.

When he kept kissing on her neck, she tried to put some space between them. "Stop it."

Her boyfriend just switched to the other side of her neck. "You haven't congratulated me yet for winning the fight—"

"That's enough!" Dominic grabbed his shoulder. "She asked you to stop."

"Back off, Luciano," he snarled, shrugging off Dom's hand.

Staring back at the gold eyes, one surrounded by a purple and blue bruise, that dared him to do something, Dominic grabbed his shoulder again, firmly this time, deciding to give him a warning.

"I said that's enough ... Kayne."

Kayne pushed away from Bristol. Turning around, he went face-to-face with Dom. "You know, if I get in one more fight at school, I'll get expelled. But I'll make a fucking exception for you, Luciano."

That black eye he sported, Dominic knew was from skipping lunch today. Kayne was always fighting with someone behind the school at a secret place they called the pit. The reason Kayne was popular at Blue Park High was from the fear he instilled. If someone much less looked at him fucking wrong, he'd make them meet him at the pit if they didn't want to get a little-bitch status put on them. When raised in poverty, all anyone had was their pride, so every sucker met him there, even if they knew they were going to lose ... And when you fought Kayne, you knew you would.

Dominic could say a lot things about Kayne, but he did know

how to fight. For a guy who'd been in too many fights to count, he had never lost a single one.

Kayne took a step forward, putting his face an inch away from Dom's, and spat right in his face. "Or do you want to take this to the pit?"

"No," Bristol said, grabbing her boyfriend's arm. She tried to back him up and calm him down. "Come on—"

"This is between us, not you, Bristol," Kayne said, pushing her a little too hard until she slammed up against the lockers.

That was all Dominic needed.

Pushing his hands out, he hit Kayne so hard on his chest that he practically knocked the wind out of him when his back met the metals lockers with a smash, giving Kayne a taste of his own medicine. "If I catch you laying your hands on her again, I'll make sure you'll never be able to fight again."

An audience was forming with the *thud* of hitting the lockers, causing Kayne to hesitate. They were so close to graduating, but the second Kayne put his hands on someone else, there were no ifs, ands, or buts about it, he would get expelled no matter how close he was to the end of the year.

Certain the audience would save Kayne from making that decision, he made a last-ditch effort to call him out on his pride. "You're too scared to fight me in the pit, aren't you, Luciano." He lifted the left side of his lip up in a smile. "My father always told me not to fuck with you, but I see you for what you are, Dominic. Behind your father and your last name, you're just a little ... *bitch.*"

Squeezing his ready fist, Dominic looked Kayne up and down, deciding he wasn't worth the risk and released his fist. "For your sake, I hope you never find out."

Pride wasn't something you had to fight for when your last name was Luciano. There was nothing he had to prove that his name didn't already say.

Giving Kayne mercy, he turned to walk away, saving the proud prick his future … until he saw the quick flash of movement from the side of his eye.

Dominic caught the fist that was coming for his head. He grabbed and twisted it until he flipped Kayne around in one swift motion, keeping the painful hold behind his back. Using his other hand, he grasped a chunk of his hair tightly in a fist to hold him up against the lockers.

Kayne might have been the best fighter at Blue Park High, but he was no match for Dom, who had been trained by the best fighter in Blue Park *period*. His secret sparring with Anthony had done him well over the years.

"See?" Dominic spoke low but deadly right into his ear. "You don't want to meet me in the pit, Kayne. I'd break your precious undefeated record in—what was that?—" Dominic pretended to count how long it took to place him in this position. "—three seconds?"

Kayne tried to push off the locker with his free hand to get out of the hold but was unsuccessful.

"I'll kill you!" he roared furiously.

Grasping his hair tighter in his hands, Dom moved his head

back an inch until he could slam Kayne's face back into the locker's little outward slits. "Then I hope they lock you up next to your dad in prison."

"Dominic, please." Bristol touched his shoulder as she cried for him to stop.

Seeing the tears that were starting to well in her eyes, he softened his grip, deciding to let Kayne go ... for her.

"Of course you'll listen to your little lovesick bitc—"

Dominic took Kayne's pinky finger from the hold he had at the boy's back and snapped the tiny appendage in two. "Next time will be your hands."

Kayne, Bristol, and the crowd that had gathered all either screamed, winced, or gasped at the suddenly quick sound of the bone breaking.

Knowing the teachers were making their way through, Dominic finally let Kayne go.

"Why the hell would you do that?" Bristol yelled at him through her tears as she went to Kayne, who helplessly held his broken fingered hand to his chest. Three horizontal cuts started to ooze blood, now accompanying his black eye. "What is wrong with you?"

Confused, Dominic took a step back, pain striking him right in the chest at seeing his friend pick her shitty boyfriend's side, the boyfriend who had just insulted her in front of the whole school. Hell, the only reason Kayne even went out with her was to piss Dominic off and to try to make him jealous. He'd had it out for

Dom ever since they were kids and got in that silly, little fight on the playground. He almost couldn't believe Bristol, until he saw the fear in her eyes.

All these years, she had never believed he was anything like the reputation his last name made him out to be. Now that she had seen it for herself, Bristol looked at him like the rest of the world saw a Luciano ... as a monster.

LUCIFER OWNS
EVERY DUMP I TAKE
DOMINIC. AGE 19

"**W**e good?"

Dom placed the two wadded stacks of bills in his thin jacket pocket. "We're good," he answered, rising from the table, then slinging the last of the drink that Anthony had given him.

The older man laughed when Dom took a gasping breath at the fire hitting the back of his throat. "That's what happens when you drink the good shit." Anthony chuckled. "I didn't give you the crap I pour when your old man comes along with you."

Dominic raised a brow at the contempt that Lucifer's strong arm didn't bother to conceal, drawing another chuckle from Anthony.

"Kid, if I was afraid of bad-mouthing Lucifer in front of you, I wouldn't have taught you how to hold your own when he goes off the rails."

Both of them knew, if Lucifer noticed that the two of them had became friends and Anthony had been teaching him the dirtier art of fighting, Lucifer wouldn't haven't trusted him to collect the money owed to him from the businesses and poor suckers that Lucifer shook down.

"You hate the punk-ass motherfucker as much as I do," Anthony noted.

That wasn't a shock. What was surprising was Anthony admitting out loud the contempt he felt.

"You're just as trapped as I am," Dominic stated, seeing the man's hatred burning, which had Anthony refilling his glass. Usually, Anthony made an effort not to exhibit the contempt he felt, just as Dom did himself. Tonight, Anthony wasn't keeping his words in check.

"Lock, stock, and barrel, Lucifer owns every dump I take."

"What does he have on you?" The weariness etched in the lined faced of the only one of Lucifer's minions who had tried to help him when he had seen the beatings Lucifer inflicted on him. Sneakily, Anthony had taught him the ins and outs of the jobs he carried out for Lucifer, as well the fighting tactics that would at least give him a chance of defending himself against his father.

Anthony picked up his drink, taking a generous swallow before slamming his glass back down. "Kid, when you decide to take your old man out, I'll tell you. Until then, it doesn't matter. It's not like you can help."

Anthony was right; he couldn't. Dominic had his hands full just keeping his brothers and sister breathing under Lucifer's merciless rule.

"I won't be a kid forever." He wasn't exactly promising to help, if the day ever came that he could, but the silent meaning was clear. Dom owed Anthony more than the man would ever know. Lucifer thought that Anthony was just a stupid bag of muscle, while Dominic saw the only person who actually gave a fuck about him. Anthony treated him like he didn't exist around Lucifer, but when he wasn't around, Anthony treated him like the son he never had.

"No, you won't. Just hope I live long enough to see that day."

Dom's concern grew at seeing the weariness become more apparent. "Are you sick?"

Anthony gave a sarcastic laugh. "Sick and tired of dealing with Lucifer. Does that count?"

Ruefully, Dom nodded. "Yes. We're both saddled with the same disease."

Anthony nodded toward a gun that was laying on the table next to the liquor bottle. "There's the vaccine. Both of us know that's what it's going to come down to. The question is"—Anthony refilled his glass—"which one of us will get the fucking pleasure."

Dom didn't have to think twice about his answer. "I will."

"You sure about that? I could do it without a guilty conscious."

"Me either." He shrugged.

"You sure?"

Seeing the life drain from Lucifer's dead body would be the highlight of his existence. "Oh, I'm sure."

"Then I guess"—Anthony took another drink—"we wait."

Dom nodded. "For now."

Going for the door, Dominic buttoned his thin jacket.

"Kid, you need a thicker jacket. It's cold out there."

He managed to scrounge around enough money to get Angel a winter coat. He still needed to get Matthias one. Winter would be over before he had enough to get one for himself.

Dominic shrugged, not wanting to admit the truth to Anthony. "Don't need one. The cold doesn't bother me."

"Take mine." Anthony wasn't buying that load of shit. "I'll get myself another one."

Dominic looked at the distinctive coat that was hanging by the door. "No, thanks."

"Take it," the gruff enforcer barked out at him in a tone that had Blue Park quaking in fear when they saw him. Then the man, who was as close to a true father that he would be granted, got out his chair to take his coat off the hook and shove it at him.

Dominic pushed it back. "What do you think Lucifer would do if he saw me wearing your coat? He wears a fucking wool coat. He knows it's freezing outside. He's trying to teach me a lesson. If I wear your leather, it'll just piss him off."

"What fucking lesson could you learn from freezing your ass off?"

Dominic's hazel eyes glowered. "That until he's ready, I'll only have what he wants me to have."

"Thanks, kid."

Confused, Dom stared at him as Anthony hung the coat back up. "What for?"

"For making me feel better about my shitty life."

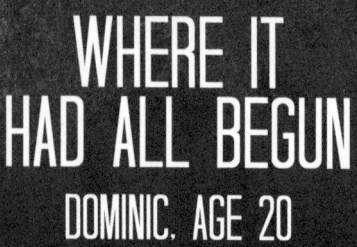

WHERE IT
HAD ALL BEGUN
DOMINIC. AGE 20

Getting out of the car, Dominic fixed the ugly, dark brown suit his father made him wear. You could practically smell the dust on it from where it had hung in the back of his father's closet for all those years. Shoulder-wise, the old suit fit, but the rest of it hung like it was still on a coat hanger from where he was so lean.

"Did I really need to come?" Dominic asked his father quietly in the parking lot. Lucifer had requested his capos to attend and show respect, and Dom was still just a soldier in the family.

"You're my son." Giving him a side-eye, he just as quietly hissed out his next words, "Now, don't ruin this fucking day for me."

He had never seen his father this happy in his life, and to see it on a day like today made Dominic sick to his stomach.

"Then what about the ones you left at home?"

Lucifer stopped to look hard into his son's eyes. "They're not the ones who will be running the family one day, are they?"

His father's question sounded like a threat, like he could change his mind who sat at the head of the family when he was dead and gone.

"No." Dominic made it clear that the Luciano throne was his and his alone. "But one will sit underneath me."

The underboss. It was all the twenty-year-old thought of obtaining. When he got the title, he would be one final step closer to the throne.

"Cassius," his father said without a second thought before walking off.

"Cassius?" a stunned Dominic repeated. "But he's only seven. How could you possibly make that decision no—"

"Because I did," Lucifer announced firmly.

"Angel and Matthias are only fifteen; you don't know what they'll be capable of. They could be better than me, and you don't even know it." Dominic paused a moment before he bravely said his next words. "You won't even give them a chance."

"Let's be clear." His father spun around so his vicious tongue could slap him in the face. "The only real threat you have for taking your place in this family is Cassius, and you fucking know it."

The heart that sat in his chest pounded at the thought of the youngest Luciano at the head of the family.

"What?" Lucifer gave him a twisted smile. "You're not going to tell me how Cassius could be better than you one day too? Or do you only stand up for your brothers who never have the chance of taking the throne?"

He was one second away from opening his mouth until he thought better of it and walked past his father, toward the Catholic church. Lucifer would have beat the shit out of him right here in front of their enemies if he had. Sure, he could admit Matthias might not have a chance of sitting on the throne, thanks to their psychopathic father, but if Lucifer wasn't scared of what Angel could become, then Dominic himself wouldn't stand a chance.

Angel being born a twin was the exact thing that could have made him a greater man than Dominic, but it was ironically the very thing that held him back. Angel wasn't gifted the opportunity like Dom to pretend that he'd never backstab his own father. It was clear in Angel's gray eyes, ever since he was a child, that he'd kill Lucifer if he ever hurt Matthias beyond irrevocable damage—and Lucifer knew it. Hell, the only reason Lucifer still walked the earth was because of the thing he hated the most—Katarina. Like Dominic, Angel hadn't blown his brains out already because of him. Protecting Matthias was the only reason Angel would never make it to the throne.

Dominic loved Cassius, but he was also afraid of his youngest sibling. And it wasn't out of fear that Cassius could be greater than him, it was out of fear that he could be worse than Lucifer. Cassius might have looked like Dominic in every way, but on the inside, he was born as fucked-up as his father. Dominic did everything he could to keep Cassius busy and away from Lucifer, and the only thing that might save his soulless life was Katarina.

She could see the darkness that lurked beneath the surface and, even at ten years old, she was trying her best to keep that darkness away by showing Cassius the difference between good and evil. It might only work because, if Cassius *was* capable of love, then he felt it for his sister.

Walking into the Catholic church, he was surprised Lucifer didn't burst into flames when he entered the sacred ground.

There were two people at the front greeting their guests, and having come in behind a small group, he and his father had to wait their turn.

Dominic knew the older man. Once a year, the two crime families of Kansas City met outside the city on equal ground to ensure the peace they created after the war. That war was where it had all begun, as it almost caused the Luciano name to cease to exist. If they hadn't come to that agreement, he and his father wouldn't be here today. Simultaneously, however, it was the reason his father treated his kids like soldiers, ruining any hopes of a normal childhood.

The man they were about to approach was Dante Caruso, his father's biggest adversary. Dominic might have actually liked the man, if he wasn't so full of himself. He had an arrogance about him, and Dominic was surprised he didn't fucking choke on it. It was clear he thought he was God's gift to the American mob, and it was only a matter of time for his day of reckoning. Dom felt genuinely bad that it had come in the form of burying his wife.

The man had thought he had it all, and the universe had humbled him. Life was funny that way. You'd think his reckoning would have come from a bullet. Instead, it took the thing Dante loved the most.

The Caruso boss had always stood tall, but today, he was a little shorter, and his piercing ice-blue gaze wasn't as intimidating with the red ring around them from the tears he had most likely shed right before this. Just like the rest of the world, even the mafia needed balance.

However, it was the girl who stood in front of Dante who drew his attention. The second he saw her, his heart had stopped; he never knew beauty like that could exist in a world so ugly.

She had blonde hair that looked like it had been spun from gold, and her tanned skin somehow made it shine brighter. Her face was so symmetrically perfect that, since she was the only one wearing white against a sea of black, Dominic, honest to God thought he was seeing an angel. Thinking he had imagined her, he shook his head to see that she wasn't the one who had tragically died too young.

His heart might have stopped, but now it beat faster with every man who greeted her. Every one of them either gave her a hug or a touch—from what they could play off as sympathy—but Dom knew they couldn't care less about her mother laying in a casket at the end of the aisle. Their eyes lit up like fucking Christmas trees to see a young girl in a pretty dress. Dominic was always surrounded by older men, and they didn't think of angels who had fallen from the sky but the ones from their dirty magazines.

If he heard another one of those grown men tell her how grown up she had gotten, he was going to shove their wagging tongues down their throats until they were shitting them out for the next week, like her father, Dante, should be doing. The Caruso boss was likely already deciding who his princess would marry out of his men, and he was probably sitting in this very room.

It was her height that gave the men the audacity to think it was okay to look at a young girl that way. Dominic didn't know how old the girl was, but she had to be somewhere around Angel and Matthias's age and was almost as tall as them too.

Strangely, Dominic felt something for the girl, as well, but it wasn't in the way the rest of the men did. What he felt, when watching the gross men look at her, was similar to the thought of his father hurting Kat. He couldn't place that feeling at first until he thought about how happy he was that Lucifer didn't claim his sister as his own, and she would never be subjected to this. He realized his feelings for the girl were protective in nature.

"Dante," Lucifer greeted him with a nod. "My son and I are sorry for your loss."

Dominic only briefly nodded to the grieving boss before his eyes went to the girl. As if she wasn't pretty enough from far away, she was more beautiful the closer he stood; her hair that looked as though it was spun from gold, complemented her emerald eyes that would give the real stone a run for its money.

"Thank you." Dante clearly had to force the words out but somehow managed to fake it before he politely introduced his daughter. "This is my daughter, Maria."

That name not only suited an angel, but it was fit for an Italian princess.

Now you want to keep her away from creepy old men? he shouted in his head, seeing the sudden death grip Dante had on his daughter's shoulders. Dominic didn't blame him from wanting to keep Lucifer away from her, but his father would rather drink acid than want a woman, or girl for that matter, who had the Caruso last name.

"It's nice to meet you, Maria." Lucifer kept up the charade.

Dom had to give her credit. Most kids, and even adults, cried at the sight of his father, but she managed to look the devil right in the eyes.

"This is my son, Dominic," he continued, introducing one boss's child to the other.

When her emerald eyes landed on him, he became transfixed at the sight. It was like they had their own light source behind them, reminding him of the stained glass windows around them as the sun shined through the painted green.

"Hello."

"Hello." Her voice came out just as angelic as her features.

Wanting to get to the others waiting to greet them, Dante moved them along. "Well, thank you for coming to pay your respects, Luciano."

It wasn't because they were in a church that Dante didn't call

Lucifer by his first name. Neither the Caruso boss, nor his men, called him by it, only ever calling the devil by his surname. No one knew why they refused to call him by his given name, but it certainly wasn't done out of respect. Nevertheless, it was still Lucifer's day, and nothing was going to ruin his mood as a slow, sinister smile touched his lips.

"Anytime."

Dominic's hazel depths lingered on her precious stone ones a little longer. There was something strange and oddly familiar about her, but before he could figure it out, his father pushed him down the aisle.

Walking down the long aisle, passing the occupied pews, every step away from the Caruso princess was harder than the last; it felt like he was trudging through mud. He didn't know why he felt like that. Maybe he wanted to go back and somehow get her out of being forced to greet the men who came in? Whatever it was, every instinct in his body tried to lure him back to her. It wasn't until they reached the end of the aisle did the instinct ease.

It was catholic tradition for the children to wear white to funerals, so evil didn't touch them, but when he saw the crisp white casket that held the boss's late wife, Melissa Caruso, there another reason. Maria didn't belong in black, just like her mother who looked peacefully asleep in a light pink dress.

Even in death, Melissa was beautiful, but it didn't compare to the large portrait of her set off to the side. Dominic couldn't help but think what a pity it was to rid the world of something so pretty when such ugliness existed.

He touched his forehead, finishing the sign of the cross over his chest, waiting for a smug Lucifer to respectfully do the same. Of course the devil refused the blessing. Dominic had to look away from his sick father, who was rejoicing this sad day.

Seeing the eighteen-year-old son of the deceased seated in the first pew alone, Dominic walked over and silently took a seat beside him. He had only met him two times, the same way he had met his father, Dante, at the once-a-year meeting. Dominic couldn't believe it when the seventeen-year-old had shown up as a made man, but then he had remembered what the kid had done to become the youngest made in the two families. Like everyone else, even Dominic had to wait to be of age, but what the oldest Caruso son had done had classified him as an adult. Even the American judicial system would have tried him as an adult, locked him up, and thrown away the key.

The only good thing that would come out of hav

ing a psychopath as a father was that Dominic would know how to deal with his future enemy when it came time. Lucifer was his greatest weapon, and the Carusos didn't even know it yet.

Both future Kansas City mob bosses sat next to each other in silence, and just like their fathers, the sons were destined for the same adversarial path.

It was strange to know your enemy before they'd become it. It was like staring into a crystal ball and seeing your future. He supposed he should feel blessed, as not many people could say that, but it felt ominous to have your whole life decided before you were even born.

Dante's son didn't have an air of arrogance like his father, but rather a cloud of darkness. Today, however, it was gone. He thought it might've been because he was forced to wear a suit that he didn't want to wear, just like he felt, but Dominic was sure they hadn't wanted to wear it for different reasons. Not only was Dominic's a size too big, but he had asked Lucifer if it was appropriate to wear brown to a funeral, even if it was dark.

Dom would have killed to wear the suit his adversary was wearing. It had been tailored to him perfectly, but it was the fact that it was all black that had him envious. Unlike the Lucianos, the Carusos always dressed in expensive Italian suits that varied in colors of black, gray, and white. The Lucianos wore clothes that looked worn, their fabrics less lux. They hardly ever wore full suits like the other family did. They'd either not have the tie, suit, or pants to complete the ensemble.

The young Caruso who sat beside him was like the Lucianos in that regard—he hated to wear suits. The only thing Dominic had seen him in was dark jeans and black T-shirts, even to their official meetings. But the suit wasn't why the dark cloud had evaporated. The air around him was replaced with ... *sorrow?*

Dominic furrowed his brows, thinking he couldn't possibly possess feelings, even for his mother. He had always thought him to be like Lucifer—incapable of loving another. Dom felt bad for the deceased and for those she left behind, but he hadn't felt an ounce of care for the eighteen-year-old ... until now.

Looking back to the beautiful woman in the casket, he spoke softly and low to the future Caruso boss for the first time. "I'm sorry about your mother, Lucca."

At first Lucca seemed shocked when he turned his head toward him, clearly not having heard someone say those words to him yet. Then the look disappeared as his blue-green eyes bore into him, forcing Dom to look into his haunting depths. "Don't act like you're sorry, Dominic."

"Was she anything like you?" he asked simply.

Lucca's brows drew together in confusion. "No." Looking back to his dead mother, the coldness in his voice left as he said, "She *was* everything I'm not."

"Then"—Dominic stood to go sit next to his father—"I truly am sorry."

"Dominic," Lucca called as Dom started to leave.

He stopped, turning to look at the enemy. He almost didn't believe it when the words "thank you" crossed his lips.

It was at that moment Dominic knew two things: the Luciano throne would be his, and the city would be his as well. The future Caruso boss had just made a critical error.

Lucca proved he was human after all.

Giving him a final nod, he went to take his seat next to his father as the ceremony was about to begin.

"Luciano." Dante came down the aisle, this time sounding a little less sad. "There's someone I wanted to introduce you to."

Father and son both stood up, turning to look at where the Caruso boss had walked up from behind them.

"My newest soldier"—a young man in a clean, black and white suit stepped out from behind Dante as he introduced him—"Salvatore Lastra."

The second Dominic saw him, he felt like he had seen him before and quickly tried to place him from his memory, thinking he had to have seen him from school since he looked so young. If he was made, then he was at least eighteen, and he doubted a day older.

When his father didn't introduce himself, he looked over to see the smirk he had all day had been wiped clean from his face.

"Dominic." He held his hand out, introducing himself when his father remained stunned. "Nice to meet you, Salvatore."

The Carusos newest recruit took his hand in a firm grip. "You can call me Sal."

The second his rough hand took his, Dominic instantly recognized a tell. Out of all the hands he'd shaken of Carusos' men, none had been as rough as his. Those were the hands of someone who had grown up in Blue Park.

"I know you, don't I?" Dom said, making all three look awkwardly between themselves before he continued. "You're from our part of town, aren't you?"

A silent sigh of relief that Dominic didn't understand washed over the men. Clearly, he was left out of something, and he didn't know what. Taking another moment to look into the young man's eyes, a memory hit him. As he fiddled with the cherry candy in his pants pocket—a habit he'd never grown out of—he knew where he'd seen him before. The street kid cleaned up good. It'd been a few years since Dom had last seen him wandering the streets a few years back, but his face, while clean-shaven, still looked young. It was certainly a small world. Little did he ever think the homeless kid he'd passed on his way to school from time to time would end up working for mafia royalty.

"Yeah." Sal adjusted his suit, looking like he himself didn't think he belonged in it. "Mr. Caruso took me off the streets of Blue Park after my mother died."

"How kind," Lucifer finally spoke through clenched teeth. "Is this *the* Great Salvatore you've been speaking of?"

Dominic had to do a fucking double-take. *No fucking way.*

At their meetings, Dante had mentioned the Great Salvatore as an associate of his. They spoke about him as if he was an urban legend who was on his way to becoming the greatest hacker to ever live. Lucifer had even used his services when they needed to get a cop off the city's payroll and onto theirs. Dominic had assumed he was an older man, not some homeless kid.

Dante wrapped an arm around Sal's shoulders like a proud father. "Yes, he is."

Lucifer's jaw flexed slightly before he held out a pale, long-fingered hand. "Nice to finally meet you, Salvatore."

His blue eyes didn't stare as kindly as they had at Dominic when he took the devil's hand. "Likewise."

Then … Dominic finally saw the little secret that he hadn't

been let in on as he noticed Sal's eyes weren't just blue; they were blueish-black.

It really is a small fucking world after all.

Going back to their seats, they watched Dante walk away and take his seat in the first pew with his children. Sal sat with the family, making it look like he was one of his sons, as well.

Dominic chose not to say anything yet, waiting until after the funeral to discuss just how much more fucked up the Luciano family could get. The only thing that made him happy about his new revelation was that his father's creepily chipper mood had turned sour. However, it quickly returned when the priest began. As if his father didn't make him sick enough, the longer the mass lasted, the bigger his smile got, while everybody else cried.

In a sea of sad faces, the only face that wasn't distraught, other than his father's, was the angel sitting in the front pew next to Lucca.

He couldn't help but watch Maria throughout the different stages of the funeral, wondering at what point she was going to cry. He thought when the choir sung the gospel song that she'd at least look sad, or when the pallbearers carried her mother's body out, but even when her dead mother was lowered into the ground, she hadn't shed a single tear.

Dominic couldn't help but laugh at the fact he had thought she was an angel.

Maria was a mafia princess, and a fucking monster, just like the rest of them.

THE EARTH BECOMING WHOLE AGAIN

t seemed like such a sin to throw dirt on such a beautiful, white casket. Every shovel of it made a hard *thud* from the impact, until it became softer as the dirt began filling up the six-feet-deep hole.

As Dominic left the graveyard, Maria exited in the opposite direction, and with the earth becoming whole again, Dominic turned to give the princess one last look.

And thus, a new beginning was created from an end.

BLUE PARK'S BIGGEST WHORE

he drive back to Blue Park was definitely going to be awkward as they got into Lucifer's old black Cadillac. It was just another thing that separated them from the Carusos—seeing all the new Cadillac models surrounding them.

When Lucifer turned the key in the ignition and the car roared to life, his smile disappeared now that the festivities were over.

"Well …" Dominic began the conversation.

"Well, what?" Lucifer snapped, driving onto the road and into the traffic erratically.

"When were you going to tell me I had yet another brother?"

"When I wanted you to fucking know."

Dominic could tell by his voice that, if he hadn't been driving, he would have slapped the shit out of him. However, the truth was obvious; Lucifer was clearly just as taken aback as he was, not over the fact that he had another son, but that his biggest enemy had taken him in.

"Why didn't you want him?" Dominic asked, looking down at his hands that were beginning to shake. He didn't think he'd every truly understood his sick father and why he did certain things. "You wanted fucking soldiers, but you let him rot on the street?"

"His mother was a whore!" Lucifer roared back. "It could have been any man's!"

"Pull over," Dominic said, feeling bile rise. "Pull the fuck over!" he yelled again when his father didn't stop, reaching over to abruptly turn the wheel. They swerved off the side of the road.

"What the—"

Lucifer hit the brakes and slammed the car into Park when Dominic jumped out of the car.

Leaning over, vomit spewed from his mouth as he barely made it out of the car.

All day he'd had to watch his father's joy that the Carusos' boss's wife had been laid to rest after being tragically murdered. And now *this shit?* In his mind, he kept replaying all the fucking times he had passed by Sal living on the street, wanting to give him change or the couple of dollars he'd had in his pocket, yet he never did. Because he used that money to buy Kat something to help with her boredom, being stuck in the basement, or to buy Angel and Matthias a pack of donuts in the morning at the gas station if they ran out of cereal. Not knowing each time he did, he'd denied his own goddammed brother.

"Are you throwing up?" Lucifer's face and voice leeched with disappointment when he came around the car to see him hurling. "Since when did I raise such a pussy!"

"I ate leftovers of DeeDee's shitty cooking this morning, and it must've given me food poisoning," Dominic quickly lied, thankful when his father believed him.

Wiping his mouth off with the back of his hand, he stood straight, facing his father. "You knew he was your son; admit it."

"I did," Lucifer finally admitted without remorse. "But it wasn't until after he was born and I saw his eyes that I knew."

"Then why didn't you bring him home?" Dominic asked, confused. Raising an army to take back the city was his father's whole purpose.

Lucifer was silent, clearly thinking until he just came out with it. "His mother was Blue Park's biggest whore! I didn't want anyone to know I had slept with her."

Sal's mother hadn't been a whore; the disgusting men who had pulled up to her on the street corner and paid to sleep with her were.

Taking a step closer to him, Dom pointed a finger at him angrily. "So, you let your son rot on the street for *years* rather than let the world know you had to *pay* for sex?"

This time, the fist that came at his face, Dominic wasn't allowed to catch. Literally and figuratively, he had to take it on the chin or his punishment would be worse.

Dominic spat out the blood that filled his mouth into the grass, still waiting for Lucifer to answer his question.

"Yes," his father finally answered coldly.

Dom was quiet at first, staring at his father blankly, until he threw his head back in laughter.

"What the fuck are you laughing at?" Lucifer hissed. "That I fucked a prostitu—"

"No." Dominic's chest still boomed with laughter, but it turned sinister the more it went on until he completely stopped. Looking into his father's black eyes, Dom gave him the same creepy smile he'd seen all day. "I think it's funny that the one son you had nothing to do with ... ended up being your greatest creation yet, and you led him right into the arms of your enemy."

The fist that met his face brought him a deep sleep ...

Running down the block, he finally made it, bending over to catch his breath.

Lucifer watched as he got out of his car.

Talking through a heavy breath from having to run across Blue Park, Dominic didn't understand why his father couldn't have just picked him up. "What was the rush that you needed to meet here so fast? I was—"

"I don't give a fuck what you were doing. You do what I want when I want," his father hissed.

Dom bit back what he really wanted to say. It was becoming harder and harder to tolerate Lucifer.

Lowering his eyes to his scuffed shoes, Dom hid the burning thoughts of wanting to take his brothers and Kat and disappear. Freedom from Lucifer and the tyranny he imposed on them beckoned him to start raising enough courage to take his life and those of his siblings in his own hands. He had been creating an escape plan, if it came down to it. After the funeral, Dom was slowly coming to the realization that he might have no option but to run away from his own destiny.

Once a week, Dominic picked up a bag of cash from Anthony, and he gauged the amount Lucifer had him transporting. The amounts increased equal to Lucifer's trust. He just needed one large payout to help them disappear to a place where Lucifer couldn't use his parental rights to drag the younger siblings back under his control if they were found.

Lucifer began walking toward an older house, expecting him to follow. Dom did. The unkept yard was just one of many on the block. Iron bars on the windows showed no one felt safe as the empty, dark sidewalks curved into a cul-de-sac. There were several cars sitting in the driveway. Dom recognized Anthony's old, lime green Buick sitting in front.

Lucifer didn't knock, going inside as if he owned the home. Walking in behind him, Dom was nearly knocked over at the strong scent of perfume and incense that had his eyes watering.

Taking in the crowded occupants of the room, he spotted

Anthony leaning back on a worn sofa with a woman who had her top more off than on.

Anthony had been the lone man in the room before their arrival, as the crowded room was filled with women of various ages, sizes, and complexions, staring at him with listless expressions that had his skin crawling.

"Took you long enough to get him here. I had to keep Lacy occupied. She was getting bored," his enforcer nonchalantly spoke, glancing toward Lucifer as he got off the couch.

Revolted, Dom was unable to hide his disgust when it was visually apparent that Anthony was aroused.

Dom turned toward his father. "What—"

The word had no more than left his lips when Dominic found Lucifer's fist swinging, striking him on the side of his nose. The hard contact immediately brought him to his knees.

Disoriented, he brought his hand to his nose, feeling the rush of blood pooling out.

The women scattered to different sides of the room, getting out of harm's way without a noise. Their silence exhibited this wasn't the first time they had been exposed to sudden physical violence. Instinctively, they were making themselves unnoticeable to keep themselves safe the only way they could.

Lucifer's face swam above him, filled with contempt, as he threw his foot out, hitting him in the ribs. "You think you're more man than me?" Lucifer roared as he kicked him again.

Dom tried to roll away from the unprovoked attack, unable to fight back as it could cost Kat's life.

"You think you can run from me ... or worse, turn my men against me? You puke your guts out because you feel sorry for a street kid who would blow your brains out at a Caruso's order. Boohoo! You're too fucking weak to ever take me on!"

Vicious kicks, one after another, had Dominic gasping for breath as Anthony watched, making no move to interfere.

"You think you have the balls to take me down? Prove it!"

Dom felt himself jerked to his feet by Lucifer's hand on the back of his jacket. Tossed forward, Dom hit a wall, making the whole house rattle before he was grabbed and forcibly led into a bedroom. Thrown down on a bed as he tried to gather his reeling senses, he saw Anthony and the woman had followed them into the room.

"Show me!" Lucifer yelled at him.

"I don't unde—"

Lucifer bent over him, placing a hand on his throat to strangle what air he had left. "Fuck the bitch ... Show me you're man enough to take what's mine."

Lucifer expects him to fuck a woman in front of him?

Revulsion filled him once again at his deranged father.

Seeing Anthony sprawling down on a chair to watch, it finally clicked in his pain-filled brain why Lucifer was so furious. Anthony had betrayed him, and Lucifer wanted him to know.

"I'm not going to fuck her," Dom gasped out as the woman came around the bed and get on next to him. He found nothing attractive about the woman, who Dom could clearly see was terrified.

"She's not good enough for me, but she's the right slut for you. That little pecker of yours has never been out of the barn door. It's time he got out to play."

Demented laughter filled the small room, making Dom want to vomit at what Lucifer was ordering him to do.

Feeling her shaking hand go to his trousers when she went to unzip them at his hips, he tried to jerk away from her touch. However, Lucifer tightened his hand on his neck, making bright spots appear in his eyes as his oxygen was cut off.

"You're going to fuck her, or I'm going to kill you," Lucifer commanded with a clenched jaw. "You're going to prove to me you'll do what I want, when I want, and how I want, or you'll be watching what I do to your precious siblings from hell's gates. I'll make the boys into the soldiers I deserve and"—his lips twisted up into a frightening sneer—"I've already promised to marry the girl off to Anthony when she becomes legal. Without you around, I won't wait. I'll give her to him now."

Dom gave in. There had never been a chance of escape from Lucifer's psychotic future for them. The only way he would ever beat Lucifer at his own game was to put his own feelings aside and become what he hated the most—his father.

Dominic forced himself to stop struggling against Lucifer.

Feeling his capitulation, Lucifer loosened his hold.

"If you expect me to fuck her, get off me," Dom wheezed out with a hiss. He didn't know how he was supposed to fuck anyone with the mess Lucifer had made out of his body, as well being completely unaroused by the woman waiting to comply to Lucifer's demands.

Lucifer got off the bed to go stand in front of the door, blocking any escape. It was a useless endeavor. Lucifer had won. He had won the minute he threatened him with Katarina. There was no way he would ever let Anthony lay a hand on her, much less spend the rest of her life married to the betraying bastard.

"Get busy," Lucifer ordered.

Dom used the corner of blanket to stem the flow of blooding from his nose and saw fear mixed with sympathy coming from the woman.

She didn't want to be in this situation any more than he did. Both knew they were pawns in Lucifer's game, and giving in was their only key to survive.

When she unzipped his pants, Dom didn't try to stop her this time, letting her slip his trousers off first, then his underwear.

"At least you took one thing after me." Lucifer's sarcasm as his eyes went to his limp dick had Dominic wanting to use the blanket to cover himself, but he didn't. He used his humiliation to fuel the hatred he felt in every pore in his being for the man he called Father.

The woman started stroking his dick, and the only thing Dom wanted was to hold down his lunch.

"If you puke, I'll slit her fucking throat and bring in another slut to get the fucking job done."

Lucifer's threat had him gagging back the bile and blood

choking him.

Closing his eyes to shut out Lucifer's and Anthony's stares, Dominic used his imagination to take himself away from the bedroom that had probably been used hundreds of times to fulfill the customers' fantasies at the brothel that Lucifer must own.

"You just going to lay there and let her do all the work?"

Dom ignored the goad, tuning his thoughts to another channel where Lucifer, Anthony, and the woman sucking his dick didn't exist.

Feeling a condom rolled onto his dick, he was almost torn back to reality, but he succeeded in staying in his own thoughts, telling himself he was strong enough to get through this punishment that Lucifer was determined to administer.

Forcing his aching ribs to work, Dom shifted enough to clumsily drag his body over the woman. Inexperienced, it took two tries to find the target, to sink his dick inside of her.

Losing his virginity in front of his father and Anthony hardened his soul enough to complete the act, as he drowned out the excited moans the woman pretended to give. She deserved a fucking Academy award, but he wasn't so naïve that he wasn't aware her pussy was dry.

Both of them in a hell of his own making, Dominic blamed himself for ever trusting Anthony and lowering his guard enough for Lucifer to see his disgust about the callous treatment Sal had received from him. Hell, his brother had been the lucky one.

Painfully heaving into a sitting position, Dom sat on the edge of the bed to reach for his pants after disposing the used condom.

"You're not done." Lucifer's black, maniac orbs looked at him before he yelled, "Amy, get your ass in here!"

He could only sit there, shell-shocked, as another woman came into the room and approached the bed, taking off her top.

"This time, make me believe you enjoyed getting some pussy."

Dominic opened his mouth to tell Lucifer to kill him, as it would be easier than having to live through this hell, but the black eyes stopping him were the precious ones in his mind—his sister's.

Defeated, he handed over what dignity he had left to hold out his hand. "Give me another condom."

Three hours and four women later, Lucifer finally stalked toward an exhausted Dominic on the bed.

His cold face stared him down as he reached out, taking Dom's sweaty chin in a death grip. "Now you can call yourself a man." Letting go, he reached into his pocket to pull out his silver money clip to start counting bills. "You know, I was worried about you when Angel and Matthias started sneaking out to fuck every girl in Blue Park, but now I see I've just kept you too busy." Lucifer sprinkled the cash down on the bed with a sinister laugh. "You thought it was funny that I fucked a hooker. Well, congrats, son, you're no better than your old man."

Finally satisfied he had humiliated him enough, Lucifer left.

Dominic's hatred for him seeped out of his every pore as he watched his audience laughingly begin to exit. Dominic had learned his lesson on trying to outsmart Lucifer. He wasn't ready to take him on... yet.

As both men put their coats back on, Dom stared at Anthony's enviously, thinking back to how he had used it to lure him into trusting him. Both men created fear just at the sight of those coats; Lucifer in his fancy wool, Anthony in his opposing leather.

Stinking of sex, cheap perfume, and cherry incense, Dominic tried to drag his sore, exhausted body into his clothes. His eyes glittered in the dark room, trying not to let a tear spill.

Dominic didn't know what hurt worse: the fact that his last bit of innocence had been taken away from him ... or that he had been betrayed by his only friend.

THE DAY DOMINIC BROKE

B *RRing.*

The house phone ringing had Lucifer answering.

Dominic never paid any mind to his father when he was on the phone, but he could feel the air in the house change, which had him listening in intently.

Looking at Lucifer, he could see his black eyes turn blacker, if that was even possible, as he stayed silent, listening to the other end of the phone.

"I'll see what I can do," Lucifer answered as harshly as he was looking at his son, then slammed the phone back on the wall.

Adrenaline rushed through Dominic's veins, instinctively knowing that whatever was coming tonight was going to end very badly. The look on Lucifer's face told him one thing, and one thing only.

He wanted blood.

Bravely, Dominic asked what he wished he didn't have to. "Who was that?"

"The school."

"Matthias, what did you do now?" he snapped over the loud shooting video game that he and his brothers were playing on the couch.

"Nothing!" Matthias nonchalantly yelled from over his shoulder.

It wasn't until Angel had paused the game did he notice the shift in the air that his twin had already caught.

Even little Cassius, who had been intently staring at the TV as they murdered Nazi zombies, turned his head too.

"Not him." When Lucifer's skinny, pale finger pointed to the floor, the fear emanating from the boys was palpable before he even said the next word. "Her!"

Fuck. Dominic breathed silently to himself, already making a fist.

Angel stood up quickly, followed by a shaky Matthias. Little Cassius, however, looked back at the paused TV.

Dominic took a step forward, seeing the basement door was in Lucifer's reach. "What did the school say?"

"They want me to come up there to talk about her grades. She's fucking stupid, isn't she?" Lucifer's cruel words whipped him.

Dom's jaw flexed, wanting to take the knife off the kitchen

counter to slit his father's throat for how he spoke about Kat when he didn't know a single damn thing about her. He'd have him buried six feet deep by morning if he wasn't still afraid the system would take his underaged siblings away. With Lucifer dead and Dominic not the head of the family yet, the fear his father put on the city would all be gone. The fear Lucifer instilled would turn to hatred, and the family would go down; there was no question about it. They would throw his ass behind bars. He was a made man now, and that was the consequence of being one … if you got caught.

"I should have never let you raise that child and gotten rid of it myself!" he roared. "Lucianos have never been dumb! We are the smartest people in this city, and you've let her taint the name!"

"Well, if you had raised her, you'd know she's not dumb," Dominic coldly told him.

"Clearly, she isn't that fucking bright if I got a call, now is she?"

Dominic opened his mouth to tell him that his ten-year-old daughter, who he didn't fucking want, was smarter than he would ever be, but he shut his mouth. He and his brothers kept that part about Kat secret. Not only did he not deserve to know his daughter was a genius, but Dominic was scared that Lucifer would feel inferior to her intelligence, making him hate her more.

"I thought so," Lucifer spat before turning for the basement door.

I'm not going to let you get her again. Dominic swore to the devil and to God Himself.

"No," Dom ordered, holding a tone that his father sometimes respected.

When Lucifer paused, he continued, making him a promise. "I'll go to the school and handle it. You will not get a call *again*."

Lucifer stared at the basement door for several moments with the tension in the room on high alert. "Fine." He turned back around, heading out the front door. "I'll be back in the morning."

What the . . .? That's it?

All the brothers let out a sigh of relief once the door closed.

"I'm gonna let Kat come up to play now." Little Cassius got up, walking to the basement door.

"No, not yet," Dom told him from over his shoulder, watching his father walk to his car, knowing Lucifer never backed down. Something felt off.

The basement door creak open, and then Cass yelled out, "Kat! Come up and play."

"No, it's not s—"

Dominic went to the basement door to hurry up and stop her, but seeing her happy, little face as she was already excitingly starting to come up the steps, he couldn't tell her no now. Knowing she hated the basement, he went against his instincts, letting her come up before their father could drive off.

Watching Kat practically skip to the couch where her twin brothers went back to sitting, her butt didn't touch the couch for a second when the front doorknob jingled.

Dominic ran to the door in a split-second, keeping it from opening. He looked over at a scared Kat who had jumped back up from off the couch.

"*Go.*" He mouthed for her to run. Every nerve ending in his body was struck with cold fear as he watched Kat run off, horrorstricken.

"What the fuck!" Lucifer hissed from the other side of the door.

Looking at his twin brothers, who had made it to the door beside him, he asked them gravely on a whisper, "Ready?"

A prepared Angel nodded, followed by a scared Matthias.

"Open this damn door! I'm going to fucking kill—"

Dominic flung open the door once he heard Kat close the basement door behind her, knowing he couldn't hold the devil off forever.

It was his brother, Angel, who jumped him first, and even though the fifteen-year-old was brave, he didn't stand a chance against his father. The back of Angel's head split on the wall the second Lucifer threw him back on it.

Dominic was thankfully quick enough to get to his father before Matthias, knowing he would be scared shitless, tried to face Lucifer.

When Lucifer reared his fist back, Dominic caught it, showing him a trick he had learned from his own enforcer.

The look of Lucifer's face switched from shock, to disbelief, and then to cold murder. The student had now become the teacher, so what did Lucifer have to do? He fought dirty.

When they had destroyed the whole house and ended up in the kitchen, Lucifer picked up the kitchen chair, smashing it over his son's head and breaking it into pieces.

Matthias didn't go into action until he saw Dominic fall to the floor. However, he was no match. Even though Lucifer had to be tired after the fight he and his oldest son had, Matthias had gone down quick. The punch his father planted on him sounded like he had possibly broken his nose.

The sound of the basement door opening had true fear setting in for Dominic. Lucifer was too crazed and hungry to get ahold of Kat after the phone call and now this.

Dom had done his best to keep their father away from her, but over the years, Lucifer had slipped past him a few times and got to her before he could protect her. In the past, he had just been in a torturing mood, but this time, he was in the mood to kill.

Shaking his head to get his thoughts back, he fought through the pain to somehow get back up. The world had become blurry from the blood that seeped into his eyes, so he didn't even notice little Cassius going out the back door and into the night.

Limping to the basement door, he could already hear her little body tumbling down the steps. Knowing Kat had probably stayed on the other side of the door to hear them fighting. He really wished she would have listened to him when he'd told her to go hide under the bed if she ever heard anything scary coming from upstairs.

When he got to the door, he used the doorframe to hold his broken body up, and when he saw the scene of her crawling across the concrete floor to get away from Lucifer, his heart broke in two.

"No!" Dominic tried to go down the steps, but his broken body fell, hitting the concrete floor with a *thud*. The last of his adrenaline shot through his body, letting him stand up to grab the back of his father's shirt as he stalked toward a crawling Kat.

Lucifer turned, spitting the words, "You can't fucking protect her from me this time," before he smacked Dom across the face with the back of his hand.

The hit on his already defeated body had him kissing the concrete again, but Dom wouldn't give up protecting her, so he tried to get up for what would be the last time until Lucifer's foot kicked him to the ground for good. However, he didn't stop there as he continued to beat his son over and over, making sure he stayed down this time.

All Dominic could do was lay there as he watched Katarina crawl underneath her bed.

He hoped for death to come, to take him away, knowing his heart wouldn't be able to watch what Lucifer would do to his precious sister, but he should have known better when his father stopped kicking him before darkness could take him away.

Internally, Dominic screamed from the top of his lungs for help as Lucifer turned to go for his target. He wanted nothing more than to close his eyes, knowing what it would do to him if he watched, but he forced himself to, not wanting his sister to go through what she was about to experience alone.

What hurt the most was that she wasn't looking at Lucifer, who was stepping closer; she was looking into his eyes, pleading for help, and there was nothing he could do about it.

When Kat's scream entered his ears as Lucifer dragged her out from under the bed, the two broken pieces of his remaining heart shattered.

Lucifer lived for one reason—to break souls. He marked the living. It was his signature he left on a soul that you could only see through someone's eyes who had been touched by Lucifer. That was why, over time, when he let Dominic out of the closet, he would stare into his eyes, looking for the mark that told him he had finally broken him.

Dominic knew it killed his father that he had yet to break him, but it was kind of ironic that the reason he hadn't yet was because the hell he'd put him through was the exact thing that made him resilient to it … until now.

For twenty years, he had lived on this earth, never letting his father get the best of him, no matter what sick torture or games he played on him. He was feeling his resolve slip now, though.

He held onto his soul for as long as he could while watching Lucifer mercilessly beat his own ten-year-old daughter. The only thing that saved her was her body protecting itself from the pain when she passed out.

Dominic didn't even watch Lucifer walk past him when he tossed Kat's body to the ground like it was a piece of trash. He only kept his eyes on her.

Time seemed to pass slowly. He didn't know how long he lay there on that concrete floor. The pain he felt in his body was unmatched to the pain that was in his heart.

It took everything he had in him to crawl over to her when he finally could. Every inch he scooted closer to her, the more his soul slipped, until he finally got to her unconscious body and rocked her in his arms like he had the first night he'd met her.

Then that was it.

For the final time, Lucifer had finally … won.

Dom sat in the chair at the tattoo parlor, taking in the pain with stride. What he felt as the tiny inked needles sunk deep into his skin was nothing compared to the day Dominic broke.

Lucifer might have won the battle, but Dom wasn't going to let him win the war. His father had made the biggest mistake of his life that day by forcing him to watch as he hit his little sister. He had finally marked him and broken a piece of his soul, but just like he had broken his wrist … it healed back stronger.

Looking down, he watched the black ink stab into his fists as the eight letter word slowly formed over his fingers.

He had promised himself two things that day …

First, Lucifer would never lay a hand on Katarina again. He had to tell the devil their little secret, and when she healed, he had brought her upstairs to the kitchen and out of the basement for the first time as Lucifer had sat, counting his money.

The mathematical prodigy had showed Lucifer how far from stupid she really was when she had counted the cash on the table without touching a bill.

"She's special . . ." The devil leaned forward, staring at the little girl, who he had never wanted to call his daughter, right in her eyes. "Like him."

"She is," Dominic confirmed. "Do not make the same mistake again by leading her right to our enemies."

Lucifer snapped his dead, black eyes back to his son's at the insult. "Is there anything else you want to fucking say?"

"She is too valuable to us." Dominic placed his hands on the table before he stood. Staring the devil down, he showed him the monster he had created. "And you will not touch her again."

And the second thing he promised himself was . . .

Lucifer would only die by the hands that now had the word O-V-E-R-C-O-M-E splayed across them.

With the door opening and the lightswitch being flipped, the man that had come in suddenly stood frozen in place.

Using his shoulder to close the apartment door, he pressed the gun at the base of Anthony's skull. "Don't fucking move," Dominic warned, using his other hand to lift Anthony's coat and take out the weapon that he always carried on him. Unloading them, he tossed the pieces across the room.

Now with only his gun in hand, he shoved Anthony to the side of the living room before carefully walking backward to the table in the middle of the room, keeping the bastard within his field of vision.

"You're making a mistake. Your old man won't be happy with you taking out his strong arm."

"Everyone's day comes," Dominic mocked him, enjoying the spurt of fear that came to his so-called friend's eyes. "Tell me, was it Lucifer's idea to get me to trust you enough to tell you my deepest, darkest secrets, or did you just betray me all on your own?"

Anthony swallowed hard as sweat began to bead on his brow. "Would it matter?"

"No … I suppose not," he admitted callously, laying his gun down on the table before slowly backing away. "Out of respect, I'm going to give you a chance to keep your title." Dominic halted with a smile, giving Anthony an advantage to the table that held the gun by a couple of inches. "Don't you think the man who deserves to be the Luciano enforcer should be able to get to the gun first?"

Anthony's eyes widened in understanding that Dominic was giving him a chance to save his life and legacy.

Dom let Antony make the first move, but when he took off, Dominic reached the gun first, sweeping it up into his hand, and pulling the trigger before the soon-to-be past enforcer had even reached the table.

Uncaringly, he watched Anthony fall backward from the bullet hole placed neatly between his eyes. Then Dom moved around the table, coldly jerking the coat off the still warm body, desensitized to the drops of blood on the huge collar.

Dominic slid the thick, brown leather jacket onto his broad shoulders before going to the door.

Turning the lights off, Dom slipped out, walking slowly down the steps, in plain view of anyone who had looked out their window or down below after having heard the gunshot. No one would be brave enough to snitch on him, especially with the mantle of protection he was wearing.

He had just taken out Lucifer's enforcer, becoming the third most powerful man in Blue Park.

BLUE PARK DEFINITELY HAS ITS PERKS
DOMINIC, AGE 23

Hangin out with Luke tonight.

Dominic read the text message he had received from his ten year old brother Cassius before sliding his phone back into his pocket and getting to the task at hand. Placing the nozzle into the gas tank of his car, Dom clicked the handle instead of watching the pennies flip away on the meter.

Screeching tires had him looking over as a city bus came to a grinding halt and a sixteen-year-old kid who he recognized getting off the bus.

As the boy walked across the parking lot, he sighted him

Keeping his face aloof, Dom didn't return the infectious grin the boy treated him to as he drew closer.

Please, not toda—

"Hi, Dom!"

"How's it going, Marco?" He decided to be polite to the kid, even though he wasn't particularly in the mood for small talk.

Marco grimaced. "Would be better if Dad didn't need me to come stock the cooler before I got home, but I can't complain."

The boy didn't know how lucky he had it to have a father like Carlos. Dom would freeze his balls off in Siberia if he was given a choice of parents.

"I better get inside before he runs out of cold beer during rush hour."

Giving the boy a slight nod, Dom removed the nozzle from his tank, following the lanky teenager inside and leaving Lucifer's car unlocked. No one was stupid enough in this crime-infested neighborhood to touch the car that Lucifer rolled around his domain in. The only reason he was allowed to drive it was because his father thought fueling the vehicle was beneath him. Soon though, Dominic would have a car of his very own.

He had seen an ad in the local newspaper for the body of an old Mustang and bought it. All his spare time and extra cash went into fixing it up to get it back to its mint condition, and now he was really close. Then his days of walking all over Blue Park or hitching a ride from his father would be over.

Entering the gas station, Dominic picked out an assortment

of candy that his brothers and Kat would divide between them and even grabbed an extra bag for Cassius to take to his friend's when they hung out at the park down the street. With his hands full, he made his way to the front of the store to get in line to pay, using his own money. Lucifer studied every purchase on his card. If he didn't approve the charge, then he would take double the amount of the purchase out of his paycheck.

Dominic eyed the man standing in front of him, noticing the jeans and black shirt before him might have been simple, but they were a lot nicer than the worn-out ones usually worn around here. Looking up, he watched the man turn his head slightly toward him and recognition dawned.

"Slumming it today, Lucca?" Dom asked, feeling stupid when Lucca glanced down at the amount of candy clutched in his hands and raised his brow.

"Passing through." Lucca shrugged, starting to advanced forward as the line toward the cash register moved and giving him a cold shoulder under what Dom would bet was at least a fifty dollar T-shirt. He could buy a pack of five of the same shirt at their local Walmart for eight bucks.

Dominic automatically looked toward the glass door when he heard the jingling bell as another customer entered. The man had a wild look on his face when he barged forward, ignoring the waiting line as he shoved his way past him, then Lucca, before thrusting aside an older woman.

"Give me your fucking money!"

Well ... shit.

Dom saw a flash of gunmetal as the robber pointed a gun at Carlos across the counter. The owner quickly began opening the register, taking out the cash inside.

Neither Dominic nor Lucca made any move to stop the robbery, seeing another man outside, blocking anyone else from coming in. Dom would let them leave, then track down the fuckers when he didn't have to worry about Carlos's face getting shot off by the robber who looked coked out of his mind, already trying to get his next fix.

Lowering his hands, he held the candy lower to his waist and waited for the robbery to play out, seeing Lucca was doing the same.

"Dad, I'm done. You—"

Startled, the robber turned at the sound of Marco's voice as the boy came from a side room to go behind the counter, unaware his father was being robbed.

The muzzle of the gun turned toward the boy, but before the robber could pull the trigger, he found a booger the size of 9mm shoved up his nose.

"Put the gun down," Dominic instructed the robber coldly, feeling the burning bite of a bullet that hit his upper arm. Unfazed, he pulled the trigger, splattering brains and gore around the counter and ceiling.

Tightening his hand on the grip of his gun, Dominic turned in one motion toward the door and the robber's accomplice, who had fired the bullet at him.

The man wasn't so high that he didn't recognize who he had just shot and who else was standing by the counter. Pure fear flashed across his face before he took off running.

Lucca made it out the door first since he was closer, but Dom was on his heels as the accomplice ran like hell, trying to disappear down the street. The fucker was sprinting, not high enough not to know he was dead man if he was caught. He had gotten far enough away that he had nearly reached the end of the block. If he managed to get around the corner, he would be able to disappear from sight. The man could have been a fucking Olympic runner; he was moving so goddamn fast that Dom could only make out the color of his red T-shirt.

Lucca raised his gun to fire, but Dominic didn't hesitate a beat.

"Don't," Dom said as he raised his gun alongside Lucca's. "He's mine."

The bullet that left his pistol at the speed of light fired before Lucca could sight his fleeing target. The man could have out run the fastest person alive, but he wasn't going to beat a bullet.

He suddenly stopped running midair, dropping to the ground facefirst.

Lucca slowly lowered his gun and turned, staring at Dominic hard with his blue-green eyes. "You shot him in the head."

"Yes, I wanted him dead," Dominic said simply. Placing his gun back at his waist, he made a smart-ass remark to the man who had been made at seventeen. "I didn't think you'd be opposed to it."

Lucca looked back to where the body had landed, seeing how

far away it was. "But it only took you one bullet."

"Lucky shot." Dom shrugged it off, then quickly changed the subject. "You could have saved me the bullet if you had caught him."

"I don't know a man alive who could have caught that fucker," Lucca told him, not insulted in the least. Putting away his own gun, he went back to staring him down.

"Maybe," Dominic agreed with a smile, unable to resist saying the next words. "But you woulda had a better shot of catching him if you put down the cigarettes once in a while."

Sure, Dom might've been lucky that Lucca had already put his gun away before making that comment and that Carlos had come out and was heading toward them.

Carlos didn't have to ask if he had taken care of the other robber trying to steal from him. "I called my brothers. They'll help me clean the mess up. You go. We'll take care of them."

Dom nodded, already seeing the body being lifted off the sidewalk sown the street and shoved into the trunk of a car. His ass wouldn't be back in Lucifer's car before he would receive a call, asking for payment for hiding the body. This side of the tracks, you had to make money anyway you could, and hiding one of the Lucianos' victims was easy money.

Dominic buttoned the cheap jacket he wore, unconcerned that he had just taken two lives or that the cops would show up any minute. What cops the Carusos didn't own, the Lucianos did.

Lucca intently watched the interaction between the two men, his face a blank mask. Taking out his wallet, he then gave Carlos a wad of bills before going back to his Cadillac without a word.

"You need me to take a look at your arm?" Carlos offered.

"It's just a graze," Dom said, aware of the stinging pain for the first time.

About to return to his father's car, he stopped when he heard Marco call out. The boy was coming out of the store, carrying two grocery bags filled with candy and chips.

"For you. Thank you."

Taking the bags, Dominic gave the teenager a curt nod as Lucca pulled away from the pumps. Curiosity about what the Caruso boss's son was doing on their side of town gave him a brief spurt of worry, but then Dominic dismissed the thought. There was nothing here that the Carusos would want. Hell, even the Lucianos didn't want to be here.

Holding the bags in one hand, he used his other to take out another gun, giving the untraceable gun to Carlos.

"I don't even know how ..." Carlos started to protest.

Dom gave the father a telling look at Marco. The owner was just fucking lucky he wouldn't have to plan a burial for his son.

"Then fucking learn."

Stepping out of the car, Lucca entered the back of the funeral home, scaring the lone night shift worker almost to death.

"Do you know who I am?" he asked, taking a hit of his cigarette.

The worker swallowed hard before slowly nodding.

"The body that was brought in discreetly earlier, where is it?"

It was like you could see the wheels turning in his head, trying to figure out who he was scared of more, the man before him or the devil. Making the decision that was going to, at least, let him live five minutes longer, he gave in. "I-I was just about to throw him in."

Smoke poured from his mouth with each word. "Let me see it."

Quickly, the worker took him to the room; it felt like entering hell. Stepping inside, he went up to the dead body that was laying on the gurney in the middle of the room.

"Is there anything else I can do for you, Mr. Caruso?" the guard asked nervously.

"No." Lucca grabbed the cigarette from between his lips and extinguished it in the bullet hole that was right between the robber's eyes. Watching the little puff of smoke float up, he took a step back. "Throw him in."

The worker hurriedly went to the head of the table, then slid the body into the waiting fire.

Pulling out the almost empty pack of cigarettes from his back jean pocket, Lucca reminded himself that he needed to get more since his first run to the gas station hadn't ended so well. Holding his last one with his lips, he took out the little pack of matches from his front pocket that had *Kansas City Casino Hotel* written on it. Flicking the little stick, it caught fire instantly, making a large flame that died down as he held it to the end of his cigarette. Lucca killed the match with a shake of his wrist as he watched the flesh in the kiln light up, burn, then slowly fall to ash.

"Our little secret?" he told the guard, taking out his wallet and handing him some cash.

"Yes!" The worker seemed so relieved, he looked like he was about to cry. "Please, no cash necessary."

Snapping his wallet closed, Lucca smiled with a little tilt of his lips. He couldn't help but think how easily it was for Dominic to get rid of the body without even trying.

Blue Park definitely has its perks.

YOU'RE NEXT
DOMINIC. AGE 26

Dominic kicked in the heavy metal door, even with the heavy package he was carrying on his shoulder.

The men had all been lined up in their spots but didn't dare look away from Lucifer, who sat on his throne behind his wooden desk.

"You're late! Where the hell hav—"

His father's voice had boomed through the warehouse, but stopped the second he saw what his son was carrying. As Dominic strode in, the line of men gasped and whispered throughout the space while their jaws dropped.

Dominic passed his usual spot in line, going right up to Lucifer's desk and dropping the dead body he carried in with a hard *thud* onto the paved floor. Then Dom turned, taking his place right in the middle of the front of the line.

Slowly, Lucifer stood, leaning over his desk and looking at the lifeless man. Then he slowly sat back down.

The man by Lucifer's side had gone pale, as white as his eyes that looked toward the door for escape.

"Try it, and I promise your death will be painful." Lucifer didn't even have to look at him to know what he was planning. He continued in his cold voice, "Now stand in front of me and tell me why I should show you mercy."

Gino shakily left the Luciano boss's side and went around the desk to face him. "I-I-I tried everything I could to find him, but I knew if I didn't tell you I took him out soon, you would …" He gulped as clear images came to his mind. Gino, who had started out brave, now begged on his knees as he stammered on, "I swear to you, I was going to kill him! You were never supposed to find out, and it was going to be like nothing ever happened once I found where he was hiding. Please, Lucifer, I beg of you, demote me or cut off my fucking hand, but please just show me mercy!"

Lucifer was silent for a moment. Then his voice was not as cold when he spoke. "I'll give you mercy, Gino."

"Thank you!" Gino's tears turned into ones of relief as he brought his hands together in prayer while he stood back up to take his coming punishment like a man. "Thank you, Lucifer."

"Well, I might give you mercy," Lucifer began as he folded his hands before him, his long fingers interlocking, "but my son will not."

Dominic took a step forward, out of the line. Then, marching to the front of Lucifer's desk, he stepped over the dead body he brought in of an undercover cop trying to end both mafia families of Kansas City.

Gino didn't even dare run, but his cries and eyes pleaded with the devil's son for mercy when he stood in front of him. "Please, Dom, show me mer—"

In a flash of light, Dominic took the dagger off his father's desk that every Luciano made man, including himself, had used to give their blood oath as they spoke the *Omertà*. It took only another flash of light for the dagger to meet Gino's neck. His hazel eyes watched the life slowly leave Gino's eyes as Dom swept the blade across his skin. The blood flowed down his neck, covering the front of his white, buttoned-up shirt and stained the gray concrete black when a puddle began to form. Dom put the old antique back in its place before Gino's body fell to the floor.

"Lucianos"—Lucifer slowly rose, presenting with his hands out wide, his proud voice echoing once more throughout the warehouse—"meet your new ... *underboss*."

Dominic turned to face the Luciano men as, one by one, they lowered their heads and bowed. As the last one displayed his respect, Dom walked to the spot Gino had once stood, taking his place at Lucifer's side. He looked out at the men from his new position before he slowly looked to the side to see his father on the throne.

You're next.

LUCA, ANGEL
AND DRAGO
DOMINIC, AGE 28

The second Dominic's phone rang, he answered it, not having to speak before his father's voice came through the line.

"Get everyone to the Switzerland warehouse *now.*"

When the beep met his ears, Dominic's hair stood up on his arms, instinctively knowing that today was the day. He quickly put his matte black Glock, the one his father had gifted him with after becoming the underboss, back together in ten seconds.

"Kat, get back down to the basement, and if you don't hear the special knock, you hide under the bed," Dominic told his sister who was no longer little anymore, as they had just celebrated her eighteenth birthday with donuts.

Looking to his youngest brother when Kat hurried to the basement, he gave him clear instructions. "Cass, get the duffle out of the closet and load it up with the money on the table. Watch the window, and if any car other than mine pulls up, get Kat and sneak out the back. Put as many miles as you can between you and this city and don't ever fucking come back. Do the same if I don't text you our codeword in three hours."

Cassius nodded before disappearing into the hallway to go get the duffle bag.

"What is it?" Angel asked on behalf of both twins who stood antsy nearby.

"It's time," Dominic said, putting the Glock behind his back. "Suit up."

Without another word, both Angel and Matthias grabbed the guns that had yet to be cleaned off the table before going to where they kept the bullets. They were now in their early twenties and had become made.

Dominic threw on his brown leather jacket that he still wore every day. It was old and worn but, somehow, the huge collar made it look regal on him.

Adjusting the sheepskin collar, he said a silent prayer for him and his siblings.

May God have mercy on their souls.

Over the years, he had known his father was slowly losing his grip with reality. His hunger to control the whole city ate Lucifer alive with every passing year. Both death and his son, who he had ironically created to be stronger and smarter than him, shortened his time on the throne.

Once Dom rose the ranks to underboss, he'd slowly taken control over Lucifer's men, one by one, until over half of them secretly followed his commands exclusively.

The last few months, Dominic had known his father had completely lost it, and he'd been preparing for this day since. Today was either going to end with him on the Luciano throne or dead from the possible war that was coming.

When he walked into the warehouse where the meetings of both families were held, he found out just how badly his father had lost it.

A girl was tied to the chair. She looked young, far too young for his father to have here.

When Dante had taken over the Caruso family, he'd made a rule that was supposed to be enforced by the Lucianos as well—children were not allowed to be touched. Mafias around the world not only killed men and women, but children if they had to. In Kansas City, you weren't up for grabs unless you were over eighteen.

Seeing the old scars that the terrified girl carried on her face, it looked like Lucifer had broken that rule years ago. It was especially obvious by the look in her light gray eyes that she had been marked by the devil.

He took a step, watching her tremble harder as he walked around her. Taking off his leather jacket, he put it around the terrified girl's shoulders, unable to watch her freeze to death in the cold warehouse for a moment longer.

Giving his brothers a knowing look, Angel and Matthias continued to guard the scarred girl from their father by walking around her in circles, while Dominic went back to the front of the warehouse, prepared to protect his men for what was coming through that door.

Every Luciano man held up their guns as the door was being beaten.

"You will await my orders. I have waited many years for this moment," Lucifer manically ordered them. "Today is the day we take back our city."

Once the door opened, Carusos came filing in, making every Luciano man behind him shake in fear and confusion that Lucifer was throwing them into an unknown war that they couldn't win.

"The Carusos! You didn't tell us it would be them!" the Lucianos backed up, whispering as the opposing family began to surround them, outnumbering them.

Dominic could hear the rattling of a chain before Sal appeared. Following the chain that Sal held in his hands, he found it connected to his father's most loyal capo, Giovanni, who no longer looked the same. The man looked like he had been tortured beyond recognition. Dominic didn't have to know by who; he knew before Sal kicked Giovanni down to his knees and revealed his oppressor, dressed in black from head to toe.

The boogieman.

The last time he had seen the Caruso underboss in a suit was at his mother's funeral, but since then, he had created his own legend throughout the years. Lucca had outgrown even his own father as the most feared man in the city.

And he was ... *for now.*

As the drama unfolded, Dominic found out all the things his father had kept hidden from him, especially over the last few months. The only sad thing was he had to hear it from his enemy's mouth as it played out in front of him. Just like the rest of his men, he had been blindsided too.

The girl who sat tied in the chair behind him was Chloe, and by the sound of it, Lucifer had developed a sick obsession with her. Dominic had never seen his father look at a woman like he did Chloe, nor speak about one like when he claimed her as his.

In disbelief, Dom didn't understand until Lucca said the words, "Chloe is *mine.*"

Lucifer's sick mind must've developed feelings for her out of jealousy. His father wanted everything and everyone who belonged to the Carusos, and this time, his obsession had gone too far.

When a fair trade was made—Giovanni for Chloe—Lucifer turned it down with laughter.

"There's not much of him left. He's better off dead. He serves no purpose to me anymore if he can't hold her precious body dow—"

POP.

Blood droplets splattered on him from Lucca pulling the trigger on the gun he had aimed at Giovanni's head.

"Kill them!" Lucifer ordered his men, but Dom stood still as the men behind him looked around, trying to decide who to follow.

His father screamed louder, "What are you doing? Kill them!"

Dominic watched Dante closely, seeing what the Caruso boss would decide, but then he looked at Lucca.

"She's yours?" Dominic asked, wanting to see something.

Lucca's blue-green eyes told him all he needed to know before he said, "She's mine."

Dante finally spoke. "Step aside, Dominic. Let us take those who should be held responsible for their crimes, and no one else will have to die ... *today.*"

"I SAID KILL THEM!"

Hearing his father's deranged voice, he hoped it was the last time he'd ever have to fucking hear it again.

It's time.

Lowering his Glock, Dom dropped it on the ground, then took a step to the side to let them through. Then, one by one, Lucifer lost his power as every Luciano man dropped their weapons, letting the metal hit the floor before stepping to the side themselves.

The power and fear his father had created now fully rested on Dominic's shoulders, which might've felt heavier, instead ... he finally felt free.

He had done it, and the funniest part was that Lucifer had done it to himself. Dom hadn't even had to get his hands dirty. Though he had wanted to be the one to kill Lucifer, he wasn't going to be able to get his hands on him since Lucca clearly wanted him so badly.

Dominic smiled at the thought of Lucifer in the boogieman's hands.

Sometimes, reality was better than dreams, after all.

Dominic walked up the steps of the home that now belonged to him. Opening the door to the only room upstairs, it was the best bedroom in the house. It wasn't tiny and the small attached bathroom made this room the most desirable. The only downside was the darkness; the only light came from the single triangle window.

Passing the threshold, Dom could feel the ownership of the room pass to him and now, it was time to make good on a promise ….

Dominic entered the room and approached the bed. He stared down at the older woman passed out who reeked of perpetual booze. Kicking the mattress that sat on the floor, she began to stir.

Raising up on an elbow, her tipsy bloodshot eyes barely opened at first.

"DeeDee…" Dominic's voice was cold as he reached into the pocket of his leather jacket and kneeled down before her.

The alcohol and sleep wore off quickly. Instinctively knowing that something had happened, DeeDee stared back at the boy she watched turn into a man.

"So, do you want help?" Raising his hand out of his pocket, he dangled a little baggie in front of her face that was filled to brim with her precious white snow… "Or, do you want to fly?"

Giving away his father to die was easy, but having to agree to the terms the Carusos demanded was not.

The first term had them handing over fifty percent of their profits.

The second would cost a Luciano woman's life, as one would be chosen to marry a Caruso to mingle the blood of the two families to cease any future wars.

The third had ensured the first two terms by keeping Angel as collateral until the terms were met.

Bang.

Bang.

Bang.

Bang.

Bang.

Bang.

Gunshots rang out, piercing the ears of the living and the skulls of the dead.

Dominic and his siblings thought the third agreement would be the hardest. It turned out they were very fucking wrong.

"You promised me!" Katarina screamed at him, uncaring of the many women who stood in their living room. "You promised me I wouldn't have to go back down there ever again!"

"I know," Dominic told her painfully and regretfully, not wanting her to have to go to the basement even for just a moment. After Lucifer's death, he had promised to never make her go down there again, but he was already breaking his promise. "But, please, it's only for a little bit."

Kat shook her head vigorously, trying not to cry. "No."

"They're here," Matthias yelled from the window, seeing the black Cadillacs pull up.

"He will choose you if he sees you, I know it." Dominic's voice started to break. "There will be nothing I can do. They'll kill Angel if I don't let them have you."

When Lucca walked through the door minutes later, Dominic instinctively knew he was fucked. They had kept Kat a secret from the Carusos, but there wasn't much the underboss didn't know in this city.

Lucca only scanned the line of Luciano women before he went searching the house. Dom's heart sank when he opened the basement door and went down. His last hope was that Drago, the Caruso that his father had shot in the chest five times and almost sent to his deathbed to get his hands on Chloe, wouldn't choose his baby sister.

When Drago had given his underboss a nod that she was the one he wanted to marry, Dominic had to choose between Katarina or Angel. He could pull the Glock out from behind his back and blow Lucca's and Drago's brains outs, and they could try to make a run for it out of the city before the Carusos found out, leaving Angel behind. Or he could let Lucca walk out that door and keep everything he had worked hard for, but it'd cost him his sister.

Dominic's fingers flexed, itching to go for the Glock at his back as Lucca walked past him.

Letting Lucca go was the hardest fucking decision of his life, but he promised himself one thing.

One day . . .

He.

Will.

Pay.

FOR THE LOVE OF GOD, BE FUCKING UGLY

The anger Dominic felt over the next few weeks was about to reach a boiling point. He had never in his existence felt so helpless, and that was saying a lot, considering the hell his father had put him through the second he was born.

One sibling already belonged to the Carusos for the foreseeable future, and now Katarina was set to join Angel.

Taking over the Luciano throne was supposed to make his life easier, not harder. The worst fucking part was that, for the first time, the Luciano siblings could finally be happy *together* ... and they had even been stripped of that.

"Some car just pulled into our driveway," Cassius had told

them, looking out the front window.

Dominic and Matthias instinctively looked at each other before Dom could ask Cassius what he wanted to know.

"Brand new Cadillac."

"Shit." Dominic pulled his Glock from behind his back and cocked it so a bullet was ready in the chamber.

Matthias's voice grew with the same worry that Dom felt in his heart. "I thought they weren't supposed to come for Kat until *after* the wedding?"

"Do you know who it is?" Dominic's tone was serious, mentally preparing himself for the worst.

"It's a Caruso, for sure," Cass answered when he saw the fancy suit, protectiveness for his sister becoming apparent in his voice. "He's opening the door for someone else now ... It's a"—Cassius seemed confused at who he was looking at—"girl?"

"Girl?"

"Yeah, some blonde in heels," Cassius described her.

"Blonde girl in heels?" Matthias quickly jumped up then ran to the window to see, the worry in his voice suddenly gone. "God ... damn ..." the twin breathed out the words upon seeing her.

Who in the fuck could that—

"It's the fucking boss's daughter," Matthias said in disbelief. "Maria Caruso."

Dominic's heart beat hard in his chest at the name. The sudden image of the fourteen-year-old girl in the white dress at her mother's funeral appeared in his mind.

"Oh." Cassius went back to the couch, no longer concerned for his sister.

"What the hell is she doing here?" Dominic thought he had been worried before, but now he really was. The boss's daughter belonged nowhere near Blue Park. He didn't want to be in a ten-foot radius of her. Dante and Lucca would kill the whole Luciano bloodline if anything happened to her. He knew that because, if he had the power Lucca held, every Caruso man would be buried twelve feet deep, because six feet was still too close to the surface for him when it came to Kat.

"Relax." Matthias, whose ass had been depressed the day Angel was handed over, suddenly looked like life no longer felt bleak.

Dominic felt it the second she took a step on the porch, his memory flooding with the strong but strange feeling he had felt for her all those years ago. It was a pull. His body was drawn to what was on the other side of the door before she even knocked.

Watching his brother's hand go to the doorknob, Dominic gave one small prayer as those feelings washed over him. *Please, for the love of God, be fucking ugly.*

And, by ugly, he meant the hunchback of Notre fucking Dame better come through that door, because every nerve ending in his body waited in anticipation to see her again. Even though he knew it would be impossible—considering how beautiful she'd been at fourteen, sending grown men into a frenzy—still, he prayed for Quasimodo ….

Matthias opened the goddamned door.

Fuck.

If he knew any better, he would walk right up, tell her to get lost, and then slam the door right in her pretty face. But the problem was, it wasn't just pretty; it was the most gorgeous fucking face he had ever seen. Anything he had realistically imagined her to look like before the door had opened was topped. At the most, he thought she'd be beautiful, kinda look like Reese Witherspoon. What he got was Reese Witherspoon from Kat's favorite movie, *Legally Blonde*, mixed with Marilyn Monroe. Maria was a goddamn sin wrapped in pretty packaging that was pulled straight from Hugh Hefner's dreams.

Matthias couldn't keep his eyes to himself either. "Hey, princess."

Any stupor Maria had put him under from seeing her again quickly vanished when a suit barreled through, pushing his brother out of the way like he owned the goddamn place. Standing up, Dominic wasn't about to be disrespected by a no-name Caruso in his home.

"Who the fuck are you?"

"He's with me." The boss's daughter entered without permission to save the poor fucker's life.

Dominic couldn't help himself when she stepped between them, his hazel depths begging him to look at her legs since she stood much taller than any typical woman. Dominic had always been tall, outgrowing most of the female teachers since sixth grade. By the time he had gone to high school, he looked like he belonged in college. When she stepped in front of him and stood just a few inches shorter than him, his eyes traveled down her lengthy body.

Her champagne dress hugged all the right places, at least what he could see of it under the big fur coat. But the best part about it was how short it was, showing off just how fucking long her tanned legs went on. The cherry on top... her high stiletto heels. Normal "good-looking" people either had a great face and a nice body, or a nice face and a great body. Maria, of course, had both. And it gave him all the more reason to get her the fuck out of here and back on her side of town where she belonged before the effect she had on him put him six feet under.

"Why the hell are you here?"

When her green eyes, that somehow shined brighter than emeralds, gave him their own once-over, Dominic's heart stopped when she appeared to like what she saw.

Shit, shit, shit.

"I, um ..." Maria paused for a moment before answering, "... to see Kat."

Crossing his arms over his chest at the mention of his sister, he hoped it would send a polite message to her that, if they came to collect, she should have brought someone besides the dipshit who stood behind her. "And what do you want with her?"

"Well, I thought she needed a wedding dress." She slightly raised her brow. "Doesn't she?"

Oh. He didn't know what he had expected her to say, but it wasn't that.

"Cassius, go get Kat."

Dominic never turned his head from hers, even though she did to study the youngest Luciano brother. Even her fucking side profile looked goddamned perfect.

Matthias must've wanted to see what the dress underneath really looked like because he asked, "Can I take your coat?"

Maria looked him dead in the eyes with a precious smile on her lips. "Touch me, and I'll kill you."

He might've actually laughed if it wasn't for the fact that every second she was here could cost them their lives.

Dominic stepped closer to her. "Does Lucca know the princess is out of her castle?"

"Do you think I would be here if he did?"

Dom lifted his eyes from hers to the Caruso soldier behind her. "Certainly not, if this is the one who brought you."

The dumbass suit proved to be dumber than Dominic thought when he didn't catch the insult at first.

"I hope the poor sucker knows whatever you promised him won't be worth it by the time Lucca gets done with him." Dom placed his eyes back on her.

"What he doesn't know won't hurt him. It can be our little secret."

Dominic had to flex his jaw to keep it from dropping to the floor at the sound of her voice dropping an octave. The brave princess had even taken her own step forward until the tip of her toed heels were just a few centimeters away, showing him that she wasn't the least bit frightened of him or his last name. Hell, Dominic might've been offended if he didn't want her to be scared of him.

The two were practically eye-fucking each other when Kat walked in.

"What are you doing here?"

It took Maria a hard second to look away from him. "I thought you might want a wedding dress for when you walk down the aisle."

"I have a white dress, but it's shor—"

"Absolutely not," Maria scoffed. "I am taking you shopping right now."

"O-Okay," Katarina warily agreed, clearly partly out of fear.

Before Dominic knew it, the words slipped right out of his mouth, "I'm going with you." Grabbing his coat, he had to let Matthias down. "Matthias, you stay here with Cassius."

Frankly, Dominic didn't trust Maria not to kill him. She could see right through his playboy façade.

Maria tried to be polite. "That won't be necces—"

But Dom had stopped her. "I'm not having Lucca find out I let you two go alone with this fucking idiot." He didn't fucking trust him to water a plant, much less watch his sister and the Caruso boss's daughter.

"Excuse m—"

"Fine," Maria quickly cut off her wannabe boyfriend.

With all of them going out the door, he saw the brand new Cadillac that he wouldn't be caught dead in, next to his black Mustang, and he had to decide just how far he wanted to go …

"You know what, Ted …" He tried to remember the name he'd

heard on the other side of the door before they had knocked.

Maria told him he was a letter off. "Todd."

"Todd," he corrected, trying to pretend he gave an actual fuck what his name was. "How about you go home, and we can all just pretend Maria snuck out by herself. I think we both know I won't touch a pretty blonde hair on her head because of what Lucca would do to me if he found out. I'm sure it's going to be similar to what he's going to fucking do to you if you don't leave."

"Bye, Todd." Maria gave him a sweet wave, clearly wanting the same thing as Dominic.

That was all that was needed for Maria's puppy dog to leave with his tail tucked between his legs.

"Aren't you cold?" a fully clothed Kat asked Maria, while closing her jacket.

Dominic tried his best not to burst out in laughter. The last ten minutes with her proved the theory he had of her when she was only fourteen. He decided to keep his laughter inside, but he was going to let Maria know he knew exactly what she was if they were about to do this so-called dance.

"You can't feel cold if your heart is dead." Dominic gave her a knowing smile before opening the passenger side door for her. "Isn't that right, princess?"

The look Maria gave him as she chose not to answer his comment let Dom know he had her wondering how he had found out her little secret so fast, but he wasn't going to tell her that just yet.

Watching Maria slide into his black leather seat was a dream he never knew he needed to come true until he saw his Mustang parked beside her Cadillac. That was another reason he had wanted Teddy to scram.

Fuck. If he was going to die by the hands of the Carusos for this, then his trip to hell was going to be worth it.

YOU NEVER STRIKE A DEAL UNTIL YOU'VE WON

Dominic pulled his black Mustang into the expensive drive. It looked like a goddamn mansion compared to his house, and it honestly could've been by the looks of it out here. The perfect white house was fit for a king, as it was spotlighted to light up how perfect the façade actually was. It was the first time he entered the Caruso family home, and coming from his side of town to this side made Dominic swear middle-class didn't even exist.

Throwing the car in Park, he supposed he should feel scared or, in the very least, nervous to walk into the enemy's den, but he wasn't. The fury he felt boiling in his veins outweighed his possible stupidity.

Katarina was set to be married one month from when she'd been chosen, and now that the day was almost here, regret and rage overcame him. Determined to save his sister from her fate of becoming a Caruso, he had called Lucca, asking for a private meeting.

He would have asked to be in Dante's presence, but Dom had a feeling it was Lucca pulling all the strings, and desperate times called for desperate measures. Getting out of the car and slamming the door shut, this was that time—he was fucking desperate.

Dominic walked straight up to the Caruso family home like he was on a mission, letting his determination flow through him. Heavily knocking on the door, there was no fucking way he was leaving this home without his sister's wedding called off.

They'll be taking me out in a body bag if they want me to lea—

The door opening had him unable to complete his vow, as his heart thudded at the image on the other side of the door.

"Hello, princess." Dominic wasn't afraid to let his eyes wander at the much different ensemble than when she'd unexpectedly arrived at his home. "I thought, even at home, you might wear heels and fur. Guess not."

Dear God, he liked what she had worn last time, but this was something else altogether. The matching pink velvet set consisted of a little tank top that displayed her midriff and tight shorts that were the size of some women's underwear. It had him almost willing to risk it all right here.

He was unashamed of his hazel eyes taking in her body, though it was a dangerous game to stare at the Caruso boss's daughter like that, much less in his home. Nevertheless, the family had taken almost everything away from him, and there wasn't much to lose, so the thoughts he had of Maria since seeing her just yesterday, and the many thoughts he planned to have of her tonight, gave him the little bit of respect he needed back.

"I don't like to be called that, Dominic," Maria told him harshly.

The way she responded definitely came as a shock to him—her green eyes lit up every time.

Maria might not liked to be called princess by other people, but from her pretty little face, she secretly liked it when he did.

"Well, that's too bad," he told her with a sly smile.

"May I help you?" Crossing her arms had her perky breasts raise higher. The motion had him about to ask her to show him the way to her bedroom.

Stepping into the doorway, he put his body an inch from hers, paying her right back for coming into his home uninvited. He couldn't help but notice she wasn't as tall as she was the last time, since she was barefoot and not in her stilettos. He had more of a height advantage, and he fucking liked it.

"Sure."

He rudely pushed past her, getting to the real and only important reason he came here—his sister. "You can take me to Lucca." His tone was serious now, his mind back on track.

Maria studied his changed demeanor before finally asking, "Is Lucca expecting y—"

"Take me to him." He was slightly rude when he said it, but he couldn't waste any more time talking to Maria. The power she held over him could have him forgetting everything.

Thankful that she seemed to silently understand his urgency, Maria show him the way.

The huge, wrought iron staircase in their foyer was only the beginning of the family's wealth. Going down a hall that led to a door, he could smell the hint of smoke, knowing the one he wanted was on the other side before she even opened the door for him.

The moment he saw the Caruso underboss patiently waiting behind his desk staring at the burning flame of his lighter, Dom didn't even notice Maria leaving, closing the door on her way out.

Not waiting to be asked to sit down, he took a seat in the chair on the other side of his desk.

"How did you know?" he asked, trying to keep his rage in check.

"Know what?" Lucca asked coldly, flipping shut his Zippo lighter.

This time, he failed when his voice came out guttural. "About Katarina."

"I have my ways—"

"No." He stopped his bullshit answer, getting frustrated that he was more interested in opening and closing the Zippo than their meeting. He hoped this would get his fucking attention. "I want the fucking truth."

Lucca flipped his lighter closed again, letting it hit the desk, then finally look at him. "You sure about that?"

"Yes …." He now feared the answer.

Smiling, it appeared Lucca didn't feel an ounce of remorse. "Cassius."

Dom's brows furrowed in confusion … until it hit him. "Luke …" he whispered the name of Cassius's friend. He'd been talking about a Luke since before Dom had run into Lucca at the gas station on his side of town. That was why Lucca had been there. "All these years?"

Lucca slowly nodded.

Dom had thought Cassius's friend was a fucking imaginary one at first, but then he figured it was just a kid from school … Not fucking Lucca Caruso.

"You … You …" Dominic's confusion quickly turned back into fury. "You know fucking everything about us, don't you?"

His blue-green eyes confirmed Dom's fears.

Dominic ran his hand roughly through his hair. "He told you everything, and there isn't a goddamn thing you don't know about us."

"He didn't know it was me," Lucca tried to excuse Cassius. "Not until I walked through the door the day Katarina was chosen."

Dom wanted to fucking kill him, suck the life out of him with his bare hands, like he had wanted to do to his father. Every time he thought it couldn't get worse, it did. He had officially reached his boiling point, as Lucca had managed to ruin every one of his brothers' lives. Angel had been taken, Matthias was slowly withering away every day without him, and all the work he did to keep Cassius away from his father was for nothing, considering he'd been hanging around someone just as fucked up. All he had untouched by the boogieman was his Kat, and now he definitely wasn't going to give her up.

"I'm not forcing my sister to marry." Pausing, he made it clearer to the underboss. "I *cannot* do it."

"*Force* is such a strong word," Lucca told him, pulling out a cigarette from his pack that sat on his desk. "We like to use the word *arranged.*"

"Call it whatever the fuck you want, Lucca, but Kat's no longer doing it, so Drago will have to pick someone else."

"Pity." Lucca flipped his lighter open to light the end of the stick he held in his mouth. He took a few quick puffs, letting smoke blow through his mouth before he continued, "I was just starting to like Angel working for me."

Dominic had to flex his jaw to keep cool.

"He's a better soldier than half my men combined, you know. Who do I have to thank for that?" Lucca paused. "Your father ... or you?"

"I don't know. You tell me?" he asked through gritted teeth, since Lucca knew so much that went on in the Luciano house.

"Doesn't matter much now." Lucca shrugged as he sat back and got comfortable in his leather chair.

The heat that came from Dominic was almost as hot as the tip of Lucca's burning cigarette. Being forced to choose between letting him kill Angel or end Katarina's future didn't feel like much of a choice.

Dominic gave him a chilling look, his voice as deadly as his stare. "Lucca, you have taken everything from me. You've taken fifty percent of our profits, my brother, and now you're taking my sister." Pausing, he decided to give the underboss a warning and remind him that he might be a Luciano, but he still held power. "There's not much else to lose."

"Trust me, Dominic"—Lucca took a hard hit off his cigarette—"there is always more to lose."

You would know. Dom desperately wanted to say what he whispered in his head, but he had to keep that card in his pocket. So, he just tried to get him to see reason. "Please, Lucca, Kat is innocent in all of this. If you talked to Cassius, then you know what it was like for her growing up. She deserves to finally be free, and she most of all deserves a future."

"What about marrying Drago would mean she wouldn't be free or have a future?" Lucca leaned forward in his chair, clearly taking offense.

Dominic's brows drew together, wondering why the fuck he needed to spell it out for him. "Because she's being forced to marry a man she doesn't wan—"

"Did Katarina tell you she didn't want to marry him?" he asked simply.

Thinking a moment, he realized she had never said a word. "No, but she wouldn't do—"

"Of course she wouldn't," Lucca stopped him. "There are many things we have to do in our lives that we don't want to, Dominic, but we do them for *family*." Taking another hit of his cigarette, he hit Dom with the cold, hard truth. "She is doing the same thing Angel is doing by being here with the Carusos, and the same thing you had to do when you agreed to the terms."

"No." Dom shook his head. "Kat didn't choose this life."

"And you did?" Lucca asked, raising a brow.

"I said the *Omertà*."

"You might've made the oath, but what choice were you given?" The underboss tapped his ashes into the crystal ashtray. "Do you honestly think you would have walked the same path if Lucifer wasn't your father?"

Not only did Dominic know the answer, but Lucca did too. Still, he continued to fight for his sister.

"Katarina is better than us, than what we are. She deserves a happy life with a great husband who will show her how special she is, not Drago."

Lucca's strange colored eyes flashed at him. "Do you know why I picked Drago, Dominic?"

"I don't know …" Dom told him, exasperated, feeling like he had reached the end of his rope to save his sister. "Because it suits one of your sick agendas? Lucifer almost killed him, so you chose him, knowing he'd pick Katarina the second he knew she was his daughter."

"No," the underboss told him wholeheartedly.

Yeah right. As far as he was concerned, he had hit the fucking nail on the head.

Dominic sat back, waiting to hear how Lucca was going to spin this shit. "Well, you tell me then, Lucca."

"Did I know Drago would pick her? Yes," Lucca told him without a hint of remorse. Crushing the butt of his cigarette into the ashtray, he looked Dominic in the eyes. "But I picked Drago because, not only is he loyal, strong, and determined, but he's the best goddamn man I have. Do you know why Lucifer was almost successful in killing him? Because he's the only man I trusted to leave Chloe in his care, and he took five bullets to the chest to try to save her."

During his speech, Dominic's rage had slightly softened at hearing Lucca talk about his man in that way, knowing each word he said about Drago was true.

Lucca continued, "I don't know a better man than Drago, inside and outside of Kansas City ... except for one."

Dominic's brows furrowed at his last line, but before he could ask who, Lucca answered.

"You."

"Oh, come on, Lucca." Dominic got up from his seat in frustration, unable to stay in the chair any longer, afraid he would jump across the desk and strangle him if he didn't put distance between them. "What are you doing? Trying to butter me the fuck up? Do me a favor, since you know every damn thing about me, let's cut the bullshit and stop the pretending between us. 'Cause, if you're going to continue to fuck me in the ass, I'd like to at least keep my dignity."

"I don't pretend, Dominic," Lucca told him, deadly serious. "I meant what I said."

"What is your game here, Lucca?" Giving him a stern look, his hazel depths searched the blue-green ones for answers to make sense of this. There was a reason why he was putting all this into motion when the underboss already had everything he could ever want—the city, the money, the throne, and Dominic on his knees, trying to save his family, thanks to his father, so ... "What is it you want?"

"You're right. I do know everything about you, Dominic ... I know the things you went through in that house, how you were raised, and what you're capable of." Lucca stood, walking slowly around the desk. He stepped right in front of Dominic. "You and me will burn this fucking city to the ground if we don't see eye to eye."

"So"—Dominic gave him a strange look, his heart accelerating—"what are you saying?"

"We work together," Lucca said simply, "and when I get my father to step down, we run this city together ... fifty-fifty."

Dom laughed then suddenly stopped. "You're fucking serious, aren't you?" When the underboss nodded, he asked, "Why?"

"I have my reasons. Now"— was all he would give him before Lucca held out a hand—"do we have a deal ... or not?"

Staring at the boogieman's outstretched hand, it were as if all the air had been sucked out of the room. Everything felt ominous as the crystal ball he had always seen his future in violently shook. The wind began to change, and not only did he get to decide which way it blew, but he could finally choose his own destiny. However, if he shook the boogieman's hand, it could be worse than shaking his hand with the devil and, from personal experience, that never went well. Then, suddenly, he came to a decision.

"Call off my sister's wedding, and we will."

Lucca only stared at him a moment then turned. "No."

"You said fifty-fifty," he told him, wondering if he should have shaken his hand first before fighting for his sister, but then he thought no, he had done the right thing. You never strike a deal until you've won, or at the very least was fair. "And you've taken everything from me. Kat is the only thing I'm asking to get back. My profits and Angel, you get to keep. You don't even need her anyway."

"But I do." He stuck another cigarette between his tilted lips. "Making Katarina a Caruso ensures our deal and that you will never betray me."

Fucking sick bastard wasn't only smart, he was right.

"What about me, though? I've taken loss after loss. What ensures *my* deal with *you?* You have to give me something that proves your deal is in good faith and that you won't stab me in the back one day."

"Unfortunately, the terms you agreed to are off the table until I replace my father, but besides those"—Lucca flipped his Zippo open, the glow from the small flame illuminating his face as he lit the end of his cigarette—"what do you want?"

It was a scenario he thought he'd never in a million years be in, so when the question was asked, his mind nearly went blank. Only a whisper of an impossible thought echoed in his mind …

"Think carefully, Dominic." Lucca's voice held a knowing warning. "You only get one choice."

Staring at the underboss, he wondered if he knew what it was

Dom was going to choose before he himself knew.

Swallowing hard, he thought, if he asked what he secretly wanted, it was going to make it real. Dominic wasn't going to be able to take it back, and until he shook Lucca's hand, he was the enemy, which made this a very dangerous game. The only thing he wanted could cause the whole deal to fall through. It was a scenario of high stakes, high rewards, and the reward could be oh so sweet while simultaneously making him and Lucca even.

Taking one deep breath, he chose. With the second, he staked his claim. "Maria."

It was an eye for an eye.

Lucca took a hard hit as he stared him in the eyes. Then he stood, leaned forward, and put out his hand again. "Deal."

Confused, Dom furrowed his brows at how quickly Lucca had agreed to it.

Just like that? Holy shit, he's even more of a cold bastard than I already thought.

Dominic stepped in front of Lucca's desk and took the boogieman's hand. "Deal."

Lucca stood as they shook hands. Looking Dom in the eyes, he sealed the deal, making them go from sworn enemies since birth to ... equal partners.

THE LAST THING HIS NAME WOULD TAKE

T*he second Dominic pulled his* hand away from Lucca's, his
heart dropped at Lucca's next words.

"Good luck with my sister." Lucca smirked. "You're going
to need it."

"What?" Dom asked, feeling his rage begin to creep back in.
"We made a deal. If Kat understands an arranged marriage, then
I'm sure Maria will too."

Amused, Lucca knocked his ashes in the tray. "Then you really
should have specified that. The only thing I planned to do was give
you my blessing and keep my father from killing you."

"No," Dominic hit his fist on Lucca's big, wooden desk. "You knew exactly what I was fucking asking for."

Lucca put a hand on his crystal ashtray, stopping it from rattling as he gave Dominic a deadly look. "If you think my sister would listen to single order I gave her, then you do not know Maria at all."

"Oh, I know Maria," Dominic made it clear.

"Then you know, if I forced her to marry you"—Lucca paused for a moment—"she would never, ever love you."

I should do it, just fucking slit his thro—

Smiling, Lucca blew out the smoke from his mouth. "And that's what you want, isn't it?"

"You know, at least we finally came to one agreement." Dominic started pacing the room again. "Your whole 'arranged,' not 'forced' marriage bit was a load of bullshit."

"There's nothing to be ashamed about, Dominic. I've got well over half my men in love with her."

Dominic pinched the bridge of his nose at another realization. "Jesus, Lucca, is that why you gave her that joke of a bodyguard? Ted?"

"Todd," Lucca corrected.

"I don't give a fuck what his name is." Dom's voice went cold. "You knew exactly how this was going to go before I walked through that door. You probably put the idea in her head that Kat needed a wedding dress right before you assigned Teddy to her."

Lucca corrected him once more, "Todd."

That was it. Dom turned, heading for the door, knowing if he didn't walk out of the room, one of them was dying tonight.

"What are you more scared of?" Lucca taunted in a haunting

voice. "That you won't be able to get Maria to fall in love with you … or that you might find out she'll never love you back?"

Dominic didn't know how the sick bastard had figured it out, but since he had, he supposed there was no longer a point in hiding it. "I'll get her to love me." Going to the door, he opened it, making a promise to Lucca Caruso and the rest of the world as he declared one last thing. "Even if it's the last fucking thing I do."

Slamming the door, he didn't even hear the "good luck" that he had been genuinely wished.

"A girl only gets to walk down the aisle for the first time once. So, it has to be designer."

"Princess has a point." Dominic grabbed the other arm that didn't have a manicured hand around Kat's. His sister might've not needed, let alone wanted, a fancy dress, but if the Carusos were going to make his sister get married then, by God, they were going to pay for it.

"Fine," Kat gave in before looking over at Maria with concern. "Did you just say, for the first time once?"

"I'm thinking my third husband, after the first two mysteriously die, will be the right one."

Dominic felt his balls wanting to shrivel up and hide inside his body. "That's good to know."

"Maria …" Kat waited for her to look at her before she continued, "I think I'm a little bit scared of you."

Maria smiled. "I'm only kidding."

Yeah fucking right. *The poor soul, aka the Caruso schmuck who married*

Maria, he prayed had tough knees because no man, and he meant no man, was going to get his dick sucked. The only reason he didn't fear his sister around the mafia princess was because it was obvious Maria liked her.

Maria might've looked at men like she wanted to stomp her stilettos on their necks, but she didn't look at women that way. Her eyes softened around them. She looked at them appreciatively, especially when she liked what they wore. As for men, he could tell how she felt about them. When her beautiful emerald eyes turned beady, he didn't have to be in her mind to know the single swirling through her brain ...

Kill all men.

And, if Lucifer hadn't been his father, and he wasn't in this line of work, he might've been a little offended. However, Dominic was man enough to know that less women wanted to keep men around. It was no wonder women were trying to figure out how to make babies without needing the Y chromosome. Hell, after having Lucifer as a father, he truly wished them all the luck in the world.

They passed designer store after designer store until it was apparent they'd arrived at a bridal store, as everything inside was white.

Entering the store, they were greeted by one beautiful-looking man. "Maria, my love, I haven't seen you in a while."

Maria and the guy gave each other a kiss on each cheek.

"I know. I've missed you."

Why does it seem like she comes here once a week ...

"Ken, I need a dress for my friend, Kat." Maria took his hand in hers to introduce them.

Dominic couldn't help but think the two looked like Barbie and Ken had come straight to life as they stood next to each other. However, in this Barbie dream house, Ken didn't like Barbie.

"And who might this handsome man be?"

Well, that definitely explains why Maria likes this man.

The mafia princess grinned at him smugly. "This is her brother, Dominic."

"Nice to meet you, Dominic." Ken gave him a wink.

Joke was on her, however, when he smiled at Ken, because it didn't bother him one bit.

Ken continued when he looked at his sister. "And you are gorgeous. Spin for me, honey; let me take a look at you."

Awkwardly, Kat spun, and Dominic had to keep himself from laughing. His sister wasn't your typical "girly girl." She loved the color pink, just as much as he did on her, so much so that she even died her hair a cute baby pink. But she also loved the color black. She appreciated girly things, but Dominic had ultimately rubbed off on her. Kat was the perfect mixture of hard and soft, sweet and badass, and Dominic couldn't be prouder of how she turned out.

"Maria, you take her to the dressing room to get her undressed while I go pull some dresses. And you, handsome, can go take a seat in the sitting area." Ken finished the orders with his eyes back on Dom.

"Thanks." Dom gave him a polite smile, not wanting him to think his nerves had anything to do with Ken's harmless flirting. Hearing him give the orders had made everything real. He was about to watch his little sister, who he raised, try on fucking wedding dresses for a man she didn't want to marry, making him feel like he was about to be vomi—

"May I offer you some champagne?" a woman offered when the three entered the dressing room area.

Dominic picked up the flute without a second thought, throwing it back like the disgusting gold liquid was a shot of fucking tequila. Picking up the second glass, he gave it to Maria before grabbing the third, this one to nurse until this hellish experience was over.

"She's not old enough to drink," he told the woman holding the tray out for Kat. It only made the woman look at him in concern when she then glanced over at Kat. "But not too young to get married," he said, not only for her but to remind himself.

Needing to go sit down before he passed out, he took a seat on the expensive, ridiculous-looking. grand velvet love seat, while Maria rolled her eyes, then took Kat to a dressing room.

Wiping his brow he took a few deep breaths, trying to calm himself. He could handle killing men and his father, so he should be able to handle this. Dom didn't know the last time he felt this sick, on the verge of throwing—

Maria coming back and taking a seat beside him miraculously kept his stomach contents down.

She took one look at him and chuckled. "Nervous?"

"No, not at all," Dominic badly lied, taking another sip of the champagne.

"Uh-huh." Maria smiled. "You sure about that?"

"Yeah." Dom shrugged. "I just had to choose death upon my whole family or marrying off my eighteen-year-old sister."

Maria had been in the middle of taking a sip of her champagne when she suddenly stopped to stare at him in disbelief.

"What?" he mocked, unafraid that he had told her something he wasn't supposed to. Dom couldn't care less about much at this point, and it wasn't like Maria was an innocent, little angel anyway.

"Does Daddy not tell you the family secrets?"

"No," Maria answered simply, still staring at him strangely. "I find things out other ways."

"If you knew, then why are you staring at me that way?"

"Because my father and his men don't exactly just come out and tell me family business," she said softly, her eyes boring into his.

Dominic could see it then, in her emerald eyes, that she was slowly starting to see him a bit differently, like her mind was beginning to change about something ... and then they heard the dressing room door open.

Clearing his throat, he looked to where he heard the sound of a dress dragging on the floor. Seeing Katarina in a white wedding dress brought his sick stomach right back.

"Hmm." Kat looked at herself thoughtfully in the mirror on the pedestal that made the dress fall perfectly around her.

Even though his stomach was doing somersaults, Dom only had to give the dress one hard glance to know it wasn't meant for her.

Shaking his head, he told her, "I don't like it."

He was thankful for his honesty when she happily went right back to the dressing room and he no longer had to look at it.

The second she shut the door, Dom couldn't help but down the contents the second his lips touched the glass.

"Here." Maria took the now empty flute out of his hand and handed over her half-full one.

Dominic stared at the outstretched glass, making sure his large hand grazed her fingertips when he took it from her. Immediately, he regretted it, as now his body screamed out for him to touch her more. "Thanks."

He couldn't say he had the same effect on her when she immediately called out for the woman to bring them more champagne.

"You don't come here often, do you, princess?" he asked sarcastically when the lady began refilling up their glasses.

Maria laughed. "N—"

"Oh, yes. Ken gives Maria a call every time a new collection arrives."

"Is that so …?" Dom asked, a sly smile touching his lips as he looked at the lying blonde.

"Thanks, Sherry," Maria said through clenched teeth after she filled up her glass.

Dom took a sip, still smiling. "It's probably good to start practicing now, if you plan to be on your fifth husband by thirty-five."

"That's not why I like to come try on the dresses. I try them on because I know I'll never wear one."

Looking over at her, he couldn't figure out what he heard in her voice. It wasn't sadness, but rather a … void.

The sound of Kat's footsteps on the pedestal had him looking back to his sister. This white dress was uglier than the first.

"No." Dom took a sip, desperately not trying to down the contents with Kat around.

Ken stood there, looking appalled, clearly no longer thinking Dominic was attractive, since they didn't share the same taste.

It was too bad, as he was sure the dress was fucking expensive and would be pretty on another girl, but not his Kat.

"The dress I have is fine, Maria," Katarina groaned, clearly not liking this experience.

He knew the dress they were talking about. It was a strapless, white dress, with a short, puffy tulle skirt. Dominic had surprised her with it when he had turned the basement into a fake high school prom. He couldn't get her to go to her high school one, since she had been like him in the "having no friends department." So, because he didn't want her to miss out on an experience like he had, he threw her, her own prom. Dom had even managed to get Lucifer out for the night so they could blare their music, and he, his brothers, and Kat had laughed and danced all night. Kat had somehow even managed to get Cassius to dance with her. To this day, it was one of his favorite memories of them all. That one memory slightly made all the other horrible other memories in that house bearable.

The tall, legged blonde suddenly stood up and went over to her. "What's wrong?"

"They're beautiful, but this just … isn't me." Kat awkwardly stood in the big white dress, staring at herself in the mirror.

"Go back in there and get this thing off," Maria quickly told her. "I'll be right back."

When Kat and Ken went back into the dressing room, Dominic watched Maria carefully as she left the dressing area on a mission, then came back a moment later with a dress in her hands.

"What do you think of this?" Maria asked, holding the dress

up in front of her.

Dominic stared up at her from the couch, his breath getting caught in his throat. "I don't like it for you"—he stood up, making her move the dress off to the side carefully, not liking to see her in that color—"but, for Kat, it's perfect."

Staring up at him, the blonde beauty looked caught off guard. She didn't leave to take the dress into the dressing room until Dominic sat back down.

When she turned her back, Dominic downed the champagne again.

Returning to her spot next to him, Maria sat down differently, like she was now aware of how close they had been sitting on the couch. Dominic had noticed it immediately. The smell of her sweet perfume had called out to him to get closer, but he'd forced himself to be a gentleman, when that was last thing he wanted to be with Maria.

He already had two different images playing through his mind; one dirty, one criminal. He'd take both, but he preferred the one where he pressed her up against the glass on the storefront window over the one where he took her in the dressing room for five minutes.

Slightly adjusting himself on the couch, he tried not to inhale too deeply, but he couldn't resist letting his legs spread wider, which put him that much closer to her.

"How come you didn't like that color on me?" Maria asked, her perfect brows slightly drawn together.

Taking the champagne glass from her hand without permission, Dominic gave her a wicked smile. "Princesses don't belong in black."

As soon as the last words left his lips, the door opened.

Kat slowly emerged, this time with a smile. Finally, she looked like herself.

Maria whispered what they were all thinking, "It's perfect."

Staring at his baby sister, he forgot why they were here. All he could see was how beautiful she looked, and how she suddenly wasn't that little baby in her pink cat onesie.

Feeling his eyes getting wet, he blinked, only able to say, "Wow," afraid he might cry if he said anything else.

While Maria started accessorizing and Ken began the alterations, they kept Kat distracted.

Dominic stood up, going to where the lady kept the champagne.

The woman politely smiled. "Would you like some mor—"

Grabbing the opened bottle that was already halfway empty, he started to walk away.

"Sir, you can't do that . . ." She gave up when he gave her a "watch me" look.

Dominic didn't give a single fuck. Lifting the bottle to his lips, he let the shitty liquid wash down his throat, as he headed to the front of the store, staying far enough away from what they were doing in the back but close enough to make sure they were safe. While watching to make sure no one entered the store, he pulled his phone out of his pocket, took a big swig, before he regretfully dialed a number.

"Yes?" a cold voice answered.

He took another drink. "I want a meeting."

"I'll have to get back with you. Dante is bu—"

"No," Dominic stopped him. "With you."

There was silence at first.

"Tomorrow night, at my home office, nine o'clock."

"Thanks. Listen …" He gripped the phone, looking back toward the dressing room, contemplating.

"I don't have all day." The cold voice was harsh.

Dominic cracked his neck from side to side. "Never mind. See you tomorrow night, Lucca."

When the dial tone clicked, he was happy he didn't rat Maria out.

Dominic had called to do the right fucking thing, to tell him where he could find his sister without Caruso protection. He thought it would show some sort of respect to the underboss. That way, when he had the meeting he wanted, Lucca might show some mercy. But then he decided to fuck it. The boogieman hadn't shown mercy a day in his goddamn life. Lucca didn't even know the meaning of the word mercy.

When Dom returned Maria, the wrath of hell would exponentially increase since withholding that information from Lucca.

At first, he didn't know why he did it, knowing the consequences would be harsh, but when the girls emerged from the back of the store almost an hour later and he saw Maria's face, he knew.

Her emerald eyes sparkled the longer she was away from her Caruso bodyguard. Maria looked content, like she was genuinely enjoying herself. He didn't want to take that away from her just yet.

Dom also might've had selfish reasons for wanting to keep her in his exclusive care … He'd already planned on driving her home much slower than when he drove them here.

Thanking God he had already tossed the bottle before they came out, he had made it up to where they stood at the cash register right when the price with far too many zeros was announced.

"Excuse me? What?" Kat's mouth dropped to the floor.

Maria didn't bat an eye as she went into her purse. "Don't worry about it. It's a gift from—"

"The Carusos."

When a black card appeared from behind them, along with that cold voice, Dominic didn't have to look back.

"I really can't accept—"

"It's okay, Kat." Throwing an arm over her shoulders, Dominic hushed her while smoothly pulling her closer to him. "It's the least they can do."

Outwardly, he kept his cool, but internally.... Shit, shit, shit.

Regret seeped in at not telling Lucca where Maria was. Making sure to keep Kat close to him as they exited the store, he was ready for the underboss to unload, but was shocked when Lucca addressed Maria and not him.

"Maria, you have five seconds to tell me why you are here."

She didn't gave a single fuck as she flipped a blonde lock behind her shoulder. "Kat needed a dress."

"And where the fuck are my men?" Lucca's voice was quiet, which made it even more lethal.

Dom waited for her answer, but when she kept silent, he was surprised to find himself answering for her.

"Kat asked me to drop her off here, and when I came in, I saw Maria alone." That part might have been a lie, but he continued with the truth, finding himself sticking up for the mafia princess. "Instead of getting her in trouble, I decided to watch her for you and was going to bring her back home safely when they were done."

The silent look Lucca gave him promised retribution for not telling him over the phone.

Maria's eyes flashed in surprise at Dom before she nodded. "I called Kat to meet me here, and then I just snuck out and took a cab."

It appeared Lucca would save the tongue-lashing for their meeting tomorrow, as he looked back at Maria with harsh, blue-green eyes. "We're leaving."

"Yep, so are we." Dom wasn't wasting any time getting them the fuck out of there. He pulled Kat in the opposite direction that Lucca was trying to pull Maria toward.

Maria waved, clearly not scared of her brother. "Bye, Kat."

"Bye. Thank you for everything." Kat smiled as he dragged her away.

"You're welcome." Maria looked at him. "Bye, Dominic."

He, however, didn't have the luxury of turning back to look at her, knowing, if he did, his body—that was screaming for him to stay—wouldn't be able to control itself. It were as if his body had become possessed around her, like it didn't belong to him, and he didn't trust to keep his feelings in check, especially when Lucca was around.

He also didn't trust his voice to say the word good-bye.

If only he had turned around, he would have seen her upset face; not saying good-bye affected on her too.

Dominic didn't know when it happened—the first time he met her at her mother's funeral, the second time after Matthias opened the door, or third time when he'd looked up at her as she held Kat's wedding dress—but he wanted her. And it wasn't just want, she was a fucking need. Dominic needed Maria to be his, and he had to have Maria need him as well.

When she placed that black wedding dress up against her, he had her move it out of the way because the only thought he had was that he wanted her in a beautiful white wedding dress . . . to marry him in.

He had envisioned it all in a split-second, from his ring on her finger to a baby in her belly; his fucking soul needed her. Dominic could feel that she was meant to be his, and his body had secretly known it since he'd first met her. Like how he knew

189

a gun belonged in his hand at the age of two, Maria belonged to him, and he was never going to be able to get a chance with her because his last name was Luciano.

It would be the last thing his name would take.

"That was rude," Kat whispered harshly.

"Don't care." Dom only slowed his pace when they were far enough from Lucca. His mind still on Maria, he almost felt bad for Ted. "That psycho is on a mission to get every man in Kansas City murdered today, and I'm sure as fuck not going to be one of them."

That was why he knew Maria was meant for him.

Dom would never have to pretend to be something he wasn't around her, or have to hide what he was or the things he did. Not only did his body cry out for hers but, for once, he wasn't afraid of being around a woman and hurting her.

Dominic had never trusted himself around women, fearing that part of Lucifer was somewhere deep inside of him, like the anger he'd passed down to him. But Dominic wasn't afraid that he'd hurt Maria, knowing he'd never be capable of it. What he feared was Maria hurting him.

"Jesus, are you drunk?" Kat asked, having to throw her arm around his waist as he slumped forward so she could keep him up on her shoulders.

"Psst ... No." Dom reached into his pocket, thanking God that weak-ass champagne had finally kicked in and that Lucca came for his sister after all. Giving Kat the keys, he hiccupped, "But you're driving."

"Oh my God, Dom." Kat shook her head. "Why exactly did you feel the need to get wasted midday?"

Because I had to watch you try on wedding dresses! And now I'll be forced to watch you walk down the aisle to marry a fucking piece of shit who just wants revenge!

However, it was much easier to sum it down to a couple hiccupped words.
"Lucca fucking Caruso."

Thinking back to yesterday, it was no wonder Lucca hadn't killed him for not telling him about Maria on the phone. This was what he wanted, and Lucca got his retribution, as Dom was now leaving without freeing his sister.

With all hope for his sister not having to marry the Caruso lost, he hadn't seen Maria at first. Not until he hit the foyer and Maria's head and eyes lifted to his from where she sat at the bottom steps of the grand staircase.

He did his best to hide his sadness from from them both. A part of him felt dirty the second he walked out of Lucca's office, taking the deal from the boogieman that didn't include his sister's freedom, regardless of how unfeasible it was.

Lucca needed Kat as a piece on his chessboard.

Passing Maria where she sat, he could see her sympathy reflected in her green eyes.

"See you at the wedding," Dom confirmed the grim reason why he had been there to speak with Lucca.

Opening the front door, he was going to walk out, but unlike last time, he allowed himself to look back at the woman he had fallen in love with, and his hopeless heart suddenly felt ... hopeful.

Dominic gave her one final look. It was time to let her know he was stiking his claim. "I'll be wanting a dance, princess."

A WEDDING...
AND A FUNERAL

Dominic adjusted his suit jacket, feeling weird that he didn't have his big leather jacket on instead. Growing up, he had always wanted to dress like a Caruso, but now that he was in an expensive rental suit expertly fit, it didn't feel right.

While others viewed his last name with disdain, Luciano was a name he had proudly earned, just like his leather jacket. To bear that name meant he'd survived the devil and hell.

Opening the door, he thought it hadn't been long since he saw that face, but it had been. The two brothers took each other in an embrace, Dominic holding him in a tight hug for a long moment, somehow missing him more than he had before, even though he was now standing in front of him.

"Let me get a look at you." Dom finally let him go to see him.

He had changed just ever so slightly. It wasn't his outer appearance as much as the metamorphosis that had taken place inside. However, seeing this half of a whole showed him just how bad off the other one had gotten.

"You look good, Angel."

"Thanks."

"They treating you right over there?" he asked, wanting to make sure what had happened when he'd first gone into the Caruso's care hadn't happened again.

After Lucifer, a new enemy to the two families had emerged. One-Shot. It was a man who possessed the same power he did with a gun. When a Caruso soldier was murdered and One-Shot took his first kill, some of the Caruso men had assumed it was Angel who'd done it, and they had ambushed him in the middle of the night, beating him within an inch of his life.

The tattooed brother gave him an assuring nod. "Yes, Lucca has done right by me."

"Good." Dominic nodded back.

Clearing his throat, the pit in his stomach ached for what he had to talk to him about. "There's something I need tell you."

Angel looked at him like a soldier.

"Dante will release you once the wedding is over," he told his brother what the Caruso boss had told him earlier.

"He is?" Angel, who had prepared for bad news, had happiness in his voice.

"Yes, he will have Kat to make sure our deal stays intact."

Suddenly, his brother's face turned into a mask of emotions. "Listen, Dominic there's something I need to t——"

"I know about Adalyn," Dom stopped him. "I'm glad you have her," he told him truthfully, having to look away, unable to meet his brother's eyes. "I need to ask something of you now."

Angel the soldier returned with a single nod.

"Don't come home." Dominic's voice wanted to break, but he kept it strong, not letting it waiver. "For as long as Katarina is a Caruso, you must be one, too." He forced himself to face his brother's eyes again, knowing he deserved the decency of being faced, man to man. "We Lucianos must stick together, even if that means we will be apart. Do you understand?"

Angel's dark gray eyes matched the sadness in his voice. "Yes."

"Good. You will make sure that not only Drago takes care of her, but that every Caruso does too." Dominic knew the cost of his ask, separating the twins would be Matthias' downfall. "The only Caruso you can trust for now is Lucca, but *do not* trust him completely, Angel. He is just one bad day away from turning into our father, and when that time comes, it'll be up to us to put Lucca down."

Swallowing hard, Angel nodded in understanding again.

Dominic took his brother in another strong hug, his voice was no longer able to keep from wavering. "Make sure she's taken care of for me, not only by Drago but by every fucking one of them."

"I will," Angel promised, giving him his word.

Letting his brother go, he quickly went for the door, needing to go to the source of his rage that was beginning to boil.

"Keep him alive for me?" Angel asked with a solemn whisper before he walked out.

Squeezing the door handle, Dominic wished he was able to give the same promise that Angel had for Katarina, but one of the Lucianos hadn't mentally survived their time in hell. "I'll try."

Dominic silently walked into the room undetected, slowly stalking the huge man he could only see from his back, with his hand on the Glock behind his back.

One bullet is all it'd take ....

His mind taunted him to take it out and pull the Glock's trigger like he desperately wanted, and he had every intention of doing so until their reflections met in the mirror.

Drago, who had been tightening his tie in the mirror, turned around, realizing he'd been snuck up on.

A lot like how Anthony was for the Luciano family, Drago De Santis was that for the Carusos. He had been often called "the tank" and bore that nickname even more so after taking five bullets to the chest, which was why he was Dante's personal bodyguard. To say he was shocked seeing Dominic standing behind him with his hand at his back was an understatement.

Dominic squeezed the grip of his Glock until his tanned knuckles turned white. "You do anything to hurt her or be any fucking less than what Lucca has said about you, you'll have wished the boogieman had come for you when I fucking kill you." Taking a deep breath, he removed his hand from his back, regretfully leaving his gun firmly in place. The only silver lining was he was finally able to make a fucking promise he would keep. "And this time, there will be no coming back, Drago. Because, unlike my father, I don't fucking miss."

Walking into the final room broke his heart, but he made sure to stay strong. Their fate had been sealed, no matter how hard Dominic tried to fight it or find a loophole. Lucca had won … this battle.

Staring at his beautiful sister all done up, he wished he didn't have to ask, "You ready?"

When Kat stood, her black, expensive gown flowed around her as she took some nervous deep breaths.

"I want you to know that, even if it meant my death, I would not let you walk down this aisle if I didn't know you could handle it," Dominic told her, his eyes boring deeply into hers.

Kat's voice came out in a whisper. "I know."

"We knew this day would come, Katarina," Dom reminded her of the many talks they'd had in the months leading up to their father's demise. They'd known Dominic's journey of taking over his father's position in the family wouldn't be an easy road, just like the road to get the Luciano throne had been daunting and long. There would be a price to pay, but Dom had promised all his siblings one thing …

I'll make the Luciano name mean something again.

She gave him an encouraging smile. "Yes, we did."

"You're going to be the one to save us all, and I couldn't be more fucking proud. They might not know what you're capable of but, one day, they will. They'll know what we are *all* capable of." Dominic finally smiled. "Make him fuckin' regret picking you, Kat … Give. Him. Hell."

"I plan on it."

He'd known the second he had picked her up in his arms the night so long ago that she would mean more than him and his brothers combined. Katarina was giving him his first step into Kansas City's new world order, and if Dominic did become king one day, it was going to be all because of her.

He held out an arm with a heavy breath, and she took it as she picked up her blood-red bouquet of roses.

The walk was long, but as the church doors swung open, it wasn't nearly as long as that painful walk down the aisle. Passing the pews in the same Catholic church he had met Maria in years ago, he was glad Kat looked the part in her gothic dress because, with each step they took, it felt like they were taking part in a wedding … and a funeral.

He felt so sick with every step closer, by the time they reached the alter, he wasn't sure he was capable of giving his little sister away. It wasn't until his eyes caught the angel dressed in white, sitting in one of the pews, was he able to give Kat one final hug.

The two siblings, who were more like father and daughter, hugged for a precious moment, and Dominic could have sworn he saw Kat's life flash in front of his eyes, from the time he first picked her up, to the time he lay broken while Lucifer beat her, and all the way to the moment they were in now.

Giving her away to Drago broke another part of his soul, but the only fucking reason he was able to do it was for the angel in white a few pews over that his body called out for.

And if he didn't get his angel …

I'll fucking kill every last one of them.

Dominic looked over to her brother, suited in black from head to toe beside her.

Starting with you, Lucca.

TO LOCK THE DOOR
OR KEEP IT UNLOCKED?

"**H**" *ave you seen the bride's* dress? She's Luciano trash, for sure."

It hadn't been the first time Dominic had heard that, and he'd bet every penny he had that it wouldn't be his last. Hell, he'd heard it about five times since the wedding reception had started, from every rich asshole and bitch in here, but by the look on Maria's pretty face, she hadn't experienced it yet.

"I thought she'd get more use out of a black dress, Luisa." Maria's green eyes glowered at the old woman, who clearly came from the Caruso side of the family based on the diamond broach she wore. "I'll tell her to wear it to your funeral."

By the look of the old bitch's face and her equally old friend, they were about to let Maria have it—until Dom let his presence known by coming up to stand behind her. Needless to say, the old bitches moved away in a hurry.

"I have to say that was better than anything I could've come up with, princess," Dominic said with a smile. It had been the first time he'd heard anyone stick up for a Luciano who didn't bear the name, and it only made him like her that much more.

Maria spun on her heels, seeing why the old women had left in a hurry.

Noticing the glass in her hand was empty, he took it, repaying the favor she had given him at the bridal boutique by placing a filled glass in her hand from the tray a waiter was carrying. He raised a brow, still smiling at the clever but ruthless words she spouted off to the women. Everyone wanted to tell off old folks who thought they could say whatever they wanted and get away with it because they were old ... but no one actually did it—except Maria.

"You really are as cold as I think you are, aren't you?"

Maria looked at her newly filled champagne glass. "What makes you think that?"

"Do you remember the last time we saw each other before all this?" Dom waved his hands around him at the extravagant reception held in the Casino Hotel that he was sure she was responsible for. *And before you walked through my front door.*

The blonde's perfect brows drew together, clearly trying to remember.

"Wow. You don't remember, do you?" Dominic had to laugh,

picking up a glass of champagne for himself.

He must've been sickly in love with her at twenty. Not even amnesia could have let him forget the first time he had thought he saw an angel walking the earth.

Confusion still marring her face, she lifted the glass to her lips. "When was it?"

Dominic was captivated by her jeweled eyes. "Dance with me, princess, and I'll tell you."

"I ..." Maria's eyes and body told him that she wanted nothing more, but her words said otherwise. "We can't. Not here in front of everyone. Our blood only mixed a few hours ago, and I think it's probably too soon for the Luciano boss to dance with the Carusos' boss's daughter."

Giving her a sinister lift of his lips, he walked off with some parting words. "Well, who said I wanted to dance with you in front everyone, anyway?"

Leaving her with a new look of confusion, he kept the smile on his face, glad he had already worked out a plan B.

He searched for Cassius, who was staring at the ice sculpture when he found him.

"So, they really are as rich as our father was telling us, aren't they?"

"Yes," Dominic told him with a solemn nod. It was the first time his youngest brother had been introduced to the other crime family. From here on out, it would be up to him to form his own opinion upon the Carusos.

Yes, Cassius might be young, but the thoughts that went on in his mind were far beyond that of a fifteen-year-old. It was the reason why he had let Cass join the first family meeting that he called once Dom had taken the Luciano throne after Angel had been taken.

Even though he hadn't spoken the *Omertà*, and still had yet to, Cassius was just as much made as the rest of them. Dominic had decided it was better to accept his nature and try to mold the darkness in him for the benefit of the family, because excluding Cassius from the family business would have caused his younger brother to begrudge him, not only as a brother but as the Luciano boss.

Cassius turned from the sculpture, letting the thoughts he had swirling in his mind disappear, as his face want back to his normal blank stare. "I take it she turned you down?"

"Yep," Dominic said with a laugh, having expected no less from the mafia princess. "You know where to find me."

The youngest Luciano nodded before Dominic walked off, going to the back of the reception area and to a black sheer curtain that was covering the door to the kitchen. None of the Carusos would have thought twice about young Cassius leading her here.

Pushing aside the curtain, he opened the door to the kitchen, where he would finish his champagne and wait. It wasn't until the door lightly swung open a few minutes later did he know that his plan B had worked.

"You're not scared, are you, princess?" he asked when she didn't dare enter the kitchen fully.

Maria took a step, letting her hand fall so the door could close them in. "Of course not."

"Good." He smiled, holding out his hand for her to take.

It was as if the world went into slow motion for a solid moment as he held his breath, waiting for her to either take it or turn him down. All he needed was for her to place her hand in his, and he would never let her go.

Her emerald eyes on his outstretched hand … she finally took it.

Holding onto her soft, slender hand, he pulled the blonde beauty to him for the first time and carefully placed his other hand at the small of her waist. His body, that had been on fire to touch her since he saw her last, finally stilled, content with a slow dance, even though his thoughts dreamed of much more.

When she didn't move fluidly with him to the music they could hear coming from the other side of the door, he looked down at her. "Why do I get the feeling you've never danced before?"

"Because I haven't." It took Maria a moment before she admitted the second part. "Not with a guy, that is."

"Just relax and listen," he coached her, knowing it had to be hard for the woman who despised all men to be led.

When she took a long, deep breath and finally began to relax, he pulled her just the littlest inch closer to him. "See? It's not so bad."

"Yeah, not for you." Her eyes might not have rolled, but her voice had.

"That's true. I'm sure I'm enjoying this more than you," he freely admitted with a laugh.

"If only your father could see you now," Maria said then

instantly regretted it. "I'm sorry. I—"

"It's all right. I'd pay good money for him to see us dancing together. I'm sure he'd fucking rather die all over again." He didn't want her to feel bad, nor hold her tongue with him. He liked that Maria said what she thought, even if it was harsh. She wasn't for the weak, but Dominic wasn't either.

Maria relaxed even more in his arms. "I take it you and he didn't get along?"

"We had a complicated relationship." There wasn't enough time in a day to explain the relationship he'd had with his father, especially not in the little amount of time he was going to get with her tonight. "How about you and your father?"

"Complicated," she agreed. "But I have a feeling yours might be more so."

"Yes, you're probably right." Dominic gripped her hand ever so slightly, causing her eyes to drift over to his inked fingers. She then glanced down to the hand at her waist, reading the word he had permanently placed into his skin.

Maria bit her bottom lip. "Cassius is like your father, isn't he?"

"You mean, like Lucca—" He paused for a single moment. "—and you."

Knowing it wasn't a question but a factual statement, she flipped it on him. "What about you? Are you like him too?" she asked, not denying her own demons.

Tilting his lips in a half-smile, he wanted to make one thing clear. "Princess, I'm nothing like my father."

Their eyes danced with each other's the same way their bodies did, and Dominic squeezed his fingers at her waist, feeling the warm flesh underneath her dress as he brought her even closer.

"Then, how did you know I was heartless? And, what does that have to do with the last time we saw each other?"

He broke their connection as he twirled her in the desolate room, taking in her white satin dress that exposed her left thigh from the large slit. It was like the grownup version of the white dress that he had first seen her in.

"I still can't believe you don't remember."

"Sorry, but I don't." Her voice clearly told him she only apologized to be polite. "I'm dancing with you like you wanted, so tell me already."

With the song ending, he was able to hear Maria was breathing just as heavily as he was.

He could do it—lean in and steal her lips in a kiss that would seal their fate forever—but the new song kept him a gentleman.

"Your mother's funeral." When that still didn't ring a bell for her, he figured he should be really fucking hurt, but thankfully, she'd only been fourteen at the time, so he didn't hold it against her. Continuing, it was time to finally tell the princess how he knew she had been born without a heart. "I knew you were heartless because you didn—"

BANG.

Unfortunately, a single bullet would not only cost a life, but it just might have costed his and Maria's future ...

All of hell breaking loose in the reception hall, and unlike everyone else who could be heard screaming and trying to run for cover, he managed to like the woman before him, run for the door.

"Are you fucking crazy?" Dominic grabbed her before she managed to reveal the secret door.

"We can't just stay in here and do nothing!" She fought him to leave.

Rolling his eyes, he lifted the pretty blonde off her pretty little heels, taking her backward through the kitchen. "If I let the boss's daughter go out there and get hurt, then my family and I are as good as dead anyway."

As he opened the deep freezer, she fought him fucking hard.

"Please, Maria," he begged her to calm down.

Her anger was seething that he hadn't let them run out to make sure their families were okay. It didn't just hurt her; it hurt him just as fucking badly. His siblings and his men were out there, but he would have never forgiven himself if he let Maria walk out that door. His instincts told him to protect her first, and he always trusted them. They had yet to steer him wrong.

Placing her back down on the floor, in the safety of the frozen box, he snatched her face in his hands to get her to understand. "You're drunk."

"No, I'm ..." Suddenly, he saw Maria realize that she was, but she continued to deny through her fumbled words. "Am not."

"You are," Dom told her firmly, deciding not to tell her that he'd made sure she was so many glasses deep before he'd even asked her to dance with him. Giving her that last glass of champagne had been for good measure. "And if I don't protect you—"

"I don't need protecting, Dominic. Why can't anyone understand that!"

Looking at the perfectly sculptured face in his hands, his voice softened with his heart. "I don't think you do, princess, but we both know, if I let you walk out of here like this, *I'm* dead, *my brothers* are dead, *Kat's* dead."

He prayed for her to understand with his begging eyes, not knowing if he could make her stay in there if she continued to resist. He didn't doubt that she could handle herself, but he couldn't risk her safety. Dominic needed to walk out of there knowing at least one person he cared about was safe.

Maria stared up at him for a few moments before she finally decided, "Fine."

Thank you. He wanted to say the words to her but didn't want her to know he would have given in.

To let Maria go when he had her in his hands almost broke his heart. He hadn't had enough time with her yet … She didn't yet know they were meant to be.

Removing his hand from her face one finger at a time, he could see, clear as day, in her eyes, that she hated it too.

"Here." Dom removed his suit jacket, wishing it had been his leather one, because he wanted to see it wrapped around her and to take her scent with it. "Take this, and I'll be back."

"You're leaving me?" A slight sadness marred her emerald eyes, making him wonder if she was beginning to feel their connection.

Wrapping the jacket over her slender shoulders, he regretted having to say his next words. "I can't sit here with my family and my men out there."

Finally, understanding shone on her face, but she had one request. "Will you make sure Leo's okay?"

With a nod, he drifted his eyes to her perfectly pouty lips. He was beginning to feel desperate to get her to see their connection. With a death grip on the jacket around her shoulders, he wanted to pull her up in a kiss that would make sure her feet stayed planted in this very room until he came back to continue where they had left off, but he'd promised himself that he would wait for Maria to ask him.

He either needed Maria's permission to place his lips on hers or she had to kiss him herself because, if he didn't, the princess with no feelings, who hated all men, might pull away before giving their kiss a chance. If that happened, she would deny them any chance and any future they were bound to have would be gone forever.

That was exactly why he had to regretfully let her go.

"I'll make sure someone comes to get you when it's safe." Walking toward the door, he couldn't allow himself to look back.

Maria instantly sensed the shift in the air. "Don't you dare lock me in here, Dominic."

Dominic opened the freezer door . . .

"I swear to God, Dominic, if I go for that door when I think it's safe and find it locked"—she paused, turning her warning into a promise—"I will never forgive you."

He never liked to look back at her, but he did this time, seeing that she meant her words wholeheartedly, before he brought the freezer door to a complete close.

Staring at the lock, he thought about how it was the only way to ensure Maria's safety and that she would live through the possible war that was on the other side of the kitchen door. If it had been Katarina, he knew what he would do.

To lock the door or keep it unlocked?

His tattooed hand hovered over the lock ...

It was like being thrown into World War III. The once beautiful reception had been destroyed.

The line had been drawn in the sand, as the two families who stood on different sides of the room waited for their orders to fire. Problem was, it wasn't a fair fight, as every Luciano member hadn't been allowed a weapon to the wedding. Dominic had instructed his men to take the risk.

Whoever had shot the gun, it hadn't been a Luciano; he'd bet his life on it. His men wouldn't defy an order, not to mention they had been checked by Caruso soldiers before they entered the door. However, judging the people on the other side of the room, there were plenty who could have.

Dominic quickly pushed past his men before the slaughtering of his family could begin. Jumping up on a now ruined table setting, he made sure his voice could be heard by every man.

"We came without guns like I promised. You checked every one of my men on the way in," he reminded the blood thirsty, adrenaline-rushed Carusos, making them look at the men who stood on the other side stood without true weapons in their hands, only holding butter knives and anything else they could swing.

"Dante, call your men down," Dominic demanded louder, as he searched for the current reigning king who was too scared to come out, "so we can deal with this man to man." Spinning on his heels, he continued his demands, but this time to his men alone. "And if it was one of my men who defied my orders, then I will hand him over to you myself."

Finally Dante appeared, his face a mask of rage, letting Dominic know this wedding wasn't going to end in a happily ever after.

Fuck.

He made a fist for the coming fight that he wasn't going to win, as they were all soon to be dead, but he planned to take a couple with him on his way to hell, starting with the ego maniac who had hid behind his own men.

Dante didn't deserve the throne. The only reason he had gotten it was the exact same reason everyone looked at him with disgust—their last names.

Lucifer might have been crazy, but one thing he was right about was his hatred for the Caruso boss, and his father was about to get his dying wish.

The hard *thud* of the ballroom doors flinging open had everyone turning their heads to see Drago storming through. He pushed through furiously, going right to his boss to quietly speak something to him. Dominic wished he knew what he had said, but by the look of Dante's face, he wasn't going to get his wish of wiping them out or . . .

Holy fuck, he was going to do it, regardless what his trusted Drago was telling him. Dante was about to blow them all to smithereens.

About to give the order for his men to fight with what they had, Dominic stopped when the ballroom door flung open again.

"Put your guns down." Lucca's voice traveled through the room, giving out the order without even speaking a word to his father.

Never thinking he'd ever thank God for seeing that asshole, Dominic jumped down from the table as soon as every weapon was lowered, and he went straight for the underboss.

Any respect he'd had for Dante vanished. It was sad to think that the boogieman was saner than the Caruso boss, yet he was. Dominic might hate Lucca, but what he had just done made him hate the bastard a little less.

The two met in the center of the room, with the dead body at their feet.

"I take it you lost him?" Dominic asked, looking down at the pitiful Caruso with the bullet hole right between his eyes.

"Yes." Lucca was still breathing heavily from the run.

"It's a shame you didn't kick the cigarette habit when I told you to all those years ago. You just might have caught him."

Lucca's blue-green eyes darted to him. "Careful, Dominic, you're still the best option we got for One-Shot."

"I guess it's a good thing you made me leave my Glock at home." Dom smiled, running a hand over his back and coming up empty.

"Lucky you." Lucca's voice then turned ominous, hinting that he might've already known the answer to, "Where exactly were you when the gun went off?"

"I could ask you the same thing." Dom raised a brow, looking down at the lifeless body. "Teddy wasn't exactly your most loyal soldier."

"Todd," the underboss couldn't help but remind him with a smile in his voice.

"Well, lucky you … you're a shit shot," Dom said smugly, looking around now for his family. "Where's Kat?"

Smiling, Lucca pulled out his pack of cigarettes from his pocket. "Drago just dragged her out of the room over his shoulder."

"Wha—"

"She's fine," Lucca assured him, flipping his Zippo open to light the end. "You got bigger problems than her right now."

"Like what?" Dom snapped.

"Like convincing my father you weren't the one who killed his man." His blue-green eyes glowed knowingly. "I'm sure someone saw you when the gun went off."

"Shit." Dominic looked around again. "Where's Leo?"

Catching the sight of the good-looking teenage boy, he left a confused Lucca behind as he went up to the Caruso who he hadn't yet spoken with.

He hadn't needed to see him sitting beside Maria at the church wedding to know they were siblings. Every Caruso sibling wasn't only gifted a perfect last name, but they came with perfectly good looks, as well.

"You good?" Dominic asked the youngest Caruso when he reached him. It was a question he hadn't yet asked his own brothers, but he knew instinctively they were fine and capable of protecting themselves.

Leo looked at him, confused for a moment, before he answered, "I'm fine."

Dominic nodded, able to see instantly that he was nothing like the other Carusos. It was no wonder Maria asked him to check on him. The kid was the same age as Cassius yet the complete opposite. He would guess Leo had taken everything but his last name from his mother.

"Go through that door." He pointed to the hidden kitchen door. "Maria's hiding in the deep freezer in the back of the kitchen."

"Maria? Hiding?" Leo looked at him with even more confusion, not believing the words he spoke.

"She had a lot to drink." Dom tried his best to explain but gave up. "Just go let her know it's safe to come out."

"Mmmhmm … sure." Leo clearly had his doubts. "I'll believe my sister is in a deep freezer, hiding for her life, when I see it."

The kid was lucky he was cute.

THIS PART IS GOING TO HURT

Lucca *sat in his smoke-filled*, blacked-out Escalade outside of the big building, watching the hundreds of people leaving. Bringing his cigarette to his lips, he searched every human who walked out, thinking he'd either missed them or it wasn't true after all …

When his blue-green depths landed on the couple exiting the coliseum, there was absolutely no way he could've miss them, as one of them looked so out of place compared to everyone else.

His hand unconsciously squeezed the steering wheel in a tight grip before he let it go to grab his cell phone. Bringing it to his ear after he hit the contact, he listened to the phone ring, his eyes never leaving his mark.

bRRing.

It wasn't hard, considering the blonde in the big fur coat stood out like a sore thumb, surrounded by hockey jerseys.

bRRing.

He lightly blew out the smoke that he held in mouth when he brought his gaze to the man walking beside her. He might've been wearing a cap, but it was shit at concealing his identity.

bRRin-

"Dominic." His cold voice greeted him before the Luciano boss could even answer.

There was a moment of silence on Dom's end, already sensing the bad news to come. "Yes?"

Flicking the butt of his cigarette out the window, Lucca looked to the hands that swung between the couple ... together. "We got a problem."

Storming into the Caruso family home, Dom shoved right past Lucca, who had opened the door. "I have to see for myself."

The underboss only sighed while closing the door.

Dominic ran up the foyer steps two at a time, making his way toward that sweet scent that led the way. By the time he reached the door, his body temperature was raging hot, but it wasn't until he flung the door open to see it for himself did he see red.

Maria was standing there, looking at her perfect reflection in the mirror, and it only took him half a second to see the happiness that had never been in her emerald eyes before.

Lucca was right; the woman who he was in love with and who was supposed to be in love with him ... loved another.

Turning to face him, she looked like she almost didn't believe he was there. "What are you doing in here?"

Dominic thought he would have turned around and never speak to her again, but something possessed him to enter the room.

Quietly shutting the door behind him, he wanted Maria to realize the mistake she had just fucking made. The blonde stomped her stilettos into the thick carpet as she walked toward him, getting pissed that he'd had the audacity to come into her bedroom unannounced. "What the hell are you doing in here, Dominic?"

"Lucca gave me permission," he promised her coldly, blocking her from exiting the room before he could say his peace.

That clearly only enraged the independent Maria more. "Then I'll scream if you don't leave."

"Scream." Dominic's dangerous hazel eyes glowed in a dare. "But you won't ever get ten minutes alone with me again, princess." When she didn't open her mouth, he took a stalking step toward her. "I didn't think you would."

Maria's green orbs slightly grew wider as she took a single step back. The girl had never backed down from anyone, but Dominic wasn't just anyone. Clearly, he had led her to believe he was, thinking the self-righteous man-hater would have loved the part of him that cared for Katarina. So, he had only shown her the part of himself that he was around Kat, but he was much more than that ...

Dominic Luciano was also the devil's son.

And if Maria had shit taste in men then, by God, he would show her the worst one.

"What do you want?" Her voice held a sliver of alarm.

"To see you, and to see if it's true." When she backed up against her bedroom wall and there was nowhere else for her to go, he continued, "If you really were falling in *love*." The last word was hard for him to say. His chest constricted in a pain that was almost as unbearable as the day he had to watch his father beat Katarina. There had been nothing more he could do that day to save his sister, and he felt that exact same hopelessness now as he stared at the beautiful Maria. "I suppose it is true."

"I don't know what you're ta—"

"Don't. You. Dare," Dominic cut her off with the same slice she had made to his chest. "Don't you dare play the fucking stupid blonde with me."

He knew she liked to do it around the Caruso men, so she could trick them and get her way. Her harmless flirting was actually a dangerous game that most likely costed Todd's life, and Dominic wasn't going to have any of it.

Something flickered in her emerald eyes as she watched him carefully.

He had let her see just how different he was from his father, from Lucca, and from her. Dominic had a fucking heart and felt full-heartedly, and that was exactly what made him more dangerous than all of them.

"How many dates did it take? Two? Three?" he asked, letting her see the pain his face and his voice.

Maria clearly had been shocked to see that he had such passionate feelings for her, but Dom knew better. She had either fought them or didn't understand. He knew, because he had done the same thing.

"I told you what would happen, Dominic." Her voice came out in a whisper before it turned to show her own hurt. "But you locked the door."

"You don't know me at all." Dominic's words came out in a growl as he punched the wall beside her. It closed her in, making her unable to run from the monster she had created.

Looking down at her, all the feelings he held for the beauty suddenly turned into utter disappointment. "And you're not the woman I thought you were at all ..."

Maria's face and body tensed, her wondrous green eyes searched for the answer of why he felt that until he spoke it from his lips.

"... not if you've chosen Kayne Evans."

Maria Caruso could have chosen any other man in the country, and he would have understood. Dominic would have bowed the fuck out graciously, because he himself didn't think he deserved a woman like her. No one did. But anyone was better than a Luciano. Except for one.

Kayne.

"You know him?" she quietly asked, confused.

"I own Blue Park, princess ... or did you forget that the second you left my worthless home?" He didn't wait for the pretentious blonde to spew the bullshit that his home wasn't worthless. "Kayne and I went to the same high school, and I know the *real* him. I know him more than you'll ever know."

Dominic didn't know what effect Kayne had over women, but he had thought Maria was smarter than that.

"So, what then? You're telling me Dominic Luciano is the better choice?" Maria's tone was sarcastic, but even her own voice betrayed her—she knew the answer before he uttered a sound.

It would hurt, but Dominic let himself finally touch her. For one second, he let himself sickly pretend she was his, that she had allowed him to touch her. With his hand in a relaxed fist, he reached up to run the back of his fingertips over her flushed cheeks. He began quickly memorizing her perfect face, as it would be the last time, which made his heart break when he gave her the answer her mind valiantly tried to deny. "I know I am."

A part of him prayed she would see it before he walked back out that door forever, but he doubted it. Maria wasn't the kind of girl who changed her mind.

Letting his hand drop from her cheek, he picked up the strand of spun gold that rested on the top of her breasts, that beckoned for him to touch, to feel because he wasn't going to get the chance again. Rubbing the silk between his fingers, it felt just how he had imagined it.

"You've haunted my dreams every night, Maria."

He knew she had the same dreams by the way she looked up at him and had yet to detest him.

Dominic could see the pleading in her eyes, and he was going to give her a taste of what she wanted ….

Leaning down, he brought his lips to her throat. Inhaling deeply, he smelled that sweet scent of vanilla up close, letting himself bathe in it for once, finally understanding why he had been so drawn to her scent—it held a little secret. A single drop of bourbon that you could only get straight from the source.

"For weeks, I have dreamed of you …" Dominic let his lips hover over her skin, careful not to touch as he neared her lips. With his hand holding her face in place, he could feel the silent little push that she tried to make for their lips to meet, but he didn't let them, keeping his a whisper away. "And you didn't even give me a chance to show you what we could be." Dominic let his lips dance along hers for a split-second. "Now …" *This part is going to hurt me just as badly as you,* he silently spoke before pulling away. Taking a step back, he finally had Maria Caruso right where every man in Kansas City wanted her. "… you will never know."

Giving her his back, he didn't dare look back as he disappeared out of her door and her life for good, without remorse.

Out of the corner of his eye, he caught Leo standing there, but he simply turned to go in the other direction. Going back down the long steps, Lucca stood waiting in the foyer, but Dom just headed for the front door.

"That's it?" the underboss taunted him.

With his hand on the doorknob, Dom paused for a moment before he violently spun back around on his heels, going right up to the boogieman to spit in his face, "What do you suggest? Drug her, take her back to my house, and lock her away until she falls in love with me?"

Lucca's blue-green eyes glowed.

"Yeah." Dominic laughed mockingly. "You're not the only one who knows secrets."

Lucca spoke through gritted teeth, "I didn't force Chloe to fall in—"

"It's called Stockholm syndrome. You should look into it sometime."

"Dominic ..." Lucca warned him that he had better tread fucking carefully, his voice coming out in a harsh whisper. "You know exactly why I had to bring Chloe here! Lucifer had already made one attempt to capture her in a mall full of witnesses, and if I had been five minutes later the day I took her, then your father would have shown her what Stockholm syndrome really fucking was." Pausing for a moment, the boogieman then gave him a warning, "Now, I get that you're pissed, but you better watch it."

Running a hand through his hair, Dom tried to take deep breaths to get the scent of Maria out of his mind. "Sorry."

"I am not saying what I did was right," Lucca admitted a truth softly, one that he had never said before, but he wasn't the least bit sorry. "But I did what I had to do, not only to protect her from her worst nightmare … but to get the woman I love."

"*Maria* is not Chloe," Dom reminded him the bit of information that he was clearly missing.

"No," Lucca agreed, his voice going dark. "But Kayne still bleeds the same as Lucifer."

Hearing footsteps hit the top of the stairs, both men fell silent when Maria graciously walked down the steps with Leo.

It took everything he had to hold his tongue when she flipped the lock he had held in his hands.

"Please don't stop on my account."

Sensing the tension that continued from upstairs, Leo excused himself out the front door. "I'll be in the car, waiting with Jerry."

"I was just leaving," Dom snapped, turning from Lucca, who had yet to be of any help in their fifty-fifty agreement, making him wonder when the hell he was going to hold up his end of the deal.

"Me, too," she retorted after flipping her gold hair that he loved so much into his face when he came up behind her.

She was fucking lucky Lucca's ass was here, otherwise he would have made her regret it.

Mumbling under his breath, his words were for him alone. "Try that when your big brother's not around, see what the fuck will happen."

Shaking his head, Dom saw that Lucca might have heard it as he went to close the door behind them. He watched as Maria took a step closer to the car that Leo was just a couple of feet away from now.

The world slid away, and all he could hear was the sound of the strange engine of the car ...

Every fiber of his being knew what was coming before it even happened. His instinct to save Maria overwhelmed him as he ran to close the distance between them.

The engine suddenly clicked, shutting off. Then there was a single moment of silence ...

Dominic wrapped his arms around Maria.

BOOM.

Dominic stood outside the hospital, letting the pouring rain beat at him. It had been one week since ...

"Leo!"

Dominic had held her tightly as she screamed her baby brother's name with a pang that went through him.

It hurt him to the core that he could only save one, that it wasn't simply a choice he made, but it was one he made without a single thought. It wouldn't have mattered anyway, since Leo was too close, and the blast would have only killed them.

Both Maria and he tensed at seeing Leo slowly stand. He had felt the sheer relief that washed through her body as he'd begun to turn, but Dominic had known better. You didn't experience hell without coming back with a few scars.

Even though Dominic knew that, it still hadn't prepared him for the damage he saw.

Turning to show his once-perfect face fully, the left side of Leo's face was no longer immaculate. A shard had impaled itself into his left eye socket, leaving the right eye in perfect physical shape, yet it was filled with pain and sheer terror—a vision that would scar Dominic for life.

The cry from the woman who still lay in his arms would somehow cut even deeper. "No!"

Watching Maria exit the hospital, it was the first time he had seen her since that wretched day. Dominic could still feel the heat that burned on his back from the explosion when he managed to shield Maria's body with his, the same way he could still feel the break in his heart that she had put there.

For not giving them a single chance.

He had been furious that day, his anger getting the best of him, but that explosion put things into perspective. And not seeing her beautiful face until right now only solidified it.

Maria took a step under the awning. It might've protected her from the rain, but it didn't protect her from the violent winds as her beautiful gold hair spun. She still looked perfect, but only almost. A part of her looked broken or lost, most of all, she looked tired.

Dom understood, as he felt it too. He had waited every day out here for her, knowing she needed space from him...

"Maria, I'm so sorry," Dominic whispered to her, holding her tightly when she began to shake while the paramedics drove away.

Something in Maria had snapped then. Pushing him back, she hit his chest. "Don't you dare act like you care or give a fuck about me after how you just talked to me."

All he could do was stand there as he watched her first tear fall ... then

another as she continued to hit him. It would be the first time the princess, made of
ice, would cry.

That was the thing about ice . . .
It eventually melted.

Dom waited there to give her one last shot to see what he saw. Both were too worn down for a fight with each other, and all that was left for him to do was hold his hand out for her and pray that she'd take it . . . .

A car pulled up between them. Dominic didn't have to look inside the navy blue Charger to know who it was. He had clocked the car waiting for her for the last thirty minutes. He knew because he had been standing out here for the last seven days.

Staring into her emerald eyes as her the hair whipped her face, he prayed for her to stop when she reached for the car door.

Please, Maria, don't do this.

"You never finished telling me how you knew I was heartless."

Hearing her beautiful voice yell out at him gave him an ounce of hope, something he hadn't felt for a very long time.

"Don't get in that car, princess, and I'll tell you," Dominic begged her, praying that her soul, that was a match to his, would hear it and come to him. She had to feel it—how much he fought going to her right now. Her body had to scream out for her to come to him too.

I beg of you, Maria . . . don't do it. There will be no going back from thi—

"Maria," he heard her name being called from inside the car.

No! His soul cried out for her when she dropped her eyes from his to the man inside the car.

He knew it the second she looked away that he had lost her … when he almost had her. He didn't watch as she got in the car, looking instead at the man who had just stolen everything from him.

Dominic didn't know what façade he had put on for Maria, but staring into the gold eyes through the dimmed window, he knew the real Kayne Evans …

And he hadn't fucking changed at all.

Watching the car drive off with his true love, the boogieman's voice echoed in his mind.

Kayne still bleeds the same as Lucifer.

MARIA WILL
NEVER FORGIVE YOU

Opening *the car door, the* man slid inside the front seat behind the wheel, only noticing the presence of another when he looked into the rearview mirror.

The man in the driver's seat didn't move a muscle. "What are you doing, Dominic?"

Dom had been in the back seat of the dark vehicle for a bit, just waiting for his mark, as he held his Glock pointing at the back of the seat.

Staring down the rearview mirror, his hazel eyes met the furiously glowing blue-green ones. "We're done, Lucca."

"Done?" Lucca coldly mocked him, his words slashing the cool air. "We haven't even begun."

"You did," he assured him, keeping his voice as steady as his gun. "You have taken everything from me … Angel … Kat … and now Mari—"

"I didn't take Maria away from you. I have been trying to help yo—"

"*Bullshit!*" Dominic's voice exploded in the car. His gun no longer steady like his voice, he waved the metal piece with each word he spoke. "You could have done something! Like you made me do with Kat!"

"I told you, Maria would never love you if I did that," the underboss gritted out through clenched teeth.

"Yes," he agreed. "But you could have kept her away from him, and you fucking know it."

Lucca went silent for several deadly moments, and then his voice lost the bite it had before, and in its place was disappointment. "I thought she would have chosen better."

"Well, she didn't." It broke his heart to say those words. Both of them knew Maria's choice was final. She had stopped hiding her relationship with Kayne when she had left publicly in his car.

Making a move, Lucca suddenly stopped when Dom placed the barrel against the back of his skull.

"I need a cigarette, all right?" Lucca slowly continued to reach into his pocket without permission, pulling out a pack, along with his Zippo. "It's not exactly like I fucking have a chance of outshooting you, even if you didn't have that gun in your hand."

Dom actually had a slight burst of laughter, his erratic brain not sure what emotion to feel next. In some way, he felt like, if the two of them hadn't been sworn enemies, they might have been friends.

Lighting up a cigarette, Lucca took a couple of hard hits before he continued, "You just didn't give it enough time; you have to keep trying with Maria."

"Time?" Dominic switched back to his angry tone and feelings of them being enemies. "How much time has she had with Kayne? I've spent my days since the wedding too busy, proving to your father that I, nor any of my men, are One-Shot. And while I've been fighting for my family's lives, you've managed to let Maria fall in love with someone else."

"I thought she knew better," Lucca hissed. "I wanted to see who she would choose."

"So, what? You wanted to test her?" Dominic's voice shook the vehicle. "This is Maria's life we're talking about here! She isn't one of your sick, little experiments. You wanted her to *choose*? Well, congratulations. She chose, and now we both will pay for it."

"You're not going to kill me."

"You should never underestimate a desperate man, Lucca." Dom's hazel eyes glowed in the night.

That was exactly where the underboss had pushed him, and that was his downfall. The worst thing to do was back a dog into a corner because, eventually, there'd be a fight.

Seeing he was serious, Lucca's strange eyes glowed back. "My father will kill you for killing me, and you know it."

"I actually think he might thank me for getting rid of his biggest enemy. What do you think?" he asked with a tilt of his lips, but Dom wasn't that naïve. "Even so, he won't let me off, but I could get him to leave my siblings out of it."

Lucca stared back at him through the rearview mirror, unafraid. "After everything you've lived through, you're just going to give up?"

"I don't have anything without Kat, and now especially without Maria." Dominic said the words with such pain that it rocked the earth itself. "You told me *fifty-fifty*, Lucca. You lied as you shook my hand and looked me in the fucking eyes."

Dom couldn't hide how cornered he was. Lucca could see it through the tiny mirror.

"If Katarina isn't happily married when I take my father's place, I will make Drago file for a divorce or let you kill him. It'll be your choice."

Dom's brows drew into a line at seeing that the underboss was fucking serious, and he wasn't just saying it because he was scared for his life.

Continuing his promise, Lucca blew out a puff of smoke. "And as for Maria, I'll—"

"Oh, come on, we both know you're not leaving this car alive," Dom stopped him. Cocking his Glock, the sound echoed throughout the small space ominously. "You don't point a gun at the boogieman and live."

It didn't matter what the underboss told him, he couldn't let him live. Dom had a better shot at facing Dante, and the father had way less of an imagination than his son.

Lucca took a long, hard hit of his burning cigarette. "I followed the car that picked up the dead body you shot outside the gas station. I visited that funeral home and told them to give me a call whenever a body needing to be discreetly disposed of was brought in. I knew every person killed by you. Every single one of your kills landed them with a bullet right between the eyes. The only one you shot from behind was the one I saw that day."

Dominic continued to listen to every word spilling from Lucca's lips.

"That was also the day I knew I would have to kill you." He crushed his cigarette in the ashtray without looking away from Dom. "The first real chance I got, I knew I'd have to take it, because no man who only took a life by looking into their eyes and possessed your skill would be happy with the shitty, little piece of this city you were given."

"Until you met *her*," Dominic said the next part of the story, letting him know he knew why he had asked for the fifty-fifty agreement.

"Yes," Lucca agreed. "The second I saw Chloe, I no longer wanted you as my enemy. What happened to my mother, *I will not* let happen to her."

"It was the day of your mother's funeral that I knew I could kill you." Dominic drifted his eyes to the loaded Glock in his hand, telling him his own story. "I thought you were like my father, but he never loved a soul. I could see the way you loved your mother when you looked at her casket. I knew you would love again … but I also knew you'd die if you lost her."

Lucca stared at him fiercely in the rearview mirror, showing Dominic just how right, but oh so wrong, he was. The man he held a gun to might not live long after the death of his soulmate, but the boogieman promised him with evil blue-green eyes that he would burn the city to the ground all by himself, destroying every living thing in its limits before he'd take the man responsible for Chloe's death to hell with him.

"Relax," Dom told him. "The gun's pointed at you, not her. My father already touched her, anyway, and I take no pleasure in hurting anyone Lucifer has marked."

Taking in his wholehearted answer, Lucca lit up another cigarette, the glow of the Zippo in the dark car lighting up his face. "There will come a day when we will make an enemy, whether its inside or outside of the city, and I'd like to have you on my side. I won't be able to protect Chloe alone."

Dom could see he still wanted them to work together, but he had yet to prove it.

"You want me and my men prepared to die for *her*, *not* to actually share the city."

"You'll want it too, you know," Lucca warned him. "You'll want me and my men prepared to die for the woman you love too."

"The woman *I love*, your men are already prepared to die for," Dominic spat behind him, letting him know it wasn't the same thing.

The underboss taunted him with the cold hard truth. "Their

love for Maria will die the second she becomes a Luciano."

"Well, it's a good thing she didn't choose me," he bit back.

Staring back down at his gun, it was time he decided what to do. "Not once did I ever consider running this city together. I promised myself long ago I would take the throne and become king." Dominic lifted his hazel depths back to the rearview mirror. "You will always need me more than I need you. You were born for this life, Lucca, but ... *I was made.*" Uncocking the gun with his last words, Dom let the boogieman go free, both with the knowledge of who truly deserved to wear the crown.

"Tell me," Dominic said, opening the car door, deciding to leave Lucca with some final words before he left, "what is it, do you think, Maria will *never* forgive you for?" He taunted the underboss, repaying him for the thoughts he had forced upon him. "For not finding out which of your men is One-Shot before Leo lost an eye ... or for not telling her who Kayne really is?"

Sitting in his Mustang, Dominic continued watching the apartment with his stomach in knots. Bile rose with each passing hour, knowing what most likely was taking place inside, yet he had to sit out here and just let it happen, no matter how much it hurt.

Once it reached five in the morning, Dom went to open his car door, needing to vomit. It had been a long time since his emotions made him sick. Right before the little contents he had placed in his stomach yesterday were about to come up, he caught a figure leaving the building.

Quietly shutting his car door, his stomach began to settle. He waited until the man in the ball cap and sweats got into his own car and pulled out of the lot before he started trailing him.

Following behind the car, he didn't use his headlights, even though the sun had yet to rise, depending on his memory, good eyesight, and the lights of the car in front of him to guide him.

He hadn't expected him to leave this early, thinking he would have had to wait to confront him until he went to work or left later in the day. It was why Dom had decided to follow him, to see where the hell he was going this early.

Not sure what he expected, when he pulled into Kansas City Park, he figured he should have guessed when the man exited the car to pull up his hood over his cap before he jogged off.

This park was much different than the one down the street from his home. Like all the other comparisons, this park sat on the rich side of town, with pretty views that assholes like to jog in early in the morning.

The man he had been watching might've been from Blue Park, but he hadn't lived there for a long time.

Figured.

It was just another way the man pretended to be something he wasn't.

Jumping out of his car, Dominic ran after him, his fury driving him to catch up with him. Then he waited until he was a few feet away before he let him know of his presence.

"Kayne!" Dom boomed out over the desolate park as the sun began to rise.

The figure in front of him looked over his shoulder before he quickly turned in surprise. "What the fuck are you doing her—"

"We need to talk," Dominic continued closing the distance between them.

Looking over his shoulder, back toward the way he had been heading before he'd been stopped, Kayne's tone went serious. "This needs to wait, Dom."

"It can't" was all he had said when his fist met Kayne's jaw. Dominic had waited twenty-something years to do that, and it felt good.

Kayne slowly wiped the blood from his mouth with anger growing in his gold eyes, but his voice stayed even. "If this is about Maria, I get it. But right now, I—"

bRRing . . .

The phone ringing in his pocket cut him off.

Pulling out his phone in a hurry, Kayne checked to see who was calling.

Dom took one look at his face and knew instinctively who it was.

"It's her, isn't it?" he asked furiously.

bRRing . . .

Kayne held up a hand. "I need you to trust me—"

bRRing . . .

"Trust you?" Dominic laughed manically. "Why don't you

answer it and tell Maria the truth about you?"

bRRi-

Kayne's finger slipped, and instead of canceling the call, he unknowingly answered it.

"What do you think she'll think about you then?" Dom asked harshly with a twisted smile.

Now Kayne finally fought back. "I planned on telling her!"

"When was that? Before or after you got done fucking her?"

Kayne took a threatening step closer to him. "You don't even know anyth—"

"I know you've been fucking jealous of me since the day we met. Was ruining Bristol's fucking life not enough for you?" Dominic pulled his Glock from his back when Kayne made a move for his pocket.

The old Kayne quickly returned to his golden eyes as words spewed from him like venom. "I should fucking kill yo—"

BANG!

The look that rested in Kayne's eyes as the phone slipped from his hand, crashing to the pavement, was the same one that had been in Leo's single eye when that explosion had taken away his other. Only, Kayne wouldn't be losing just an eye.

Kayne looked down to the hole that had been placed in his chest. Covering the wound with his hand, blood flowed through his fingers as fresh raindrops began to lightly touch their skin.

Dominic caught him before his knees hit the soon-to-be wet pavement as death came to greet him. Then, letting his body fall completely to the ground, his unremorseful hazel eyes unconsciously went to the phone that was lit up with Maria's name.

He watched the raindrops hit the screen as it sat in a puddle of blood, knowing she had heard it all and now she sat waiting on the other end of the line.

Picking up the shattered phone that had fallen to the ground, he heard her unsteady, "Hello …?"

He gripped the phone with blood-soaked hands that even the rain would be unable to wash away, while staring at the dead body before him. He breathed heavily, trying to catch his breath after that confrontation.

He knew what it would do to her when she heard whose voice it was coming from the other end … but Dominic did it anyway.

"Hello, Maria."

I'LL KILL YOU

Maria *had been sitting motionless* on the floor in Kayne's apartment for what seemed like hours. The only light coming into the bedroom was from the window she stared out of. She had been so irrevocably numb and out of it that she hadn't even heard she was no longer alone.

"Maria ..." a dark voice spoke from behind her in the doorway.

Knowing who the voice belonged to, she still had to turn to look at him. She couldn't believe the set of balls that man had on him to come here after what he had *done*.

"Leave," Maria hissed at him, giving the brave man a warning that he shouldn't underestimate her.

"No," he answered simply.

"You have five seconds to leave, or so help me God"—Maria

glowered at him, promising she'd make her next words true—"I'll kill you, Dominic."

Standing in the doorframe, Dom crossed his arms. "I'm not leaving without you. We need to get out of here."

Maria moved like a flash of lightning. Grabbing one of her heels from where Kayne had placed them beside the bed that he had held her all night in, she stood mere inches away from Dominic as she pressed the end of her stiletto lightly into his neck.

"You just couldn't see me fucking happy with Kayne, could you? You couldn't handle that you lost, that I fell in love with him and not you."

"What you felt for Kayne wasn't love, princess." Dominic's hazel eyes bore into hers, unafraid.

"And you suppose I felt it for you?" She snickered evilly. After their dance, Maria had one fucking dream about the man standing before her and she was more interested if Dominic really did have the dimples when he smiled, over anything else that happened in that dream. "I never felt a thing for you, Dominic Luciano, and I never fucking will." Pressing her pointy heel deeper into his tanned skin, she continued, "I won't even feel hate for you when I get done killing you. You don't even deserve that after what you've done."

"I deserve to die," Dom told her wholeheartedly, pressing his own neck into her heel. "But not for this."

"You lied," Maria whispered, feeling disbelief that she had ever believed a word out of his mouth. "You lied when you told me you were nothing like your father. *You're worse.*" Her words lashed him like a hot whip across his face. "At least Lucifer knew he was a monster … You act so fucking righteous you've let yourself believe you're not."

"Probably so." Not even Dominic could hide the slight hurt in his eyes at her words. "But the only thing I regret is ever thinking you could love me."

She lifted her eyes to the single drop of blood trickling down his neck as she came to a decision. "I'm not going to kill you. I want you to suffer with the thought that I'd rather love a dead man and be alone for the rest of my life than ever love you." Releasing the heel from his neck, she lifted her lashes back up for her eyes to meet his once more. "Now get the fuck out of here and out of my life, because I swear to God, Dominic, if I ever see you again, I'll take the thing you love most and kill it … just like you did me."

If Dominic and the rest of the world thought she was cold before … *they haven't seen nothing yet.*

With one last look, Dominic didn't even look at her the same. It was as if he was suddenly void of any and all emotion for her.

"Good-bye, Maria."

Watching the Luciano boss walk away, a part of her hadn't believed the words when he had said them before. This time … she knew he fucking meant them.

Maria stared down at the glittering city below. Like her older brother, Lucca, she enjoyed the view, often visiting his office at the

Casino Hotel whenever he wasn't around to be alone.

Unlike their father, who had hated it whenever she'd snuck into his office when she'd been a child, Lucca never mentioned it bothering him, even though he knew she did so without permission. As she got older, she had stopped sneaking into her father's office and found herself in her brother's.

She weirdly felt welcomed here, not only by Lucca but by the very room itself. The four walls and the things it held had a presence. It all brought her a peacefulness she didn't get anywhere else.

The office door opening behind her reminded her that she could only borrow the room for the small moments in time that she needed it, that it would never belong to her, and would always be the owner's, who now stood quietly beside her.

Taking her eyes away from the view, she looked over to her brother, watching him stare out into the night.

"You're working with him, aren't you?" Maria might have asked the question, but she only did so to make him to speak the words out loud. She already knew its validity, though he had never told her.

It was unlike him. Yes, Lucca kept secrets from her, but he also spilled a lot of them to her whenever he needed to think out loud or bend her ear. This particular information, she thought he would have told her. Made men business wasn't her business, thanks to being born a woman, but Lucca had always given her a little piece of a dream, making her a part of it. Lately, however, he looked at her no differently than how her father looked at her.

Lucca didn't even look away from the city when he answered, "Yes."

"And you're going to continue to work with Dominic, aren't you?" she asked, again already knowing the answer.

"Yes."

"He killed Kayne!" Maria lashed out, wanting him to look at her. "He fucking murdered the man I love, and you couldn't care le—"

"No, he didn't," Lucca's controlled voice cut through her scream. Turning, with his blue-green eyes locked on her, he stared at her unrelentingly.

The next two words out of his mouth would change her life forever ...

"I did."

Maria thought her knees were going to give out from sheer shock as she watched the city lights dance upon his face. Not a single thought came to her brain, only the action of swinging her hand to harshly slap his face.

Lucca's face turned back toward the city from the hard slap that his sister had landed.

"How could you?" she demanded, watching his cheek turn red before the scratch from her manicured fingernail began to draw blood.

Lifting a finger to his cheek, he touched the cut, sweeping up a drop of red liquid. He stared at his stained fingertip, then simply rubbed the blood away between two fingers. "I did it for your own good."

This time, when she tried to slap him, he caught her hand.

Lucca held her manicured hand firmly in his. "I let you have one, Maria." Giving her flesh a slight squeeze, he made himself clear. "And that was the only one you're ever going to fucking get."

She couldn't believe she had ever respected Lucca and, like Dominic, she had one thought. *He's no different than our father.*

Maria snatched her hand back from his grasp. "You had no fucking right to decide what's good for me. I loved hi—"

"What you had with him wasn't love, Maria," Lucca spat cynically in her face. "That was infatuation with the first man you fucking laid your eyes on who could never be controlled by our father or me."

"And how did that make you feel"—snidely, she snickered at him—"when a high school teacher didn't bow down to you in fear?" She had to look away from the brother who she had once trusted. "No wonder you killed him."

"That's not why he died …" Lucca's dark voice ricocheted in the room. The second truth she was about to hear would be harder than the first revelation. "Kayne was a…"

YEARS AGO…

Dominic drove down the dark road, the pavement made even darker with the rain pelting down. About to turn the corner, Dom flicked his lights off before pulling to the side to park. Cutting his engine, he unzipped his coat, putting his gun within easy reach in case the person he was meeting had something else on his agenda instead of the information he wanted to impart.

A cold rush of air filtered inside the warm car as the door opened. The darkness enveloped the silhouetted figure.

Dominic stared at the hooded man as he turned to face him after shutting the door. "Your father, Carlos, won't be happy to find you sneaking out to meet me at this time of night."

"I waited until he was asleep."

Warily, Dom kept his eyes on the Marco's hands as he slunk farther down in his seat.

"I needed to talk to you."

"So you said in your text. What's up?" Even in the dark, Dom could tell how frightened the kid was. He was trying hard not to be seen inside his car. At three in the morning, no one was stupid enough to be out during the howling rain unless they had to be.

Dominic was too familiar with the fear Marco was exhibiting for him not to know it wasn't manufactured to distract him into a sneak attack from one of the Luciano's enemies.

"What's up?" Dom asked again in a more authoritative voice, trying to ease the boy's fear.

Marco finally started speaking. "My uncle Luis got in a fight with my aunt last weekend and ended up in jail."

"You need to borrow bail money off Lucifer?" Dom frowned, about to kick his ass out of the car with a threatening warning, liking the kid enough not to want to see him become in debt to Lucifer.

"No," Marco hastened to correct him.

Dominic didn't know where the conversation was going, becoming more curious about what Marco was trying to explain.

"The cops put Luis in holding until my dad could post bail. He wasn't alone. He had company waiting to be bailed out."

"Who?"

"Gabriel Evans."

"Kayne Evans father?" Dom wasn't surprised. Gabriel was locked up more time in jail than out.

"Yes."

"You had me come out in the pouring rain just to tell me something that happens all the time?" Dominic started to kick the kid out of the car, reaching for the key to turn it back on.

"No." Marco shook his head. "I had you come out because he was bailed out but refused to leave."

That got his attention. He moved his hand away from the key. "He *wanted* to stay in jail?"

"He was yelling that he wasn't going to take any help from a cop, even if it was his piece of shit son."

Dom sucked in his breath. Kayne was a cop? Dominic knew Gabriel wasn't talking about his other son.

"Luis sure he heard him right?"

"Oh, he's sure. Luis said they had to taze Gabriel to get his drunk-ass out of the cell."

Dom raised a brow. "You sure they didn't take him to the morgue instead of releasing him?"

"I checked him out in the morning at the gas station when he came for another bottle. I'm sure."

"Who else knows?" Dom asked the kid hastily.

"No one." Marco started to shake his head again. "My uncle Luis hit the road, afraid he'd get deported."

Dominic didn't believe that for a second. "If Luis knows, then your whole family knows."

Marco just kept shaking his head. "I was the one who picked Luis up from the jail, and I told him to keep his mouth shut or Lucifer would cut his tongue out."

That Dom believed. "You tell anyone?"

"No, just you," Marco swore.

"Do me a favor." Dominic took out the wad of bills in his pockets, peeling off two hundred dollar bills, then held them out to the kid. "Let's keep it that way." No one would believe Blue Park's biggest drunk's son, Kayne Evans, had become a cop without proof.

Marco wouldn't take the money. "I don't want your money. I owe you my life."

Dom didn't argue with the truth. Returning the money to his pocket, he was inwardly relieved he wouldn't have to make up an excuse to Lucifer for being short on the expected amount. "We'll call it even. Thanks for the info."

"Sure thing, Dom," he immediately agreed, starting to get out of the car.

"You graduate next week, don't you?"

"Yes. I got a scholarship, too, out of state."

Dominic decided to impart some advice. "Convince your dad to move with you and forget you were ever a part of this shit yard, kid."

"You're lying ..." **Maria's harsh tone** drifted off the second she turned back to look at him for his blasphemy when the word cop passed her brother's lips. One look into his eyes, and she saw the truth.

Lucca looked at her pitifully. "How does it feel to know the man you claimed to love didn't tell you the one thing that would make you despise him?"

"How do you know?" she whispered, racking her brain to think of how she had been deceived.

"Because I know," the underboss told her. "Very few did. He was given the perfect cover, one the family wouldn't even expect. I assume, since they never lucked out with men who were made, they would try to do it through the children. Nero, Amo, and Vincent were all in his class. Leo was his last shot, but then ... he met you."

Maria felt her knees wanting to give out again as the world slowly spun, thinking about every moment she had shared with Kayne.

It was as if Lucca could read her thoughts. "Your relationship and everything you shared with that man was *a lie.*"

"No ... it can't be. Kayne loved me." That she believed wholeheartedly. The way he treated her, talked to her were all things out of love. She had been around men her whole life, and they'd only wanted her for two things—sex or power. Maria was beautiful, but it didn't compare to her last name. To marry the boss's daughter could grant money, a job, security, and respect from the man who held the city in the palm of his hands. Kayne had been the opposite of those men. She felt it in her bones.

"I'm sure he did," Lucca told her truthfully, looking at her. "But you wouldn't have."

It's true. Even her own conscience told her what she was trying to fight. Maria would have never given Kayne the time of day if she had known he was a cop, let alone try to take her family down. Therefore, Lucca was right.

It had all been a *lie.*

"Why the fuck didn't you tell me?" she hissed.

"I wanted to see who you would choose." Lucca showed her his utter disappointment. "I hoped you knew better."

Maria's hand burned with wanting to slap the so-called boogieman again, but even she wasn't stupid enough to try it for the third time.

"Why?" she demanded. "What was so fucking important to know that you risked him getting any information out of me ... and our bond?"

"To see where you fit," Lucca stated with glowing eyes that matched the city lights that still danced upon his skin. "Or where you *once* fit in the family."

Maria shook her head angrily, knowing he wasn't talking about their blood. "And now I don't?"

"Nope." Lucca's cold voice ended her dreams with a harsh slap of reality. "Not when you were prepared to throw your life away and everything you stood for, for a man your brain couldn't decipher was love or lust. And especially not when there was another man who could have given you everything your little black heart could ever desire." His eyes whispered the unspoken word, the one thing she wanted—*power*—before he continued, "And, somehow, on top of all that, he was the one who *truly* loved you."

"Dominic loves me for my last name and what you could give hi—"

"He fell in love with you the moment he fucking met you," Lucca snapped, losing control of his voice before he coolly evened it back out. "And if you believe anything other than that, then I'm glad you chose wrong."

"How do you even know …?" She trailed off, watching her brother take out a much-needed cigarette.

Flipping open his Zippo, he lit the end of the stick that he held between his lips. "He didn't take his fucking eyes off you at our mother's funeral, but when I picked you up from the bridal shop, he tried too hard *not* to look at you."

Her brows drew together in thought, being reminded of their mother's funeral. That certain point in time kept being brought up. She had still to learn why Dom—

Making herself shut down those curious thoughts, she looked back out the full-length window. "It doesn't matter anymore."

Drawing a long hit off his cigarette, Lucca narrowed his blue-green gaze on her. "You don't fucking deserve him," he brutally told her, blowing out a puff of smoke that rolled over her body slowly. "Picking Kayne Evans over Dominic Luciano is the biggest mistake you'll ever make, Maria. I only hope, when you learn to regret it, it won't be too late for you."

Maria wasn't the type to walk away, but her heels started gliding her across the room, unable to respond to Lucca's harsh reality. She didn't know how to act, feel, or think after the events of the week. First Leo and now Kayne … She could only process one feeling.

Numbness.

Grabbing the silver knob, she wanted to give the boogieman a reminder that he wasn't all he thought he was. "You don't know everything, Lucca."

POOR LEO

"You get to go home soon," Maria's soft words filled the white, sterile space, hoping he would finally talk to her.

Looking at her perfect baby brother, she saw the white gauze that covered his left eye concealed his only imperfection. It hid the gruesome hole that would never be filled again, but it wasn't the only thing that wouldn't be the same.

Before the explosion, Leo was everything that she and the rest of the Caruso siblings weren't—funny, charming, sweet, and kind were only the beginning of his appeal. He was the only one to take after their mother, and that was why he was the only person left on this earth who Maria felt any love for. He gave her hope that not all men were bad. Just 99.9 percent of them.

However, staring at Leo's single blank stare, she could no longer find the baby brother she had once known. He hadn't spoken a single word to her since she entered his hospital room and had barely spoken to her at all after telling him what had happened.

All that was left of poor Leo at the moment was a shell of what he used to be.

"Kayne's dead," Maria blurted out, hoping to get some sort of reaction out of him since he had been his English teacher. When that information didn't give her a response, she continued on, hoping to shock him at some point. "Lucca killed him because, apparently, he was an undercover cop and not because I"—She paused a moment, needing to correct the words that had been about to roll off her tongue.—"*thought* I was in love with him."

She didn't know why she was telling him this. At first it was because she was trying to garner some sort of a response from him, but now she only kept talking because it felt therapeutic, and it felt no differently talking to Leo in this moment than it did if she was talking to a wall or the wind.

Closing her eyes, she tried to decipher her numbness, to see which part of it hurt the most—that Kayne had fooled her, his death, or ...

"I don't think I'll ever forgive Lucca for what he did. Not for taking his life, but for not telling me who Kayne was."

Opening her eyes when she heard movement, she thought she might be getting a response, but Leo was only reaching his hand out for the cup of water on his hospital bedside table.

Reaching out slowly, Leo tried to grab the Styrofoam cup,

but when his hand clenched, it came up empty. His hand-eye coordination had been totally affected since losing his left eye. The doctor had told him it would take a while for him to adjust to his new sight.

"Let me help." Maria got up from the chair, going to his side quickly.

"No, I can ..." Leo frustratingly spoke his first words to her this evening, trying to grab the cup again and knocking it over, spilling the water all over the table.

"Don't worry about it; I'll clean it u—"

"Just leave me the fuck alone!" Leo screamed, swiping his hand across the table and sending the cup and the rest of its contents flying across the room.

She froze in place. It was the first emotion she had seen from him since the accident and the first time she had ever seen her little brother angry like this *ever*.

Looking into the single blue eye, Maria realized his frustrations. He wanted her to stop babying him, but she was only trying to help.

When she didn't leave at his outburst, Leo sighed, going back to staring out the side window, hiding the left side of his face again.

Taking a deep breath, she sat down on the edge of his bed, seeing Leo retreat to the shell he had become.

"I'll never forgive *him* either," Maria whispered to the universe, going back to talking about her problems because she sensed it might help. Leo only had people around him focusing on his problems, the constant reminder that he was no longer whole eating him alive. "Dominic locked me in that freezer proving that, not only did he not trust me, but that I can't ever trust him."

"No, he didn't."

Goose bumps coated her skin, though she didn't know if they were from the fact that Leo was talking to her or from what he said.

"What?" she whispered.

Leo turned his head away from the window to face her fully, reminding her why they were here. "The door was unlocked."

YOU BETTER PRAY FOR
YOUR SOUL...ASSHOLE

It *took everything Maria had* to knock on the fucking door, her knuckles lightly hitting the wood. She glanced over her shoulder, second-guessed taking the taxi here from the hospital. Thinking he wasn't going to answer, the door suddenly flung open. However, it wasn't who she expected.

Last time she was here Angel's other half opened the door, but this time, his twin didn't look the same. The hallows under his eyes were filled with darkness that matched his grave, gray eyes. She had seen a brief moment of hope when he first opened the door, clearly wanting to see someone else, but then it disappeared at the sight of her. The playboy mask he usually wore had slipped, revealing the real Matthias underneath.

The door being shut in her face had Maria's jaw dropping to the porch.

Excuse m—

She was ready to beat the door down when the door flung open once again. This time by a different brother.

Watching Matthias walk slowly down a hall behind the other brother, she was about to give him a piece of her mind when Cassius drew her attention.

"Sorry, he's not feeling well lately."

Maria's eyes went to Dominic's mini-me before they shifted back to Matthias, noticing for the first time how sullenly he walked into a room before he slammed the door.

"Is he all right?" she found herself asking sympathetically to the most disliked Luciano.k90o=,p[l'

Katarina, she loved. Angel, she respected. Matthias, annoyed her. Dominic … was complicated. The one in front of her, she knew nothing about, other than he was a little Lucifer in the making.

"I don't know," Cassius told her truthfully without an ounce of emotion. "You can come in," the young kid told her, stepping to the side. "Dom will be mad at me for letting you in, but I know he'll kill me if I don't."

Letting her heels hit the old wooden floor, she stepped inside the Luciano home. Last time she was there, she hadn't paid too much attention to the home, enamored instead by the oldest Luciano brother and too busy looking at him.

At first glance it was old and rundown, a house people wouldn't want to step in, but looking at it now, she noticed how clean it was. Usually, old homes with ancient appliances and furniture had layers of dirt in places impossible to get rid of, but she didn't see anything wrong with it, other than it needed updating.

"Dom should be home soon," Cassius told her, closing the front door. "Want to watch my show with me?"

"Sure." Maria nodded, already watching the youngest Luciano walk to the couch before she even answered.

Sitting down on the brown, leather couch next to him, she raised a brow when her gaze shifted to the little TV screen from the sound of bullets being fired. "And this is …?" she asked, watching a swarm of zombies get nailed in the head.

"*The Walking Dead.*" Cassius, who had his hazel eyes glued to the screen, gave her a quick glance. "You've never seen it, have you?"

Maria motioned to her baby blue dress and nude heels. "What? I don't dress the part, so how could I possibly watch it?"

"No," Cassius told her, nodding toward the screen that had a greasy but badass-looking man shooting a crossbow into a zombie's eye. "If you don't know who Darryl is, then you've never seen it."

"Oh," Maria muttered, glad she didn't have to hate this Luciano *yet*. "I was about to tell you I left my apocalypse clothes at the dry cleaners." Telling her lame joke, Maria studied Dom's mini-me, hoping he'd laugh. As much as she didn't want to admit it, her curiosity was killing her over finding out whether the dirty dream about Dominic was true. If the kid smiled and showed a dimple, then she was pretty sure she'd have her answer.

But Cassius didn't even break a smile, much less a laugh. Hell, Leo at least gave her a pitying chuckle, even when her jokes missed the mark.

"If you had them, you shouldn't wear them anyway. My brother likes the way you dress, you know."

"Matthias ..." Maria rolled her eyes. The wannabe playboy had made it very obvious he had when he asked to take her coat when she came here the first time. "I know he's—"

"No," the young Luciano stopped her, shrugging. "Dom."

He does ...? A slow smile tilted her lips that she was unable to hide.

Making a mental note of that information, her smile disappeared when she watched the Darryl character pull the arrow out of the zombie's eye, taking it with it.

Normally, that stuff didn't bother her, but with what had happened to Leo, that particular action was a little too real.

"I see where Kat gets her taste in TV shows."

"What did she have you watch?" he asked curiously.

"Deadly Women."

Cassius gave her another glance and nodded. "I thought you'd like that show."

"Oh, I did," Maria assured him. Unlike this show, it was a documentary about women killing men, even though they didn't deserve it. That wasn't the point, though. It, at least, portrayed women who didn't run scared.

"Well, you'll like this part coming up." Cassius nodded back toward the TV so she wouldn't miss it.

Staring at the television screen, she watched a woman with glistening, ebony skin pull a katana out of the sleeve she carried on her back. Walking right up to the pack of deadly, gruesome zombies, she swiftly began decapitating them, one by one, as her dreads swung around her with each kill.

"Who is that?" Maria asked, unable to pull her eyes from the TV.

"Kat and Dom's favorite character." If Maria had turned her head, she would have seen Cassius' little smile before it quickly vanished. "Michonne."

Looking at him a second too late, she raised a brow. "Got any popcorn?"

"I think Kat still has a stash here," he said, getting up to throw a bag of popcorn into the microwave.

Maria's eyes were glued to the TV as *The Walking Dead* marathon continued.

The bowl of popcorn was long gone by the time Maria glanced down at her phone to see what time it was. What had her squinting her eyes was the fact that she didn't have any missed calls or texts. Usually, Lucca would have blown up her phone by now, knowing she didn't have a suit with her. After telling him she no longer wanted or needed protection, he hadn't bothered her. Hell, she hadn't even talked to him since the night she slapped him, and she wasn't planning to. Not to mention she hadn't talked to her father after telling him she danced with the Luciano boss. She was sure he now knew that Kayne was a cop, so the chances of her father ever speaking to her again were slim to none. But she was okay with it. Her brother, on the other hand, she tried to deny it bothered her as she blackened her cell phone screen.

Looking back at the TV, Maria watched the group of the living rub zombie guts over themselves so they could trick the dead into thinking they were one of them.

"Something bad is going to happen, huh?" she asked.

"Just watc—"

The front door opening had a heartless Maria's heart pumping.

Not having seen a car outside, Dominic couldn't hide his shock seeing Maria sitting on the couch. However, the surprise quickly wore off and in its place was a cold chill that even Cassius didn't miss.

"What are you doing here, Maria?"

She didn't like the way the words left his lips, like seeing her was an inconvenience. It hurt a part of her pride, even if she was the one who had come here to extend an olive branch. And only *if* that was what she was doing …

Frankly, she didn't know what she was doing, other than …

"We're watching *The Walking Dead*." She matched his cool tone, turning back to the TV and looking away from the man who she'd promised to kill the next time she saw him.

"I see that," he grumbled, glancing at the TV. He had no more than put his eyes back on her when he shot a glance to the TV. "Cass, change the channel."

"But the best part's coming u—"

"*Now, Cassius,*" Dominic ordered firmly, storming into the living room.

"Gore doesn't bother her." The little Luciano shrugged, not looking away from the screen.

Maria, on the other hand, looked between the TV and Dom, trying to figure out what his deal was and what was so bad that was about to happen.

"I said, *change it.*" Dominic snatched the remote from Cassius before quickly changing the channel right after a gun went off. He then took a deep, calming breath and held out the remote for his brother to take in truce. "Listen, you can watch anything else right now, but not that, okay?"

Cassius stared up at him for a moment, then nodded as he took the remote.

Scrutinizing Dom, she watched him carefully walk back to the door. Maria wasn't sure what was wrong with him, but then she supposed it probably had a lot to do with her strolling in unannounced.

Getting up from the couch, she quickly followed behind him, afraid he was about to walk out the door. When he started taking off his jacket, she was relieved. Maria couldn't help but notice the thin, black T-shirt he wore underneath that stretched over his broad shoulders as he slipped it off. It was his tanned arms, however, that had her staring. She had never noticed just how fit he was, since she always saw him with that infamous jacket on. She couldn't quite remember if she had ever seen him without it, other than when he had given his suit jacket to her in the freezer, and he'd been wearing a long-sleeved dress shirt underneath.

Her palm itched to touch his bicep, to feel the muscles underneath. It was the first time she felt something other than … numb.

"What do you want, Maria?" he asked, hanging his leather jacket up on the coat rack.

Rubbing her hand down her dress, she smoothed the odd feeling away. "I wanted to talk."

He didn't even look at her when he turned to go into the kitchen. "Talk, or murder me with your heel?"

"Uh …" Maria glanced back at Cassius, who was watching a different murder program, back at the couch.

Following Dom to the connecting kitchen, she kept her voice low in the small house. "Maybe we should talk somewhere alone."

"It's all right," he told her, opening the fridge. "There isn't anything Cass hasn't heard, and he's not paying us any attention, anyway."

"Okay." She cleared her throat, not knowing where to start. When she watched him take out the milk and drink straight from the carton, she couldn't keep her disgust hidden. "Ew."

"Ew, what?" he asked, placing the milk back in the fridge like he hadn't just tainted it.

"You can't do th—"

"I just did," Dom said before she could finish.

"That's disgusting. Everyone drinks from that container." Maria went to the fridge, wanting to throw it out.

"There's more disgusting things that go on in a house with

three brothers; trust me." He snapped the fridge door closed before she could grab the milk. "Plus, this is my home and, clearly, not yours, princess. So, why don't you go back to your castle and guard your own damn milk?"

The way he said *princess* reminded her how everyone else called her that. It sounded derogatory, and not the way he used to say it, making her insides heat up.

Dominic went to the kitchen table, pulling out the hidden Glock under his T-shirt before sitting down.

Frustrated, she contemplated just walking out the door—this definitely wasn't easy for her. Instead, she took a seat in front him. "I'm trying to talk to you …."

Dom continued to give her the cold shoulder as he started to break down his gun. Watching him ignore her hurt Maria more than she'd like to admit, but thinking back to how horribly she had talked to him the last time, she wouldn't get any sleep tonight if she didn't try.

"Why didn't you tell me that you weren't the one who killed Kayne?" Her voice came out as a whisper.

Picking up a rag off the table, he wiped down the parts of his gun he had separated. It took him several long moments when he finally spoke. "Would you have believed me?"

"I … don't know," she answered truthfully. Carefully, she watched him, entranced with the way he was caring for his weapon. "But you should have at least given me the chance to believe you."

"I didn't tell you because"—Dominic finally looked up from

what he was doing to meet her eyes—"I wasn't sure I wouldn't have done it myself."

Maria swallowed, listening to him recount Kayne's final moments.

"I had the gun in my hand, Maria. I might not have been the one to take his life, but I can't promise you I wouldn't have done the same as Lucca did five seconds later."

Nodding, she took his answer for what it was—the truth. It might not have been what she wanted to hear, but she wanted the truth. It was something her father had never given her when it came to this profession.

"Why didn't you tell me he was a cop? I deserved to know, and you had no right to keep that from me, Dominic." That was what upset her the most—the secrets the men kept from her. It was exhausting and demeaning, especially when it concerned her. Maria didn't know what the men were trying to "save" her from, but it certainly hadn't helped the little bit of heart she had when it shattered into even tinier pieces. The irony was, the more they tried to protect Maria, the more hurt she got.

She might have been backstabbed by Kayne, but Dominic and Lucca had betrayed her just as badly.

When she watched his hazel eyes drifted back to his task, Maria became furious that he hadn't answered her, going back to giving her the cold shoulder.

"Fine," she snapped, jumping up from the table.

Maria couldn't believe it when she made it to the front door and he had yet to stop her. Normally, she would have flung the door open and stormed out, but putting her hand on the doorknob, slowly turning it, she realized she shouldn't have called his bluff

Come on ....

"Don't." Dominic's commanding voice had her freezing in place.

Maria hid her smile, but it was wiped clean off when she turned at the sound of a chair screeching to see Dom's serious expression and imposing stance. His hazel depths scorched her. He didn't take them off her for a second.

"Leave, Cassius."

Cass did as followed, quietly turning off the TV, then getting up.

Maria pressed her back up against the door as Dom's fierce gaze kept her from leaving. Her breath caught in her throat, knowing that, as soon as Cassius left the room, she would be in deep shit with the way Dominic was looking at her.

A bedroom door closing down the hall told her that they were alone, making every hair on her body stand up.

"By the time I found out you and Kayne had a thing, it was already too fucking late." Dominic's heated words were almost as hot as his stare. Slowly, he stalked toward her, closing the distance between them as he continued. "I wanted you to fucking choose *me* over Kayne. Not because you found out he was a cop and I was your second option, but because I was the *only* option."

It was unbearable to keep her eyes on his, seeing how badly she hurt Dom by choosing Kayne over him. He didn't even try to hide his pain.

Lucca was right ... Dominic was madly in love with her, and

she completely missed it. Maybe it was because the idea of her and him ever being together was absolutely insane, considering who their fathers were. But the last thing she truly expected was for Dominic to wholeheartedly love her. She wrongly assumed that, because his last name was Luciano, his intentions would be to use her. Instead, she ended up in the arms of a man who had done exactly that.

I'd rather love a dead man and be alone for the rest of my life than ever love you.

Maria's words struck her like a high-speed Mack truck.

She finally drifted her jeweled eyes to his chest, no longer able to look at the pain in his. Maria had known she would hurt him before she'd said those words. She had *wanted* him to hurt, just as badly as he had hurt her by killing Kayne … or so she thought.

"I—"

Dominic lifted her chin, forcing her gaze back to his. "Don't you dare apologize for something you don't mean, princess."

The pain in his eyes suddenly subsided as she watched his lips barely tilt to one side. She looked at his cheek to see if a dimple would appear, waiting on pins and needles, holding her breath ….

"You're a shit liar," he teased as he bent his head down closer to hers. Moving her chin with his forefinger and thumb, he lifted her face up slightly, stretching out her long, delicate neck so he could take her lips more easily.

Maria's brain told her this wasn't right, as it was too soon after Kayne's death, but *holy fuck*, her body told her it was *so* … right. Her lips begged her to close the little distance between them.

So, she did the sane thing, choosing somewhere in between her mind and body by holding perfectly still. She might not have been shoving her tongue down his throat like a part of her wanted to, but she wasn't stopping him either.

Her eyelids started to drift closed in anticipation when he tilted his head to the side … right before his lips came a millimeter closer to hers. His hot breath hit her waiting pout when he murmured the words, "I'm taking you home."

Maria's eyelids shot back open as he smugly backed away from her, but somehow she expertly managed to make sure he knew it hadn't bothered her.

You better pray for your soul … asshole.

PRINCESS, DON'T MAKE PROMISES YOU CAN'T KEEP

T*he lights on his blacked-out* Mustang flashed as he unlocked the car doors with his key fob as they exited his house.

"Thanks." She gave him a sweet smile that Dominic saw right through when he opened the car door for her.

"Uh-huh," he mumbled under his breath, watching her get in.

Maria waited until after he swung the door shut to dart him an evil glare, closing her inside the tinted cover of the blacked out windows while she buckled her seat belt and watched him walk to the other side of the car. She made sure to wipe her promise of retribution clean off her face when he opened the driver's side door.

The confines of the two-door car suddenly got smaller the

second Dominic slid behind the wheel, reminding her again just how big he was and how glorious he smelled when his fiery scent assailed her nose.

Wasting no time, he roared the engine to life with the flick of his wrist before quickly pulling out and onto the road.

"So, which poor sucker did you talk into dropping you off at my house and leaving you there?"

"None." She shrugged nonchalantly. "I took a taxi here."

"Right," Dominic said sarcastically, thinking she didn't want to give up a name, considering the last one who had done it took a bullet between the eyes.

"I'm serious." She watched his tanned right hand as he changed gears. "I really did take a taxi."

"Does Lucca know where you—"

"I told Lucca I'm done with having one of his men follow my every move."

Dom was about to bust out in laughter, but then he gave a quick glance over at her. "You're fucking serious, aren't you?"

"Yes." Crossing her arms, she raised a brow. "You think I need a big, strong Caruso protecting me too?"

"No," Dom answered, clearly reminiscing to when a heel was pressed against his throat. "I just can't believe Lucca listened."

Looking out the window, she watched Blue Park pass by. "Well, it was a long time coming …." And it had been. Her whole life had been spent with a man in a suit following ten steps behind her. She hadn't been able to go anywhere or do anything unless it was approved of by her father or brother. Yes, Maria might have been born with a tiara on her head, but it came with a cost. A normal childhood … sleepovers, friends, a real college experience. Being a "normal" girl for once was something she had never experienced until … Kayne.

"Having someone watch your back isn't a bad thing, you know. Especially considering One-Shot."

"And if that was the case, I'd be fine with it," she agreed, looking back at his profile. "But it's the controlling aspect I have a problem with. Imagine having someone decide when and where you are allowed to go at all times since you were born. It gets kind of old, especially when you get to watch your brothers do what they want."

"I understand." He nodded, feeling for her. "But I'm sure Lucca's overprotectiveness comes from what happened to your mother."

"You know, you talk about my brother like my father doesn't exist, right?" Maria's brows furrowed. "You are aware that Lucca is the underboss?" she asked, knowing full well he knew and reminding him of that little fact.

The engine was all she could hear through Dom's silence. She could tell he was thinking carefully about what to say.

"Your father has yet to earn my respect," he answered rather truthfully to the Caruso boss's daughter.

He's got a set of balls on him …

Smiling to herself, she thought about how she could get him killed for those words alone. Luckily for him, she appreciated not only his brutal honesty but that he trusted her enough to tell her that. Her smile, however, quickly faded with another thought. "How exactly did Lucca earn your trust? By killing Kayne?"

"Trust and respect are two different things, princess." He shot her a look so she'd know that he was being truthful. "Lucca earned my respect the day he was made, but I've yet to give him my trust completely."

That answer only showed Maria just how much Dominic disliked her father ... but the feeling was mutual at the moment.

"Maria"—Dom gripped the leather of the steering wheel tighter—"I might not be sorry about Kayne, but I am sorry about the part I played in hurting you. I should have put my pride aside and told you who he was. You had no way of knowing when he had the whole city fooled."

Maria looked forward, to the dark city road ahead, only able to manage a nod to let him know she accepted his apology. It wasn't easy, considering every made man treated her the same, but she accepted it because she could see he meant it.

My own brother couldn't even fucking apologize to me.

"Why did you come?" he asked curiously, changing gears again. "Lucca let me know that he told you he was the one who did it ... and you didn't come to see me then."

That was another reason she had accepted his apology—Maria was starting to see that she might be able to trust Dom after all. "Leo finally told me that you didn't lock the door."

"I see." Dominic's voice couldn't hide its smile like his face had. "Do you mean by *finally told you*, you finally asked if I did it instead of assuming?"

You know what . . . She decided it was best not to tell him that she hadn't asked Leo; he'd been correcting her when she did exactly as Dom said—assumed.

Maria turned on the radio to avoid answering, which most likely told him all he needed to know.

Hearing the song playing, she immediately changed the station.

"What are you doing?" he asked, giving her the side-eye as he changed it back. "That's Johnny Cash."

Maria looked at him dumbly. "So?"

"Jesus." The look on his face showed that he was more offended at her music taste than her choice in men. "You don't change it when one of his songs come on. It's a rule."

"That you made," she told him, raising her hand to change the station again.

"Maria." Dom let go of the shift to grab her hand before she could do it. "Don't make me pull over."

She slowly drifted her emerald eyes to the strong, tatted hand that held her slender one. "What are you going to do?" she asked with a heavy breath.

"There's only one way to find out, princess," Dominic said, letting his own eyes drift off the road to gaze down her body. With his hand still capturing hers, he brought their connection to her lap, placing their hands on her exposed thigh until he abruptly let go. "If you're brave enough to try it."

Keeping herself from rolling her eyes was near impossible.

Dominic was proving to be a lot harder to pay back for that "almost kiss." She thought she had him, until Dom made her think that he was about to hold her hand. Clearly, she needed to crank up the heat.

Shifting in her seat, her baby blue dress rose higher up her toned thighs as she pointed her knees toward Dom. "I like your car."

Dominic might not have turned his head from the road, but he certainly shifted his eyes, being less obvious as he dragged his depths up her tanned legs.

"Thanks. I worked on it for a long time before I finished it."

"Really?" Maria asked seriously, forgetting her mission for a moment. She didn't know much about cars, considering whenever someone in the family needed one, they just bought it brand new off the lot. She hadn't taken Dominic as the mechanic type. Looking around the interior of the car, it all seemed new to her. "I thought you just bought it like this."

"No." Dom laughed. "Every car you see in Blue Park has been pieced together in some way. Most of them with duct tape and a prayer."

Looking at his hands, she admired the lettering of his tattoos as he held the wheel and gear shift. "Does that mean everyone knows how to fix them?"

"No, but a lot do, because finding a good mechanic, who doesn't try to scam you, doesn't come cheap."

She was still entranced by his tatted hands when he downshifted, making a sharp turn. "And that's why you learned?"

"Something like that," Dom told her before changing the subject. "Which Cadillac do you drive?"

"I took a taxi here, remember?" Maria reminded him, acting like her next words weren't a big deal. "I never learned."

The offended face Dom made showed that her admission had clearly shaken him to his core. This time, he broke his own rule by turning the radio off, along with Johnny Cash, so he could show her how serious this was.

"You don't know how to fucking drive?"

With her tone of voice, she let him know she didn't think it was such a big deal. "No, I've always been driven by one of my father's men."

Dom was still in disbelief, glancing over from the road to her several times. "Have you ever tried?"

"Nope." Maria shrugged. "Never really wanted to."

"Wow," he mumbled under his breath, drawing his brows together as he started realizing just how smothered she'd been. "Maybe getting some space to yourself will be a good thing."

"I think so."

Getting back on track, Maria lightly flipped her gold hair behind her exposed shoulder. To him, it looked like she was just getting it out of the way, but its effect on him, she knew, would have him silently pleading.

She'd mastered the art of flirting into her only weapon against her father's men. For the most part, it was harmless; she only did the littlest bit to entice them to get her way. It never took a lot for men, just a flip of her hair or eye contact would do. But Dominic was different. She needed to pull out all the stops in order to pay him back for that little stunt at his house.

Usually, she never much enjoyed the act of flirting; her only satisfaction was when it paid off. But, when Dominic watched the slinky movement from out of the side of his eye, he drove slower just the *tiniest* bit ....

It was fun.

"You still haven't told me why you thought I was heartless," she finally commented, hoping he'd give her the answer she had been dying to hear.

"I don't think it. I *know* it, princess," he reminded her how she couldn't put him under any delusion that she was anything other than that. "And I'm not going to tell you."

Maria's voice couldn't even hide her disappointment. "Why not?"

"Well, what fun would that be for me?"

His playful voice and the confident expression on his face had her wondering if she was the one doing the flirting when her stomach summersaulted.

"Well"—she matched his tone while looking over at the Luciano boss through her lashes—"I could make it fun for you."

Braking at a stop sign, Dominic gave her his full attention, turning to face her. He lifted his hand off the shift to capture her chin once more. Letting his eyes slide down from her eyes to her luscious lips, he had her chest rising and falling heavily before he spoke in a low voice that didn't come out sensually like she had thought it would, but instead with a threatening warning. "Princess, don't make promises you can't keep."

The second he let go of her chin, Dominic went back to driving as if nothing had happened, letting Maria know she had been fooled again.

No amount of prayers was going to save this man now ….

ONE LONG NIGHT

P*ulling in front of the* Casino Hotel, Dom parked the car. "You sure you don't want me to drop you off at your house?"

"Yep, I've been staying here lately," she assured him.

Maria hadn't been back to the house since Leo lost his eye. Plus, it was really hard to avoid Lucca in the same house. At least at the hotel they stayed in separate penthouses.

He nodded, seeming to understand. "I'll wait here and watch you go in, then."

"Or …" Maria looked at the hand with the letters O-V-E-R splayed on his fingers that were still resting over the gear shift. Reaching out, she lightly let her soft fingers trail over the top of his hand. "You could come up and make sure I safely get to my room."

Dominic dropped his eyes to his hand, watching her smooth her fingers over his rougher skin. "Yeah right," he scoffed, not buying her innuendo, but he didn't pull his hand away from her either.

"I'm making good on my promise," she threw back his words, trying to prove her earlier "I can make it fun for you" statement.

"I-I don't think that's a good idea, Maria." His sudden husky voice revealed he thought otherwise.

Maria continued her strokes, her breathy voice telling him she wanted the same thing. "Something could happen to me on the way up."

Putting her eyes back on Dom, she could see the turmoil in his mind, weighing his options and determining if he was ready to risk it all.

"Is there a back wa—"

"Come on." The mafia princess smiled at the supposed big, bad Luciano boss as she opened the car door and put a long, toned leg out. Looking back over her shoulder, she raised a manicured brow. "You're not scared, are you?" Getting out of the car, she closed the door of his Mustang with a smile.

The decision Dom faced would take big, ginormous, *blue* balls to walk into her father's business right through the fucking front door with his daughter. So she had to create a challenge that would be hard for the Luciano boss to back down from.

It took only a few seconds before he cut the engine off, and a ballsy, but brave, Dominic got out of the car, meeting Maria on the other side. "If you get me killed for this, so help me Go—"

"You don't think it'll be worth it?" she asked through heavy lashes as she sultrily began for door.

Maria couldn't make out if Dom mumbled a silent prayer or a death threat under his breath when he followed her.

Giving him a polite smile as he held the door to the Casino Hotel open for her, she thought he might have turned back, but glancing over her shoulder, she was surprised to see him still following just one step behind her as she led the way.

In the crowded casino, Maria reached back, twirling her pinky with his. It was like a little secret, not enough of a connection to garner any attention, but it showed Dom that she was very serious.

Dominic looked down at their interlocking fingers for a second, then brought his head back up to look through the crowd.

Shocked that he didn't break their connection, she was even more shocked by the way the littlest contact made her feel all hot inside. Her tiny acts was going well past flirting . . . She blamed it on having to stare at his hands for the last thirty minutes. His tattoos intrigued her, which was why she had touched his hand in the car. It had only made her selfishly crave more.

The two went up the escalators that took them off the casino floor, their little connection still intact, while both avoided each other's eyes, knowing the cameras on the ceiling were watching them.

Stepping off the escalator, Maria gave the security guard who checked hotel key cards a smile as she took Dominic to an elevator behind him, without the guard's approval.

The big, bald man who worked for her father did a double-take, watching Maria and Dominic walk past. Too stunned to question or do anything, considering who she was, he just stood there.

Untwining her pinky from his, she started putting in the code for the elevator to take them to the penthouse without stopping.

"Don't show me that," Dominic urged with frustration. "If anything ever happens, I'll be blamed for it."

"Don't worry." She pressed the last button, letting him see. "I trust you."

"Jesus, Maria." Dominic held the bridge of his nose, clearly telling himself mentally that this was a bad idea as the door slid closed.

"Quit worrying," she coaxed softly, wrapping a hand around his leather-jacketed arm. She started to press her body against his, but he took a step away, backing into the corner of the elevator.

His frustrations continued. "There's a fucking camera in here."

"What day is it?"

Dom looked at her like she was crazy. "Tuesday. Why?"

"If it's Tuesday night, then Sal's working, and that means he's the one watching us right now." Maria waved at the camera with a smile before she gave him a nice view of her middle finger.

Rubbing his head like he had a headache, Dominic clearly hated to ask the question. "I take it you're mad at him too?"

"No, I just don't like him," Maria answered simply. Already knowing what he would ask next, she elaborated, "He likes to kiss Lucca's *and* my father's asses."

Holding a finger up to the ceiling, he asked a question he seemed to already know. "I guess there's audio in here, too, huh?"

"Possibly." She swept her tongue along her bottom lip as she pressed her body into his successfully since he had nowhere else to go. Instantly feeling the warmth off him through her thin dress, she met his eyes. What she was doing was definitely not considered her normal flirting, not with how it was beginning to make her feel, but she was still curious about one thing.

"Why did you get so upset with Cassius for not changing the channel?"

Shrugging, Dominic averted his eyes to the climbing floor numbers. "I just don't like that show, is all."

Staring up at him, she carefully watched his face. "Oh."

Kat and Dom's favorite character. She remembered Cassius's words, knowing full well Dominic liked that show. It was his one and only lie of the night, but the question was: *Why?*

The dinging of the door sliding back open meant they were greeted by another Caruso who watched this floor and who now knew Dominic was here with Maria.

"Hi, Ed." Maria grabbed Dom's arm in order to pull him along.

Dominic gave the man a nod as they passed.

"Bye, Ed."

Again, the Caruso guard did and said nothing, clearly shocked.

"You're in for one long night, princess"—Dominic shot her a heated glance—"because I'm not fucking coming out of here alive."

Doing what she wanted to do downstairs, she intertwined all her fingers with his. "I promise, I'll make it worth it."

Both quickly walked to her door, where she put her cell phone up to the lock, eager to get inside. Opening the door, Maria went in, letting her hand fall from his as soon as she crossed the threshold.

Maria gave him the sweetest smile, not letting him in any farther. "Have a nice night."

Asshole.

Staring at the door that was slammed hard in his face, Dominic felt his blood begin to boil. He didn't know who he hated more in this moment—the little man-eater who was proud of herself, or himself for fucking knowing better.

Sure, he might have started their little flirting game, but she damn sure finished it.

At first, Dominic wanted her to pay for what she'd done to him, make her realize the mistake she made by proving she felt something for him. But now his own game had turned on him, bringing back everything he felt for her in a rush.

Maria was fucking cruel. He had seen her with Ted-Teddy-Todd, or whatever the fuck, knowing she had turned him into a helpless puppy, but he'd bet everything he fucking had that she hadn't flirted with him like *that* to get her way. That was *not* flirting; that was a con. She was no woman; she was one of the best conmen he had ever seen. Maria had just led him on—on a criminal scale. Sure, he might've led her on a bit, too, but he was actually going to fuck her, if that was what she wanted, because that was damn sure what he wanted!

The only goddamn reason Dominic had fallen for it was because in no way had he thought Maria would make him walk through the front fucking door of Dante's business to fuck his daughter and risk his life ....

Banging on the door, Dom roared, knowing she could damn well hear him. "You're going to pay for thi—"

"Girl trouble?" was asked from behind him in a cold but cunning voice.

Violently snapping his head back toward the man he knew, he made his eyes into slits. "If I did, I wouldn't take girl advice from you, Ted Bundy."

Lucca, who stood in the doorway to his place, gave him a sly grin. "Wasn't Ted Bundy married?"

Dom told him what he thought of that by flipping him off. "I better get to walk out of here, or so help me Go—"

"You will," Lucca assured him with a nod.

Starting to walk away, Dominic shot the underboss a serious look. "Prepare your men for the bad news."

Lucca slightly drew his brows together. "What news?"

"That Maria Caruso is *mine*."

Maria walked into her place, satisfied, with a smile on her face. Ignoring the beating on the door, she walked up the stairs, humming a tune to drown out Dom's heated words that suddenly stopped.

Dominic had tried to play a game that Maria had invented.

Sure, it wasn't fair, as the scales were slightly tipped in her favor, but it sure had been a hell of a lot of fun.

Hell, even Maria was second-guessing leaving Dom out in the cold. Her harmless flirting was no longer harmless when she ignited a fire within, but that strange little lie that Dominic told her in the elevator had officially stopped her from making a mistake she could regret ....

This penthouse was the biggest one in the Casino Hotel, as it was built large enough for the Caruso family. She and her siblings had grown up between here and their family home, but Maria had always preferred it here. She'd thought it was fun navigating through the casino as a child; sneaking into the secret one in the basement when she wasn't allowed had been even more fun. The sneaking around had stopped when she turned eighteen, and even though it wasn't legal for her to gamble, she was able to gamble in the illegal one underneath. Being here made her feel closer to what she dreamed of, being in the mafia world and not outside of it—because she was a woman. This penthouse also had more personality and her favorite view in the world—Kansas City.

Walking into her bedroom, she dropped down on the edge of her bed, taking off her heels, then laying back on her silk sheets, wanting to see something before she got ready for bed.

Maria grabbed her phone and typed in the episode of *The Walking Dead* that she and Cassius had been watching when Dominic had made him to turn it off.

Fast-forwarding through the episode, she got to the part right before he changed the channel. When she saw the gun fire, she jumped when she saw who it hit.

Maria could watch anything. Her cold, dead heart kept her from even reacting from the scariest of jump scares to *Old Yeller* getting shot. But this scene was too real as she watched the blood drip down his face.

The character was a young boy named Carl … and the bullet had gone right through his eye.

The elevator was already open and waiting for him when he made it down the hall and passed the guard Ed. And when he turned to get on the elevator there was another Caruso waiting.

Dominic did a full stop, staring at the blackish-blue eyes of the brother who had been taken away from him—Salvatore.

Taking a step onto the elevator, Dom didn't say a word, and neither did Sal, as he put in the code. They might've had the same blood, but this brother, Dominic didn't know.

He likes to kiss Lucca's and my father's asses.

One of them, he semi put his trust into, but the other didn't even have his respect. If Sal kissed Dante's ass, then blood brother or no, Dominic couldn't trust him, no matter how badly it hurt him.

His siblings were his only weak point. It would be naïve to think Sal wouldn't use him, especially with what Lucifer had done to him. Truthfully, Dom wouldn't blame him. Sal had an origin story that rivaled his, and until Dominic figured him out, Sal was no brother of his.

Both watched the elevator door slide close.

Keeping his head forward, he looked at the numbers that began to fall as he broke the tense silence. "How's it going?"

"Can't complain." Sal gave a quick spin of the keys in his hand that was hooked on his finger. "You?"

Dominic gave a little shrug. "Could be better." That was an understatement, compared to what Maria tricked him into believing he should have been doing right now.

Dom missed the little tug on Sal's lips as they continued their silent journey, the only noise in the tight box was the sound of the keys clashing into each other with each twirl.

Nearing the end of the ride, Sal gave the keys in his hand one last spin around his finger, catching them so the only thing that could be heard was his voice. "So, Maria, huh?"

Dominic looked away from the digital display above the doors to look over at a smiling Sal, knowing exactly what he meant. He answered just as the door slid open. "Yep."

Putting his eyes back forward, Dom walked off the elevator.

"Dominic …."

He stopped, turning back to look at The Great Salvatore who was beginning to disappear as the doors slowly started to close. Dominic didn't know if the look on Sal's face was one of pity or delight.

"Good luck."

Maria awoke in the middle of the night, not from one of her good dreams—the ones she'd had of Kayne and Dom—but from a nightmare. Feeling wetness on her pillow, she sat up and touched a finger to her cheek. It was ... wet?

She had been crying in her nightmare. Only, it hadn't been a nightmare. Maria's mind replayed the scene over and over again of the car blowing up and Leo losing an eye.

Watching the scene from the show had drudged up all the feelings of hate, fear, and loss that she made herself subdue. It was as though Dominic had known it would affect her. He had gotten mad at Cassius when he didn't change the channel, because he had wanted to spare her feelings.

As badly as Maria hurt him, Dominic didn't want to see her hurt.

Her choices were now coming back to haunt her.

Maria grabbed her phone off her nightstand, hitting the contact that had once put a smile on her face. It went right to voicemail.

"This is Kayne Evans. Leave a message, and I'll get back to you as soon as I can."

Beep.

She was silent at first. Hearing the voice of a ghost who she thought she loved brought a single tear to her eye.

"You lied to me, Kayne." Maria clutched her black heart as she rocked on the bed. "How could you do that to me?"

The ding from his nightstand had him reaching over to pull out the cracked phone that had disrupted the darkness.

One new voicemail.

Putting it up to his ear, his heart sank as he listened to the woman he loved cry into the phone over another man.

Darkness fell over him again as Dominic clicked off the phone.

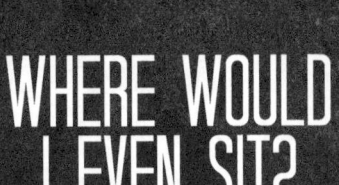

WHERE WOULD
I EVEN SIT?

Dominic sat in the back corner of the pizza restaurant, watching people enter and exit the establishment. Not yet seeing who he was meeting, he reached for his cell phone to see what time it was … again.

Hearing the sound of the tiny bell, he lifted his hazel eyes to the door. It felt like déjà vu watching the woman enter. She had hardly aged in the ten years since he last saw her.

Dom immediately stood up, seeing her serious expression turn into a smile when she glanced around the restaurant and saw him rising from the booth against the wall. Dom couldn't be sure because of the distance separating them, but he thought she gave a small sob as she rushed toward him.

Catching her easily when she threw herself into his arms, he gave her a light hug. "Good to see you, Bristol."

"You, too." Bristol closed her eyes. "I've missed you."

"I missed you too." Pulling her back to arm's length, he stared down at her. "You look good."

"I wish." She looked over him just as critically. "I see why I fell in love with you in grade school. You've become better looking in your old age."

Dominic rolled his eyes at her, then motioned for her to take a seat in the booth. Sliding in across from her, he turned to look for the waitress, catching her attention before turning back to Bristol.

Ordering a pitcher of beer and a medium pizza, he waited until the waitress was gone before he nodded toward her left hand. "No ring? I thought you would be married by now. The men in Florida must be stupid if they let you get by them."

Bristol gave him a sad smile. "I haven't had the best of luck with men."

He gave her a smile that was just as sad, knowing what she meant. "You didn't love me, Bristol. You felt sorry for me, and when I didn't need your pity anymore, you latched onto Kayne. You thought you could fix what was broken in us and, in return, you were hurt."

"I wasn't hurt," she denied with a waver in her soft voice.

"Weren't you? I don't blame you leaving Blue Park after graduating, but you haven't even been back to visit, not even for the holidays. I had to look at my phone twice to make sure it was you who texted me to meet you here."

Bristol gave him a smile. "This place brings back good memories for me. Do you remember coming here and working on our projects together?"

"I remember," Dom told her. "But I also remember when we stopped coming here because of Kayne."

"I was trying to make you jealous," Bristol admitted as the waitress approached with their beer and pizza. After the waitress left, Bristol stared down at the pizza instead of looking at him. "You put me in the friend category, and you weren't budging me from that spot. I thought, if I could make you jealous enough, at least it would be a step forward. Instead, I took seven steps backward and stupidly lost our friendship."

Pouring both of them a glass of the frothy beer, Dom tried to think of something to say without hurting her. Once upon a time, he wouldn't have understood the pain of jealousy, but Maria had shown him the agony firsthand that night she spent with Kayne.

Bristol reached out, tapping his left hand before he could touch his beer. "I don't see a ring on your finger, either."

"I haven't had the best of luck with women either." Dom quickly changed the subject from his personal life. "So, what brought you back to Blue Park? How long are you stayin—"

"I'm moving back."

Dominic almost dropped his beer. "Why in the fuck would you do that?" He could see her disappointment at his reaction as Bristol reached for her mug of beer. "I didn't mean it to come out like that."

"It's okay, Dom. I know you didn't have the same feelings for me that I had for you."

Taking the plates, she placed a large slice on one, setting it in front of him before taking a smaller slice for herself. "I hope it tastes as good as it used to. I've been imagining how good it would taste since I got off the plane."

Dominic took a bite as she began eating hers. "How's the pizza?"

"Better than I remembered," Bristol said, taking another huge bite.

"You gonna tell me you're moving back to Blue Park because of the pizza?" he jokingly asked, taking another slice for himself.

"No. I'm moving back because my mother told me Kayne is dead."

This time, Dom did drop the contents in his hand, the pizza hitting the plate. "Why does it matter if he is alive or dead? Was the breakup that bad?"

"Pretty fucking bad," Bristol admitted, grabbing another slice. "That's why I had to talk to you before word gets around. I don't know how many people Kayne told about our breakup, and once news gets around that I'm back, I don't want you to hear any rumors before I have a chance to explain."

"What rumors? We aren't in high school anymore—"

"I didn't come home back home by myself." Bristol paused. "My son is with me."

"Your son? Why would that matter ...? " Dom trailed off, seeing her embarrassed expression. The wheels finally clicked in place. "Kayne's the father; that's why you waited to come back until after he died."

She swallowed hard as her cheeks turned a bright shade of red. "Yes."

"Oh ..." he said slowly.

"Kayne broke up with me the day I found out I was pregnant. He told me it was because I was getting too serious and he was leaving for college. He said it would make the break easier." Bristol gave a bitter laugh. "I knew he wanted his freedom to do whatever the hell he wanted to, so I gave him his freedom."

For once, Dominic actually felt bad for Kayne. Being sent to his grave without even knowing he had a son was harsh.

"You still should have told him, Bristol."

Looking down at her plate, her voice cracked as a single tear slid down her face. "I know."

Reaching out, Dom took her hand ....

Ding.

Maria knocked on the front door in a hurry, still knocking when it opened.

"I need to speak to Dom."

It was the second day in a row she'd shown up on their doorstep.

The first time, she failed. Now she was trying to make things right so she could sleep in peace for once.

"He's not here," Cassius told her.

"When is he going to be back?" It was midday, and he could take all night again. "It's important."

Cassius looked toward the driveway. "Well, I could take you to him."

"Thanks," Maria answered gratefully, relieved she wouldn't have to wait all night to clean her conscience.

Yesterday she didn't know what the hell she was doing, but today, she felt strangely antsy to see him, and she didn't like the feeling.

Walking down the driveway, she headed toward the passenger side door of the car parked there, having taken a taxi here yet again, but when Cassius didn't go in the direction and instead grabbed a bike, Maria looked at him strangely. "What are you doing?"

Cassius straddled it, balancing the metal between his legs. "Taking you to see Dom."

"Uh, no." Maria shook her head matter-of-factly. "Why can't we take this?"

"That's Matthias's car, he'll kill me, besides I haven't bothered to get my permit yet."

"There is no way in hell I'm getting on that thing. Where would I even sit?"

"Right here." Cassius patted the handlebars. "Do you want to see Dom or not?"

Maria thought for several moments before she stomped forward in defeat.

The young Luciano held out his hand. "Give me your heels."

Okay, now this was going too far. Her shoes never came off her feet for anything. If they did, then that activity wasn't for her.

"Excuse me?"

"If we crash, they'll break your ankles. Come on." He snapped a finger, trying to get her to hurry.

"*If we crash?*" Maria lifted a leg, pulling the first one off then the other, already regretting this. "How about you don't make us crash?"

"I'll do what I can," he told her, grabbing the shoe from her hand, then sliding the toe part of the stiletto onto the end of the handlebar.

Her mouth dropped open, watching him shove it roughly into the handlebar so it would fit tightly. "Those are Jimmy Choo!" Holding her other one hostage, she continued, "I'll just wear the—"

"It won't matter what the fuck they are"—Cassius snatched the heel out of her hand—"when they're cutting it off your foot in the emergency room after your ankle snaps in half."

Maria slit her eyes, watching her newly most hated Luciano destroy her brand new Jimmy Choos.

"Come on." Cassius patted the handlebars again, this time with a slight tilt to his lips.

"I can't believe you don't have a permit." Maria turned, beginning to awkwardly place her ass on the uncomfortable handlebars. All her brothers had been on the DMV's doorstep on their fifteenth birthday.

"And where's your car?" he asked, holding the bike in place for her to safely get on. "Aren't you like twenty-five?"

I'm twenty-two, you little shi—

"I liked you better when you didn't talk as much," Maria grumbled. Placing her bare feet on the foot pegs that stuck out from the center of the front wheel, she thought about how this didn't feel safe at all. "You know, I didn't think you'd be above breaking the law …"

"I'm not." Cassius placed the sole of his shoe on the pedal. "But there's one thing you should know if you're going to be with Dom."

"I don't— *AH!*" Maria's protest turned into a scream. She held on for dear life when he suddenly kicked off, sending them down the driveway

"You don't fuck with a man's car."

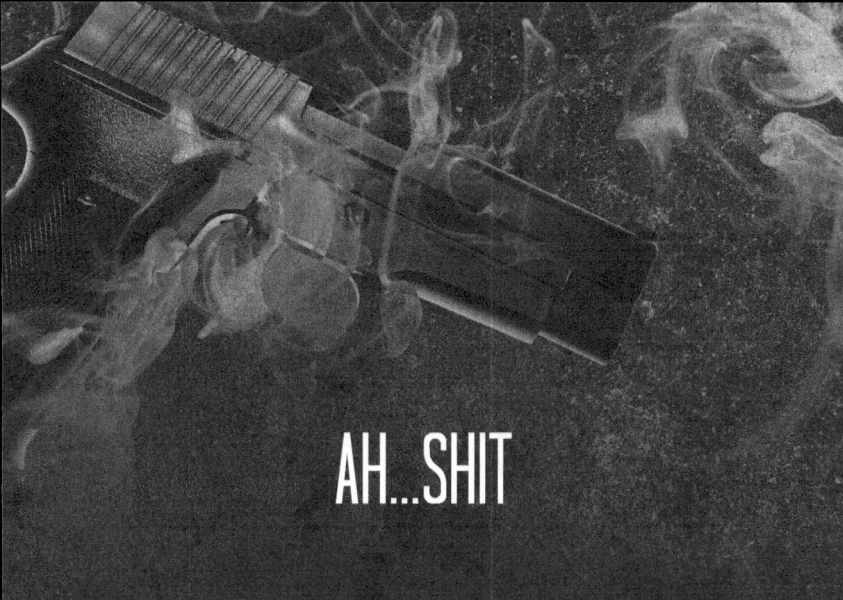

AH...SHIT

*T*hank God.

Maria jumped off the bike as soon as Cassius pulled up in front of the pizza joint after seeing Dominic's Mustang out front. Snatching her poor heels off the handlebars, she slid them back on her feet. "How'd you know he was here?"

Cassius touched a finger to his temple. "I know things."

Maria stared at him strangely. The young Luciano just reminded her of her brother Lucca for some odd reason.

Feeling back to normal with her shoes on, she smoothed down her dress. "Thanks. I think I'll get Dominic to take me back."

"I think I'll wait out here … to make sure."

"Suit yourself," Maria told him from over her shoulder, knowing there was no fucking way in hell she was getting back on that thing.

Walking up to the door, she grabbed the handle and swung the door open.

Ding.

Out of habit, Dominic looked over at the person who had just walked through the door. He almost thought it was a fucking illusion at first. There was no way in hell Maria Caruso was here, staring right at him ….

The pissed off look that crossed her face confirmed she was very much real.

Dom's eyes went back to the hand he held in his on the other side of the table.

Ah … shit.

Ding.

The bell went off above her head as she slammed the door back open, on her way out. Her stomach had sunk the second she had seen Dominic's hand resting over another woman's hand.

Cassius's face said it all before his words did. "Back so soo—"

"Maria!" Dominic called out from behind her as he flew through the glass door.

Walking toward Cass's bike, she didn't turn back until a hand grabbed her arm, forcing her to turn back around and face him.

"It wasn't what it looked like. She—"

"Why should I care what it looked like?" Maria snatched her arm out of his grasp. "It's not like we're together," she told him coldly, heading back toward the bike.

Snatching her arm again, he spun her around so quickly that her dress lightly twirled as he pulled her close until their bodies touched. "Don't pretend like you don't care," Dominic said fiercely to her pretty face that was an inch away from his, showing her that he could see right through her façade. "If you didn't care, you wouldn't have walked out like that."

"I don't," Maria said the words, looking into his hazel eyes without an ounce of emotion. "Now let me go, and if you touch me like that again, I'll show you just how tall the heels I'm wearing are today."

Slowly, Dominic removed his hand from her, not letting her go out of fear, but because she asked.

Spinning back on her heels, there was one thing Maria wasn't okay with, and that was being manhandled.

"Why are you here in Blue Park, princess?" he asked, walking behind her with every step. "There's a reason you came back."

"Well, apparently, it was stupid," she spat back, knowing he was trying to rile her up. Quickly, she tossed off her heels.

"What are you doing?" he asked, watching the action, then practically flinching when she bent down to pick them up at the speed of light.

"Don't worry." Maria hurriedly slid one on Cassius's bike like he had before. "I'm not going to use them on you ... yet."

Dominic stared at her in shock, just now noticing how the fuck she had gotten there. "You came here on this?"

"Yep," Maria growled, shoving the other Jimmy Choo on forcefully. *I can't believe I fucking came here.*

"I'll deal with you later." His hazel eyes glowered at his pleased-looking brother sitting on the bike. "Don't you let her leave till I get back home."

"Oh, I'll be long gone," Maria reminded him that she was right fucking there, jumping back up on the handlebars.

Once Maria was settled, Cassius slightly backed up the bike so he could maneuver around Dominic who stood in front of them.

Maria gave him a smile. "Your date is waiting for you."

Suddenly, Dominic reached out, grabbing the handlebars and dragging the bike with the two of them on it right back to him.

With wide eyes, Maria stared at Dom, whose face was an inch from hers as he bent down, caging her in with his arms. He didn't dare touch her, like she had warned.

"How does it feel?" Dominic's taunting words sent chills up her body. "That's only a *taste* of what *you* made me feel."

For the first time, Maria was speechless. She swallowed hard, staring into all the emotions that he clearly felt in his hazel depths.

"Bristol is a frien—"

"*Bristol* ..." Maria mouthed as she slid her eyes from his to the beautiful blonde standing behind him and off to the side. "That's a pretty name for a pretty girl."

Dom turned his head to see Bristol standing there, then let go of the bike.

Looking back at him, Maria felt the bike reverse again. "Bye, Dominic."

She was grateful when Cassius kicked off and they rolled away. The sick feeling in her stomach grew tenfold when Dom simply let her go.

Maria returned her eyes to the blonde. What she had said about Bristol, she meant wholeheartedly. The gorgeous woman proved Dominic definitely had a type. He could claim she was a friend all he wanted, but she saw the hurt look in her eyes when he called Bristol just a friend. Maria couldn't blame her either, but she wasn't going to let Dominic fool her into thinking there wasn't anything there when she had walked into the restaurant to find him holding her hand.

Maria had never been jealous of another girl in her life. It went against everything she believed in to pit herself against another woman, and she damn sure wasn't going to start now.

As they rode down the sidewalk, Maria watched their surroundings pass her by while Cassius pedaled them through Blue Park.

Turning to look back at him, Maria wasn't too happy with the youngest Luciano either. "You knew he was with her."

Cass didn't answer.

Now he goes back to not talking?

"Stop the bike," Maria told him from over her shoulder. When he continued to ignore her, she yelled, "You either stop the bike, Cass, or I jump!"

Cassius slowed before hitting the brakes. "What are you doing?" he asked, watching her hop off, then taking her shoes off the end of the handles.

Sliding on the left then right of her stretched-out Jimmy Choos, she then reached into her bra to pull out her cell phone. Maria loved her purses, but there was no way in hell she'd bring a Birken to Blue Park. Both times she'd come down here via taxi, she'd stuffed her phone and some cash in her lacy bra. Her expensive shoes, however, were the exception, as there was no way she was leaving the house without them.

"What the ...?" Maria patted her left breast. Her phone was nowhere to be found. The last time she had felt it was when ... "*Ugh!*"

Cassius raised a knowing brow. "Problem?"

"No." She shot daggers at the mini-me and swore internally at the man who had pickpocketed the phone off her without her even knowing. The bastard must have stolen it from her when he held her close to his body. She hadn't noticed because the grip he had on her arm was more concerning. It was probably easy fucking pickings as the dress was a bit too tight up top, and she had to repeatedly shove it back down on the way here to conceal the phone.

"I'll walk home."

"No, you're not." Cassius's tone told her he thought it was a joke.

So, Maria did the logical thing and started walking.

"Come on," Cassius griped, watching her get about twenty feet until he rolled his eyes and caught up with her. "You won't make it five miles in those things."

"Watch me," she spat as if she said the words "bite me." Maria had gone endless miles in a mall with them on her feet, so the little know-it-all couldn't have been more wrong.

"All right." Cass shrugged, letting the princess walk if that was what she wanted.

Walking another twenty feet, she watched Cassius slowly pedal the bike beside her like he was bored.

"I can walk home all by myself, you know."

"You sure about that?" he questioned without even looking over at her.

Maria furrowed her brows, seeming to understand what he meant. Looking around the neighborhood they were passing through, she saw bars through every window and several fenced-in houses with big dogs wandering the yards, barking as they passed.

"I'll be fine," she assured him. "I can take care of myself."

He looked at her smugly, then glanced down to her feet. "So I've heard."

"See? I'll be fine. Good-bye."

"Do you see that big guy over there?"

Maria looked toward an older man who Cass nodded toward. He was bald and huge, grilling in his front lawn while staring her down.

"That's Big Vic." Cassius continued pedaling beside her without a care in the world. "He got out of prison a month ago for murder.

What do you think your chances are shoving your heel into that huge fucking neck?"

Crossing her arms, she saw the prison tats that marked his face come into view. "And you think if you stick around, that'll keep me safe? You're like thirteen ...." She paid him back for the earlier comment.

"Fifteen," he corrected. "But, nope, it'll keep those assholes behind us from touching you."

Maria regretfully glanced over her shoulder, seeing three sketchy men in their late twenties tailing them. They had better luck fighting off Big Vic from prison than those three. A slight alarm went through her, but she didn't feel the need to have to run yet as the men were still quite a ways back.

"Don't worry; they won't touch you as long as I'm here," Cassius assured her, sensing her thoughts.

Again, Maria stared back at the *fifteen-year-old* boy. "What makes you think that?"

"Because I'm Lucifer's son and the spitting image of Dom. They'd have to either be fucking stupid or asking for a death wish to touch you while you're with me."

Glancing back again, they appeared to be closer. "You sure about that?"

"I've snuck out of the house and walked these streets since I five, so ... yeah," Cassius assured her once more without a hint of worry. "I'm sure."

Unfortunately, that didn't mean much coming from the little

Lucifer in the making.

Cass gave the man over the fence a nod. "Hey, Vic."

"Hey, Cass." Big Vic gave him a warm smile with a wave. "Tell Dom I said thanks for the homecoming present."

"Will do."

Maria's mouth fell open, then quickly snapped back into place, thinking it had to be a joke. She had seen real murderers, but on the inside, that man was a Teddy bear.

"Yeah … he seems real dangero—"

"He went to prison for killing the man who raped his daughter."

Maria kept her mouth shut now, understanding. "Oh."

Cassius still kept trailing along. "Like I said, he wasn't the one you should worry about."

Again, she looked back over her shoulder, and again, they were even closer. "Since you were two, huh?"

"Yes." Cassius shot her an ominous look with a raised brow. "Sound familiar?"

Maria stopped, staring over at him. She wondered how the hell he would know about her wandering problem around her father's casino when she was just a kid. "You're really starting to creep me out." Looking back, she felt their presence sneak closer. She was either going to make a run for it or get back on his bike. "You know, you're not very convincing, considering they're still following us."

"That's because they're following you, not me." Cassius pedaled his bike faster. "They've been too busy staring at your legs and ass that they have yet to recognize me from the back." Crossing in front of her, he slowly circled around her.

The second the three men saw his face, they scurried like three blind mice down a cross street.

Laughing, Maria looked at him, impressed.

"Don't worry, that won't last much longer." Cassius resumed his riding spot beside her. "Once Dom gets the word out that you two are together, Blue Park will be safer than any place on your side of Kansas City."

Maria found the last part of that statement interesting ... until she remembered the first. "Me and Dominic are not getting to—"

"Yeah, yeah, yeah," Cassius said, wanting her to save those words for someone who believed it. "Now, can you please jump back on so we can get home already?"

"No." Maria flipped her gold hair behind a shoulder. "I'm still mad at you for not warning me about his little date back there before I made a fool of myself."

"Is this the part where you want me to apologize?" he asked seriously, making Maria look over at him.

She realized how much older he looked, but just how young he still was. It was like a child asking if he was in trouble, like his father Lucifer and her brother Lucca, Cass's emotions weren't just stunted, they were nonexistent. He hadn't yet mastered blending in, like bumping into someone at the supermarket and saying "sorry" because it was the polite thing to do. It was what people like Cassius needed to learn to survive so they could live undetected as a danger to society. Maria knew ... because she was one too.

"You never have to apologize to me unless you mean it," she told him, not wanting him to feel like he had to pretend with her. However, someone was working with him, trying to help keep him accountable, so much so that he was aware to ask the question if he should apologize.

"Is Dom the one helping you?"

Knowing what she meant, Cassius shook his head. "Kat."

"Oh." Maria smiled inwardly to herself. It meant Cass trusted her, and that strangely made her feel ... happy.

Stopping, she tossed off her heels, hopefully for the last time. "How about we make a deal?" Picking up her shoes, she went to stand in front of his stopped bike. "Tell me why you wanted me to see Dominic with her, and I'll let you give me a ride back to your house ... Deal?"

It took Cassius a moment before he gave a single nod of agreement. "I knew, if you didn't see them together, you would never be able to really understand what Dom was talking about when he told you that you hurt him by choosing somebody else." On paper, what Cassius said might've been deep, but his blank eyes and even tone reminded her that wasn't the case on the inside. "Those are just words to people like us. They hold no meaning."

Staring right through the windows of his soul, Maria couldn't find anything in the young boy.

Cassius was soulless.

Sliding her heels back on the bike, she jumped back on the handlebars, accepting his answer without a word. For someone who was a lot like him, that answer kind of stung.

Back on their way, Cassius waited until he was at a higher speed to take one shoe off the bar and launch it into someone's yard. By the time Maria had noticed, he had already snatched off the other one.

Watching her brand new Jimmy Choos being launched hurt a hell of a lot worse the second time as the yard it landed in had a Rottweiler that had just found its newest chew toy.

"You little motherfu—"

"Oh, shut up." Cassius kept pedaling so she couldn't jump off to stupidly try to retrieve them. "I knew you were just using me for a little ride. Your ass would have started walking the second we got there."

Maria snapped her neck forward furiously. He was right, but that wasn't the point. This Luciano suddenly got knocked down to dead last.

"You're lucky if I don't kill you when I get off this thing."

Cassius actually laughed. "Why the hell do you think I threw those?"

"That won't be why," she hissed at him as the wind hit her face. "I gotta wait three years."

WHERE HER HEART
WAS SUPPOSED TO BE

As *soon as Cassius came* to a stop, Maria jumped off. Having to walk barefoot on the filthy ground made her livid. Seeing that only Matthias's car sat in the driveway meant Dominic wasn't back yet, and she didn't know if that made her happy or more pissed.

Storming into the unlocked house, she left Cassius behind, who was still getting off his bike in the dust. Maria went right up to the phone on the wall in the kitchen and started dialing a number. She pressed the last number right when Cassius ripped the cord out of the wall.

"You little …" Maria grumbled, unable to finish the sentence to his evil but cute face. *Shit!*

Storming down the hall, she needed a different method. Throwing open the bedroom door, she walked right into the dark room casting light from the hallway inside.

Maria suddenly stopped when the light illuminated his sleeping face glow. Even in what should be a peaceful sleep, the dark circles under his eyes highlighted that his dreams were haunted.

"What time is it?" she whispered very quietly over to Cassius, who was following her through the house. "Isn't it a little late to still be sleeping?" Her tone wasn't judgmental, but held a bit of worry.

"Matthias"—Cassius took a second to finish his answer— "works kinda late."

Maria's emerald gaze slightly softened, staring at his sleeping face. She kind of felt … bad for what she was going to have to do.

Bursting through the room, she went right up to his nightstand.

"What the …?" Matthias groggily opened his eyes before they flew open. "The fuck are you doing here?"

"Looking for your phone, sleepyhead. Where is it?" she snapped, her kind demeanor toward him had clearly been left at the door.

Quickly, Matthias got out from under his covers and exited the bed on the other side. Holding up his hand, he dangled the rectangle. "You mean this?"

Maria slowly turned her head from the nightstand to the Luciano brother with intent to kill, but when her eyes landed on him, the emotion dissipated at his sight.

Matthias was only wearing a thin pair of shorts. Waist up, his body was on display. She had seen his twin, Angel, whom they shared mirror-imaging tattoos, but she had never seen him unclothed. She assumed the twins had more tattoos, as their fingers, hands, and necks were fully inked until they disappeared under clothes ... but not this many.

Maria couldn't see a patch of pale skin other than his face.

"Like what you see?" Matthias's playboy façade had returned.

"No," she told him truthfully. Even her voice made it clear that she wasn't staring from lust but curiosity. "I just didn't take you as a masochist."

Matthias's mask slipped at her words, shocked that Maria had called him out with one look.

"I can understand Angel being able to take pain," she continued, still staring at all the ink that covered every inch of his skin. They were beautiful but ... looked very painful. The amount of hours he'd had to sit in a chair as a needle constantly beat into his skin was almost unimaginable for a person his age, which was maybe a year older than herself. That kind of ink took a lifetime, not years. "But not you."

Matthias smiled. "Then you'll be shocked to find out it wasn't Angel who first wanted them, princess."

She drew her brows together for a second, then her curiosity disappeared. "Don't call me that," Maria hissed

"Why?" Matthias's smile remained with his gloat. "You let Dom call you that."

"Yeah, not for long." She took a step closer to the end of the bed so she could go around and snatch the device from him. "Now, hand over the phone."

"Don't do it," Cassius told him, standing by the door, watching it all unfold. "Dom doesn't want her leaving."

When Matthias seemed happy about that, Maria gave him a final warning. "Last chance …."

Matthias practically laughed. "Or what?"

"I wouldn't—" Cassius's warning stopped the second Maria moved.

Taking a shortcut, Maria jumped on his bed.

Fear set in Matthias's eyes, but before she could cross the bed and jump him, he shoved the phone down the front of his shorts.

Maria was about to take a flying leap, but watching that action, she had never stopped so fast in her life.

"If you want it, you'll have to come and get it," the fully tatted brother teased her.

"Ew, no." Maria jumped back off the bed and in the direction she had come, realizing Dominic was right—there were scarier things that went on in this house with three brothers. That was fucking saying a lot coming from her. She'd been raised with three brothers of her own, but they were nothing compared to the Lucianos. She was about to rip her hair out from having to deal with them. At home, it was her three brothers that had to deal with her.

Maria suddenly realized she had whipped her brothers into shape, for the most part. They knew not to be gross around her and had learned the hard way not to get their disgusting germs anywhere near her food.

Boys were gross, teen boys were even grosser, and young men still were. Lucca's, and especially Nero's, girlfriends should be thanking her for her handiwork, because God knew how much worse Nero would have turned out where girls were concerned if it wasn't for her. These Luciano brothers were proving her to be right.

Matthias looked offended as he watched her leave the room.

Seeing stairs, Maria made a run for them, deciding to try her luck for a phone up there. Getting to the top of the old creaky steps, she found it strange that there was only one door when she should have found it stranger that Cassius and Matthias hadn't followed her up.

Maria turned the rusty doorknob. Creaking open the door, the room was dim and only lighted by a single, odd-shaped window. The room was canted due to the roofline angling down, but that wasn't the only thing strange about it.

There was an unavoidable feeling that emanated from within the room; she felt it the second she walked in. There weren't many things in there—only a bed and nightstand—but the energy was insurmountable. Standing in the center of the room, it was like being right between good and evil.

Or heaven and hell.

Turning away from the eerie feeling, Maria went back to trying to get the fuck out of there. With nothing around, she reached out for the nightstand, hoping to find something ….

The door coming to a creaky close behind her had her quickly dropping her hand and turning around, seeing Dominic's back.

Instantly, she knew whose room she was in.

It didn't feel like it would be Dom's, as the only warmth in the room came from what she had missed seeing, but now the fiery smells enveloped her.

After shutting the door, Dominic reached above the doorframe, grabbing an old, intricate silver key that was resting on the lip. He pushed it into the doorknob, then turned it. Taking out the key in the now locked door, he placed it back.

Maria was tall but not tall enough to get it from its spot, even if she were wearing heels. Not wearing heels gave her absolutely no fucking chance.

When Dominic slowly turned around, her breath caught in her throat—his presence telling her that she just might've pushed him too far. Dom had clearly reached the end of his rope. The slack he had given her had run out. The moment reminded her of the night he came to her house and confronted her about Kayne.

"I-I ..." Her words came out breathy at first, but she quickly righted herself. "I want my phone back, Dominic."

Dominic took an intimidating step forward. "Tell me why you came here, Maria, and I will."

Crossing her arms, she wasn't going to let him intimidate her. "I told you, it was stupid."

"It only became stupid to you when you saw me with another woman." Dominic gave her an incisive look. "So, that means it had to do with your feelings ... for me."

Maria shot him a cold look. "What feelings?"

"My father is the only one of your kind that I've seen truly heartless." Strolling into the room, he stood a foot in front of her. "Lucca somehow loves Chloe."

"And Cassius?" Maria asked with a raised brow.

Dom didn't try to hide the fact that his youngest brother was touched by darkness. "I know Cassius cares for Kat, but I'm not sure if he will ever feel love."

Maria wasn't sure Cassius would either.

Putting distance between them, she turned, taking a seat on the edge of the bed. "Well, I hate to break it to you, but you were right; I don't have feelings."

"I know you are capable of love. I've seen it."

Maria looked back toward Dom as he caught her emerald eyes and held them captive.

"You want to know how I knew you were heartless, princess?" Dominic stalked toward her. "I watched a fourteen-year-old girl watch her mother get buried, and she didn't shed a single tear."

How did he . . .? Maria tried to avert her eyes, hiding her lie, but the hold he held on them made it impossible. "That doesn't mean anythi—"

"It does . . . when Lucca did." Dominic stepped in front of her, making her crane her neck to look up at him as he towered over her. "Tell me, princess. When you were told she was dead, did you even cry then?"

That was a secret she wanted to keep from the world.

A little Maria had stared at her shoes for half the funeral, trying to look sad. At one point, when a single tear had fallen out of the corner of Lucca's eye before he quickly wiped it away, she had known just how fucked up she was. There was a type of guilt she carried for not being able to shed a tear for her beautiful, dead mother. It had proven just how inhuman—no, monstrous—she truly was.

Maria forced her eyes from his, looking at the ground as she whispered her admission, "No. Like I said, you were right."

"I thought so, too"—Dom took a seat beside her on the bed—"until I saw you cry for Leo."

She didn't say anything, continuing to stare at the old floorboards, not wanting to be reminded of that wretched day.

"And Kayne ..." he continued with a brokenness in his voice.

Maria looked over at him strangely, wondering why he had suddenly changed his mind from when he had told her, *What you felt with Kayne wasn't love, princess.*

Getting up, she'd had enough of this game. "Dominic, give me my phone and let me the fuck out of here. I want to leave *now*."

"No." Dom lazed back on the bed, making himself comfortable. "I said I would give you your phone back after you tell me why you came."

"Fine," Maria simply said, going to find something to knock the key down from its place. She opened a door to see a little attached bath.

Dominic suddenly sat back up. "What are you doing?"

Snatching a toothbrush, she hoped he liked the taste of dust.

"I know you feel it," he taunted, standing in the bathroom

doorframe and blocking her from leaving. "Otherwise, you wouldn't have walked out after seeing me with Bristol."

Furious, Maria ducked under his arm and squeezed past him.

"You're just fucking scared because seeing her with me made you realize you do have feelings for me."

Using the toothbrush, she quickly tried to swipe down the key, being forced to still, listening to his words.

"Hurts, doesn't it?"

The key fell off the ledge and onto the floor. Dropping the toothbrush, she picked up the little old key with shaky hands, trying to manage to get it in the lock.

"Hurts to see the person you love with someone else, and there's nothing you can fucking do about it."

The key slipped into the lock.

Dominic's rough voice became strangled. "But I promise you this, Maria, whatever it made you feel will never fucking compare to the pain you caused me by choosing Kayne."

Maria snapped. Letting go of the key, she violently spun back around and stomped back toward Dominic, who stood in the middle of the room. Giving his chest a hard shove, she spat her words at him like venom. "You expect me to know how to fucking feel when you said it yourself—my heart is dead. Every time I'm around you, Dominic, my body screams at me to touch you, to choose you ... but I never feel a single thing here." Maria placed a shaky hand over where her heart was supposed to be. "But I did with Kayne."

In his eyes, she could see his hope turning to heartbreak all over again in a split-second, but she kept going.

"But what I didn't know was that the little twitch I felt in my *cold, dead* heart was trying to tell me he *wasn't* the one for me."

Maria's breaths were heavy from being forced to share her feelings that she didn't want to admit, but she needed to finish. "I have never done anything with my heart. My gut has led me to the decisions I've made in my life, and I haven't regretted a single fucking thing until Kayne. So, you and Lucca were right; I didn't love him. But how the fuck was I supposed to know that?" she cried angrily up at him.

Dominic stared back at her, stunned, not knowing what to say.

"I came back to tell you what I should have done yesterday. To tell you I'm sorry, Dominic. I'm sorry for anything and everything I did to hurt you. For choosing Kayne, and especially the horrible things I said to you. You didn't deserve that ... but I don't deserve this either." Going to the bedroom door, she turned the lock before looking back at a dazed Dominic, needing to say one last thing as she opened the door. "This game we're playing was fun at first, but I'm done."

Running down the steps quickly, going through the house, she was afraid that, if she looked back or Dom caught up with her, she wouldn't leave—and that was the one thing she needed to do.

They were doing nothing but trying to hurt the other, and she knew if they didn't stop soon, Dominic would be the one to get hurt. When that happened, she would never be able to face him again. It was already too hard to look at him after what she'd done.

She was never going to fucking forgive herself for picking Kayne. Not because Kayne had hurt her for deceiving her, but because she had hurt Dominic.

Walking into the living room, she saw a dressed Matthias. "You want to see Angel?"

Matthias nodded.

"Then get your keys now and let's go," Maria told him, throwing open the front door.

Matthias wasted no time, meeting her at the car with his keys in hand.

Throwing herself into the car, she took a long, deep breath as relief came over her. As the bellowing emotions tried to burst through her iced core, like the day Leo had gotten hurt, she felt on the verge of a breakdown after the events of the day.

Turning the key in the ignition, Matthias threw the car in Reverse, knowing he'd defy Dom's orders.

Maria watched Dominic appear at the front door, watching her leave.

"You don't deserve him," Matthias told her, throwing his car in Drive.

Looking away from Dominic, she couldn't watch his heartbreak any longer. "Why do you think I'm leaving."

ONE THING WE DON'T FUCK WITH IS GHOSTS

"**C**an you slow the hell** down?" Maria gripped the oh-shit handle in the car, her long, almond-shape nails piercing her palm from holding so tightly. "You might have a death wish, but personally, I like living."

Matthias shot her a hot look before adjusting his speed to just above the legal limit.

Releasing her death grip, Maria let him know she hadn't missed that look he gave her. "Quit acting so shocked that I've figured you out. You're not as hard to read as you think you are. Everyone you and Angel fooled are just idiots."

Gripping the wheel, Matthias's jaw flexed. His voice was quiet when he spoke, and Maria no longer saw the mask he usually put on around her. "You don't know me."

"I know you can't sleep at night, and you're obviously not scared of the dark, since your room was pitch black, which means what you fear is in your dreams. You're codependent on your twin and have deteriorated since Angel left. So, my guess is, whatever you're scared of, Angel protected you from. Just like how he's protected you your whole life by letting everyone believe he was the weaker twin when, in fact, you were all along." Maria looked over at him pitifully. "How did I do?"

Matthias continued staring at the road, the sadness in his dark gray eyes visible. "You really are a cold-hearted bitch, aren't you?"

Not offended by the jab, she answered what he was clearly thinking—*how did I know?* "People often mistake the quiet ones for being weak, when it's the ones who are the loudest and appear to be the happiest who are trying to overcompensate." Maria took her eyes off a sad Matthias to look out the window at the passing surroundings. "I've had to hide my evilness; you hide your depression."

It was quiet for several, long moments before Matthias finally spoke. "And you don't try to hide that anymore?"

Maria knew it was a question, that he was honestly curious. It was clear he was trying to find an answer to help himself. She told him the truth. "No, not anymore."

"Why?"

"The only reason I ever hid who I was, was because I had to.

People are scared of those like me, and they should be. You, on the other hand, are scared of people finding out who you really are because you're afraid of being judged and being treated differently." Maria bore her emerald eyes fiercely into the broken gray ones. "Not everyone is born with armor, Matthias. Being weak is only a bad thing when you're too stubborn to ask for help."

Having to turn back to the road, his silence said a thousand words.

"It's not your fault, you know." She started to strangely feel for him again. Afraid she might've been too harsh, she felt the need to make him feel better. "It's the stigma society created that makes it hard for you to talk about."

Matthias's continued silence made it clear that he wasn't ready to talk about it, so Maria gave it up for now. He knew where to find her when he was ready.

"Slow down," Maria said, looking out the window. She hadn't been to Blue Park a lot, but she didn't remember seeing those gates before. "Stop the car."

"Here?" Matthias looked at her like she was fucking crazy but still pulled over. "Why would you—"

Maria got out of the car, taking a few steps toward the huge, vine-covered gates that had the letter B written on them in iron. You could tell they didn't used to be that color of rust, but years of dirt had coated the cursive letter.

"I wouldn't go any farther …" Matthias warned behind her, taking a seat on the hood of his car.

"Why?" she asked, not turning to look at him, but instead

trying to look through the vines. She could see the long drive and the old, overgrown stone fountain that no longer spit water. Far behind that, at the end of the drive, she saw the massive, gloomy house that had been boarded up.

"Because it's haunted."

Maria looked at the gray home closer for another second before turning back to go sit beside Matthias on the hood of his car. "And you believe that?"

"I mean, it looks pretty fucking creepy to me," he told her. "What? Have you never heard the story about Blue Manor?"

Shaking her head, she continued to stare at the home that sat right before the line that separated Blue Park from Kansas City. A couple more seconds in the car, and she would have been in Caruso territory.

"The story goes that the last family who lived there were all brutally murdered one night by a man who went in to steal a trunk of money the house was built on. Some think the murderer was successful and others think he never found it. But the legend is, anyone who goes in to try to find the money never comes out alive, because the ghosts of the murdered family are guarding it."

Maria curiously stared at the bit of the spooky home she could see. "Do you know anyone who's gone in it?"

"Hell no." Matthias continued to look at her, wondering if they were staring at the same place. "No one in Blue Park is dumb enough to try it."

Maria brought her eyes to Matthias. "So, you're telling me all of

Blue Park are scared of a little ghost story?" Most of Kansas City's hardest criminals came from here.

"Yes," he told her blankly. "We've been desensitized to many things at birth—guns, murder, drugs—but one thing we don't fuck with is *ghosts*. That shit is for the rich and dumb."

Maria glared at him. "Just because I don't believe in ghosts doesn't make me stupid."

He waved a hand toward the gate. "Then, by all means, be my guest."

Maria went back to staring through the vined gate, but she didn't get up.

"So, can we go now?" Matthias got off the hood, going back to the driver's side door without waiting for an answer. "This place gives me the fucking creeps."

"Aw … poor baby." Maria pretended to cry for him as she jumped down from the hood to go to her side. "The only house that gives me the creeps is the one you all live in." Dominic's bedroom still didn't sit right with her.

Matthias threw open his car door. With a serious expression, he reminded her that he was the one who had to live in it. "Tell me about it."

THE INDENTATION SHE
PRAYED WOULD BE THERE

Maria sat on the couch in the Caruso family penthouse, watching the television quietly play next to a sleeping Leo. She had been there, too afraid to get up, as it might wake him, but she didn't mind. She liked watching Leo sleep. It was when he was awake that she worried.

Sleep was Leo's only escape from his reflection.

Hearing a knock on the door, Maria quickly but softly got up, thankfully without waking her brother. Looking through the peephole, she stood on the other side of the door, hoping that he just might go away.

When she saw his fist pull back for another knock about to

pound the door, Maria urgently opened it. "Shh … Leo's sleeping."

"All right, jeez." Dominic stared at her like she was a crazed new mother who hadn't gotten peace in weeks, but he didn't dare speak above a whisper. "You left without your phone, and I wanted to give it back."

"I know," Maria gritted out, watching him pull it out of his pocket. She moved to snatch her device from his hand. "I sent someone to go get i—"

"And I told him to fuck off," Dominic said, not letting her take it from his grasp.

"You told Vincent to fuck off?" she asked curiously with a smile, forgetting her phone for a second.

"Yeah, he's a little prick." Dom made it clear what he thought of the young Caruso soldier. "Is he always such an ass?"

"Why do you think I sent him?" Maria finally snatched the phone from his hand.

Dominic glared at her. "You're lucky I didn't kill him, Maria."

"I knew that was the worst-case scenario, yet it was what I hoped for." Maria gave him a disappointed look before starting to close the door.

Within an inch of it shutting, Dom stopped her by shoving his foot between the crack.

"He looked familiar …" He thought a second before it finally clicked. "You sent the Caruso consigliere's son to my home!" Dominic whispered harshly. "Are you fucking crazy? If I had even laid a hand on that kid, like I wanted, my ass—"

"Oh, stop being so dramatic." Maria shushed him with a roll of her eyes. "You would have not only done me a favor of never having to hear his mouth again, but you would have done Lucca one too."

"You're psychotic. You know that, right?" Dom said, glaring at her.

"I'm aware." Maria went to slam the door again, but this time Dominic stopped it with his hand. "May I help you?"

"I came by to give you the phone this morning, but you weren't here. I would have come last night, but I thought you needed some space."

Maria took a breath, trying to be polite for one second. "I was at the hospital. They discharged Leo today." *Okay, long enough.* "And he's finally asleep now. So, if you don't mind? Good-bye."

Dominic didn't let her shut the door again.

"What the hell is your prob—"

"Princess, you have two choices. Option one: you let me inside so we can *quietly* talk." Dominic glowered at her. "Or option two: I stand out here all night ... *not* so quietly."

Maria narrowed her eyes into beady little slits that told him every fucking cursed thought she had of him—*motherfucking asswipe, dick-headed bi—*

"Fine!" she grumbled. "But be quiet."

"No problem." Dominic blew through the door and past her, letting her know, if he had wanted to come in at the beginning of the conversation, he could have.

Bitch! she finished her last thought as she quietly shut the door he left behind him.

Walking into the living room that he showed himself to, Maria saw Dominic's concern of a sleeping Leo.

"Will he be all right?"

"Physically, yes," she answered with a bit of sadness in her voice.

Going up the glass stairs, she motioned for him when he still didn't move from watching Leo. "Come on."

Staring at him for another second, Dominic then followed behind Maria, through the penthouse and to a bedroom that was obviously hers. The champagne silk bedding and matching, sheer, floor to ceiling curtains were obviously for extravagance and not for modesty as the city lights twinkled below.

"*Wow,*" Dominic mouthed, going to the window and looking down at the best view in all of Kansas City.

Maria had watched him curiously for a second. It was a view she stared at almost every day and it still amazed her. But to watch someone experience it for the first time tugged at her lips.

After setting her phone down, she slowly walked up beside him, her emerald gaze not going to the city but to his face. She liked the way the colors danced on his tan features, how the light moved through his brown hair, and mostly how the green in his hazel eyes glowed. Dominic was more than handsome … he was beautiful. The life he led made him look rough around the edges, and the full, but short, scruffy beard, along with his coat and hand tattoos only made him ooze that much more of a don't-fuck-with-me appearance. But the stern look he constantly held in his eyes and brows that caused the two lines between his brows to cut deep, all disappeared when he relaxed ... like he was right now.

Underneath it all, if Dominic had been born outside of this city and the mafia world, he would have been behind a camera or on a catwalk, just like she would have been. Both of them might have looked like models, but only Maria got the luxury to keep it up. The money she was born into, and the endless time of not having to work, afforded her things she wanted to do to be the most beautiful woman in Kansas City. She had never seen Dominic in a different jacket than the one he wore now, and still he was easily the hottest man in town.

"One thing about you, Carusos"—Dominic reached out, touching the glass with a fingertip as he stared at the other tall buildings around—"you sure are fucking brave."

Smiling, she drifted her eyes to his cheeks. Carefully she studied them, trying to find the indentation she prayed would be there from her dreams. If the dimples were there, it only solidified his beauty. "They're bulletproof. All of them are."

"So, brave and smart." He dropped his finger from the glass, finally looking away from the city and to her. "I'm sorry that I put you through hell yesterday."

The pure apology that slipped from his mouth stunned her for a moment. "It's all right," she assured him.

"And I'm really sorry about Cass throwing your heels. I—"

"You didn't get mad at him, did you?" she asked before he could finish. Dom seemed pissed enough when Cassius had taken her to see him at the restaurant.

He stared at her strangely, seeing the worry in her eyes about whether he punished Cassius or not. "No, I didn't," he soothed before a fire lit in his eyes. "But I should have. I liked those. They were new, weren't they?"

"Yes." Maria laughed. "And good, because Cassius was actually trying to help you, you know."

"Yeah, he told me." Dominic went back to looking at the city, knowing she meant about forcing her to feel the pain she had caused him. "But I wouldn't have wanted you to see that, or feel anything close to the pain I felt. I only ever wanted you to understand my pain, but I wouldn't ever want you hurt by it."

Maria's throat suddenly became tight. "But Cassius was right; I would have never understood without seeing you with her. She is pretty …."

"Don't talk like that," he demanded.

"Like what?" Maria was confused. "I meant what I said. She is very pretty."

"I know you meant what you said." Dominic didn't think she was trying to be malicious in any way, knowing her girl code went too deep. Taking a step closer to her, he forced her small, pointy chin higher under a tatted finger. "But I don't want you talking about me liking another woman *ever.*"

Maria raised a brow. "You don't like her?"

He shook his head, staring down into her jeweled eyes. "No."

"What's wrong with her?" Maria glared up at him, appearing

offended. "She's beautiful."

Dominic's eyes went down to her pouty lips. "She's not you, princess."

His admission made her stomach do a somersault, but Maria couldn't help whispering the obvious. "But she's in love with you …."

Seeing she needed to hear the story and not wanting to keep secrets, he let his finger drop from her chin as he began. "Bristol and I went to school together our whole lives, and she was not only my only friend in school but in all of Blue Park. When I realized she developed feelings for me, I should have cut her off, but I … couldn't. I didn't have anyone else, and Bristol made me feel like I was almost a normal kid when I talked to her. I didn't want to lose that and the only friend I had. So I turned her down over and over, and I selfishly had to watch her heartbreak every time I did. I swear to you, throughout our friendship, I've never once kissed her or gave her any sign to think we were anything but friends. You could ask her yourself, and she would tell you. But"—Dominic cleared his throat, having to look away from her face and to the city below— "you're not the only one who chose Kayne over me."

Instantly Maria's stomach sank. The story that he was telling her to give her a peace of mind was taking a turn.

"We all grew up together in Blue Park. Me and Kayne never got along in school. There're multiple reasons, but it mostly came down to our fathers. But when Bristol started dating Kayne senior year, I knew she had done it, at first, to make me jealous, in hopes that it would make me realize I loved her. But Kayne had gone out with her for the same reason. Bristol wasn't his type. He wanted easy and available all throughout high school. He used her the same way she used him. The only difference was"—Dominic looked back sadly into Maria's eyes—"Bristol fell for him in the end."

Swallowing down the bile that tried to rise from the pit of her stomach, Maria realized her part in letting history repeat itself ten years later.

Dominic was right; Kayne had never changed from the boy who had grown up in Blue Park. He just became a man from Blue Park instead.

"W-Why are you telling me this?" she asked, sensing the ultimate "but." She knew Dominic no longer wanted to hurt her or guilt her anymore for choosing Kayne, *so why is he telling me this?*

"Because, Bristol has a son …."

"Oh," Maria breathed. "And I'm guessing he's about nine or ten years old?"

Dominic nodded solemnly. "I just didn't want you to find out and not hear it from me."

"Okay." She nodded. "Thank you for telling me."

"If it makes you feel any better, Kayne didn't kn—"

"It's okay," Maria told him again.

Dom raised a brow. "It doesn't bother you—"

"No," she told him truthfully, her own words shocking her. That piece inside of her that thought she had loved Kayne died the second she had found out that he lied to her. Anything she felt since were aftershocks. They were mostly the fury she held against him for using her. "It doesn't."

"All right." Dominic lifted her chin once more with his tatted finger only, this time, *he smiled.*

Holy . . . fuck.

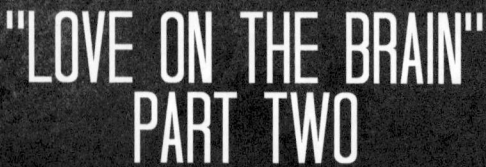

"LOVE ON THE BRAIN"
PART TWO

"**W**hat?" *Dominic asked, still staring* at her with that smile that made her stomach flutter.

Apparently, her "holy fuck" hadn't been spoken in her head.

"Y-You have dimples …."

"I'm aware." He laughed, raising her chin higher. Dominic liked looking at her long neck stretched out to him. "I feel like I should be offended you never noticed before."

"I don't think you ever smiled for me," she told him breathlessly. Raising her hand, she let the pad of her fingers gently rub over and dip into the perfect indention. "This might sound really strange,

Dominic, but I think I dreamed about you." Maria couldn't believe her admission until it was too late. The only thing that saved her were the next words that passed Dominic's lips.

Putting his forehead against hers, his breath was heavy. "Oh, princess, I have too."

Letting her fingers go from his cheek to the nape of his neck, she let her hand graze through his thick hair until she took ahold of it when he denied her seeking lips. Maria's voice came out frustrated when she said, "This is the part where you kiss me."

"No." Dominic smiled wider, making his dimples deeper. "This is the part where you *beg* me to kiss you."

Maria's mouth dropped open, starting to pull away. "*Excuse me?*"

Laughing, he strengthened his hold on her by gripping the small of her waist, pulling her to his body and not letting her go anywhere. Then Dominic tilted her chin to one side before he dipped his head to her now exposed neck. He let his lips trail up from the base to top, his hot breath tantalizing the sensitive flesh as he spoke, "I promised myself that I would only kiss you after you gave me permission."

Maria's head slightly fell back, enjoying whatever the fuck he was doing to her. Everything burned like the scent he carried, and she desperately wanted Dominic to put it out. "Well, in case you missed it, this is me giving you permission."

"I know." He tilted her head to the other side with a finger, but this time when he dipped into the needy flesh, he didn't give it the same attention as the other side. Slowly licking the part of her neck that he hadn't been able to resist, he then sucked the wet flesh between his lips. "But now I want to hear how you sound when you beg."

Neve—

Dominic repeated the same motion, now higher up her neck, making the ice princess shiver and turn into a puddle into his arms.

"Please!" she cried out.

Pressing his lips into the part of her neck that now glistened, he smiled. "Please, what?"

"Please, kiss me," she begged, sweeping her tongue over her wanting lips in order to soothe them. "Please."

Dominic suddenly grabbed the back of her head, protecting her head as he shoved them up against the strong glass window.

It wasn't the action of hitting the glass that knocked her breath away, as it would take a lot to break her. It was Dominic. The need and want he displayed for her already told her he wasn't planning on being tender. That was what made her unable to breathe well before his lips came crashing down on hers.

This wasn't a tender first kiss between two lovers; this was a violent kiss that only ended with the other taking your soul.

It was no wonder Dominic wouldn't kiss her without permission. It was clear he thought they were meant to be, and it was as if he predicted this would happen. Maria, however, really wished he would have started with this. It would have saved her a lot of trouble.

Letting her tongue sink into his hot mouth, the fire in her belly sunk lower when he savagely sucked, capturing it there for his to keep forever, if he so pleased.

Maria ran her hands up his chest. Not giving a single fuck that they had only shared their first kiss, she quickly ripped off his jacket, letting it fall to the floor. Dominic kissed her deeper, his tongue taking a dive into her mouth.

Repaying the favor, because she was nice, of course, Maria mimicked him, sucking his thicker tongue into her mouth. She wasn't as gentle with her teeth as he had been.

Both of them had clearly decided to *fuck it* in that moment. They would fuck with their clothes on, then later without. Both of them were at a dire point of need, unable to wait any longer to put out the fires that had begun to sear their souls together as one.

Maria reached her manicured hands to his jeans, unbuttoning them. She was about a second away from seeing the scene from her dream come to life as her hungry eyes eagerly waited for his dick to come jutting out—

Her eyes suddenly closed shut when a callused middle finger slipped between her folds.

He had found nothing underneath the silky satin short set she wore, discovering her more than wet with need.

Maria opened her eyes when his finger left her.

She thought Dominic had already reached the pentacle of hotness, but then she watched him slip his middle finger into his mouth, sucking her juices off in one, satisfying second.

"Tell me, princess"—licking off the last of her, Dominic's sexy demeanor would have been terrifying for the weak—"how did your dream go?"

One thing was for certain...

Taking his hand, she brought his middle finger to her lips before sucking his long finger to the back of her throat with the tight seal she created as she slowly pulled it out from her mouth.

... Maria had finally met her match.

At first, Dom was shocked as he watched her action, but then desire fired in his hazel eyes brighter, to a scorching point, when his wet finger hit the cold air. Capturing her lips with his again, she wanted him to see just how ready this princess was for him when he slipped two fingers suddenly deep into her pussy.

The noise that escaped Maria's mouth was somewhere between a shriek and a shrill as her whole body tensed.

Immediately, Dominic pulled his fingers out, taking a step back from her. "I'm sorry, I didn't mean to—"

"It's okay." Maria's body and voice cried out for him to come back to her. "You didn't hurt me."

It was an obvious lie that Dom didn't believe, having heard and felt her reaction.

A strange look and feeling came over him. "Maria, have you never—"

"I have," Maria lied again. She closed the little distance he had put between, going up on her tiptoes to kiss him while wrapping her arms around his neck. She tried to bring them back to where they had been. She had high hopes for her "Love on the Brain" part two.

Grabbing her arms, he pulled her hands down from the back of his neck. "You're lying."

"No, I'm no—"

"Stop it, Maria," he demanded. Then confusion hit every part of his face. "I thought you and Kayne …." Dom couldn't finish that sentence.

"No." Maria awkwardly crossed her arms. She hadn't wanted to be reminded of the man who had previously made them a triangle, but now she couldn't help compare the two, seeing the differences between them, especially their kisses.

Kayne had kissed tenderly; Dominic did not. Her own body reacted differently to the two men. Any fire Kayne Evans had put in her could be extinguished; Dominic Luciano's fire, however, could not. But she didn't exactly want to be reminded of her dead never-ex lover at this point in time, and certainly not like this.

"You assumed."

"Maria, I don't give a fuck what you did with him or anyone else, for that matter. That's not what I'm trying to get at," Dominic told her honestly. Softening, he gently unwrapped her crossed arms, taking her hands in his and rubbing the back of her hand with his thumb. "I just didn't know that you've never been with someone … I just don't understand why you would lie about something like that."

Truthfully, Maria hadn't known it would be that fucking obvious, or hurt in that way. She had expected it to feel uncomfortable at first, but the way Dominic had plunged in was what had her shrieking out in shock before she could bite back the pain. Unfortunately, being an ice princess made her ice over in more than one way. It wasn't until Kayne had she started to thaw, and now Dominic set her ablaze.

She could tell he immediately regretted it and felt responsible for causing her any pain without checking to see what she could handle, but Maria didn't blame him. Both of them wanted the same thing urgently, and it wasn't like she planned to place tender butterfly kisses on his dick either.

"I only lied"—Maria sought his lips, kissing him, wanting to get back to what they had been doing, her body still very much in fucking need—"because I didn't want you to stop."

Dominic kissed her precious lips hard for several moments, then made himself pull back. "Princess, you have to stop."

"No, I don't." She smiled, taking his lips again. She managed to get her tongue halfway down his throat again when he pulled away ... again. "Why are you doing this?" she asked frustratingly, knowing their teasing games were well over, and if they weren't, this was beyond cruel. "Why the hell does finding out I'm a virgin change anything?"

Dominic stared into her jeweled eyes. "It changes everything."

"No, it doesn't." She backed away from him.

Seeing that she was getting upset, he let her see his own frustration. "Don't think I don't want to. Because, trust me, princess, I do."

"Then what's the problem? Because, five seconds ago, I was perfectly fine to fuck."

"I watched my father belittle, beat, and even murder the women who carried his unborn children. He hated women, because he mistook their kindness as weakness, and being opinionated was being a bitch." Dominic looked at her proudly and laughed. "He would have hated you."

Maria stood stunned as she continued to listen.

"He didn't want daughters, and the only reason Kat is here today is because he would have lost the best soldier he had if he didn't let me care for her. I did the best I could to protect her and care for her, along with all my brothers. But do you know why I never once even pretended to think I could have a relationship with Bristol, or with any other woman, for that matter?"

Maria didn't answer, her silence her only response allowing him the time to tell her.

"I would have rather been alone until my last dying breath, having never loved than force someone into the life that I was forced to lead. This isn't the life I would have chosen, Maria, but it is the path I was given, and I started walking it to right my father's wrongs." Dominic's hazel eyes suddenly glowed, revealing the man who had become the Luciano boss for a reason. "But now I walk it because I'm good at it. I've become addicted to it. The danger, the *power* ..." His haunting voice trailed off for a moment, showing just how addicted he was to it. "All of it.

"And that is why I swore to myself I would never subject someone to this life, because you were right when you told me I was worse than my father. Lucifer did the things he did because he was born sick. I believed I did the things I have done because mine and my family's lives depended on it. Now that he's gone, I am not so sure of that anymore. I can't walk away from this life, and I never will. But I would never forgive myself if it hurts the woman I love."

Maria watched his tatted hand reach out to her. Letting him take her hand, she studied his inked, rough fingers, intertwining them with her slender, manicured ones.

"Then I met you ... and I don't think you being with me is going to change much about your life, Maria Caruso." Dominic stared down at their interlocking fingers with her, seeing how opposite they looked, not only on the outside but the blood underneath. "But my life will."

"So ..." Maria slowly moved her gaze from where they were tethered, up his body, until she got to his eyes. "Why exactly are you not fucking me right now?"

Dominic smiled at her need at first, but it quickly disappeared, showing how serious he was. "Because I'm in love with you, princess—" Taking the hand he held, he brought it up to his lips, placing a light kiss on the back of her smooth flesh. "—and I want you to marry me."

I—

Maria's mind went blank, never thinking she would hear those words in her life. She even thought she had heard him wrong, that Dominic could not possibly be ser—

"You're being serious, aren't you?"

"Yes."

A part of Maria actually felt bad to do this ... "Dominic, I can't marry you." Taking her hand away from his, she needed to make this clear. "That's fine if you believe in marriage, but I don't. I tried on those wedding dresses for a reason; because I never thought I would want to spend the rest of my life with someone, and because even if I did want it, I would never do it. For me to stand in a church and freely give myself over to a man is not something I call romantic. I thought you of all people would understand."

"I don't want to marry you for the reasons my sister had to marry Drago." Dominic was quick to understand what she meant by the last comment. "Why I want to marry you has nothing to do with our last names and everything to do with how I feel about you."

"Again"—Maria's mind and body were getting even more confused—"what exactly does this have to do with us having sex?"

"Because I might go to hell, princess, but I would never do anything to take you with me."

"Not only am I unsure if I believe in heaven and hell, but I certainly don't believe that having sex before marriage makes you unworthy to go there, even if it's real." That made Maria angry. Virginity was a notion created by men that didn't pertain to them, and if it did, wasn't it ironic how a woman's body gave a clear sign and a man's didn't? If heaven and hell existed, then Maria believed God was unfortunately a man for that sole reason alone.

"Come on, I don't mean it like that." Dominic tried to get her to see where he was coming from. "You might not believe in heaven and hell, Maria, but I do. I would have never allowed myself to touch you if I thought you were a virgin. I already don't think I deserve you for the things I've done in my life, and I will not allow myself to let my crimes taint you."

"Taint me?" she whispered. Dominic was a confident man, but she could see that he didn't hold parts of himself in high regard. All of it was starting to make sense. "Dominic, I'm not …" She searched for the correct word, but it was simply, "Good." Maria forced his powerful eyes, but held demons behind, them to hers. "You know that, right?"

He lifted his hand to let his inked knuckles lightly sweep her high cheek. "You are, Maria."

"I'm not," she assured him. "There is nothing you have done that would shock me, let alone concern me. You may think my body is pure, but it's not. I've not only stood idly by and watched horrible things happen, but I've done horrible things too."

"Princess, I will not give you my sins."

"Okay." Maria took a sultry step forward so she could hover her lips over his. Her warm breath promised a kiss that would send them to their knees with her words. "Then let's make one together."

"That's not the only reason, you know …." Dominic lightly slid his hand up her exposed thigh, to her waist, over a breast, until he finally reached to her neck. Placing his hand softly at the bottom of her throat, he said, "If I don't marry you before I fuck you, then you never will."

Excuse m—

When she went to move away, he ever so slightly tightened his grip on her neck, keeping her in place.

"Right now, you want me for one reason and one reason only—I can give you something that you have never gotten before, princess, and trust me, I want it, too, but I also want forever with you."

"So, you're blackmailing me into marrying you?" she asked with a raised brow, wanting to hate the man who stood before her, with all of her being screaming out in pain for him.

"Hmm . . ." he mumbled curiously. "Would you judge a woman for wanting to wait until marriage?"

"No." She looked at him curiously back with a smile, already knowing the answer. "But are you a virgin, Dominic Luciano?"

Dom looked at her fiercely, letting her know he was no angel. "No."

"Then we're good." Maria tried to go back to kissing him, but he stopped her. Still sexually frustrated with the man who had put her into this position and who had been perfectly fine with it before he found out she had never been touched in that way, her voice was somewhere between desperation, plea, and anger when she said, "I don't care about my virginity, Dominic."

Picking up his jacket off the floor, Dominic started to leave. "You may not, Maria, but I do."

YOUR CHOICE, MARIA

"**N**eed some help?"

"I got i—"

Maria was shushed when some of the bags she was holding slipped out of her hands and into tattooed ones, despite her refusal.

"Thanks, Angel."

Gripping the bags as they entered the elevator, he put in the code to take them up to the penthouse level. "No problem."

It had been a few days since she and Dominic had last seen each other … and Maria had desperately needed to stress shop. Going to the mall was therapeutic, and she really needed the time alone to think but also *not* think.

Leo had gone over to their brother's, Nero, and Elle's place, wanting to spend time with him and give her a break, which she appreciated.

Shopping hadn't solved her problems, but they definitely put them on mute for a few hours. Plus, it was a whole new experience to get to shop alone for the first time.

Not only was the ride up the elevator silent, but the walk to her penthouse. She liked that quality about this Luciano brother the most, as Angel only spoke what was needed to be said.

Managing to open the door with her phone, Maria and Angel entered. Setting her bags down by the bottom of the stairs, she didn't want to inconvenience him any longer.

"You can set them here, and I'll take them up later."

Angel nodded, setting them down beside the bags she had carried up.

"Thank you," she told him again.

"You're welcome."

Watching him turn to leave, she stared at his back, contemplating, and when he got closer to the door, her voice made the decision for her. "Angel?"

"Yeah?" he answered, turning back around.

"Do you think we could talk for a few minutes …?" Maria twirled her fingers for the first time. By Angel's expression, he had noticed the strange fiddling act from her. "It's about Dominic."

He hesitated for a moment then came back to her. "All right."

Honestly, Maria didn't know where to start or what she was even trying to ask. "I'm not sure if you know anything about me and—"

"I'm aware," Angel told her. "Cassius actually has a big mouth sometimes."

"I'm gathering that," she bit out, but thankfully got to skip to the part where she didn't know how to explain her and Dominic's relationship to an even a more awkward part …

"Whatever it is you want to say, Maria, say it. We don't keep secrets between us."

"Dominic asked me to marry him," she blurted out the strange words that were still hard for her to grasp. "And, while I understand his feelings for me, the reason is more than that." Maria tried to politely navigate the topic without it being too weird, as she was talking to Dominic's brother. "He mentioned Lucifer's behavior toward women, but I think he wants to marry me … to save my soul? He won't *do* anything with me until we are —"

Immediately, Angel understood. "Has my brother told you anything else about our childhood?"

She tried to remember but only came up with, "Just that he helped care for all of you."

Placing his hands slickly into his pockets, Angel moved his eyes from her to the floor. "Lucifer wasn't a kind man. Not to anyone, and especially not to his children. Whatever you've heard about Lucifer, he did it and then some. While others have had one unfortunate meeting with the devil, we had to live with him every day with no escape. Dominic is five years older than me …" Angel's eyes no longer met the floor. Holding her eyes with his haunting gray orbs, he showed her whatever imagination she had wasn't enough for what they had endured.

Maria had never once seen Angel angry, but she could see the fury just below the surface that he held in.

"*Five. Years.*" He spoke the harsh words with pain. "Dominic had to live on this earth with our father alone, and I will never know how he survived it." The pride that shone in his eyes demonstrated how much he not only loved his older brother but how much respect he held for him. "Not one of us would have survived without him, but he would have survived just fine without us ... if not better."

Standing eerily still, she hung onto every word the Luciano brother spoke, knowing that somehow, something even worse was coming.

"Dominic is nothing like me and Matthias when it comes to women. Mostly because he was old enough to see and recognize our father's behavior toward women at his worst, when he was trying to father as many sons as possible.

"Thanks to Lucifer, we all believe ourselves to not be worthy in some way. For the longest time, Dominic in particular, believed that since Lucifer was horrible to women, somewhere deep down, it would be that way for him too. He was so afraid to even touch a woman.

"Lucifer did many things to hold power and control over us any way we could. He believed we belonged to him, that he could do whatever he pleased with us, if he thought it would serve his purpose in owning mind, body ... and soul. One of the cruelest acts he committed was against Dom when he was twenty years old."

Maria took a shuddering breath.

Angel's strong voice fell sullenly. "Some people don't get to choose how or when they lose their virginity ... and Dominic was one of those unfortunate souls."

She wanted to dig her long nails into her chest so she could rip out her dead heart and make a hole that could never be filled for the man she was starting to develop true feelings for, no matter how much she denied it.

"It is Dominic's story to tell when he is ready, but if he's worried about your soul or anything else, for that matter, it's because he didn't get a choice, and Dominic would never allow himself to touch a woman if he thought he could harm or *taint* them in any way"—he used the word Dom himself had used—"like he had done to him."

Maria nodded solemnly, her mouth too dry to speak.

"If you want to be with Dominic, then that is your choice, Maria, but you must understand that he will do *anything* to protect the ones he loves, no matter what that is."

Finally, Maria found her words. "Thank you, Angel."

Nodding, Angel then went for the door, but he had one last thing to say. "Dom did more than care for us. He was a brother, a father, a friend, and our savior."

Knocking on the door, a sleepy Matthias finally swung it open a few minutes later.

"You do know how to pick up a phone and call, right?"

"But what kind of fun would that be?" She smiled, coming in right past him without waiting for his permission to enter.

Matthias became quickly annoyed. "Aren't you tired of taking taxis?"

"Aren't you tired in general?" she replied, crossing her arms, before answering, "And no." *It sure as hell beats having someone watch my every move.*

"Well, if you would call Dom, he would actually come to you, but since you don't ..." Matthias gave her an all-knowing look, reading her like she had hurtfully described him last time. "I think it's because you secretly like it here in Blue Park. So, what exactly are you running from? Is living in a castle not all it's cracked up to be?"

Maria's eyes turned into slits. "Is Dominic here or not?" Truthfully, she didn't have a smart-ass comment, because mostly, what he had said was true.

He couldn't help but smile because he'd gotten her. "No."

"Okay, then I'll wait." She let the annoying twin know she wasn't going anywhere, which tipped the smile right off his face. "Where's Cassius?"

"I'm sure he's up in Dom's room." Matthias told her, heading back to his room. "Get your boyfriend to make you a key already."

She rolled her eyes. "He's not my—"

"And Maria"—stopping her lie, Matthias shot her an evil glare from his doorway—"learn how to fucking drive."

At least he wasn't fucking dumb, because as soon as she took one step, Matthias quickly shut his bedroom door before she heard the lock on the other side click.

Maria wanted to call him every name in the book, but she didn't as she passed his bedroom door. Instead, she actually smiled.

Going up the steps, Maria was confused as to why Cassius would be in Dom's room and was even more confused when she opened the bedroom door to find him not there. About to walk back out to go find him, she noticed the strangely shaped window was cracked open.

Walking up to it, she saw the back of the younger figure sitting on a little flat part of the roof that went straight out from under the window seal. "Cassius?"

Turning, he saw Maria. "What are you doing?"

"Coming out to join you."

"Well, be careful," Cassius complained, taking her hand to make sure she didn't trip. "You should have taken those things off before you came out here."

"Last time I did that, you gave a dog a thousand-dollar chew toy," Maria reminded him, taking a seat on the roof beside him.

Cass gave a side smile. "Oh, right."

Seeing the little dent in the side of the cheek that lifted, Maria's mouth dropped open. "You have dimples too?"

"Don't remind me," he grumbled as his smile quickly dropped.

"What do you mean? They're adorable," Maria said in awe. They were hot on Dom, but on Cassius, they were cutest fucking thing in the world. They made the devilish boy finally look his age. They didn't suit his personality, but that was also what made them so charming.

"So adorable that Kat would always pinch my cheeks to see

them." He rubbed his little cheek, getting rid of the ghost pain.

"Well, from what I could see, they're not as deep as Dominic's." Maria laughed. "I'm sure she just wanted to get a good look."

Cassius shook his head. "Mine aren't as deep as Dom's, because he smiles all the time."

"Oh, I see." Maria understood he was implying his dimples weren't as trained as Dom's because he rarely smiled. "Kat was just trying to see them."

He gave one last rub of his cheek for good measure. "Yep."

"So, is this your usual spot?" Maria asked, staring out at the land that surrounded the home. It was a decent amount of property, but it just looked bleak and sad. There was hardly any grass. "'Cause, if so, this view sucks."

"I don't know … I've always liked it up here." Cassius shrugged, looking up at the sky as the sun started to set. "It's pretty nice out here at night."

"Yeah, maybe." It was much different than the night view she was used to.

"Does Dominic's room not creep you out, though?"

"No … it was my father's before Dom's."

Well, no wonder it creeped her out.

"Did you and your father get along?" Maria asked softly, trying to pry.

Cass gave his answer in a simple shrug.

Seeing that this Luciano didn't want to answer made her even more curious about their father/son relationship. Maria knew how the other Luciano siblings felt about their father, but the youngest one, she did not. She didn't want to force it out of him, though, like Angel had said about Dominic ….

Cassius would tell his story when he was ready.

"Um, excuse me …?" Maria's green eyes caught something. Leaning over, she picked it up from out of the gutter. "What is this?" Of course she knew what it was, but it was a rhetorical question.

His eyes grew wide. "Uh … You're not going to tell Dom, are you?"

Maria gave him a stern look. "That depends. Are you going to keep doing it?"

Cassius answered without a blink of his eye, "No."

She didn't doubt the Luciano could easily lie. Rolling her eyes, she scolded him, "Smoking kills, you know? And you could at least try to hide it. How dumb can you be to do it right outside of your brother's window without even trying to hide the evidence?" Taking the butt of the stick, she shoved it in his pocket for him to throw away later, "And don't litter, that's not cool, either."

"Thanks." He gave her an appreciative look that she wouldn't tell on him. "I promise I don't do it often."

"That's how it starts, though," she continued her mothering rant. "My brother smokes, and it was only a cigarette every on—" Suddenly, Maria stopped, staring at Cassius with a scrutinizing gaze. It all suddenly clicked. "You talk to Lucca, don't you?"

"Yes." Again, he didn't deny it, but Maria didn't miss the little flex in his jaw.

"That's how you knew I used to wander around when I was a little girl." Maria continued to stare at him strangely. "How long have you been talking to him?"

"A long time …." His voice turned from nothingness to holding the littlest bit of anger. "I thought he was my friend."

"What happened?"

Cassius's brows furrowed deeply, looking out at the falling sun. "I didn't know who he was, and he used information I gave him against us."

"Katarina," Maria whispered, the last piece falling in place.

He didn't even have to nod his head. "He betrayed me."

"He betrayed me too," she told him, seeing how hurt he was. It was like looking in a mirror.

"He did?" Cassius asked, looking back to her.

"Yes."

"Are you going to forgive him?" he asked.

"I don't know," she answered honestly, looking away from the sunset to him. "Are you?"

Cassius shook his head confidently, but Maria saw how he had to think about it first. "But you should, though," he finally admitted. "He's your brother, and he cares about you."

"Really?" Maria smiled. "What else has he told you about me?"

"Well, he told me your name was Mia," he huffed before dropping his anger to slightly tilt his lips. "But he also said you were evil, spent too much money, but that you were also pretty cool."

Maria couldn't help but laugh. "Well, that's awfully accurate."

"I think so too," Cassius agreed with another smile that showed his little hint of a dimple.

Ugh. As much as this family made her pull her hair out, the more she came over here, the more attached she started to feel.

Maria always thought she just wanted to be alone, but now she'd had her alone time—*finally*—and with only Leo living with her, it turned out she was kind of missing her brothers and how they were always in each other's faces, even though it used to annoy the piss out of her.

"Are you going to marry Dom?" Cassius bluntly asked her.

Maria thought for several shocking moments until she finally knew what to say. "I—"

The window creaking behind them had Maria and Cassius turning their heads.

"Maria?"

Staring at a confused Dominic, she slightly melted upon seeing his handsome face. Maria hadn't known until this moment how much she had missed him these past few days.

"Well, I'll see you later." Cassius slightly raised his eyebrows at her before getting up to go back through the window to leave them alone.

Looking at the hand he held out to her, she grabbed it as she stood on the shaky ground and carefully made her way to the window.

Grabbing her waist tightly, he lifted her down in one swift, light motion until her stilettos reached safe ground once again.

Maria stared helplessly up at him. The act he had just done

made her stomach flutter, and when he let her waist go, she could see that the time she spent apart from Dominic had affected him as well. He seemed sad when he had left her place, and now he appeared even more so.

Dominic avoided her eyes, taking a seat on the edge of his bed. He looked tired as he rubbed his eyes.

Taking a step toward him, she could see that he hardly slept, making that hole in her chest that much deeper. Maria stretched out her hand, spreading her fingers through his hair.

At her touch, Dom suddenly opened his eyes and was even more surprised when he found her arms wrapping around his neck.

"I'm sorry," she whispered into his ear as she hugged him.

Wrapping his arms around her waist, he sat her down on his leg. "For what, princess?"

"For not understanding, listening, judging you, not coming to see you sooner—" She stopped, not wanting to make herself look worse.

"It's okay," he murmured, letting his thumb smooth back and forth over her exposed thigh that he held.

When she kept her face burrowed into his neck, Dominic sensed something was off. "Maria, what's wrong?"

Wanting to continue to stay there a little longer, she wasn't sure she could look him in the eyes. She liked the way his skin smelled even more fiery up close, and it hurt to look Dom in the eyes when he was sad or, worse, heartbroken.

"I talked to Angel," she spoke into his skin, hating she even had to say this to him, hating this fucking happened to him. "He didn't tell me what exactly happened, but he told me that you didn't get to choose your first time."

Dominic continued his thumb motion on her thigh. "Oh."

"Are you upset he told me?"

"No," he assured her sweetly, "I'm not upset. I would have told you eventually."

Maria squeezed him tighter as her throat closed. "I'm so sorry that happened to you."

"It's all right. It happened a long time ago." He placed a kiss on her shoulder. "There's no reason to be upset, princess. I'm not anymore."

"Well, you're nicer than me. I'll never get over it."

Dom chuckled at his black-hearted princess's joke, knowing it was true. "Maria."

She lifted her head from his neck, knowing he wanted to see her eyes.

"I just want you to know that the only reason I want to protect your virginity is because I didn't get to protect mine."

"I know," she told him before placing her face back in the crook of his neck, liking how warm he was there. "But you taking my virginity, with or without a stupid piece of paper, isn't protecting it, because it's something *I want. I choose.*"

"I understand, and I'm glad you trust me with it, but"—Dominic smiled—"you're still going to have to wait till after we're married."

Maria brought her face out of neck again. "Confident, aren't we?"

"Yes." Dominic showed her his dimples that she loved so much. "I'm going to get you to marry me, Maria Caruso, even if it's the last thing I do."

"Well"—she brought her lips closer to his—"you're going to be waiting a long time."

"That's fine."

"You prepared to wait that long for me?" She teasingly brought her lips even closer to his without letting them touch.

"I'm a patient man," he teased back, showing no signs of mercy. "You're the one who's going to break, princess."

Maria let their lips only touch for a second before she pulled away. "Never."

Dominic laughed, and when she placed her face back in his neck, he gave her another sweet, tender kiss on her shoulder, whispering a promise onto her skin. "I'll wait forever for you, princess."

"Good luck," she told him with a yawn after her long day, and watching him look sleepy made her look sleepy.

Going to her pink strappy heels that matched her monochromatic pink dress, Dominic took his time carefully removing them.

Maria was already breaking, getting turned on by watching him take off her heels. It was the way he grabbed them and pointed her feet to show off her white toenail polish that had her about ready to say vows here and now.

"Don't." Maria moved her naked foot before he could grab it after he had taken both heels off. "I get to wear heels twenty-four seven for a reason."

He looked at her confused.

"The bottom of my feet are tough," she informed him, letting him know the downside to being able to withstand the pain. "You can touch my feet in heels, but you don't want to touch them without."

"Well, that's too bad," Dominic said, taking her foot in his hand anyway. "You'll have to get used to it."

Ugh, Maria wanted to melt, liking the way he touched her feet, slightly massaging them as if he could rub them into being soft again.

"You know, you could at least take me on a date before asking me to marry you," she grumbled, wanting to jump his bones already.

"You're right." He laughed, seeing that he was making it hard for her already. He stopped, picked her up in his arms, and looked down at her with his dimples on display. "How about tomorrow night?"

"That works," she answered, not expecting that response but knowing she would be at the spa in the Casino Hotel first thing in the morning getting a pedicure.

When he placed her down on the bed, Maria made herself comfortable on her side, putting her hands underneath her face. As Dominic lay down, he took the same position, only opposite. Both of them lay facing each other with a small space separating them from head to toe as they stared at each other.

"You're so beautiful," he told her achingly without reaching out to touch her.

Something about him telling her those words meant more when he said them without touching her.

All her life men had stared at her with only one thing on their minds and told her things they thought would make something happen between them. It was ironic that the one man she desperately wanted to fuck wouldn't, because he was giving her the one thing she had wished everyone else gave her—respect.

Dominic was being respectful to her and a true gentleman, but that somehow made her want him even more. And the things she wanted him to do to her were neither respectful or gentlemanly in the least.

But this moment felt precious in a way, and she didn't want to ruin that. All Maria wanted to do was understand him more.

He called her beautiful, but Maria believed she was ugly. On the outside, yes, Maria knew she was beautiful, but that wasn't what really mattered. Those things faded with time and were shallow, *like me*.

There was a reason why Maria presented herself so gorgeously on the outside—because the inside was hideous.

Dominic was different, though. He was not only beautiful on the outside, but on the inside, he was just as, if not more, breathtaking … and in their cruel world, that was all that would ever matter.

"Can I ask you a question?" she asked softly.

"Yes."

Even though Dominic had answered like she could ask him anything, Maria still hoped her question was okay to ask. "Did you sleep with anyone after what happened to you?"

"Yes." He nodded just a little bit over his hands. "I've been with lots of women, Maria," he admitted honestly. "The first four were not my choosing, but I thought, somehow, I could undo what happened to me by sleeping with women of my choosing. So, I drowned those first four out by fucking women over and over, but it never worked. Most of the women I slept with were in that first year. It's been a long time since I've been with someone, but every woman I was with didn't live here and wasn't untouched, like me. We both did it to help forget whatever it was we were running from. It was never out of love and only to serve a purpose."

She could hear it in Dom's voice and see it in his eyes that he used to be ashamed of what had happened to him and the things he did to cope with it, but he wasn't anymore. He had healed, which allowed him to speak so openly now.

Maria's silence had him continuing. "If you're worried, I am clean. I've been tested and, like I said, I haven't been with someone—"

"I'm not," she assured him with a shush, putting a stop to his fears. "That wasn't a worry in my mind at all." Maria knew he would have never come close to sleeping with her if he even *thought* he could give her something. "You've never explained anything that happened in your past to me, Dominic. I only ever want to hear about it when you want to tell me."

"Okay." He gave her little smile ... before it slowly disappeared.

Maria listened as Dominic told her in depth about the night he lost his virginity. He told her everything, and no story had ever made her feel such strong emotions of anger, sadness, and hurt, but she continued to listen as they both stayed perfectly still. She learned a lot about Dominic that night, but one night wasn't long enough to tell twenty-eight years of abuse. Sleep would come first ...

KETCHUP IS SEASONING

The sun coming up stirred Maria to wake, but before opening her eyes, her first thought was that Dom would be gone. The trauma of waking up and not seeing the last man she'd shared a bed with remained. But there Dominic was, fast asleep, peaceful.

Smiling, she stared at him a moment longer, then quietly and very carefully got up, grabbing her heels before leaving the room and going down the creaky steps.

Passing a little bathroom, she took a few minutes for herself and cleaned up a bit. Slipping her shoes back on, she left the tiny bathroom, heading down the hall, keeping herself from loudly clicking her heels. She about made it to the living area without even so much as a peep when she saw a someone she didn't know in the kitchen. The "peep" hadn't come from Maria, but the older woman who screamed at the sight of her.

"Holy shit." The woman gasped for air. "You scared the piss out of me."

"Sorry about that." Maria stared at her curiously. "Who are you?"

"I'm DeeDee." She smiled, looking at her yesterday's dress and heels. "Are you one of Matthias's friends?"

"Ew, no." She practically gagged, knowing what she meant by "friend." "I'm one of Dominic's."

"Dom's?" DeeDee looked at her in disbelief. "That's strange."

"Yes." She nodded, finding the way the woman was looking at her stranger.

"Well, come sit down, sweetie." DeeDee came to her and took her arm, leading her to the kitchen table. "I'll make you some breakfast. Would you like some orange juice?"

Watching her go to the fridge, she remembered Dominic drinking from the milk carton, and while she didn't mind swapping spit with him, she wasn't about to swap it with the other two brothers. "Water's good, actually."

"All right." She went to make her a glass of water. "How do eggs and toast sound?"

"Good."

"The boys will be hungry when they wake, so I'll make plenty."

"Thank you." Maria smiled when she placed the water down in front of her. Staring at the glass, Maria asked, "What was strange?"

"Oh." DeeDee laughed it off like it was no big deal. "He's just never brought a girl here before, is all."

Tapping the glass, she asked another one, "Have you known him a long time?"

"Since he was just a baby." She smiled happily, reminiscing his cute, little face as she started cooking the eggs. "I've watched all the kids grow up now, but Dom lets me stay around to help clean the house and get the groceries."

Maria warmed at hearing her talk about him.

"He's a good man," DeeDee assured her before realizing … "What's your name, sweetie?"

"Maria." She gave the kind woman another smile. "And I know."

Ugh, she was getting soft the longer she stayed around here.

By the time they talked a bit more, with Maria mostly asking questions about little Dom, the woman had no sooner started making a plate for her when Matthias entered the kitchen.

"I wouldn't do that," he warned her, strolling in.

Maria looked at him in confusion. "Do what?"

"Eat that," Matthias said, going to the fridge to look at what else they had. "DeeDee can't cook for shit."

That's rud—

"Oh please," the woman shushed him, hitting his upper arm. "I cook fine; don't worry."

At first, Maria thought Matthias was being a dick, but when she had set the plate down in front of her, Maria looked down at the eggs strangely—they weren't the expected yellow color. Hell, now she wasn't even sure if she should eat them, but the way the older woman was waiting for her to take a bite, she hated to be a bitch;

they were just eggs ... *What was so hard about that?*

Taking a small bite, she instantly spit them back out onto the plate with no remorse.

"You shouldn't have done that." Dominic laughed, entering the room. "She can't cook for shit."

Gulping down her water, she didn't even look at the woman sympathetically for the crime she had committed against those eggs. "I'm sorry, DeeDee, but it's true."

The woman didn't seem to take offense. "Well, that's okay. They'll get eaten."

By who? A dog?

Placing a jar of jelly down in front of her that he got from the fridge, along with a butter knife, Dominic gave her a sympathetic look. "Don't worry; the toast is fine to eat. DeeDee just thinks ketchup is seasoning."

"Ketchup!" She took another swig of water, wondering why the fuck she thought it was okay to eat red-tinted eggs in the first place. Maria hadn't let it touch her tongue long enough to even know what the fuck it was, but one thing she was sure of was that DeeDee belonged in jail.

Cassius had come in silently, taking her plate of the gross eggs. "I'll eat 'em."

Maria watched him take a seat beside her at the table. "You are not about to—"

"They taste fine to me," he said, shoving in a mouthful.

"That's vile," she scolded him. Both he and DeeDee needed to be locked up.

"Sorry, we don't have a personal chef here for you like I'm sure you're used to," Matthias grumbled, still staring into the fridge like something good or different was going to appear.

"We don't have one," Maria threw back. Taking her toast from the plate Cassius had stolen, she began smearing the jelly on top once Dominic finished coating his next to her. "Lucca does most of the cooking."

All three brothers stopped what they were doing to stare at her.

"What?" She looked at each one of them weirdly.

Matthias was the one to quickly go back to what he was doing. "Nothing."

It became clear that where Matthias liked to push her buttons, he wouldn't dare push the boogieman's.

She took a bite of her toast, deciding to surprise them even more with the truth. "He's a really good cook, actually. You would die to eat one of his steaks. He cooks it in a hot pan on the stove just like a renowned chef would. He makes them a perfect medium rare and lets them rest till just the right amount of blood coats your plate when you cut each piece with a knife for you to dip it in." She gave them all a bright smile. "Maybe I could ask you all over for din—"

"That's all right," Matthias choked out. "I think we'll pass."

"Suit yourself." She shrugged, taking another bite of her toast but quickly swallowed when she saw what the twin brother was doing. "Can you please not do that?"

Gulping down the orange juice from the carton, he came up for air. "Why not?"

"Because I'd like to be able to drink something other than water when I come over here?" she snapped back without even a thought of what she was asking. She hadn't realized until Dominic looked over at her with a smug expression. Maria had planned to keep coming back ....

"No," Matthias simply responded, going to take another large drink, but Dom got up from the table, taking the carton out of his hand. He set it down on the counter, along with a glass on the counter for him. "Use a glass. And that goes for you, too, Cass," he instructed, turning to look at Cassius taking his last bite.

"All right." Cass gave him a nod.

"Jesus, next, she'll be having us put down the toilet seat—"

"That too," Dominic informed them.

I think I'm in l—

"Oh my God." Matthias glared evilly at her and not his brother, who was starting to make the rules.

Maria smiled happily back at the pissed-off brother, flipping her gold locks behind a shoulder as they both mentally flicked each other off.

When DeeDee filled up Cass's plate with the rest of the eggs, Maria's stomach turned.

"I need to get home," she informed Dominic, because she had a date at the spa before she could go on their actual date tonight. Plus, she wanted to spend a few hours with Leo, as all the siblings were taking turns being with him.

"Matthias will give you a ride back to the Casino Hotel." Seeing the massive eye roll, Dom continued before his brother could bitch. "I have a few things I need to handle today before I see you tonight."

"Okay," Maria told him, understanding. It wouldn't be great for her either, but if it pissed Matthias off, it worked out for her.

"I'll pick you up at six," Dominic informed her with a smile as he walked back to where she sat at the table. Leaning down, he forced her chin up for a quick kiss with an inked finger. "And wear white, princess."

Maria's green eyes went wide as she watched him walk away just as quickly as he had kissed her. Her cheeks actually might have flushed, but she was too embarrassed to touch them in front of everyone. The only thing that saved her was that DeeDee was the only one who seemed to care. It was clear on the woman's face that she hadn't believed Maria when she'd told her she was Dominic's friend … but now she did.

"Can I go?" Cass asked before Dom could leave the room.

Dominic stopped for a moment to turn around. "Not today."

"It's okay if he wants to come," Maria offered. "I don't min—"

"No, I need him to go to work with me today," Dominic told her.

Nodding, Cassius didn't seem to mind going with Dom. "Okay."

Maria glanced between the two brothers, finding that strange ….

"Come on, your highness." Matthias opened the front door and took a dramatic bow. "Your chariot awaits!"

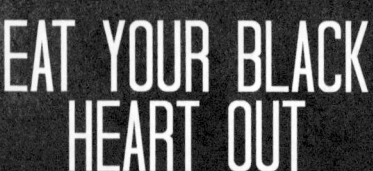

EAT YOUR BLACK
HEART OUT

Hearing the knock on the door, Maria couldn't help but smile as she checked herself out in the mirror. Her feet were as smooth as a baby's bottom, and her toes and nails were freshly painted white … just like Dominic had wanted, but that was where it ended.

He had wanted her dressed in white, like a pretty bride, but Maria made it perfectly clear what she wanted. Smoothing her very tight, form-fitting dress down her body, it hugged every curve and left absolutely nothing up to the imagination as it was … nude. And not just any nude, *her* exact nude that matched her tanned skin perfectly. From a distance, you would do a double-take, thinking she was naked when, in fact, she was not. Up close, however, the dress could pass for lingerie as the part that hugged her breasts was lacy and appeared almost see-through, as it was actually a built-in bustier creating two perfect, high-placed mounds.

If Dominic wasn't going to fuck her until she had a ring on her finger, she was going to make him pay *hard*.

Hearing another knock, Maria picked up her small rhinestone clutch that matched the long rhinestone clip she had in her blonde hair that kept the right side of her softly curled hair behind her shoulder. Clicking her super skinny nude stilettos on the floor, she opened the door.

"Dear"—Dominic's widened hazel eyes slid down her body slowly—"God." Clearing his throat, he actually had to wipe his brow. "I-I thought I asked you to wear white."

"You don't like it?" she asked with a smile.

"No, you know I do, princess." Dominic gritted the words out, clearly struggling. "But that's the problem."

Licking her bottom lip, she gave him a hot look. "Well, I thought we could skip the white."

Knowing exactly what she meant, Dominic craned her neck up like he liked to do with his finger. It was clear he liked the way she had done her hair as he had the view of her long neck on display.

Leaning down, he whispered huskily into her exposed ear, "Next time I ask you to wear a certain color, princess ... do it."

"Or what?" she challenged with a raised, newly perfected manicured brow.

Placing a kiss on her neck, he gave her a promise, "If you're brave enough to do it when we're married, you'll find out."

Suddenly, the thought of marriage isn't so ba—

Maria internally shook the thought away. "You could always give me a prequel …"

Groaning, he had to pull away after kissing her neck once more. "I would, but then we'd be late for what I have planned."

Maria took his hand, twirling his fingers in hers, trying to pull him closer and into her place. "Or we could skip right over your plans and get right to mine?"

His rich hazel eyes glowed for a moment as he leaned back down to place the lightest kiss on her full lips, careful not to smudge her lip gloss. "Not a chance, princess." He smiled, giving her a view of his dimples right before he took ahold of her hand and started dragging her in the opposite direction she wanted to go.

Internally screaming, Maria started walking beside him, unhappily.

Staring at the gorgeous man who had her begging to be fucked, there was only one explanation at this point …

Dominic was a fucking saint.

This time, as the two made it through the Casino Hotel, they didn't try to hide the fact that they were holding each other's hands. They made it more than obvious how they felt about the other, not only to the cameras but to anyone around. As they walked, the people parted, giving them a wide berth to stare in either awe or jealousy of the gorgeous couple who looked straight out of a *James Bond* film. However, it wasn't your stereotypical *Bond* movie, as it looked as if a Bond girl had either dumped or killed James for the bad guy in the film.

Dominic wasn't dressed in Caruso fashion, which would have made him more like *James Bond*; he kept his signature look with his leather jacket. The only difference tonight were the dark, expensive-looking jeans and the brown suede boots that Maria had never seen him wear.

Walking out of the hotel, Dominic's Mustang was parked right out front. He unlocked the car and, with a couple of flashes of the headlights, he opened the passenger side door for her to get in.

Maria expertly slid into the leather seats, looking like a million bucks, and it was clear Dominic was in love with the sight.

Some men wouldn't let their women walk out of the house wearing what Maria was wearing, but Dominic wasn't some men. Men might look at her, but there was always going to be men staring at Maria, even if she was wearing a brown paper sack, and she was on his arm, not theirs.

Shutting the door after another glance of her shiny, tanned legs, Dom got in behind the wheel and quickly drove off.

Goddamn, Maria loved that fiery, earthy scent that she felt wrap around her every time she was in his car. This and his bedroom were the only places that amplified his otherwise light scent that she could never get enough of.

Maria couldn't help but eye Dom as he switched gears, even though she was trying to take her mind off the sexual tension. Why, every time he was near her, did she feel like the biggest slut on the planet?

"Stop that." Dominic's guttural voice echoed in the small confines of the car.

Maria's emerald gaze went to the steering wheel he was gripping tightly. "Stop what?"

"Moving your legs like that," he ordered as he glanced out of the side of his eyes while he drove. "You're doing that on purpose."

Actually, she wasn't. She kept moving her silky legs to try to get comfortable, because the only thing she kept imagining was sitting on his dic—

"I don't know what you're talking about," she said helplessly with a pearly white smile. There was no way in hell she was going to tell him that just watching him drive was making her consider marrying him. She didn't want Dom to know she was the one closest to breaking. She had never been more thankful for buying that lotion with gold shimmer in it. She was going to have to buy stock in the company.

Wanting him to be closer to the pain she was in, she trailed her freshly shaped, long nails along the tatted hand that kept hold of the gear shift. "We may need to get you a car that isn't a stick shift."

"What? You don't think I know how to multitask?" Dominic let his hand wander up her thigh, getting closer to the hem of her short dress. With his widely spread hand, he stopped to squeeze her flesh in a tight grip that sent Maria's body up in flames before he let go to put his hand back on the shift. "Not a chance, princess." He made it clear there was no other car he would drive.

Maria silently agreed, not able to picture him driving anything else. Plus, she liked the show, just not the way it made her feel when she couldn't be satisfied. She desperately needed to clear her thoughts and the raging fire brewing in her belly, so she put her mind on something else that she had wondered about all day.

"This morning"—Maria looked over at him curiously—"when you said Cassius was going to work with you, you don't mean like *family* business, do you?"

Dominic's silence met her question, which answered her question.

Shocked wasn't even the word to describe the look on her face. "He's fifteen, which makes him the youngest ..." She trailed off at the thought. Lucca had been the youngest to be made at seventeen. You weren't made unless you were a man, and her brother had only did so because he proved without irrevocable doubt that he was no longer a child.

Cassius wasn't. There was a hint of a childlike charm still in him. She had seen it.

"I've not let him speak the oath," Dominic spoke the words stoically. "But I know him, Maria. If I shut him out of the family business, Cassius *will* resent me. I spent my whole life trying to end my father's reign, and I will not have the strength to do what would need to be done a second time."

A cold chill went up her spine, knowing what he meant by that.

"To do everything I possibly can to keep Cass from turning into our father will not only delay the inevitable, but I could end up creating something worse in the process."

Maria knew it was a dangerous game he was playing. It was like playing with fire, and Dominic himself knew it.

"I felt no love with my father, but I'd take my own life before I'd take my brother's."

Hearing the fear of what his brother could become, along with the pain it would cause him if he did so, Maria placed her hand over Dominic's that hovered over the shift and gave it a light squeeze, letting him know she supported him in his decision.

The truth was, there was no right or wrong way to care for Cassius. However, she did know Dom was right. Maria resented her own father for the same reasons.

"It'll be okay," she told him strongly, though she wasn't sure of it. Just like Dominic wasn't. But she'd do everything in her power to help him keep Cassius from walking too far down that dark path he was on. "He's your full brother isn't he?" Maria dared to ask the question she figured out once she had seen Cassius smile, when Dom looked at her strangely she let him in on how she figured it out. "He has dimples too. They're genetic."

Maria didn't need to tell him the rest, because Dominic already knew it. None of Lucifer's other children had them, which meant most likely he wasn't the one with them and since the two brother's looked so much alike and nothing at all like their father, it only meant they had to share the same mother as well.

At his nod, Dominic already answered before Maria could ask her next question. "She isn't alive… none of our mothers are."

"I'm sorr-"

"Don't be." He assured her, letting her know it was another thing he made peace with. "It's hard to miss something you never had."

Maria truly felt for the little boy who seemed to have never had a chance at a normal childhood but she also knew the man he had become didn't want pity. One thing he made clear about Lucifer: women didn't belong in his world.

Letting go of his shifting hand after another squeeze, Maria turned on the radio, only to be greeted to another country song and station. It seemed to be the only music he listened to, and not just Johnny Cash. *What the—*

"You don't listen to country, do you?"

He gave her a side-eye. "Yes."

"*Dominic. Luciano*," she annunciated his name in disbelief, "listens to country?"

"Yes. What's wrong with that?"

"Nothing …" *Per say.* It was just odd. "Just not what I, or I think anyone, would actually expect."

Smiling, Dominic was glad he could surprise her. "Growing up, I was obsessed with old westerns."

Maria looked at him in even more shock, while clearly trying not to burst out in laughter. "So, you wanted to be … a cowboy?"

"No, not particularly," Dominic corrected her, not appreciating Maria's sly smile. "An outlaw."

"Mmhmm." Maria's smile grew bigger. "But aren't outlaws just bad *cowboys*?"

Dominic's eyes started to turn to slits, but Maria wasn't done with her teasing.

"So, let me get this right ... you like guns, listen to country music"—Maria's laughter could no longer be held back as she giggled through the last part uncontrollably—"and instead of driving a horse, you drive a Mustang, but you don't think you secretly wanted to be a cowboy?"

"I think," Dominic harshly gritted out, "if you don't stop laughing, princess, I'll show you how they often treated women in the westerns."

"What?" Maria continued to giggle. She was actually about to ruin her makeup if she didn't stop. "Respectfully?"

"That depends ...." His voice came out as a warning.

Quickly, she dried a tear that had fallen. "On what?"

Dominic's eyes slowly slid down her body. "Who the male lead was."

Suddenly, Maria no longer laughed.

Hiding his smile, Dominic pulled into an empty parking lot.

"What are you doing?" she asked.

Parking, it wasn't exactly what Maria was hoping for.

"I'm going to teach you how to drive."

"Uh ... that's okay," Maria turned down the offer.

He couldn't believe she had done that. "You're telling me you don't even want to try?"

Exactly. "Yep."

"Why?"

Maria turned to face him, deciding to give him the bitchy truth. "Because, as cliché as it makes me, I personally like being driven around. Telling men where I want to go, when I want to go, gets me off. Is that what you want to hear?"

Okay, that last part wasn't exactly true, but he didn't need to know that.

Dominic had to blink several times. Then, clearing his throat, he tried a different tactic. "Maria, never getting behind a wheel is"—Dominic searched for the word—"sinful. Everyone should feel what it's like at least once."

Seeing how serious he felt about it, she raised a brow. "And you're really going to trust me to drive *your* car?" It was obvious this car was his baby. Cassius had made that pretty clear.

"Yes. Just imagine the car you could buy if you did learn," he added to entice her.

Damn. Dom did know her well.

Maria was already planning which sweet ride she would buy when they got out to switch seats.

"This should do. Nothing for you to sideswipe or rear-end," Dom joked, closing the passenger side door.

"Don't worry about my confidence before I even start," Maria said with snark, staring at the stick-shift car.

"I have every confidence you can achieve anything you want to do."

Pacified, Maria buckled her seat belt as Dom did his.

Maria smiled. "Good save."

"I have my moments."

Damn. There were those dimples again . . . .

Patiently, Dominic went over the gears and the pedals before giving her another dose of his dimples.

"Do you think you're ready to give it a try?" He gave her a considering look.

"I guess as ready as I'll ever be." Unexpectedly, Maria became excited about trying the new experience. She placed her hands in the position on the wheel that Dominic had showed her, even though she had sarcastically told him she hadn't seen his in the position.

"All right. Put the car in neutral with your right foot on the brake," he instructed. "Put your left foot on the clutch all the way to the floorboard. Go ahead and shift to first gear … That's good. Slowly, take your foot off the brake."

"This isn't so hard." Maria smiled toward him.

"It isn't too hard," Dom agreed. "Maria, when I said take your foot off the brake slowly, it didn't mean not to move it at all."

"Oh, okay." Maria moved her foot and her head jerked back.

"Brake!" Dominic yelled. "Not the clutch—the brake! Your right foot!"

Now her head fell forward at the sudden stop. Proudly, she turned toward Dom. "I stopped it."

"Yes"—he managed to keep his voice even—"you did."

Did she see a glint of fear in his eyes, or was she just imagining it?

"What's next?" Maria asked eagerly.

Dominic wasn't as eager.

"Let's get the first step perfected before moving on."

"What's wrong with the way I did it?"

"Other than you didn't take your foot off the brake slowly?" he quipped. "Or you couldn't tell your left foot from the right?"

With her green eyes, she glared over at him. "Are you being *sarcastic?*"

Silence met her question.

"I was just nervous. I'll do better this time."

"Okay." Dom didn't seem as laidback as he placed a hand on the dashboard to brace himself. "Let's give it another try."

She couldn't keep from rolling her eyes at his hand placement. "Don't be so dramatic."

He simply ignored her insult. "Okay, what gear are you in?"

Maria narrowed her eyes into slits. "Neutral."

"And … which pedal is your right foot—"

"It's going to be shoved up your ass if you don't quit treating me like a child," Maria threatened before giving him the answer he wanted. "My right foot is on the fucking brake."

"Good." Dominic let out a breath. "Now, *slowly* ease your right foot off the *bra*—brake, Maria!"

Her head went back again as the car jerked forward.

"That's the clutch!"

The car kept rolling forward. *Can cars be possessed?* It took her two more attempts before she could bring the car to a stop.

"Park the car," he ordered hastily.

Maria quickly did as he asked.

"That's enough," Dom gritted out between clenched teeth.

Another perfect brow raised at how quickly Dominic had changed his stance on her learning to drive. "That's it?"

"Yes," Dominic said, already opening his car door.

Unbuckling her seat belt, she switched seats and put her ass back in the passenger seat much sooner than he had expected.

Even though Maria had an inkling driving wasn't meant for her … "Maybe I need to try an automati—"

"No, you don't," Dominic informed, glad to be back behind the wheel. "Eat your little black heart out by having men drive you around."

Maria laughed. "I tried to tell you."

"Well, you were right. I just thought you would have been sick of having to ride in taxis lately."

"I mean, well, technically, I've been getting Uber Black," she told him that she had been getting her rides from the premium side of the car service. "But yes, it's not as nice as having one of Lucca's men driving me around, but that would mean I'd have to go back to having a bodyguard."

"And you still think that would be a bad thing?" he asked, putting his Mustang in first gear. Their little One-Shot problem had yet to be solved.

"Yes, I don't need anyone else getting hurt or dying for me," Maria told him, her mind made. "Especially considering I just buried my fourth bodyguard—"

The tires screeching to a halt had Maria thanking God she wore a seat belt, even though they were in an empty parking lot, as her head jerked forward. "What the fuck, Dominic!"

Dom's voice shook the car. "FOUR?"

HIGH-MAINTENANCE BITCH

"**Y**ou *took me to a* car museum?" Maria asked as they entered
the building, seeing all the old-fashioned cars filling the
space. "You were supposed to take me out to dinner."

"Has anyone ever told you that you're high maintenance?"
Dominic placed a proprietary arm around her waist as they waited
in line behind multiple couples.

"Well, you don't call me princess for nothing."

"No, I don't." Dom laughed. "What's wrong? You don't like it?"

"I just never knew there were so many people interested in old
cars." Bored, Maria tried to force an interest in something Dominic
obviously had. "Which one is your favorite?"

"I don't know. I've never really looked around."

Inwardly, Maria groaned. She was going to have to put on her game face and pretend she was going to be enthralled with each car that had been restored, just so she might get lucky at the end of the night.

Moving forward in line, she heard a couple in front of them give their names to the staff behind the counter.

"You have to have a reservation to look at cars?" Maria gave a brief glance around. "I've seen it all. Let's go."

Dominic gave an exasperated breath while keeping her firmly in place beside him with the hand on her waist. "Maria, give it a chance."

"That's what I'm doing. Let's go hit a drive-thru and eat at my place." Maria gave a silent groan when the line moved and the couple went around the side and down a stairwell. "There're even *more* cars downstairs?"

Jesus. By the time they got out of there, Maria would be gray before losing her virginity.

Her question was asked to Dom's back as he moved forward. Maria was so hungry she wished now she had eaten the ketchup eggs.

"Luciano."

The worker gave a nod, not looking up from her computer. "You're right on time. Go ahead."

Dom nodded his own head. "Thank you."

Finding herself being ushered down the steps, she was relieved she had no intention of marrying Dominic. *What man in this universe would rather spend the night at a museum over getting their brains fucke—*

Suddenly, Maria had to grab onto Dom's arm at the end of the steps as the light became so dim she could barely see. "How are we supposed to see the cars in the dark?"

As the words came out of her mouth, a light appeared as they walked farther along. Drawing nearer, she could see a hostess waiting for them. Gaping, Maria followed the hostess as she traversed them through tables glowing in the candlelight.

Wow . . . For the first time tonight, Maria was speechless.

"Still want to go back to your apartment?" Dominic grinned, holding a chair out for her.

Maria gave him her sweetest smile. "Right after I eat, I do."

Dom's dimples appeared as he took a seat across from her.

"You keep smiling at me like that, and I'm going to change my mind again," she warned.

"Too late," Dominic said as a bread basket was placed down on the table. "Once you taste that, you won't be leaving."

Maria peeled back the linen covering the bread to take a warm slice. Picking up her bread knife, she smeared butter on it before taking a bite. "Mmm . . ." she moaned. "You're right."

"I'm glad you like it, princess," he said, taking his own slice of heaven as she looked over the menu.

"What's good?"

Dominic shrugged. "Not sure."

"You've never been here before?" she asked as she arched her brow.

"No," he told her simply. "I've been saving this place for someone special."

Ugh. Maria wanted him to say dirty things to her, not sweet things that made her contemplate marrying him.

Taking another small bite of the bread, Maria nearly choked on it at the way he was staring at her in the candlelight. Teasingly, Maria leaned a bit forward. "If the food is as good as the bread, Mr. Luciano, you just might get lucky tonight."

"Actually, there's a bar on the lower level. I thought we could go get a few drinks and check it out, if you'd like?"

In other words, he was trying to stall and tire her out.

After the waiter came to take their orders then left, Maria gave the place another glance around. "Dominic, you know you didn't have to go to all this trouble. I don't have to have all these bells and whistles." Yes, Maria *might be* a stuck-up, high-maintenance bitch, but she wasn't interested in Dominic to get nice things or money. She had that stuff and didn't want more of it. She was looking for something different.

"Something tells me McDonalds wouldn't haven't convinced you to marry me, princess."

"This won't either," she admitted.

"I know," Dominic revealed. "I just wanted to show you how nice of a time we could have together."

Dom was sucking her under with a charm she'd had no idea he was capable of.

Reaching over the table, she traced over the letter C. "So, about those male leads in your old westerns …."

There was a slight tug of his lips. "What would you like to know, princess?"

She traced over to the O now. "How did they treat their

women?"

"Well, there's John Wayne," Dominic began, watching her trace the letters inked into his skin. "And he's mostly the respectful type."

"How romantic." She went to the letter M.

"Then there's Clint Eastwood ..." Dominic's voice dropped deathly quiet as his hazel eyes glowed in the candlelight. "And he isn't *so* much."

Finally, she went to the E. "And which one are you?"

"I guess you'll either have to marry me or watch them with me to find out, princess."

Maria countered, "I think that's something a woman should know about a man before she agrees to marry him."

Not that she was or anything.

A slow flash of his dimples told him he thought otherwise. "Then you better start watching them."

"Actually," Maria drawled in a breath, keeping him in suspense, "no."

"Why not?" He laughed.

"Because, I have a feeling you won't be the Netflix and chill type." Maria sighed. "And plus, I already know you're neither of them."

Dominic raised a brow. "So, you know who John Wayne and Clint Eastwood are?"

She smiled. "Possibly."

"How is that?" Not even Dominic took her as being able to sit through a western to know what characters they typically played.

Stopping her tracing, she pulled her hand away. "Well, that's for me to know and you to find out."

Dom stared at her, as if the answer was written on her forehead, but he couldn't see the small writing.

Snatching her hand before she could drop it from the table, he held it in his. "Tell me."

"What's in it for me?" she purred.

Turning her palm over, he started his own light tracings. "What do you want?"

Maria's eyes trailed down to his motion. "You spending the night at my place."

"You trying to get me carried out in a body bag?"

Maria slowly shook her head. "You wouldn't be any good to me dead."

"I will"—Dominic sent shivers up her palm to her arm—"as you long as you understand I'm not going to have sex with you before we're married."

It was time to try a different tactic. "Do you know how many men would die if I made them that offer?"

"Tell me who they are, and I'll make it happen, princess."

Maria was shocked at his words. "You would let me sleep with them?"

"No." He lifted his eyes from her palm to her hungry eyes. "I would help them die."

"Oh …" Maria caught her breath. "Then that's okay."

Smiling, he gave the middle of her palm a little pinch. "You're a vicious little thing."

Maria hadn't flinched, too enthralled at what he was doing. "It doesn't bother you?"

"No." He showed her the hunger in his own eyes. "It turns me on."

"You turn me on," Maria admitted eagerly. "Want to forget dinner and go fuck?"

Flipping her hand back over, he touched her ring finger. "Not until I put a wedding band here."

"I'd rather have your dick in my—"

Maria broke off as their salads arrived.

"Behave," Dominic said quietly once they were alone again.

Maria, however, wasn't so quiet. "My dad would tell you I was never good at behaving."

Picking up his fork, it was clear Maria wouldn't have expected his answer. "Princess, you can be as bad as you want to be, and I won't ever say no to you."

Dammit. Dominic was getting harder and harder to resist when he was trying woo her with such glorious freedom, but even Maria knew that was just a ruse.

"Right. Like I believe that. Once you have your ring on my finger, you'll turn into all the other overprotective men in my life."

"No, I won't." Dominic made an oath to her right then and there. "Just imagine, Maria ... you can do and be anything you want with me."

Holding her breath, she could see just how truthful he was behind his hazel eyes. "Ring size, six."

AN IMPOSSIBLE
MAN TO SEDUCE

"**Y**ou *told me you wanted* to go to the bar here, Maria," Dominic warned her in a guttural voice, in an effort to let her know she still wasn't going to get her way as they made it to her door.

"We are." Maria pulled out her phone from her clutch to unlock the door. "I just need to freshen up first."

"Uh-huh." Clearly, he didn't believe her. And it was probably for good reason.

While Maria did have a much better drinking spot here at the Casino Hotel, she planned to woo Dominic into her bed.

Who could blame her? *Dominic is hot AF.*

Smiling, Maria opened the door, and they both went inside.

"I'll wait here," he informed her, going to the living room.

Maria gave him a sultry smile. "You can come wait up in my room, if you'd like?"

"Not a chance, princess," he said, showing his dimples while he took a seat in a big velvet chair.

Maria huffed out a long, exasperated breath. "You're an impossible man to seduce, Dominic Luciano, I hope you know that."

"Well, maybe"—Dom sat back lazily in the chair, spreading his arms over the arms of the chair, making himself comfortable—"you're not trying hard enough, Maria Caruso."

She thought she was dreaming for a second, about to wave the white flag of trying to seduce him. That sensual look Dom was giving her told her otherwise—Dominic clearly enjoyed her endless teasing, and he didn't want it to stop. If he thought she wasn't trying hard enough, he was in for *her* world of pain.

Maria sashayed over to him until just a foot away. Lifting her leg, she placed the toe of her stiletto on his lower abdomen, making the pointy heel hover over his dick, all while she balanced on the other thin nude heel. "Scared?" she asked with an arched brow.

"No, I trust you." Dominic took his hand off the arm of the chair to let his palm wander up and down her long, silky leg that went on for days. Leaning down, he then placed a kiss on her inner thigh. "And you wouldn't dare, princess," he said with a smile.

That was true. There was no way she would hurt the one part of him she wanted the most.

Dom slid his hand from her upper thigh, down the length of her leg, until he reached her heel. Maria stared at him curiously as he admired her feet in her shoes, before he grabbed her heel with one hand so it couldn't puncture him as he brought her leg closer with the other. The tight grip he had on her kept her from falling while she perfectly balanced on one stilettoed foot.

Leaning forward again, his eyes went to the nice, little view he had with the rising hem of her dress. Keeping his eyes on her see-through, nude, lacy thong, he kissed her inner thigh. "I know you didn't mean it"—Dominic gripped her thigh tighter—"when you told me your ring size, but I know I'm getting you to think about it, princess." He kissed her thigh even higher, his face closer to her pretty, little pussy. "How much longer do you think you're going to be able to last?"

Those little kisses almost caused Maria's head to fall back.

"You mean, how much longer are *you* going to be able to last?"

Dom licked the silky flesh in one, long stroke before he pulled away with a smile.

Crying internally when his lips left her thigh and he didn't continue, she leaned forward, placing one knee beside his thigh and lifted the other until she straddled his lap. It wasn't Maria who kissed him first; it was Dom who took her pouty lips as hostage.

Kissing Dominic felt like getting burned—it hurt to kiss him—but it only hurt worse pulling away from the flames. It was better to deal with the initial shock of pain until you got used to it. Controlling the flames hurt a hell of a lot less than being burned alive.

Dom slipped his hands under her dress and up her thigh to her ass, bringing the tight hem up to her lower waist, completely revealing her thin thong that concealed absolutely nothing. Taking his bottom lip to suck between two teeth, Maria found herself begging when her exposed ass cheeks were gripped tightly in each of his hands. "Please ...."

"Please, what?" Dom asked, wanting her to continue to beg.

Not only did Maria's body cry, but so did her voice, needing him to take the pain away. "Please, I can't take it anymore."

"I'm still not going to fuck you, princess."

When he took his hands off her ass, she thought he was going to stop them from continuing, but he placed his hand at the bottom of her neck, craning her neck upward to him.

Dominic placed a possessive kiss on her lips. "But I'll give you a taste."

Maria's next thought was utter bliss when she felt his other hand cover her pussy. Dominic began by petting her softly through the thin material until he slid his thumb under the lace to find her throbbing button. She laid her head on Dom's shoulder at the relief he was giving her, as he rubbed her in a motion that soothed the tingling while at the same time built the flame higher.

With one little finger, Dom was wrecking her resolve to be the seducer, becoming the seduced instead. When another finger slid inside her thong, she hissed a plea for, "More!"

"Here?" he asked with a smile, knowing damn well where.

Her nails bit into the arms of the chair to keep herself from tearing him to shreds at the overwhelming lust that was setting her pussy on fire, deepening when Dominic's other hand went to the heel of her shoe, spreading her thighs wider and higher. Twisting and turning as his fingers moved slickly over her had her reaching down to flick her tongue out to taste the side of his neck.

Her hips began pumping back hard and fast against the fingers that were plowing through her pussy. Dominic was making her hot as fuck. The ice princess was melting into a puddle, and all it took were two fingers in the right area to have her panting for more. "Dom …"

"Come for me, princess."

Four words and Maria began shuddering in an orgasm, ensnaring her in a web that she didn't want to escape. Taking several hot breaths, Maria kissed Dominic softly, thanking him before massaging her tongue over his bottom lip, wetting it.

My turn.

Maria's heated gaze stayed on him as she went to his jeans and started to lower herself. His tatted finger went to her chin, stopping her from moving.

"You don't want me to repay the favor?" she asked breathlessly, wetting her own bottom lip.

Dom kept his finger in place. "No, princess."

"But I want to." She went to lower herself again, practically imagining him in her mouth, but Dom held in her place.

"Thank you for the offer—" He gave her pouting lips a kiss.

"—but I don't want you touching me till after we're married."

"Why?" It didn't seem very fair that he couldn't get any relief.

His hazel gaze was unyielding. "I told you, princess. I'm not going to taint you."

Maria no longer fought him, resting her head on his forehead. She wanted to tell him that he could never give her his sins, that he wasn't saving her or keeping her soul from going to hell by letting her touch him. It would be impossible, because even though he didn't think of himself as pure, Maria could see that he was. He was kind, good, and true, and because of those exact characteristics she knew it was pointless to try to change his mind.

Admitting defeat, she needed a distraction before he drove her insane with need. If not, she was in for one hell of a long night.

"So"—Maria took one last, long, calming breath to bring her temperature back down—"do you still want that drink?"

IT'S A TRAP

"**M**aria, something tells me *I'm* not supposed to see what's behind that door." Dominic's jaw flexed, wondering why the fuck he stupidly got off the elevator with her on the basement floor. And if that wasn't suicidal enough, he fucking allowed himself to walk beside her as they went down a long, creepy hallway to a suspicious door.

She's not going to be happy until her ass gets me killed.

Maria had to knock on the door twice, making it even more fucking clear to him *that I'm not supposed to be here!*

The door opened a small crack as one of Dante's men exited to block the door, crossing his arms, physically telling them they weren't welcome. Well, one of them wasn't.

This shit isn't worth—

"Come on." Maria stared up at the bastard like he was dumb. "Do you really think your boss doesn't know who his own daughter is *dating*?"

Dominic's hand melted in hers. He liked the way those words sounded leaving her lips, making it all worth it. But then she ripped her hand from his.

"Fine." Maria opened her clutch. "I'm sure Dante would love to be bothered at this hour." As she unlocked her phone, the guard remained stoic, seeming call her bluff ….

Maria, think of something quick, he encouraged via telepathy, which they obviously didn't share, because he knew damn well she wasn't calling her father.

Watching her work the situation, all Dom knew was that Maria Caruso was everything he ever dreamed of—in a wet one or a romantic one—but she was going to be the death of him. He was sure of it. Never in his life had he ever tried to be more respectful to a woman, only for her to want pure, unadulterated sex. The woman was a sex-deprived lioness on the hunt for his dick, and all he wanted was a little ring on her finger to allow him to sleep at night with his morals intact, then wake up to her every day for the rest of his life. What was so wrong with that? Was that shit not romantic? Because it sure as hell felt romantic to him, but clearly not to the only goddamn woman on the planet who didn't have a romantic bone in her body.

Maria's version of romance was straight out of a porno, and while that was fucking great for him, it was only great *after* they were married. He could only turn down a woman like Maria so many times. Soon he was going to be the one that fucking broke.

Pressing his earpiece closer to his ear, the Caruso goon gave a nod and his okay, then opened the door for them.

Taking an internal sigh of relief that Maria's bluff wasn't called, Dominic wondered who or what had made him open the door.

His sigh was short-lived, since he only had more problems coming.

Dominic tried to keep his face impassive at the sight of an underground, illegal casino, but that all went to hell at the sight of the lingerie-clad women everywhere, serving the men playing at the tables.

"Maria"—Dominic took a long, hard swallow—"I don't want to be here."

"Oh please." She started dragging him into the dark place that smelled of cigars, booze, and women. "I'm not going to let my father hurt you."

Snapping his eyes to the floor, his voice snapped along with it. "I'm not worried about your father! I'm worried about you shoving a fucking heel into my neck!"

"Why would I do that?"

It's a trap. This is a motherfucking, goddamn trap, and he had let Maria walk him right into it—a strip club with his significant other, no less. Only, he wasn't with just any significant other; he was with Maria fucking shove-a-heel-into-your-neck-but-it's-okay-'cause-I'm-pretty Caruso.

He didn't know whether he was supposed to acknowledge the

half-naked women, or if he was supposed to pretend they weren't there. Contemplating which option wouldn't end in blood, he kept his mouth shut, letting her death grip on his hand lead him to an empty table.

This is a lose-lose situation, boys, he internally spoke to all men out there who might somehow be listening in for advice on what to do in this situation, because he just had to be the first to sail through these rocky waters—especially with a psychotic blonde who would have no problem killing a man in his sleep.

Hand to God, he didn't want to look at another woman besides her, either clothed or unclothed. Maria was far fucking enough for him to handle … in every department, looks, brains, personality. She ticked all his boxes except for one—the box that said she didn't want to see him dead, because clearly she did.

Either way, this was a fucking test to see how he'd react around other women, and she could play dumb all she wanted, but Dominic couldn't help wondering why he couldn't have fallen in love with someone "normal."

A normal woman would have tested him with the standard, "Hey, honey, do you think she's pretty?" Even the most moronic of men could answer that question correctly.

Throwing the man who repeatedly proposed to her into a room full of half-naked women was a new level of crazy. Even the fucking Pope wouldn't be able to keep from looking. He'd bet the straightest woman alive would be looking! Only a blind man would survive this situation, and Dom wasn't fucking blind.

He kept his eyes to the ground, blindly being led to the table, and had already felt three sets of breasts touch him in passing.

Sitting at an empty table next to Maria, he saw the dealer on the other side of the table was also wearing something scandalous.

"I'll take care of the table; you go on break," a woman told the dealer from behind.

Watching the first dealer leave, the woman behind her came into focu—

Holy Mother of God! I am going to die tonight, aren't I?

"Hey, buttercup." A woman with the biggest set of tits looked sweetly at Maria, picking up the deck of cards on the table. She began to shuffle at the speed of light as her eyes went to him. "And who is this you have with you?"

"This is Dominic." Maria glanced over at him with a smile. "Dominic, this is Sadie. She's a pit boss, but for me, she makes the return back to dealing."

Eyes, keep your eyes up! Dom gave the woman a brief nod.

"So"—Sadie gave Dominic a good once-over—"who is this? Mr. Prada or Mr. Choo?"

Obviously that was an inside joke between the two, but Dominic pretty much understood the reference, even though he wished he hadn't.

"I don't know. Which one do you think?"

Both women stared at him, trying to figure out which designer he reminded them of the most, while Maria didn't seem to mind that Sadie had mentioned Kayne in code name.

"I don't think either," Sadie finally concluded. "He's a red bottom man if I've ever seen one."

"You're right," Maria agreed, staring at him like he was a piece of meat. "He's definitely Mr. Louboutin."

Even though Dominic got it that Christian Louboutin was at the top of the shoe pyramid, and while he appreciated the comment, he was starting to feel a little warm in here.

Fuck, am I sweating?

"Cherry, I need some limes, a shot of tequila, and"—Sadie looked at Dom—"what would you lik—"

"Water."

Sadie gave him a pitiful look. "Make it two shots of tequila and two waters, Cherry."

With the woman going off and Sadie finishing shuffling, Dominic pulled out his money clip from his back pocket.

"I got this." Maria placed her hand over his, stopping him from pulling it out. "We'll split a thousand, Sadie, and put it on my father's tab."

"Absolutely no—"

Maria snatched the money clip full of cash and tossed it into her clutch before laying it back down on the table.

You're going to get me ki—

"You got it, babe." Sadie extracted the chips, placing five hundred worth in front of each of them.

You both *are going to get me killed.* Dominic glared at Maria, not touching the chips.

"You worry too much," Maria told him, putting a fifty dollar chip in the circle for him after doing hers. "I never lose at blackjack. By the time we leave, you'll be able to buy me whatever ring I want."

Giving her thigh a squeeze under the table, Dom was a weak man when it came to this woman. He knew he had D-U-M-B-A-S-S spelled out on his forehead, but he couldn't help feeling his heart swell when she talked about a ring, even though he knew she wasn't serious. Maria from a week ago wouldn't have been able to joke about something like that.

"Ring?" Sadie asked, dealing out the cards.

"Dominic asked me to marry him," Maria told her the information freely, like it wasn't a big deal.

"Several times, actually," he added at his own expense, wanting to remind his blonde seductress.

"Ah, so he's got body and brains," the pit boss complimented, not so much to him but to Maria. "I knew it would take a hell of a man to snatch you up, Maria, but damn …."

"Oh, we're not getting married," Maria told her as she tapped the table to hit her fifteen against Sadie's three.

Giving her another card, which was a measly two, they continued to speak like he wasn't fucking here. "You turned him down?"

Again, Dominic was the one to answer. "Several times, actually."

Maria and Sadie gave slight chuckles as their waitress came back.

Cherry stood between them, setting their drinks down. Dom didn't like the way the woman rubbed her breasts on his shoulder as she set them down, so he moved slightly to the side, out of her reach, to give her the hint, and even though he kept his face to his cards, he could feel her lingering stare.

Reading the room, Dominic understood that was probably the norm around here. They needed their tips and to feed their families, but if she did it again after his silent warning, he would call the woman ou—

"He ain't here for you or any other bitch I got working here," Sadie hissed, scolding the woman and making it clear not only to Cherry but to anyone else who looked at him or rubbed up on him in passing. "You will bring them their drinks, and that's it. I will slap the shit out of you if I see you touch or continue to stare at Maria's man like that again."

If Dom had had any water in his mouth, he would have spit it out. It was no wonder Sadie and Maria got along.

Cherry's eyes immediately went to Maria's. "I-I'm sorry. I didn't know."

Leaning over, Maria turned Dominic's face, grabbing his chin with her fingers so she could place a hard kiss on his lips. It took his breath away, and if he hadn't already, he would have fallen in love with her at the next words out of her mouth….

"Now you do." Maria gave the waitress a warning look.

Maria's man. He fucking liked the sound of that. He gave her thigh another squeeze under the table.

"Yes. Sorry." Cherry nodded before walking off, making it known she wouldn't make that mistake again. No woman who worked down there would make that mistake again.

Dominic finally relaxe—

Maria shot back her tequila in a second, then sucked the lime into her mouth in another.

Dear God . . . Watching her suck that lime until there was nothing left made him adjust in his seat. She was making him pay for not letting her wrap her pretty mouth around his dick, and Dominic silently asked God why he had morals in the first place. He wasn't a fucking saint!

Taking a few giant gulps of his water, he waved to stand on his twenty.

"So, why aren't you marrying him?" Sadie asked, getting back to their conversation about him that didn't particularly include him talking.

"You know how I feel about marriage," Maria told her with a flip of her hair. "I just want him to fuck m—"

Dom slipped his hand over her loud mouth, whispering to her quietly, "Let's not do this here, princess."

She already had an audience of men at the other tables trying to listen in, as well as the women working, who were still shocked Maria Caruso had come here with a man.

He didn't let her mouth go until she silently nodded.

A smiling Sadie flipped the card under her three to reveal a ten, right before she dealt herself an eight.

Watching her father's money that Maria made them gamble get taken with the house's perfect twenty-one, he gave Maria a death glare. "I thought you said you didn't lose," Dom ground out. There was no way in hell he was going to touch these chip—

"She just got lucky," Maria assured him, sliding the chips she gave him in the circle and making him bet again. "Are you going to drink this?"

Watching her point to the second tequila shot, he wanted to tell her, "*hell no*," but he went with a simple, "No." There was no way he'd feel comfortable drinking down here. Alcohol would make his eyelids heavy, and Maria wasn't going to catch his eyes slipping below the neck unless they were on her, which he never hid anyway.

Not fucking her—because God knew he wanted to—was the only way he was ever getting Maria to marry him, and he *was* getting her to marry him. Maria was his future wife, and she had to get the fuck over it.

Plus, he wasn't going to give her his sin—

Maria sucked the lime as if for dear life after downing the second shot.

Fuck me, he groaned inwardly, the tightness in his jeans becoming unbearable. *Could this night get any worse?*

Sadie dealt them new cards, but the hand was short-lived as she flipped over an ace with her ten down.

Dominic was in for a long fucking night.

MARIA THE DRUNK VIRGIN

"I'm sorry, *honey, but it's* time for me to cut you off," Sadie said when Maria asked to take out another thousand from her father's account.

Giving the pit boss a silent thank you, Dom took the shot of tequila from Maria's hand before she could throw it back. "Yes, I think we've had enough fun for one night."

A very intoxicated Maria pouted. "But we haven't gotten enough to pay for my ring yet."

"Oh, that's all right, princess," he assured her. "I have a feeling there won't be much of a wedding if we don't stop gambling with money that isn't ours."

"We can always"—she hiccupped—"gamble with Lucca's money instead."

"As fun as that sounds"—Dominic helped her ass out of the chair—"it's time to go."

"Oh my God!" Maria gasped, looking at a worker pass by before she ran after her. "I love your shoes."

Shaking his head, he kept his eyes on her while he picked up her unattended clutch off the table. Opening it, he retrieved his money clip full of cash. Counting out hundreds, he placed the thousand Maria took from her father down on the table.

Sadie took the cash with a smile.

Placing a few more bills on the table, he slid them over to her.

"Drinks are on the house." Sadie slid the money back to him. "And if you tip Cherry or any other woman down here ever, they could get the wrong idea."

Understanding that she was probably right, he slid the money back to her. "For you. Thank you for giving Maria a good time."

The pit boss hadn't made him feel uncomfortable when she stared at him or commented on his looks. It hadn't been to impress him; it was to compliment Maria. And if it somehow made the woman he wanted to marry actually contemplate marrying him, then Sadie was worth every dime he had.

Sadie placed her hand on the cash, sliding it back over more seriously this time. "Thank you, but the only money I take is from Mr. Caruso."

After a moment, Dominic nodded. Then, picking up the cash, he put it back in his clip and slid it back into his jean pocket.

"Did you see how pretty her shoes were?" Maria asked him,

coming back after getting the info on the shoes. "She was so pretty, too, wasn't she?"

Taking the shot he hadn't let Maria drink, he welcomed the burn down his throat. "Not as pretty as you, princess."

Honestly, Maria would have been offended on the woman's behalf if he had said she wasn't attractive, so he went with the truth.

Sadie gave him a sympathetic look. "Have a good night … Mr. Luciano."

Dom was surprised to find she knew who he was. "You, too."

"And Maria, honey." Sadie waited until Maria focused on her to give her a piece of advice. "Marry him."

Smiling to himself, Dominic took a speechless Maria by the waist as he navigated them out of the underground space. Somehow, even a drunk Maria was still able to walk on skinny heels. He just had to make sure it was in a straight line.

Pressing the elevator button, he dragged her in, then hit the combination of buttons Maria had once revealed to him before the door closed to take them to the top.

"I had *so* much fun." Maria slipped her arms under his jacket to wrap around his waist. "Now we can have even more fun."

"No." He laughed, showing his dimples and giving her the deep kiss a drunk Maria wanted. "But I'm glad you had fun, princess. I'm shocked you managed to get me in."

"Oh, I didn't." Maria turned in his arms to put her back to his chest. Waving at the camera, she was giving the man watching a show. "Ass kisser did."

Dom stared at where Maria waved. "I see."

The door sliding open brought his thoughts back to getting Maria in her bed safely.

Waving Maria's clutch at the man who guarded the top floor last time, the Caruso soldier looked even more shocked than he was before at the state she was in.

Quickly getting her to her door, he pulled her phone out to unlock it, feeling the stares of the concerned soldier. Managing to open the door with a now limp Maria, he waited until they were inside before he swept her off her feet.

"Woo!" Maria giggled, wrapping her arms around his neck.

Cradling her in his arms, he took Maria through the living room and up the steps, as it was much safer for the both of them that way. And even though she had absolutely tried to drive him nuts tonight, he still had a smile on his face at seeing how happy she was.

A laughing and smiling Maria slowly disappeared. Touching a dimple with her finger, her tone went serious. "Have I told you how handsome you are?"

"No." Dom laughed, kicking open her bedroom door. "That must mean you're drunker than I thought."

Maria tightened her arms around his neck, pressing her breasts into him. She kissed his dimple sweetly at first until the tip of her tongue filled the hole. "Or just the right amount of drunk."

Oh God, he loved the way that felt, but still, he let his morals win out.

"You do know I'm the one who has to be drunk in order for

you to take advantage of me, right?"

Being plopped down onto her champagne silk sheets, Maria laughed even harder. "Oh."

Shaking his head, Dominic took a seat on the edge of the bed and began taking off her tall heels. Doing so, he noticed how much brighter the white polish was. "You must've gotten your feet done after you left this morning, huh?"

"Now they're as soft as a baby's bottom," she assured him.

"I see," he said after getting the second one off. "Did you do that for me?"

Maria proudly raised up on her elbows. "Yep."

"That was very sweet of you."

"I'm a very giving person," she hiccupped the words out.

Uh-huh. Dom tried not to laugh at how cute she was being. Drunk Maria might just be his favorite Maria.

Seeing the lotion on the bedside table, he picked it up to squeeze out a good size amount. "Well, we can't let it be all for nothing."

"Oh my God," Maria groaned, letting her head fall back once his strong hands began rubbing the thick, white lotion into her foot. "You know you're making it very hard to keep turning you down."

"Then don't," he said simply, working it into the sole of her foot.

"But I told you I don't believe in marriage."

Dom at least liked her stubbornness. "Well, if you don't believe in marriage, then I'm sure you believe in divorce, which you can do at any time, princess."

"Hmm …" Her brows furrowed, clearly not thinking about

that option, but she quickly shook it out of her head. "I'd still rather skip to the fun part."

Laughing, he squeezed more lotion out. "Oh, I know, princess."

When his hands went to her neglected foot, Maria fell back off her elbows, falling onto the soft bed. "I think you might just be the perfect man, Dominic Luciano."

"Obviously, not perfect enough," he whispered under his breath, rubbing her precious feet that he adored between his hands.

Maria raised back on her elbows. She was still very much intoxicated, but it appeared, for a moment, that she wasn't when she turned serious. "Did you really mean it when you told me I could do and be anything I wanted if I married you?"

Dominic held her hazy emerald eyes in his, making her an oath. "I would never lie to you, princess."

He could see on her face; she wanted to believe it, but a part of her just couldn't.

Falling back on the bed again, she huffed, trying to hide the sadness in her voice. "You may say that now, but all men treat me the same in the end."

Rubbing the last bit of lotion into her heel, Dominic stood slowly, and removed his jacket. "Do you know why I wear this coat every day?"

Maria shook her head, seeming to have been curious of it herself.

"I learned a hard lesson many years ago." He gripped the leather in his hands. "I took it off a dead man who betrayed me, and I've worn it every day since to remind me to never trust a soul again. And I haven't …" Dominic held his most prized possession out to her. "Until now."

Maria's eyes wildly stared up at him and to his outstretched jacket.

"Take it," he encouraged her.

"Dominic, I don—"

"I want you to keep it, and when you decide to marry me, for however long that might take, then and only then can you give it back."

Reaching out for the jacket, she tenderly took the soft leather in her hands, as it was a clear sign of his trust. Dominic wanted her to trust him as much as he trusted her, and when he got his jacket back, he expected her trust with it.

Holding it to her, Maria inhaled the fiery scent it carried. "Thank you."

"You're welcome." He gave her a quick sight of his dimples, but it was regretfully time to go.

Pulling back the covers for her, Maria's happiness faded. "You're leaving me?"

"That's usually what happens at the end of a date, princess."

"Not at the end of good ones," said Maria the drunk virgin, who obviously had no fucking experience at all, but yet appeared to still know exactly what to do as she went to her knees to rub a hand over his thin-shirted chest. "You told me you would stay."

"No," Dominic corrected her, placing his hands on her hips, "I told you I would stay if you told me how you knew about John Wayne and Clint Eastwood in old westerns, and you haven't."

"Well, I can't give up my sources." She pouted.

"Okay." Dom captured her bottom lip between his teeth for a tender bite. "I wasn't staying, anyway, because I don't trust you to not con me into fucking you when you're drunk."

"Smart man." Maria darted her tongue out to give a playful lick to his lips. "Anyway, I can just convince you to fuck my brains out instead?"

Jesus Christ, his dick somehow went harder every time she talked dirty. Even though his mind said yes, he regretfully said the word, "No."

"Okay," Maria grumbled when he tried to shove her under the covers. "Can I at least take this dress off first?"

Taking a cooling breath, he nodded as he went to turn around.

"I need you to help me," Maria said pitifully, pathetically trying to reach the zipper in the back. Giving him her back, she looked back over her shoulder through full lashes. "Please?"

God, the woman knew exactly what she was doing, but Dominic would help, although it'd probably be another fucking thing he would regret.

Sweeping her soft, golden hair off her back and over her shoulder, Dominic slowly pulled the tiny zipper down. His breath caught in his throat when he made it to the middle of her back to find she wasn't wearing a bra, and his breathing only got worse when the zipper reached the bottom of her waist.

The line that went down the small of her back, he wanted to desperately run his tongue down, but when he watched her shimmy down the dress to reveal her thong, Dominic had a whole new dream come to his mind.

The thoughts he had about Maria were dirtier than hers, and that said a lot. It was everything he could do to keep his hands to his sides, when all he wanted was to ram her head in the pillow as he fucked her from behind.

He was jealous of the nude thong, wanting to delve his tongue between her perfect ass cheeks as he licked the length of the string from her ass to her pussy.

Still on her knees, she unwound the dress from the bottom of her legs before she picked up Dom's jacket, holding the warm side to her as she slowly turned back around.

Knowing her nearly naked body was under his coat was a dream that sent his heart racing. Dom was strong ... but he wasn't that strong.

Maria crawled up to him, not stopping until her body was plastered to his. She let go of the coat that held up between them, so she could wrap her arms back around his neck. One wrong move, and the jacket would slip, then there would be nothing separating her body from his.

Taking her lips in a hot kiss, he dueled her tongue with his as he felt his resolve begin to slip along with the jacket ....

"Please, Maria," Dominic groaned as he pulled his lips from hers and held her body tightly to him so the jacket wouldn't fall. "I don't have the strength to turn you down anymore."

With his forehead resting on hers, mixed with their heavy

breaths, Maria understood what he was asking, and even though it was clear she didn't want to do it, she let go of his neck and grabbed the jacket, then pulled back.

Regretting it already, Maria lay down on the bed in a sexually frustrated huff. "You owe me for this. *Big time.*"

Staring down at her on the silky sheets with nothing but his jacket covering her, Dominic definitely regretted it more when he covered her with the comforter to tuck her into bed.

Getting his thoughts under control, along with his self-control, he sat back down on the edge of her bed. "I do," he said, seeing how pissed she was. Dom smiled as he leaned down to steal a sweet kiss from her lips, "How about dinner tomorrow at Kat's? She invited me to come over to spend time with her and—" Dom hated to say the word.

"Drago." Maria helped him out with a smile, taking mercy on him from saying *husband.*

"So, will you come with me?" he asked again when she didn't answer.

"Are you sure I should come? It's not a family thing?"

"Don't worry." Dom stole another kiss. "You will be soon."

If there was one thing Maria liked, it was obviously confidence.

Stealing some of her own kisses, Maria finally agreed, seeing how important it was to him. "I will, but that doesn't exactly make up for you not fucking me."

"I'll see if I can make it up to you somehow," he promised.

"I have an idea how you can make it up right now." Maria

grabbed his hair, pulling him into another deep kiss that Dom had to stop.

Exasperated and drunk, Maria threw her head back on the bed. "What's wrong with me? What have you done to me?"

Dominic couldn't help but laugh, pushing the strands of golden hair out of her face. He felt a little bad for her. "Princess, you're horny. I know you might be foreign to the feeling, but you just need a good fuck."

Maria went to open her mouth—

"After we're married," he concluded.

"Fine," Maria hiccupped, only giving in because the alcohol was now starting to cause her lids to fall.

"Goodnight, Maria." Dom gave one last tender kiss on her lips. "I love you."

Maria's eyelids fell completely, barely able to manage the words, "Goodnight, Domin …"

Smiling at a sleeping Maria, he let the back of his fingers rub her cheeks for a moment, not wanting to leave her. He knew he had it bad for her, but he didn't think it was this possible to fall so hard for someone. However, Dom should have known he would. He was a man who, when he loved, he loved hard.

Picking up her heels and dress, he regretfully left her side. Quietly, he went to another door in her room that he knew must've been a closet, but jeez, he didn't think it would look like *this*. Half of it was ceiling to floor in clothes and the other half was ceiling to floor in purses and shoes. If this was her closet here, he wondered what her closet at her family home looked like.

Dom laid her dress down on a velvet bench in the middle of the closet that he figured was where she put on her shoes before he went to put her heels in the only spot that wasn't filled.

While he could look in here all night of the things he looked forward to seeing her wear, he took particular interest in her heels. He picked out about five or so pairs that he would be asking to see her in before he went to leave.

About to turn the closet light off, his eye was caught by the only black item he could see. Walking over to it, Dom pulled the hanger off the rack to take a look at it.

Smiling, Dominic still somehow found a way to love Maria even more … while staring at the suit jacket that he had given her when he had left her in the freezer.

Maria might've claimed to have loved Kayne, but it was *his* jacket hanging in her closet.

HELLO, AGAIN...

Closing the door to **Maria's** penthouse quietly, Dominic walked a foot in the other direction and beat on a door. He didn't treat the person who lived there with the same respect.

When the door opened, it appeared even the boogieman slept, as Lucca emerged, promising death with his eyes. "You better have a good fucking reason to wake me u—"

"Four?" Dominic roared, uncaring about the underboss's precious sleep. "*Four* of your men have bit the dust protecting her, and you're fucking letting Maria prance around Kansas City wherever she pleases?"

Lucca crossed his arms over his chest. "In case you fucking missed it, she hasn't talked to me since I told her I offed her last boyfriend." He gave him a silent promise he could do the same to boyfriend number two. "She doesn't want my protection anymore."

Dom spat at him furiously, "That doesn't mean you fucking listen to her!"

"If you feel that way, why don't you get one of *your* fucking men to watch her."

When Lucca went to shut his door, Dominic put his hand out, stopping him. "I can't. I promised her I wouldn't," he admitted, looking defeated before pleading. "She won't listen to reason that it will never be safe for her not to have her back watched."

Understanding what he was asking, Lucca gave him a pitiful look. "And you think I can?"

"Yes." Dom nodded. "She respects you. She will listen. I don't want her suffocated again. I just want someone to watch her back." He would never want Maria to have to go back to listening to what every man in her life told her to do. He only wanted her safe because, whether she liked it or not, she was born into royalty.

Lucca raised a brow. "You haven't talked to Angel lately, have you?"

Frustrated, Dominic looked at the underboss, confused and questioning if he was even listening. "What does my brother have to fucking do wit—"

"If you had"—Lucca stopped him with his cold voice—"then you would know he's been following her."

Oh. Dom's fears calmed. Staring at the underboss, he gave him a grateful look. "Thank you."

"No problem." Lucca smiled, watching him walk away, now

slightly embarrassed. "I'd be thanking your brother, though. Angel told me Maria's been a real pain in the ass, running after you."

Looking back over his shoulder, he gave the underboss a smile of his own. "I'll do that."

Hearing the door slam behind him, Dominic walked down the hall, glad he had been able to ruin Lucca's night.

When he got to the elevator, he could hear the jingle of keys before he even turned the corner.

"Hello again… Dominic," Sal greeted him as he stood there, waiting for his arrival.

He nodded, entering the elevator. "Hello."

Sal pressed the buttons to take them to the casino floor, and the doors slowly slid to a close. "Did you have a nice night?"

"I did," Dom said, watching the numbers fall.

Sal gave a quick twirl to his keys. "Good."

Sliding his eyes to him, Dom dared to ask the question since the second he'd been allowed into the underground casino. "Why'd you do it?"

"I didn't do it for you." Sal spoke over the clang of metal. "I did it for her."

Surprised, Dom couldn't help but remind him of a little fact. "But she calls you an ass kisser."

"Has she told you how her father hoped for us to marry when we were just kids?"

"No …" Dom whispered, not knowing how to feel about that fact. "And this has to do with her calling you an ass kisser how?"

A slow smile touched Sal's lips. "Well, I just thought you'd know better than anyone that siblings fight."

Dominic smiled himself. Sal didn't tell him that information about Dante wanting them to marry to make him jealous. He told him to let him know Maria and Sal thought of each other as nothing more than brother and sister.

Dominic took a step forward, standing in front of the brother whom he never got to know, and he held his hand out.

"I hope Dante does get his wish after all." The great Salvatore shook his hand. "A son of Lucifer should marry his daughter."

"I hope so," Dom told him as the elevator door opened.

Dropping their hands, Dom exited, but as the door slid closed Dom stopped it.

Pushing the elevator open with his hand, he looked at the man who shared his same blood. "I didn't know who you were," he promised with shame in his eyes, remembering every single time he had passed a little homeless boy on the street. "Lucifer didn't tell me until after I met you and, by then, I knew you were better off here."

Staring into the blackish-blue orbs, Dom thought he would see hatred in them; it was what he deserved. But Sal spoke the words that set his soul free from the one thing Dominic had yet been able to forgive himself for.

"I know."

The sun shining through her tall windows had Maria's hands going to her throbbing head. It took her a minute of waking up until she smelled Dominic's fiery scent, along with the warmth of wool wrapping her up under the covers.

Reaching under, she found Dominic's jacket that she had slept with, as she began to slowly remember the night before. It was one of the best nights she ever had, and she could only compare it to one ...

Maria picked up her phone. Dialing, she held the phone up to her ear with a shaky hand as she listened to a ghost.

"This is Kayne Evans, leave a message, and I'll get back to you as soon as I can."

Beep.

Holding the jacket to her furiously, she tried not to cry. "I trusted you ...."

Hearing the phone ding in his nightstand, Dominic wanted to pretend that he hadn't heard it. He wished he had thrown the phone out. That way, he would have never known the woman he was in love with was still in love with another man.

Dominic knew what Maria was doing. She had put their relationship strictly on a sexual level and was too afraid to put the little emotions she carried back at stake. Her first love had hurt her, and now Dom was paying the price. All Maria was willing to give was her body in order not to chance feeling that wretched pain again.

When Maria had asked why she wanted him so badly, he didn't have the heart to tell her the truth. The words would have hurt her, just as much as him.

Staring at the nightstand, Dominic felt like a sick bastard for keeping the phone.

And he was an even sicker one now as he listened to the message that he knew would only break his heart.

Dominic would just have to keep praying for the day Maria stopped calling Kayne.

DINNER FROM HELL

"**W**ho the hell gets up at this time of day?" Maria muttered, trying not to trigger another round of pain by making her vocal cords work.

"It's seven p.m.," Dom informed her as they walked the short distance to Kat and Drago's place.

"I think I'm getting sick," she complained, trying to focus, despite the drilling going on under her scalp.

"It's called a hangover, princess."

"What I'm experiencing isn't a hangover; it's more like a prelude to death." Mistakes had been made. The first was using alcohol to curtail her fascination with Dom's male parts, after he refused to budge on his stance of premarital sex. The second mistake she made was opening her door when he had come to get her tonight, and at the moment, the final seemed the worst: never buying a pair of flats.

Not even Dom's dimples could soothe her pain. "I think it was tequila shot number five that I warned you—"

"Try telling me that before shot number five next time," Maria said through a fake smile. Grabbing the crook of his arm to help balance herself, they reached Kat and Drago's apartment.

"What are you doing?" he asked.

"Trying to get my balance."

"As much as I love those heels on you, princess"— Dom steadied her by holding onto her waist—"it might've been better to have picked a pair closer to the floor."

His suggestion was met with a feral glare. "Dom, sweetie, do you want to die tonight?"

Touching her forehead and cheeks, he grew concerned. "You feel that bad?"

"Yes." Maria felt only the tiniest bit bad about giving him a pain-filled glance. She tried to pull off a helpless look, hoping it would get her in his pants. "I'm only able to stand here with you because you asked me to have dinner with you and your sister."

"Maria"—Dominic's eyes sliced her open—"are you trying to use the sympathy card to lure me into bed with you?"

"Would it work?" Cunning eyes stared at him, watching his reaction.

"Nope," he told her without an ounce of sympathy. "I gave you my ultimatum."

"Why give in when I'm enjoying negotiating with you?" she cooed.

Dominic knocked on the door to end the inevitable conversation, showing what he thought of her negotiating skills.

Kat must have been waiting for their arrival, since she immediately opened the door. However, Maria couldn't miss the shock on her face.

Did he not tell her I was coming . . .?

Kat smiled, keeping her—obviously curious—thoughts to herself. "Come in. Dinner's almost ready."

Maria had clearly been wrong. Kat had been told; she just hadn't believed it.

Trust me, I don't either.

Coming inside their home, Maria stood to the side as Kat gave Dom a hug before closing the door. Watching the brother and sister together was an eye opener for her. The affection between the two was apparent.

"Where's your jacket?" Kat asked, finding it strange to see her brother without it.

"I left it at home," Dom said before changing the subject. "What's for dinner?"

The excitement on the baby-pink-haired woman was apparent. "Your favorite; parmesan chicken with lemon rice."

Kat, what are you doing? Maria internally screamed at her, as Katarina was the only girl in her friend group who had been wifed up, but ironically didn't act it. Now it appeared her friend was getting loved up more and more every day.

Moving farther into the apartment, Drago, however, seemed taken back she'd been invited to dinner. "What the hell is she doing here?" Drago grumbled.

Maria flipped her hair behind her shoulder. "I came to try your wife's cooking."

"You've never wanted to fucking try it before."

How long has she been cooking for him? Katarina might've been more domesticated than she thought.

"I was scared she might've poisoned it and, well ... you're still alive, unfortunately."

Drago's eyes went a furious shade of red.

With his eyes dancing between the two, Dominic leaned over, quietly asking Maria, "I take it you don't like him either?"

"No," Maria and Drago answered in unison.

Laughing and ignoring them, Katarina walked back into the kitchen to finish cooking.

Oh, she's good. It was obvious his precious little wife wasn't that domesticated after all. She still had some bite left in her.

Getting the picture himself, Drago looked at Kat. "Why is she here?"

Dominic whispered into her ear privately, "I knew I fell in love with you for a reason."

Kat's big brother might put up with Drago, but he still didn't like him.

"Oh God." Drago looked like he was about to gag. "I need a minute ..."

Maria smiled at him sweetly as he walked out of the apartment. "Oopsie," she said with a laugh, knowing Dom's whispered confession was overheard.

Going over to Kat, Maria slid herself up on the counter to get a good look at her partner in crime. "Conveniently forgot to mention that I was coming as your brother's date, huh?"

"It must've slipped my mind," Kat commented innocently as she pretended to wipe sweat off her brow. "It's so hard being a wife."

"You know what?" Dominic backed away from the kitchen slowly. "I'm gonna go see if I can get him to come back."

"Take your time!" Maria yelled as the door flung open.

As soon as it closed, both girls laughed until they cried.

"Her?" Drago asked when he saw Dominic come out into the hallway. "Are you fucking crazy?"

"What's wrong with Maria?" The warning in Dominic's voice told Drago to tread carefully.

Drago, however, didn't give a fuck, giving him a warning of his own. "I know you might think you're a bad motherfucker, Dominic, but that girl is going to chew you up and spit you out."

"Probably," Dom agreed. "But what do you care?"

"I've taken my fair share to protect that woman, and I'm grateful to live the tale, but I have never seen Maria let a man stand that close to her, so that means she must like your ass too." Drago looked close to tears. "I already have to deal with her as Kat's friend, but I don't need to see her at the Luciano family functions. That was my only freedom from her."

Dominic laughed now. He just got a two for one. Not only was he going to get himself a wife, but he was going to make Drago rue the day he ever picked Katarina.

Drago waited patiently until he stopped laughing then said, "You know what?" He was the one to laugh now. "Good luck."

"The way Drago feels about you, I'd almost be concerned that he might actually like you deep down, but no." Kat laughed, wiping a tear away. "He just doesn't like you."

Maria laughed, wiping her own tear, "Ugh, when I was growing up, my father used to tell me this bullshit that, when a boy picked on you, it meant he had a crush on you. It used to make me so mad."

"Not Dom." Kat shook her head with a smile at an old memory. "I had a teacher tell me that once because a boy wouldn't stop picking on me at school, and my brother got so mad, when he dropped me off in the morning, he came into my class and told the teacher, very loudly, 'that boy is not picking on my sister because he likes her, he's picking on her because he's a fucking bully.' My teacher got so scared and said she would handle it. And, I kid you not, on the way out, Dom stared at the boy who wouldn't leave me alone and said, 'I already did.' And he was right; that little asswipe never picked on me again."

"D-Dominic told you that?" Maria asked in disbelief, feeling her chest get tighter. "He did that?"

"Yep," Katarina said proudly. "After that point, I learned to stand up for myself, but I don't think I would have if I hadn't seen him do it first."

"You and Dominic are close, aren't you?" It was too obvious to miss. She had seen him with his brothers, but with Kat, he was different. Maria didn't think it would be possible for a man like that to exist, but *he really is the perfect man.* It was either the fact he had watched Lucifer abuse women, or having to care for a sister at a young age, or maybe a combination of both that made him that way.

"I'm close to all my brothers, but Dom has a special place in my heart," Kat agreed. "He's been more like a father to me."

Considering who Katarina's real father was, even Maria's cold soul shuddered at what it must have been like living in the same home with the deranged madman.

"When I think of Dom, a father figure doesn't come to my mind."

Katarina suddenly stopped what she was doing. "You really do like him, don't you?"

"I think so," Maria whispered, shocking herself. "Thinking about giving me a sisterly warning?" she asked, wondering if Kat approved, since they'd become good friends in a short amount of time.

"No." Kat laughed. "I want Dom to be as happy as I am, and he looks it with you, Maria."

That made Maria feel fuzzy inside, but she couldn't help herself from asking, "Are you? You didn't exactly pick out Drago on your own."

"I didn't, but I also knew Dom would never have let me marry him if he had any doubts about the type of man Drago was."

Maria felt bad to say the next part. "Dominic didn't have any more choice than you were given, Katarina."

Kat gave her an assured look. "Dom is protecting all of us. If I didn't marry Drago, then it would have put my other brothers in danger. He would never put one over the other. We all serve our family, and each of my brothers had paid their dues. By marrying Drago I paid mine. For the first time, I was given the opportunity to be a solution instead of a problem that had to be protected from Lucifer. Without Dom, I wouldn't even be alive; Lucifer wanted *soldiers*. I was no more to him than an annoyance that often kept his best soldier too occupied. I lost count of the beatings Dom took for me, or Angel and Matthias anytime one of us set him off."

"Nothing personal, but I'm glad he's dead," Maria said, trying to conceal the tightening in her chest from hearing Kat talk about her brother that way.

Slipping off the counter, a strange thought occurred to Maria. "Did Cassius ... ever take beatings for you?"

"No," Katarina told her after a few silent moments. "He didn't."

Seeing that she offered no more information, Maria quickly changed the subject but was sure to keep her voice down to a whisper in case the boys were about to come back in. "Can you tell me more about Dominic's old westerns?"

Laughing, Kat wasn't able to divulge any more information for her to scare Dom with about her old western knowledge.

"Good?" Maria asked Drago with a raised brow when the men walked back inside. She was offering him a truce ... at least for the night.

"Good," Drago accepted, clearly in a better mood than when he left, making Maria wonder what Dominic said.

While Drago helped his wife finish up, Dom volunteered to set the table, and when Maria went to help, he made her sit down, knowing she still had a hangover.

Ugh! Everything he did was making her contemplate saying *fuck it* and marrying him already. *He's right, there's always divorce.*

Sitting there, Maria didn't miss the way Dominic questioned Katarina about her day and activities. Big brother was finding out for himself that Drago was taking care of Kat.

She watched Dominic take notice of Drago, measuring how relaxed he was and unconcerned about what Kat would disclose.

"Dinner's ready. Everyone have a seat." Kat proudly set a serving platter on the table.

It was then Maria realized that Katarina didn't go through all this trouble to just cook for her husband; she went through all this trouble to make him happy. Like when Lucca did it for Chloe. Maria obviously preferred the societal roles to be reversed and to have a man in the kitchen, but she now understood. If Katarina was happy, then Maria was happy, and that meant so was Dominic.

Staring at the dish, she had to give Kat credit. It looked like a picture in a magazine. Maria sat next to Dominic at the table and waited for the men to attack the food, but when they looked at her, she realized they were letting her serve herself first.

Spooning a small portion of the parmesan chicken on her plate, she passed the platter to Dominic before she took a helping of the lemon rice.

Politely, she waited until everyone had filled their plates before she took a bite. *Oh God*, it was almost as bad as the ketchup eggs. She had to count to ten to give herself the courage to swallow.

"It's delicious, Kat."

Maria stared at Drago's plate to make sure they were both eating the same food. *Excuse m*—

"I don't know how you do it," Dominic complimented. "It gets better every time you make it."

The fuck? The food was so bad she guessed there was no place to go but up.

Blushing from the compliments, Kat gave her a questioning glance. "Maria? How's the food?"

Was something wrong with her taste buds? The dish tasted like soured lemons, and that was the best part of the dish. The rice wasn't done, and the chicken was hard as a brick.

Maria shoved another spoonful in her mouth to keep from answering. "Mmmhmm …."

See? Maria could be nice. She was sure if Dominic and Drago weren't in the room, she would have told Kat it tasted fucking nasty, but she didn't. Hell, she was sure Dominic would have told his sister, as he had no problem admitting DeeDee's food was gross. Instead, she literally had to eat her words.

"I'm glad you like it." A happy Kat continued eating. "It's easy to make. I'll give you the recipe if you want?"

433

Maria gave her a thumbs-up, afraid she would vomit up what she had just forced down. Had the alcohol she drank last night fried her tongue, making it unable to differentiate between good and fucking vile?

"I wanted to make Drago's favorite, but he convinced me that Dom would be disappointed."

Maria gulped down half the water in her glass. "What's your favorite, Drago?"

Maybe if she started talking, no one would notice she wasn't eating.

Drago talked with a big mouthful, "Deconstructed apple cherry ham steak."

What the fuck?! Drawing a blank at what she could say in response to anything deconstructed, she could only watch as both Drago and Dom refilled their plates.

Taking tiny bites and refilling her glasses twice, Maria was able to get through the meal with the silent promise that she was fucking murdering Dominic after they got out of there. This was payback for last night, and she knew it.

One thing was for sure, she was right when she said Katarina was poisoning Drago. Maria started to feel a little bad for the man she despised.

"You're in for a treat tonight, Maria," Kat said, rising from the table. "I made Dom's favorite dessert, too." Going to the refrigerator, Kat came back with a pie. "Grasshopper pie."

She would bite a fucking bullet before she was taking a bite of the gorgeous pie that Katarina was cutting into large slices.

Maria hastily shook her head. "None for me. You know I don't do too many carbs, and I've been on a diet."

Katarina looked at her in disappointment, which had both men looking at her like she had kicked a helpless kitten.

Oh my God! Maria cried internally and almost broke, but thankfully, her bitchy side saved the fucking day. "What's in it …? So I can count to see if I have any calories left." If lemon was an ingredient, she was out.

Kat started naming them off. "Chocolate cookies …"

I like cookies.

"Butter …"

Butter always makes everything better.

"Half-and-half."

Half of what?

"Heavy cream and marshmallows."

Hmm …..

How could Kat screw up something that sounded so tasty? If she hadn't just eaten the fucking dinner from hell, Maria would have already taken a slice of the pie that the men were scarfing down.

Kat continued, "It has two liquors …"

Sign me up for that bad boy.

"Crème of cacao …"

That's chocolate, right?

Eye-fucking the pie, Maria started to reach for her dessert plate.

"Crème de Menthe."

She would never doubt her bitchy side again. "Shoot, that would make me way over." Maria pretended to act bummed, but she continued to sell it even more. "And after last night, I swore to Dominic I'd never touch alcohol again."

"You sure?"

"Oh yes," Maria told a precious Kat before she smiled graciously. "Since it's Dom's favorite, let him have him have my slice."

"There's enough for each of them to have another slice," Kat said, giving each of the men more. "I don't like the taste. It reminds me of mouthwash. DeeDee used to make it for us when we were growing up, then stopped making it."

Gee, I wonder why . . ..

"I only started making it because Dom enjoyed it when she did, and Drago loves it too." Katarina shrugged as if there were no accounting for men's taste.

When the men stopped eating, Maria would have laughed at their pained expressions if she still didn't have that fucking sour lemon taste in her mouth. While she had eaten the food to be polite for Dominic's sake—and, to be real, she wasn't sure she hadn't been on the fritz because of the alcohol she had consumed the night before—there was only one reason the men resumed scarfing the pie down—pure love for Kat.

Maria knew she was fucked when Dominic asked for the last slice of pie and Drago began to turn a sickly green. He was taking the bullet for the team. How could the mighty be toppled by something as simple as grasshopper pie?

Lowering her gaze to her ring finger, it felt . . . empty.

Damn.

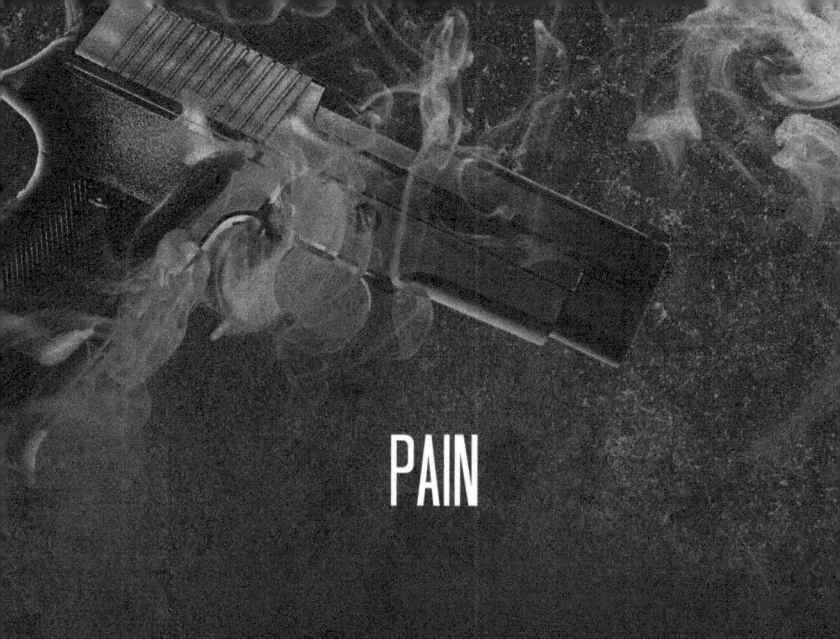

PAIN

As soon as the door shut, Maria's smile dropped as she glared at Dominic and furiously whispered at him, "That's how you repay me for not fucking me?"

"Shh!" Dom whispered back even harsher while he dragged her down the hall back to her place. "Okay, maybe I should have given you a heads-up that her cooking is worse than DeeDee's, but I knew if I told you that, you wouldn't have fucking come!"

"Why did you want me there?" Maria stuck out her tongue and tried to wipe the taste out of her mouth with her hand. "To violate my fucking mouth?"

"No, princess." Dom laughed before his tone went serious as they reached her place. "It would have felt wrong to be there without you."

Oh gosh, here we go again. Dominic saying the right fucking thing!

"Next time you want to have dinner with Kat and Drago"—
Maria reached up, lightly grabbing his chin like she had last night
in the casino—"I'm catering, or you tell her I'm dead." She placed
a light kiss on his lips.

Dominic gave her another kiss, revealing his dimples that she
loved to see. "All right."

Opening the door to her apartment, Maria gave him one last
kiss. "Goodnight, Dominic."

"That's it?" he asked, confused. "You're not going to try to
scheme your way into getting me in your apartment and then into
fucking you?"

Wow, if she didn't know better, she would think he might be a
little bit offended.

Maria shook her head with a slow smile. "Nope."

"Really?" he asked, now clearly offended.

"Why?" Maria raised a perfect brow. "Would it work?"

"N-No." Dom ran a quick hand through his hair, seeming to be
the one who was sexually frustrated tonight. "It's just unlike you."
Putting a hand back to her cheek, he felt to see if she was warm. "Are
you sure you're okay?"

"Yes," she assured him but tried her best to give a good yawn.
"I'm still sleepy after last night."

Dominic didn't look like he'd give her an Academy Award
anytime soon, but he thankfully didn't question her. "All right.
Goodnight, Maria." Leaning down, Dom placed her a tender kiss on
her cheek before his lips went to her ear to remind her of something

he never wanted her to forget. "I love you, Maria."

Swallowing, the tightness that had been in her chest went to her throat. "Goodnight."

Why did it hurt so fucking badly that she couldn't tell him those three words back? And it only made her hurt worse to have to shut the door on him when she wanted nothing more than to have Dominic spend the night with her.

But there was someone Maria needed to see ....

Knocking on the door, she waited for permission to enter, instead of just entering like she used to.

"Come in."

Hearing the dark voice, she slowly opened the door. It felt like forever since she had come in this room, and it felt even longer since she'd last spoken to the man behind the desk.

In the middle of lighting his cigarette, he did a double-take, seeing it was her before Lucca leaned back in his leather chair. "Long time, no see."

Maria took a seat down in front of him. She had avoided her brother since the last time they had spoken. Even before he murdered Kayne, they weren't in good standing, because he had yet to find One-Shot, the man who had taken their baby brother's eye.

"I didn't come to apologize," she let him know off the bat.

Lucca blew out a puff of smoke. "I didn't think you did."

"I'm here because … Dominic asked me to marry him," she said the words way easier to Lucca than Angel, but it was clear by his lack of response that he already knew. "Not surprised?"

"No," he told her honestly. "But you didn't come here for my blessing"—leaning forward, his blue-green eyes glowed—"so why are you really here, Maria?"

Taking a deep breath, Maria wasn't sure if she could get the words to come out of her mouth, until they did.

"How are you with her?" she whispered heartbrokenly into his eyes. "How do you allow yourself to even be with Chloe with what you are?" Not only did Maria's eyes trail down to the floor, but so did her fallen voice. "How am I …?"

Lucca understood what she was asking, having already gone through the same feelings when he had chosen the beautifully scarred Chloe. It hurt for something so evil to touch something so pure, and it was the only time they could feel pain.

"Maria, you will never deserve Dominic. Just how I will never deserve Chloe," he said the words just as unsympathetically as she had, but neither of them meant any ill will. "But we will spend the rest of our lives trying." The look he gave her was one of sympathy, as he left his sister to his office to think and to be alone.

"What do you get out of me marrying Dominic?" Maria asked without turning away from the sparkling city.

Lucca smiled at her back. "I guess there's only way to find out …."

HER GUT

Creaking up the stairs, Maria held her heels in one hand so they wouldn't wake anyone in the house. It wasn't until she had turned the doorknob and opened the door did she think what she was doing through.

"Jesus, Maria!" Dominic roared, dropping his gun to the floor. It proved how scared he had gotten when he tightly wound his arms around Maria. "I could have fucking shot you."

"I'm sorry," she quickly apologized, giving him a death-grip hug of her own after she dropped her heels to the floor. She had never felt so close to death before. Even feeling the heat from an explosion hadn't compare to the cold metal of a gun to your head. She didn't know if she was telling this part to him or herself. "You didn't, though, so it's okay."

"How did you even get in?" he asked, still hugging her to him and shaking.

"Angel gave me a key."

Letting her go, he stared down at her. "You found out he was following you."

"Yes. Don't worry, I know you weren't supposed to know anything about it. I just thought I'd save him the trouble of having to tail me and let him give me a ride instead."

"Well, I'll kill him." Dom hugged her to him again. "And if you ever fucking try to surprise me again, princess, wear the fucking heels next time."

"I will," she assured him. Giving him a kiss, she tried to soothe his fears and tell him it was okay, as he clearly had been more scared than she.

"You're wearing my jacket." Dominic remarked, looking down at her. He took in the sight but his brows quickly furrowed in confusion. "You're wearing the same outfit from …" He saw the tired expression on her face. "Maria, have you been up all night?"

"I couldn't sleep," she admitted as she looked out the window to see the sun had yet to rise.

Worry marred his beautiful face. "Is something wrong, princess?"

Maria slowly slipped her arms from the warmth of Dominic's jacket. Holding the soft leather in her hands, she stared at it instead of meeting his fierce gaze. "I want you to promise me, Dominic. I want you to swear on your life that you meant it when you said I could *do* anything, *be* anything if I marry you."

Making his oath again, he could only hope this time she would believe him without a shadow of a doubt. "I swear to you, Maria, on everything I love, and on my life, that I meant those words and any other words I have told you."

"I'm scared ..." she whispered, squeezing his jacket that she had yet to hand over. "I'm scared of going against everything I believe in, that it might change me." Maria took a shuddering breath. "But most importantly, I'm scared I will end up hurting you."

"Maria, when I tell you I love you, I don't expect to hear those words back, not from the little girl who couldn't even cry at her mother's funeral. All I know is that, deep down, you care for me, and that will *always* be good enough. I am only asking for you to take a chance on me."

Maria raised her eyes from the jacket to look into Dominic's intense ones, seeing he spoke the complete and utter truth. She had come to a decision before coming here, but it wasn't until now that she fully committed as she slowly held out his jacket to him.

Staring at his outstretched jacket, he knew the offer came with Maria's complete trust and faith, along with something else ... "You know, if I take that jacket, I expect you to marry me, princess?"

Slowly, Maria nodded.

Dominic didn't take the jacket. Instead, he took her. Wrapping his arms around her waist, he picked her up and took her to his bed. "Finally."

"Does this mean you're going to fuck me now?" she asked,

getting excited when he laid her down on his bed and came crashing down on top of her.

"Sorry, princess"—Dom began stealing kisses all over her face before he moved to her neck—"but you're still going to have to wait."

Maria internally cried with need. The only thing that had her not externally showing her disappointment was because when he had said "finally," he hadn't meant it in the way Maria had thought, which meant he was finally glad she had agreed to marry him.

"How did you know you wanted to marry me so quickly?" she asked. The thought of marriage was so foreign to her. She didn't understand how he could even ask her a question like that so fast. Yes, Dominic was right; she did care for him, but she could have spent the rest of her life as a couple with him and been happy at that. Both Maria and Dom knew she was marrying him to soothe his fears and satisfy his wants, not hers.

"Maria, I knew I was in love with you before you even walked through my door eight years after I had first met you." Rolling off her, he lay beside her now as he reached into his nightstand to pull something out ...

Her emerald eyes widened at the sight of the little, round, pink crushed velvet box as he untied the bow on top.

"I saw this in the window of a jewelry store after we left the bridal shop to pick out Kat's wedding dress." Opening the box, he revealed a shiny ring that somehow still caught the light in a dark room. "And even though I was drunk when I passed it, I knew that, once I sobered up, I would be back to buy it."

"You ..." Maria's breath caught in her throat. "You had it this whole time?"

"Yes," he said, taking it out of the box before he slid it on her finger, "I did."

Staring down at the most perfect, size six ring, she felt her eyes go a little misty. "It's a princess cut."

"I know, princess." He rolled back over top of her and kissed her lips with a dimpled smile. "Do you like it?"

"No." Maria shook her head, not looking at the handsome face, but to the beautiful gold ring that held a huge, crystal clear diamond. "I love it."

Kissing her deeply, both Dominic and her knew that was the closest she was going to get to telling him she loved him for now, and yet it still made him the happiest man in the world.

"I would have asked you to marry me again," he said after sweeping a tongue over a pouty bottom lip, "but I was afraid of getting turned down *again*."

Maria gave the same attention to his bottom lip with a hinted smile. "You should ask me now."

"Maria Caruso"—his fierce but very loving gaze returned, as his hazel eyes bore into hers—"will you marry me?"

"I will, on one condition."

"Anything," he promised without even having to hear it, but Maria was unsure how he would react.

"I don't change my last name."

"Princess"—Dominic reached up to touch the back of his tatted fingers to her cheeks—"I would have never allowed you to do such a thing."

Closing her eyes for a moment after feeling the somersault in her gut, she opened them only to shove him off her so she could get up and take him with her.

"What are you doing?" he asked with a laugh while she tried to drag him out of bed.

Interlocking their hands that were opposite in every way possible, inside and outside, Maria could no longer hold out. "We got a wedding to plan *fast*."

A CHANGED WOMAN

"A *hhhh!" The collective screams of* three girls erupted when she showed them the ring.

"Ha!" Lake shoved a finger in her face. "I knew you were secretly like us."

Adalyn did as well. "Ha! Ha! Ha! Ha! Maria is no different than us! She likes boys too!"

Katarina shook her head, smiling. "Oh, how the mighty has fallen."

The other two girls, however, stood there in utter shock.

"Y-you're getting married?" Chloe asked, blinking to see if this was real fucking life.

"Before us?" Elle stood there, unmoving, most likely wondering why she had put in the most work and been with her man the longest, yet she didn't have anything to show for it.

Maria understood why Elle and Chloe were shocked—because she was like them. She also understood why Kat wasn't. However, she didn't understand the reaction from the other two. "Why are you two not shocked?" She looked at the two best friends, Lake and Adalyn.

"Because I've seen him, Maria," Lake kept reminded her just how similar they were underneath, no matter how much she denied her boy crazy side. "I don't need to know anything else."

Adalyn wiggled her brows, clearly thinking about her man, Angel. "The Luciano brothers are hot as fuck, huh?"

"Ew." Kat tried not to gag.

"Nope," Maria told her. "Just the one is."

"Holy shit." Elle looked at her as if she could see the wild thoughts behind Maria's emerald eyes. "You really are getting married ..."

"Yep," she confirmed sharply before she dropped another bomb on them. "Tomorrow."

"Ahhhhh!" Another shriek roared out, this time between all five.

"*Tomorrow?*" Elle's mouth dropped. "Why so soon?"

"Uh ...." Maria looked over at Kat.

"Are you sure you're not rushing into it?" Chloe asked, concerned for her friend, who'd recently been through a lot.

"Kat, cover your ears," Maria instructed.

Katarina immediately held a gruesome face as she hummed with her hands over her ears, instinctively knowing she didn't want to hear anything that was about to come out of Maria's mouth.

"He won't fuck me till after we're married."

"Oh ..." Chloe was the one who spoke first, her eyes growing wide.

"So, you're telling me he's respectful *and* hot?" Lake's face was a picture of disbelief, as she tried to keep her swooning to a minimum. It was understandable, as she was dating Vincent.

"Did you try?" Adalyn asked in horror.

"*Try?*" Lake was the one that slapped the back of her head. "Look at her. Maria doesn't have to *try* anything."

Maria appreciated the compliment, but she understood what Adalyn meant.

"Trust me." She looked them dead in the eyes, remembering all the endless things she did to try to get Dom in her bed. "*I TRIED.*"

"Oh," Chloe said again, and Maria didn't miss the sympathetic look, now understanding why she was eager to get married.

Adalyn took Maria's hand in all seriousness. "Honey, I am so sorry."

"I think it's sweet," Elle said with a sweet smile, her mood instantly changing. The hopeless romantic at heart was easily swayed.

"What can we do?" Lake asked as they were all now on board for mission "Get Maria Fucked."

Maria put Katarina's arms down as it was safe now to listen. "Now, we have some fun."

"Why are they screaming over there?" Nero asked in concern, hearing the screams on the other side of the wall. "Are they all right?"

"They're fine." Lucca stopped him from getting up before he

looked at Dominic to continue. "You were saying?"

Dom looked around the room that consisted of his and Maria's close family of men. While she was breaking it down to the girls in the next apartment over, Dominic was breaking it down to the men. *Why, you might ask?* Because his future wife was a psychopath who had insisted it be done this way.

Dominic just got to the fucking chase. "Maria and I are getting married ... tomorrow."

The Caruso side of the room went silent, while Lucca and the Luciano brothers smiled as they watched the reactions around the room.

"You're marrying my sister?" Nero asked, confused.

Dominic nodded. "Yes."

"*Maria Caruso?*" he asked just to make sure Dom had it correct.

"Yes."

"And she is doing this *willingly?*" Nero didn't ask the question to the Luciano boss but to his brother.

Lucca nodded to confirm. "Trust me; she is."

Looking at Nero, Dominic could tell he still didn't believe it, needing to see it for himself.

Dominic couldn't help but notice the one-eyed Caruso brother sat in the back of the room quietly, unfazed.

"Oh, great." Vincent sat back in a huff, hearing the girls let out another scream of excitement. "You know what this means?" He looked at Nero and Angel sullenly. "They're going to expect us to put out too."

Dominic snapped his head to the little prick that was neither a brother or friend of his or Maria's. "Why the fuck are you even here?"

"Because my girl's over there, screaming out a fucking lung." Vincent threw a cocky thumb in the direction the screams were coming from before he patted the back of the man sitting next to him. "And me and Nero are friends, so I just followed him in here, because I wasn't going to be left out of whatever the fuck was going on."

Nero scooted his chair away from Vincent's, clearly not wanting to claim him as a friend at the moment.

"Well, now you know." Dominic nodded toward the door. "Good-bye."

"Hell no, I ain't going nowhe—"

"You do not want me to touch this asshole," Dominic warned, looking at the underboss.

Lucca didn't make a move.

Thankfully for Vincent's sake, Drago got up ….

"Okay, fine!" Vincent yelled before Drago could touch him. "Maria asked me to be here."

Dominic and Lucca furrowed their brows as they both had the same thought …

Why?

"Maria and Dom, sitting in *a tree, k-i-s-s-i-n-g …"* The girls behind her sung in unison as they danced and taunted the blonde who had sworn she would never let a man break her into marriage.

"*First comes love . . .*"

Luckily for them, Maria felt a little less coldhearted today with a ring on her finger.

"*Then comes marriage . . .*"

It really fucking sucked to eat crow.

"*Then comes the baby in a . . .*" All the girls trailed down the hallway after Maria when she threw open the apartment door to find all the men sitting there, waiting.

"Hello, boys." Maria waltzed in with the prettiest smile on her face. "Now that you've heard the news …." She went right up to Dominic and planted a big kiss on his lips to get it all right out of the way.

All the girls gasped.

"Holy shit …" Nero quickly realized that it wasn't a joke, as he had never seen his sister touch a man before, let alone kiss one. "I think I'm gonna be sick."

"Don't worry." Drago made a weird face after seeing it. "I needed a minute too."

"Oh, shut up." Maria rolled her eyes at her dramatic brother. "Like I haven't seen your tongue down Elle's throat enough."

Even though Maria had let him go, Dominic was still a bit thrown off by her kiss.

"Anyway," Maria got back to why they were all here, "I thought you boys could have a little bachelor party while the girls and I go out to have my bachelorette." She quickly waved as she turned to leave with four very excited girls. "Okay, bye!"

"No." Lucca's grave voice had all the girls stopping but her.

This time, Dominic tried. "Come back here, Maria."

Maria stopped, wondering if Dominic's dick was going to be worth it. She decided it was as she turned back around.

Nero almost fell out of his seat. "Oh my God."

Passing Dominic, she went right up to Lucca, knowing it wasn't her future husband who minded if they went out.

"We can all go out together." It wasn't her brother who spoke, but the underboss.

Maria simply said one word. "No."

"Maria," Lucca said her name in warning that he was trying to be understanding. "I can't have you girls go out unprotected."

"Fine." She already knew Lucca would never let Chloe go out without a guard. It was time to counter. "We'll take Vincent. You all don't want him anyway."

"Well, I might want to stay, depending on what kind of bachelor party we're talki—"

"It won't be that kind of party," Dominic hissed before turning to agree. "Fine by me."

Lucca shook his head. "He's an idiot."

"Actually, I'd love to go." Vincent got up to wrap an arm around Lake. "They'll probably have more fun anyway."

"He's an idiot, but he's crazy," Maria told Lucca, knowing he wasn't worthless when it came down to it.

"One isn't enough for all you girls," Lucca denied her again.

"Amo's not busy." With a smile, Maria said the name of the man who wasn't there.

She was very interested to find out if Lucca was going to let Amo watch over Chloe.

Lucca flexed his jaw, but when he didn't turn it down right away, Maria thought she just might have him ....

"I'll be with her. I won't let anything happen," she promised.

"Where are you going?" Lucca finally asked, seeming to relent as everyone watched Maria talk the boogieman into getting her way.

"Oh, you know, dress shopping. That's about it." That was all Maria was willing to give away.

The whole room was shocked as Lucca, reached into his pocket to pull out a black credit card.

Really?

And so was Maria as she stared at the card, knowing, in a weird way, it was him asking for forgiveness. He was extending an olive branch to put their brother/sister bond back to where it had been before everything had happened. If she took it, apology accepted.

Sliding the card out of his hand, she thought about how she missed him. "Thank you."

"You're welcome." Lucca's deep breath told her she had her brother back, but no sooner did the mask slip back to the underboss. "I want updates every hour, and you all back by midnight."

"Then I want rules too," Maria countered. "Vincent and Amo have to stay ten steps back at all times, and they are not allowed to talk to us."

"Deal." Lucca nodded, liking the last part, before turning to the pretty boy, who made them all want to pull their hair out. "Talk or touch Lake while you're out, and I'll kill you."

Vincent looked at them like they were crazy. "Lake's my girlfr—"

"Not tonight she isn't." Maria gave him a wicked smile that had all the boyfriends scared.

"Maria," Lucca began to warn her again, then decided to give up. "Try not to get in too much trouble."

"I'm a changed woman." Maria sweetly smiled as she went back to kiss Dominic.

Still not used to the sight, Nero had to look away. He and the other men got up to speak with their girlfriends, out of fear for what Maria had planned for them.

"You're not worried?" Maria asked, wrapping her arms around Dominic.

"No." He laughed, showing his dimples. "Should I be?"

"Nope." Maria gave him another tender peck. "Should I?"

"No," Dom assured her, leaning down to whisper in her ear, "your dress better be white this time, princess."

"No promises ..." she teased, letting him go. Then she began separating the couples and taking the girls.

Lucca had let Chloe go first. He seemed to not be worried at all, which meant he either was the most nervous and didn't want to show it or he really trusted Chloe.

Drago was next, but he was only nervous because he was afraid

Maria would get Kat's ass in trouble, since the two of them together weren't a good mix for men.

Angel was nervous, knowing Adalyn was boy crazy, like Lake, and he knew if men strippers were involved, it could be bad.

Nero was the most nervous, however, knowing the type of shit his sister was capable of. He straight-out didn't trust Maria, then his trust dipped in Elle because, when he went to kiss her, Elle had turned, giving her his cheek.

Internally Maria laughed, wondering how long it would take him to realize why.

And Vincent thought he was fine, because he was going to be joining them. Little did he know he wasn't going to have the least bit fun.

"Maria ..." Lucca called her name for the last time. "End up in jail, and I'll let you rot there on the night before your wedding while I bail Chloe out."

A WHOLE LOT OF GLITTER

"**A** *re we getting strippers?*" *Cassius* asked as soon as the door closed behind the women.

"No." Dominic threw over his shoulder to him.

"I hear there's a pretty sweet spot in the basement." Matthias raised his brows in excitement.

"Hell no," Dominic said, still traumatized from his last event. He then made one thing clear to all the men in the room. "No girls."

Matthias looked at him in offense. "No brother of mine can have a bachelor party without any girls. You're getting married tomorrow; you won't get this chance again."

"Are you forgetting who I'm marrying?" Dom looked at him like he was crazy. "Because there will be no fucking wedding."

"Well, this is going to be fucking lame," Matthias huffed out bored already.

Not saying a word, Leo stood and headed up the steps while everyone in the room looked at him sympathetically.

Well, almost everyone.

"Where is he going?" Cassius asked as he narrowed his eyes at his back.

"His room." Lucca was the one to answer. "He's got a bunch of video g—"

"Cool." Cass immediately stood to follow after him.

Dominic didn't miss the cold shoulder Cassius gave Lucca, nor the look the underboss had given back.

When there was a knock on the door, Nero got up to answer it, and when he came back, he had a shit-eating grin on his face.

Dominic didn't know what was so fucking funny until two women sashayed into the room.

Oh no.

"Howdy, partners." Two sexy voices escaped the mouths of girls dressed in cowgirl outfits as they tipped their hats. They both went for their toy guns at their low, exposed hips as the blonde said, "We're looking for an outlaw who goes by the name Dominic Luciano."

The posse of girls walked into the bridal shop with huge smiles on their faces, while Amo and Vincent walked in behind them angrily, as they were not allowed to speak.

"Maria, my darling." Ken came over to give her a kiss on each cheek before he gave one to Katarina. "How was the wedding?"

"It was ... great." Kat left out the part where it ended in death.

"You've brought me so many pretty girls." He eyed them all enviously. "Which one is the lucky lady today?"

Maria smiled from ear to ear. "Me."

Ken almost passed out from shock, but then he suddenly remembered. "It was that man you were with last time, huh? Kat's brother. What was his name—Dominic! Oh, girl, I fell in love with him too." He didn't even wait for an answer, instead he just held out his hand for a high-five.

Maria gave him high-five, and he clasped their hands together, already dragging her to the back, excited to get started.

"Sherry, pop the good shit. Our girl is finally getting married!" Ken screamed as they all walked to the back to the couch outside the dressing rooms. It were as though he had waited forever to say those words as he clasped his hands together. "Maria, this is it. What kind of dress do we want?"

Both of them knew her days of coming into the bridal shop to try on wedding dresses for fun were over, that this was it—the last wedding dress she would ever wear, and it had to be perfect.

"Kat, cover your ears," Maria announced.

"Oh God," Kat mumbled as she quickly did the same thing she had earlier.

Everyone looked at her in concern, while Amo and Vincent just looked confused.

"Ken"—Maria clearly knew exactly what she was looking for—"give me the sluttiest dress you got."

"He is." Dominic quickly pointed at Matthias before anyone could call him out.

Matthias was about to correct him, wanting his about-to-be married brother to have a last bit of fun, but then the girls sauntered over to him.

"Dominic Luciano, you are a wanted man on account of being one ... bad ... boy." The imposter cowgirls began rubbing their hands down his shirt. "How do you plead?"

Matthias sat back with pure lust in his eyes. "Guilty as fuck."

After Maria picked her dress, Sherry handed out more celebratory champagne, but stopped herself when she got to Kat. "Oh wait, you're not old enough, are you? Dang it, I was—"

"No, she is," Maria lied, even though the only one old enough to legally drink was her. It couldn't be called a bachelorette party without a little champagne.

"Okay, good, I was worried for a second. Sorry about that."

While Maria was glad that worked, she could see something was wrong with Sherry. She had come in here dozens of times but had never seen her off like this.

"Sherry? Is everything all right?"

"Yes." She continued handing out the champagne but knew Maria wasn't going to take that answer from her, so she dropped her brave face. "I'm sorry. I just found out my boyfriend cheated on me."

"Oh no, honey."

"I'm so sorry."

All the girls consoled her for a moment.

Maria only had one question. "What's his name?"

"Did you do this?" **Dom** asked Lucca as he stood the second Matthias's lap dance started.

"Nope."

Seeing the underboss answered truthfully didn't explain why he was heading for the door. "Where the hell are you going, then?"

"Don't worry." Lucca smiled. "I'll be back."

"Maria, what are we doing here?" Adalyn asked for the hundredth time. "Since when do you, or any of us, like sports?"

"And this is supposed to be a *bachelorette* party," Lake said with emphasis. "Where are the boys?"

"Oh, they're coming," Maria assured her with a smile as they took their seats. The best part about it was Vincent and Amo had to take their seats a row behind them—and they actually thought they were about to enjoy a game.

As soon as the hockey players slid out onto the ice, the girls eyes slightly glinted.

"They're awfully covered up," Adalyn said, still not seeing the full picture yet.

Katarina was making herself comfy, knowing exactly why they were there. "You're about to find out why."

"Maria, if we leave now, we can still turn this night around. We need to get you some real men …." Lake's voice trailed off as the puck flew across the ice.

Vincent no longer looked at the men playing on the ice. "Oh hell n—"

"Ow!" Elle and Chloe jumped at the same time with a collective cringe, but by the fifth hit, even they couldn't pull their eyes away.

"Maria"—Adalyn swallowed as she watched the smack cam's zoomed-in view to see the fine-looking men with anger issues under the helmets—"I'm sorry I ever fucking doubted you."

Hockey was and always would be a contact sport.

Dominic filled glasses with the hard liquor he found in the cabinet. "Drago, did you do this?"

"Fuck no." He took the glass that Dom had filled. "Do I need to remind you that your sister took a fucking baseball bat to my kitchen?"

I hope she does it again.

He looked over at his brother. "Angel?"

"Do you see my ass in there?" he griped as he picked up a glass.

All the men turned to see Matthias's shirt getting ripped off.

Nero swiped a glass, quickly downing the contents, before he tapped the glass for Dom to fill it back up.

"You're not twenty-one?" he suddenly realized.

"Dominic Luciano is really asking me if I'm of drinking age? Really?" Nero looked at him like he was fucking crazy.

He supposed the kid had a point ….

"I'm an adult and, trust me, there are worse things I've done," Nero assured him before he waved a hand at the two cowgirls riding Matthias like he was a horse. "And I'm stuck in here with this while I got a girlfriend out with your future wife doing God knows what—"

Dominic quickly refilled Nero's glass, and they all took a drink.

Trying to turn their attention away from what was going on in the living room, Dom stared into his glass. "Does Sal not come to events?"

They invited Sal, but like Katarina's wedding, he was a no-show to their so-called bachelor party and probably wasn't going to attend their wedding too.

Drago took another sip. "He doesn't leave from behind his computer much."

As Dom nodded, the door opening had the men turning their heads to see Lucca walk back in.

Seeing him holding out a wad of cash, the two girls suddenly stopped dancing on Matthias.

"What are you doing?" Matthias practically cried in frustration to Lucca.

"Get going." Lucca's cold voice had the girls grabbing the money and leaving.

"What the fuck?" Matthias watched them leave with tears in his eyes. For a moment, he had clearly forgotten who he was talking to. "Why'd you do that?"

"Come on." Lucca waved his head at all of them. "Let's go."

By the time the girls left, they were all laughing and had each picked their favorite hockey player who they now sported their last names and numbers on the back of the new jersey's they were wearing.

"Did you see Bolton punch that guy's helmet right off?" Lake asked, still imagining the scene in her head. "He can really play some hockey," she commented like a single one of them knew or even cared about the skill the sport demanded.

Vincent glared at that name on the back of his girlfriend's jersey as he grumbled ten steps behind. "Bolton, can really get this foot up his as—"

Ding!

Maria pulled out her phone, seeing a text from her favorite little ass kisser.

"What is it?" Chloe asked when she could see the wheels turning in Maria's evil head.

"Girls, we are going to need a whole lot of glitter."

An upset Matthias cheered up when they got off the elevator at the basement floor. "Thank you, God."

Throwing a look at Lucca, Dominic didn't know how much clearer he needed to make it. Herded down the hallway, he had to be practically shoved through the door. "I told you I didn't want—"

He shut his mouth the second he saw the underground casino was empty. Only two tables with dealers and two waitress remained, and they were fully clothed.

"Hello again, Mr. Luciano," Sadie said with a smile as he and Lucca sat down and were immediately served drinks. "I heard the good news that you're taking my girl off the market."

Dominic might have intended the words to the pit boss, but he was looking at Lucca when he said, "Thank you."

"Are we supposed to stop this?" Vincent didn't move his fearful eyes off the girls when he asked his friend.

Amo didn't have the same concern he did. "Was it in any of the rules Lucca gave you?"

"Well, no, but—"

"Then nah." Amo relaxed back on the hood of their Escalade. "I say we let this shit play out."

"Whose car is this?" Chloe asked, scared.

Maria watched as Kat worked on getting the car unlocked. "Sherry's ex-boyfriend's."

"What the hell, Maria!" Not-so-sweet Elle hissed at her, "You want us to commit a felony?"

"No." Maria shook the big bags of glitter in a rainbow assortment. "We're just going to add some sparkle."

"Got it." Kat opened the door before unlocking all the others.

Giving a bag to each girl, none of them looked too eager to start, except for Kat.

"Don't worry." Maria tore open the bag with her teeth, then started dumping the contents into the driver's seat. "This is perfectly *legal* property damage."

Katarina began dumping it into the carpets and smushing it in with her hands so it couldn't be easily vacuumed out.

Maria addressed the rest of the girls one last time, "He cheated on her with *her sister*."

"Fuck it." Lake started pouring hers into the cupholders.

Adalyn got the cracks between the seat. "Oh, hell no."

"Asshole." Elle hit the back seats.

"Sometimes"—Chloe pulled the visor down a bit so the next

time he pulled it down it would rain glitter——"you get what you deserve."

If there is ever a doubt ... *glitter is always the answer.*

Maria opened the door with the girls in tow at exactly the same time she told Lucca they would when she texted him after glittering the cheater's car. That poor sucker was in for a rude awakening once he realized what all girls knew——glitter was a nightmare to clean. He would be reminded of his exploits even by the hundredth car wash, and having to explain the glitter situation was going to be even better.

Walking into the penthouse, the boys and her place looked exactly like she had left it, except Leo and Cassius were nowhere in sight.

"Howdy, partner." The words fell from Maria's lips with a smile when she looked at Dominic.

Instantly, Dominic knew exactly who had sent the strippers.

"Are you fucking kidding me?" Matthias cried in frustration. "*She* got them, and we turned them down!"

"Got what?" Elle asked, coming over to Nero, not giving him a kiss.

Maria could see the men growing nervous, but seeing the glow in Lucca's eyes, she decided to spare them. "I bought the guys cakes."

"Got any left?" Amo asked.

"We didn't keep them," Matthias hissed again.

The girls stared at their men strangely.

Maria decided to save them again. "They were shaped inappropriately."

Vincent looked at the men, appalled. "And you all didn't fucking keep them?"

Ignoring his friend, Nero looked down at Elle. "Why are you wearing a jersey?"

All the men looked at their prospective woman with scrutinizing gazes, knowing ...

"You hate sports." Angel narrowed his eyes on Adalyn, stating the obvious for all the men in the room.

"You took them to a hockey game?" Lucca asked Maria while staring down a blushing Chloe.

"Yep," she said proudly as she closed the distance between her and Dominic.

Drago couldn't look away from his pink-haired wife as he asked the question that was on every man's mind. "Why the hell would you all go to a hockey game?"

"Maria, honey"—Dominic lifted her chin with a smile, seeming to be the only one who knew exactly why they had gone—"why didn't you tell me you liked to watch men fight?"

Maria raised an excited brow. "Is that your way of telling me you fight?"

"Oh, princess"—he brought his lips closer to hers—"you have no fucking idea."

KICK HIS ASS

The girls watched the men move the furniture out of the way with a mixture of emotions. After finding out why they had taken a little trip to the hockey game, the men looked at their women slightly differently, and when the Caruso men overheard Dominic telling Maria he could fight, they wanted him to prove it. All of Kansas City knew of Dom's skills as a gunman, but only those from Blue Park knew the brutality of his fists.

Maria watched Dominic stand in the middle of the room as everyone sat in a big circle. The action even had Cassius and Leo coming down from upstairs to see what the hell was going on.

The Luciano boss looked at the men around the room when no one came up to face him. "Any takers?"

Just as she suspected, the men were all talk and no action.

Vincent was lucky he had looks, because the dumbass stood as he gave Lake a look like *I've got this*.

"Sit your ass back down," Dominic told him, knowing there would be no competition. It would be like hitting a helpless bab—

"What? Are you fucking scared?" Vincent gave him his pretty boy smile.

"Dominic …" Maria spoke from behind him, "kick his ass."

Dom nodded, agreeing to the slaughter.

"On the count of three," Maria began. "One …"

Dom and Vincent drew close but maintained a four-inch distance between them.

"Two …"

Vincent raised his fists up in a fighting position while Dom remained relaxed.

"Three …"

"Let's go, motherfucke—"

Vincent took one step forward, and it was his last, as Dominic punched the pretty boy so hard right in the face that he immediately fell backward like a ton of bricks, unable to finish his sentence.

The only ones who didn't collectively jump from watching the action were Dom's siblings, Maria, Drago, and Lucca.

"Vincent!" Lake was beside her boyfriend in an instance. "Your nose is bleeding."

"I think he fucking broke it!" Vincent touched it as he came to.

"Sorry about that," Dominic told him, obviously not sorry. "Who's next?"

None of the men came for—

"I will." Amo stood, taking Vincent's place, as he was off on the sidelines, being nursed by his girlfriend. The respect from the men in the room went up for Amo.

Dom nodded again, agreeing to the fight right out the gate, which made Maria realize he had probably been waiting to get his hands on Amo after what he had done to Angel.

Angel sat back, smiling.

"I got a hundred on Dom. Any takers?" Mathias immediately called out.

"I'll take that bet." Dumbass Vincent couldn't resist, while his girlfriend held a bag of peas over his nose. Pulling out his wallet, he bet on Amo.

Maria couldn't help but notice Lucca and Chloe. They sat farther away from anyone and the Luciano brothers didn't come close to the scarred girl, all of them keeping their distance out of respect for her and the underboss after what their father had done to her. But she was solely focused on Amo, while Lucca hid a smile that Amo was about to get his ass kicked.

Wanting to get the hot show on the road, Maria began the countdown, "One ..."

Amo eyed Dominic in confidence.

"Two ..."

Dominic stared him down. "You wanting to fight to show off in front of the girls or because I'm a Luciano?"

The room went deathly silent at Maria's ... "Three."

Amo rushed toward Dom like a bull in a china shop, his eyes on Dom's hands. Unlike Vincent, Amo was a better match, body-wise, as De Santis men were huge, but even though he might not look his age, Dom was too experienced for him.

Dominic waited until the last second before he took a small step to the side, stopping the big man from running when he grabbed his neck. Holding it in his grasp, he watched Amo's shocked face as he reared back his fist, punching Amo in the small of his back and sending the man to his knees.

Fuck hockey, this was the hottest fucking thing she had ever seen in her life.

"Did you break his neck?" Nero went to help Amo, but his hand was shoved away as Amo got to his feet like a ninety-year-old.

"Want another round?" Dom offered.

With one hand on his back and the other on his neck, Amo shook his head. "Not if I'm working tomorrow."

Dominic held out a hand, and Amo stared at it for a moment, shocked, before he shook it and squashed the bad blood between them.

Matthias snatched the cash unrepentantly from Vincent's poor hands. He had plans of getting richer.

"Who's next?"

Drago slowly stood, moving to stand in front of Dominic, as every breath halted in the room.

Now this would actually be a fucking fight.

While Dominic had trained under the Luciano enforcer, Drago

the motherfucking tank De Santis, had come from a long line of the best soldiers a Caruso had to offer. If the Carusos handed out that title, then Drago would own it.

Katarina's face dropped. She had been enjoying the fights, but even she couldn't hide her nerves.

"Okay, new ground rules," Maria called out. "No hitting in the face or below the waist. We're getting married tomorrow, and I need his face to be pretty for the pictures, and ... the other thing for tomorrow night."

"Now you say that?" Vincent's ground out with the peas attached to his face. He was going to have a rude awakening when he looked in the mirror to see he was sporting a hell of a black eye.

Nero was still gagging. "I could have lived without hearing that, but I bet five hundred on Drago." He took out his wallet.

"I'll fucking take that bet," Matthias called out, sticking with his brother for the win.

"Drago can take him," Leo spoke his first words of the night.

Cassius shook his head at him. "Not a fucking chance."

"Maybe we should call it a night, Maria." Kat was clearly trying to stop the fight.

Maria sympathized with Katarina's dilemma. She was on the losing side, whichever man won. But Maria knew Dominic would enjoy getting a few shots in on Drago for choosing his sister for his revenge and without any consequences from Lucca. This was her present to Dominic, now that she thought about it.

"One ..." Maria began the countdown before Kat could

convince her husband to pull out.

The two men stared at each other without moving.

"Two …" Maria's throat went dry in anticipation. She just hoped she wouldn't regret this. "Three."

The men began circling each other, waiting for the other to strike first. Maria finally had to blink, and as soon as she did, that was when they struck.

Both men had their arms wrapped around the other, and she could see their muscles straining as both tried to gain the advantage. Arms straining, they broke apart to circle each other again, each looking for a weakness to hit. Drago went first with a left hook to Dominic's ribs, and Dom countered, swinging his fist out to plant an undercut blow right below Drago's chin.

"No face punches!" Kat reminded her brother.

"Technically, below the chin isn't the face; it's the throat," Maria told her as they both held each other's hands tightly.

Drago returned the punch with a right hook to Dominic's cheekbone while he shielded his ribs with his right hand.

"We said no face punches!" Maria hissed now.

"They really wouldn't hurt each other, would they?" Kat asked anxiously.

"I'm sure they won't …" Maria tried to lie to herself, hating that she encouraged this. Well, at least on the night before her wedding.

During the next series of hits the men traded, neither man grimaced nor made a noise of pain, each taking the hit and coming back stronger.

Kat squeaked in fear when Dom's knuckles split Drago's lip and blood formed around his mouth.

The blood loss didn't make Drago lose his temper. Instead, the man went left then right before he grabbed Dominic by the waist to lift him off his feet and throw them down on the ground.

Maria let out a light scream as she would have sworn she had watched it in slow motion. Thinking he would be dead from them both being huge and falling to the ground, she was surprised when Dominic wasn't fazed and had maneuvered himself on top of Drago somehow.

"That's enough!" Maria screeched out, standing. She and everyone else in there could see the only way the fight was going to end was in death. Mentally both men didn't know how to give up, and their bodies weren't willing to either.

Dominic reared his fist back, not wavering at her words, while the grip Drago had on Dom's neck seized.

After a tense moment, Dom got off him, then held out a hand to help his brother-in-law to his feet. Drago took it.

"Great, a tie," Matthias ground out, staring at the money he had hoped would be in his hands, as he watched Nero put it back in his wallet. "My brother has disappointed me yet again."

"Okay, put the furniture back," Maria ordered, not wanting to take any more chances with Dominic's face.

Going to him, Maria touched his swelling cheekbone. "I thought I said no going for the face?" Maria hissed over the moving furniture to Drago, who was getting looked over by Kat.

"It's fine, Maria," Dom assured her with a laugh. "I did throw the cheap shot first."

"No, you hit under his chin." Snatching the peas from Vincent's broken nose as he passed, she placed it on Dom's cheek where it was more important. "Now look at what you did to his face, and our wedding's tomorrow."

"Well, I got shot at mine," Drago reminded her as he wiped the blood from his mouth. "It'll make for a great memory."

Rolling her eyes, she went back to Dom's poor face. She had to admit, somehow, the man only looked hotter. Maria swiped her tongue over her bottom lip. "You know ... I would have said yes a lot sooner if I'd known you could do that."

"I'm out," Nero said, grabbing Elle's hand after the furniture had been put back. "This is still too fucking weird for me."

Everyone was slightly scared by the hot glances between the soon to be married couple. It had them all wanting to leave.

"Hey." Vincent stopped them before anyone could leave to ask the question that could put him in his grave. "How come you didn't offer to fight him, Lucca?"

Everyone went deathly silent, waiting for the boogieman's verbal or physical response to the idiot. All of them assumed they were about to witness a murder; even Chloe stood nervously beside him. What none of them expected was the underboss's simple response.

"Because ... I wouldn't have won."

Unbothered, Lucca wrapped his arm around his fiancée's shoulders as they headed for the door, and all of them watched him walk away.

That was the difference that separated leaders from soldiers. Leaders knew when to surrender in order to succeed, and it was a wisdom nearly every man in the room needed to learn.

Lucca was cold, calculating, and cunning, and while Dominic would have won a match in brawn, Maria knew ... Lucca would beat him any day in a game of chess.

"Adalyn ..." Finally, it was Angel who noticed. "Why are you covered in glitter?"

ALL YOU'LL EVER
CARE TO KNOW

"**A**nything else you're hiding from me that I'll find extremely fucking hot?" Maria asked as soon as they were alone.

Dominic put his tatted hands on her waist as he pulled her to him. "Oh, you'll find that out tomorrow night, princess."

"You could show me now." She darted her tongue out to lick his lips. "I promise you, after that, I'll still marry you."

"I know you will." He laughed, knowing her too well. "But no."

Catching sight of his dimples, Maria moved her tongue to the precious dent. "You sure about that?"

"No," he gritted out, loving that action from her, but he still held strong. "That's why I need to go."

Maria pulled her head back. "You're not going to stay with me tonight?"

"I can't, Maria. I'm sorry." Internally, Dominic wanted to cry just as much as her, yet he stood strongly behind his moral code. "One more night, princess, is all I'm asking. Then I swear to you we won't have to sleep apart again."

Wanting nothing more than to con him into getting into her bed, Maria knew she could easily get him to break since the wedding was only one day away. And even though she didn't care about her virginity, she respected the fact that he did.

Staring into his hazel eyes, she wanted another oath. "Promise?"

"I promise, princess." He made the easiest promise he would ever make as he sealed it with a kiss. "Now you really have to let me go."

"Fine," she grumbled, taking her lips off his. He seemed to be in a hurry to go somewhere ... "Did you like your bachelor party present?" Maria asked with a smile, trying to stall, as he walked them to her door.

"No, but Matthias appreciated it for the little bit they were here."

"You sent them away?" she asked, confused.

"Yes," Dom said before correcting, "Well, technically, Lucca did."

"Why?" Maria couldn't believe it. "Did you even get a turn?"

Dominic stopped at her door, looking at her like she was crazy. "So, they weren't a joke? You seriously wanted strippers here?"

"Yes, it was a *bachelor party*." She spelled it out for him like Lake had earlier in the night. "The outfits might have been the joke, but I wanted you to have fun."

"Woman, I will never fucking understand you." Dom shook his head like he had a headache for a second.

"I watched a hockey game; fair is fair."

"Maria, you watched fully clothed men fight where you can't see any faces. That's why you like it. And trust me; while a part of me is grateful you can't stand a man to touch you or for you to really to gaze upon any man, I don't exactly take pleasure in women touching me for money."

Oh . . . Maria felt like a fucking idiot. "I'm sorry. I should have thought about—"

"It's okay. You don't have to apologize," he assured her sweetly. "You were trying to do something nice, and I appreciate the thought, and Matthias really fucking appreciated it." Dominic laughed. "I haven't seen him that happy all year. Plus, the cowgirl outfits were a nice touch."

Maria smiled. "I thought you would like that."

"I did, but let me make one thing clear, princess." Dominic craned her neck with a finger. "The only girl I ever want to touch or look at in something dressed like that is you."

Her eyes rolled to the back of her head at his words and when he put his mouth on her neck.

"Wait . . ." Dominic removed his lips from her neck, seeing her skin sparkle up close. "Why are you glittery?"

Maria quickly opened her door and started shoving him out like she had after Angel asked that question to Adalyn.

He was no longer as eager to leave. "Are you sure you all didn't go to a strip clu—"

"I'll see you at the altar." Maria gave him one last kiss that stole his thoughts and breath away in an instant. Pleased with herself, she shut the door. "Goodnight."

Dominic left smiling, wishing he had gotten the chance to tell her he loved her one last time before they were married. But as he walked down the hall, his thoughts went to his upcoming meeting. He just hoped he came out of it alive ….

"Why are you here, Dominic?" the man behind the desk, smoking a cigar, asked after several awkward moments.

Dom knew this wasn't going to end well, and even though Lucca had told him he would handle his father, Dominic still needed to face him, man-to-man. If he didn't have the balls to face his fiancé's father, then he didn't deserve to marry her at all.

"Dante, I came to you out of respect to tell you—"

"That you're fucking my daughter?" Dante finished for him. "You think I don't know what is going on in my own damn business? You've been prancing around here with her for days."

Flexing his jaw, Dominic managed to keep his cool, even with the boss's blatant disrespect for a situation where he didn't have the correct facts.

Beginning again, he spoke the words harshly so he would not be interrupted this time. "I came here to tell you that I'm *marrying* your daughter."

Dante impassively puffed on his cigar.

"You already know," Dominic said, not seeing any additional hatred in the man's ice-blue eyes than what was already there.

He'd been more upset at the thought he was fucking his daughter under his roof than marrying her. Like everyone else, Dante was no different, assuming a man with the last name Luciano had bad intentions. Dominic Luciano had shown more respect to the Caruso boss's daughter than his own soldiers, and it wouldn't matter if he told him, Dante wouldn't believe it.

"Unfortunately, my son has already informed me." Grabbing the cigar from his mouth, he almost crushed it. "You should have listened to Lucca when he told you not to come see me. Whatever it is you want from me, Dominic, I'm not fucking interested. You can see yourself out."

Nodding, Dom stood up, seeing that Lucca had been right, but the second his back turned, he turned right back around to face Dante a second time. "I didn't come here as the Luciano boss; I came here as a man to speak with the father of the woman I love."

"She hasn't told you?" he asked, putting the cigar back to his mouth.

Dom's brows furrowed. "Told me what?"

"When she cleared your name as One-Shot, I told Maria, if she saw you again, she would be dead to me." The boss blew out a puff of smoke. "I knew no dance with my daughter would be harmless, and I was right."

The rage that flowed through Dominic took everything he had to not let his fist meet that man's face.

It hadn't only been Lucca who had told him not to see him; Maria has said it as well. It was no wonder she didn't want to invite him to the wedding. Dom didn't want her to regret it one day, and it was part of the reason why he'd come, in hopes her father would be there to see his only daughter marry. Then again, Maria didn't look at him as a father anymore—and there was no way she could after he'd disowned her.

"Those are unforgivable words, Dante, words you will come to regret once your son takes every last thing from you. When that happens, I want you to remember that it was *you* who managed to destroy the only precious thing you would have had left—and you did it all on your own."

"You *do not* know what it's like to father a child." Dante's cigar crashed as he hit his hands to the desk and stood. "And you *do not* know what it's fucking like to have your daughter marry the son of the man who murdered your wife."

"You don't care to know a thing about me, Dante." Dominic released his clenched fist as he went to the door. Dante would never see past the seven-letter name ... "My father being Lucifer is all you'll ever care to know."

THE TRUTH OF IT ALL

If *it was up to* Maria, they would have gone to the courthouse and tied the knot right after that ring was put on her finger. An imitation Elvis Presley could have married her for all she fucking cared, but Dominic wouldn't allow it. He didn't want a wedding that was a joke or one that looked like it was a spur-of-the-moment decision, even if it was. Maria, however, never saw herself committing to spending an eternity with a man in a church for everyone to witness. Hell, Maria hadn't seen herself marrying anyone *ever*. So, they had compromised. They would have a small wedding for only family, not a joining of the two mafia families.

It was safer, as well, since One-Shot was still at-large. Another big meeting of the families would only end in more bloodshed as tensions were still high. It worked out for Maria, because a wedding was never what she wanted, and all Dominic wanted was a ceremony that held meaning, and if his siblings were there and he was marrying Maria, then that was all he cared about.

In only a month's time, Maria had pulled off the biggest wedding for Katarina and Drago, so pulling off a little one in a day wasn't so hard. Plus, she had people for that. The joys of her family owning the biggest Hotel Casino in Kansas City meant they held multiple weddings a year. The small ceremony and reception was easily set up in a matter of hours. The only decor Maria wanted was the view.

Her father might not have approved of the wedding, but Lucca did, and he gladly let her have the wedding she wanted.

Maria stared at herself in the mirror. She had tried on so many wedding dresses through the years and dressed up every day of her life. She could have bought the most expensive and prettiest dress in the world, but it wouldn't have mattered to her. Maria wasn't looking for beauty.

Looking down at her white dress, it wasn't really a dress at all, as it was two pieces. The light sheer skirt sat high on her waist and cascaded down her long legs, allowing the slightest hint of her tanned skin. Underneath she wore a bodysuit that hugged every curve, reminiscent of the nude dress she had worn on their date. It was low-cut and made of the thinnest lace, displaying her perfect breasts. The dress was so perfect, it even held a secret that she couldn't wait to reveal to Dominic at the end of the night.

She had her makeup perfected with her favorite nude lipstick and soft glam eye look with wings. Her gold hair had been perfectly curled, then tousled in a light wave. Now she only needed one last thing ….

Maria went into her closet to get a pair of heels but immediately stopped when she saw a box sitting on her velvet bench in the middle of the room.

She read the note that laid on top.

For my princess. I love you.
- Your soon-to-be first husband

Maria couldn't keep the smile off her face as she carefully laid down the card, then picked up the box. Having bought thousands of pairs of shoes, she knew what would be waiting, but nothing prepared her for the perfection inside.

The stilettos were sky-high with the classic pointed toe, and they were encrusted in Swarovski crystals that glittered as she slid them on her feet, but it was the red bottoms that proved he had taste.

Maria Caruso was truly marrying the perfect man …

For me.

For the first time, Dominic wore a true Italian suit that was fit for a Caruso but tailored to him. He had shoes, but staring down at the box, he figured he might just be changing them when he picked up the note.

For my red bottom man.

Love, your princess.

Opening the top of the box, he saw expensive men's black dress shoes by Maria's favorite brand—Louboutin.

Smiling, Dominic couldn't believe they both had bought coordinating gifts without even knowing it. Now he and his bride would have matching blood-dripped shoes.

Dominic Luciano was truly marrying the perfect woman ...

For me.

Descending the steps, Maria was just about to open the door to go to her wedding when the front door suddenly opened.

"Dad?" She stood in place, stunned to see him. It immediately wore off when she remembered those three words. "Sorry I didn't invite you to my funeral. I must've forgot."

"Maria, I came to talk to you," he said as she tried to pass by him.

"I'm *dead to you*, remembe—"

"Please." He motioned for the couch. "I have a few things I need to say."

Taking in her father's sincere tone, she took a seat on the couch, wanting to hear what he had to say.

Dante unbuttoned his jacket as he sat down beside her. It took him a few moments to find the right words. "I don't know Dominic, but I did know his father, and while I can't hold a son accountable for his father's sins, you can't expect me to be able to get over the fact that Lucifer took the love of my life away. When I see Dominic, I see Lucifer, I see the man who took my wife away from me."

"Then you should have gotten to know him," Maria said the words so unforgivingly. "Because then you wouldn't see Lucifer at all."

"That would take time, Maria," Dante tried to get her to understand. "Time I plan to take as I work with him as the new Luciano boss."

Maria raised a brow, seeing the answer already on her father's face. "But not as my husband."

"You're a Caruso; I expected you to marry one of my men."

"No, you wanted me married to Sal," Maria corrected him. "Tell me, how is it that you can justify me marrying one son of Lucifer's but not the other? When you look at Sal, do you see Lucifer?"

"When I look at Sal, I see the boy I took off the street who Lucifer had let rot. He fathered him, yet he didn't raise him like he did his other children. When I look at Sal, I see a son."

"And I see a brother," Maria told him what he could not understand. "If you expected me to fall for one of your soldiers, then you shouldn't have raised me around them."

"Probably," he agreed.

Still seeing the disappointment, Maria knew she was missing something. "Why is it really that you will never be able to accept me and Dominic?"

Dom was a made man, sure from the wrong side, but the families were supposed to be joining together as one. Her marrying Dominic only solidified that fact, which was why Lucca had encouraged it.

Dante clearly had been holding in a secret, as his ice-blue eyes pierced her soul before he revealed the truth of it all. "Dominic does not have pure Italian blood."

Maria drew her brows together, but before she could speak, her father continued.

"We like our names to represent our Italian heritage, but have you never wondered how his children's names differ from ours? Dominic, Angel, Matthias, Cassius are all names of … Spanish descent." Dante finally broke the secret that not many Carusos knew. "Spanish women held the only qualities Lucifer admired and respected enough in women to father children."

Dominic and Cassius's looks suddenly made sense, while the other children had taken theirs from their father.

Maria couldn't believe that this was why her father didn't approve of their marriage and that he thought she was supposed to suddenly see Dominic differently.

"This is why you don't approve? Because Dominic isn't *Italian* enough for you? Well, thank God you don't allow women into your organization, so what the hell do you care?"

"Lineage is everything, Maria." He warned that any children from their union wouldn't be able to become made.

Yes, she did know. The mafia went back generations in this country, and no matter where you were located, the only way you could become made in an Italian mafia was being one hundred percent Italian. It was the most basic requirement, written in stone long ago, and it hadn't been changed or challenged …

Yet.

"I find it funny how the biggest piece of shit that ever walked this earth is somehow less nearsighted than you. Lucifer was smart to let go of the old ways, because yours are going to be the death of you."

Both of them knew Chloe didn't have an ounce of Italian blood running through her veins, yet it wouldn't keep Lucca from marrying her or fathering children with her, and having his children become made. That stupid rule was going to end with her father's reign, and they both knew it.

"When I took control of this family, I made a promise to uphold those values, and I will until my reign ends." Dante spoke with finality, the blood oath he made upheld. "I cannot show support for this wedding, because then I go back on that oath. My men and the many men I've had to turn down because of the blood in their veins … it isn't fair to those people that I give you an exception because you're my daughter."

Maria understood. Her father was stuck in his old ways and felt bound in blood to uphold the sacred family rules, but she was *his* daughter.

"You had no fucking trouble supporting Drago."

"Katarina has no record of where she came from. Not even her own family knows who her mother was. Can I *assume* she is of Spanish descent based upon his previous relationships? Yes. But there is no proof, and she looks every bit of her father. My men would never question it."

"Then Sal?" she asked frustratingly. "You would have supported that fucking union."

"Salvatore Lastra is one hundred percent Italian. I can take his mother back generations." Dante made it very clear. "The one Italian son Lucifer had, he gave up."

Let it go, she whispered to herself.

Maria had reached the end of her rope. There was nothing more she could say to get her father to approve of her marriage, so she had nothing more to say to him. The one thing she knew about her father was that he would never change. It was why he had his hand in making her who she was, why she stood so strongly as a woman who wanted to be taken seriously and to hold power in this family. If twenty-two years hadn't proved he wouldn't change his ways because she was a woman, Dante wasn't going to change his ways about Dominic not being of full Italian descent in the next five minutes.

"I'm sorry that I can't be there." Dante stood solemnly, saying the words that he truly meant as he went for the door. "But I hope you two enjoy my wedding gift."

Maria didn't know what she expected, but it hadn't been the emotions she felt as she sat there alone. She had been fine with her father not attending her wedding before he had come in, but now she couldn't help but feel hurt that her father refused to walk his daughter down the aisle. He chose *the family* over his own family yet again, and this time ... it truly hurt.

She had to fight down the tears as she went for the door. Maria was already running late, and while she needed a good cry, she wouldn't allow herself one.

Opening the door, Maria's emerald green eyes were already on the verge of tears before she saw the man waiting behind the door. He held the same emotions in his cold heart that were in hers right now.

"Maria"—Lucca held out his arm—"may *I* walk you down the aisle?"

THE LETTER M

As *Maria walked down the* aisle alongside her brother, she felt as if she was floating on air from being up so high in the open sky. The sun was beginning to set, and the glittering city below was starting to sparkle. At the top of the Casino Hotel, with just the few people they had shared the day with before, made this the only acceptable and most perfect wedding in her eyes.

Looking at Dominic as she took each step, made her cold, dead heart feel as if it had been hit with a defibrillator from the possessive way he was staring at her.

Dom held his tatted hand out as she approached …

Taking his hand, she wasn't sure she would ever let go.

Both men gave each other a nod as her brother took her bouquet, then went to take a seat next to his fiancée. Dante might not accept the validity of their union in the *family*, but Lucca was making sure it was.

Clasping both their hands together, the contact sent an electric charge through her at the firm hold Dominic had on her, showing her that she wasn't the only one who planned to never let go.

"You look beautiful, princess," he whispered the words for only her to hear.

"Thank you." Maria took in the sight of him as he stood in a suit that made him somehow look hotter than ever. She let him see with her eyes just what she thought of him. "You do too."

Maria and Dominic stood in front of their families, alone, at the top of the city. The only other participating member was the one neither Maria nor Dominic had expected to be there.

Sal normally didn't come out from behind his computer, always watching the cameras, trying to find One-Shot, but he made an appearance in a way none of them had expected . . . .

Clearing his throat, Sal began, "Dominic and Maria have chosen us, those special and most important to them, to witness and celebrate the beginning of their life together. Today, as we create this marriage, we also create a new bond and a new sense of family, one that will undoubtedly include all who are present here today.

"Do you, Dominic Luciano, choose Maria Caruso to be your partner in life, to support and respect her in her successes as well as her failures, to care for her in sickness and in health, to nurture her, and to grow with her throughout the seasons of your life together?"

Dominic's hazel eyes made her an oath. "I do."

"Do you, Maria Caruso, choose Dominic Luciano to be your partner in life, to support and respect him in his successes as well as his failures, to care for him in sickness and in health, to nurture him, and to grow with him throughout the seasons of your life together?"

"I do," Maria said the words she never thought she'd say as she made her oath to him.

Reaching into his pocket, Sal gave the ring to a brother.

Taking the ring, Dominic began with glossy eyes. "Through this ring," he said, sliding it onto her slender finger, "I accept you as my wife, now and for all time."

Maria stared down at her finger, seeing the ring that he had chosen for her. The gold intricate band with small diamonds throughout sat on top of her engagement ring like a crown.

Sal went to his other pocket, handing the ring she had chosen for Dominic to a sister.

"Through this ring"—Maria slid the thick gold band that was encrusted in tiny diamonds that was fit for a king over the letter M, as if their destiny had already been decided long ago—"I accept you as my husband, now and for all time."

"Before us no longer stands Maria and Dominic alone, but one couple about to embark on a new future," Sal spoke over the sniffling of the girls. "One that they hope you will share in and be a part of as their marriage journey begins and lasts long after the celebration ends tonight. I now pronounce you husband and wife." Grinning from ear to ear, he concluded, "Dom, you may now kiss your bride."

Maria's heels left the ground when Dominic swept her up in his arms. Her new husband didn't hold anything back, giving her a passionate kiss that had her wondering if the stars that were now overhead were closer than they appeared.

A GIFT FROM
MY FATHER

Walking into their small reception, hand in hand, Maria finally found out what gift her father had gotten them for their wedding as she heard the voice sing.

The girls who had tears in their eyes on top of the building now sat with fresh tears in their eyes for a whole different reason.

Jordan James started out at fifteen years old as every girl's young heartthrob. In his later twenties now, he had been through ups and downs throughout his very successful career, but three things stayed the same—he had one hell of a voice, a massive fanbase who would always support him, and he was drop-dead gorgeous.

The celebrity had frequented the Casino Hotel throughout the years whenever he was in the city for a concert, and her father had always taken great care of him. Maria guessed he must've gotten in the red while he was here, and this was how he planned to pay his debt.

Jordan liked booze, gambling, women, and everything else in his playboy rich lifestyle—which had landed him in hot water. Needless to say, the underground casino was his favorite place to be.

Every girl's dream would be to either marry the singer or have him sing at her wedding, and somehow, if it all wasn't perfect enough, Maria's first dance with Dominic as husband and wife would be just that.

Leading her onto the dance floor, Dom wrapped his hand around her waist while he lifted up the hand they were holding. Swaying to the beautiful song, he smiled as he leaned his head down toward her ear. "Thank you for wearing white this time, princess."

"No promises for next time. I'd personally like to find out what would happen if I didn't."

"I have no doubt that you will." Dominic laughed. "I wasn't aware we would have such great guest appearances, but I suppose I should have guessed, since I was marrying you."

"Yes, well, apparently, Sal is an ordained minister now." She laughed herself. "I wonder how long that took to print off his computer and what happened to the person who was supposed to be marrying us."

"I loved it," he admitted to her so sweetly. "It made marrying you that much more special to me, Maria."

"Me, too," she agreed, finding herself happy that he was happy.

Motioning her head toward the singer, she addressed their second elusive guest, "And that is a gift from my father."

His brows slightly furrowed. "It is?"

"Yes … He appreciates the lower level festivities and must've owed my father a favor."

"I see." Dom smiled. "My sister is crying. She was obsessed with him when his first song came out. I couldn't get her to quit singing that stupid song."

She gave a quick look around. "I think all the girls are crying."

"But not you." He spun her. "Does not even Jordan James have an effect on Maria Caruso?"

"He's not my type. I only have one of those." Her skirt lightly twirled around her. "You."

He tapped the ring he had just put on her finger with the hands that were in the air. "I know, I have proof."

Staring at their hands, she couldn't get over how they looked together. "I love my ring. It's so beautiful."

"I thought my princess needed a crown."

Ugh. The way he treated her and the things he said just made her melt more every day.

Kissing her on the cheek, he thanked her for his. "And I love mine, even though something tells me I'd hate to know how much it cost."

"Kat helped me pick it out yesterday." She could immediately see how much more special it now was to him. The Lucianos weren't afraid of jewelry. The bigger, the better. They loved thick, weighty pieces, and Maria wanted him to have the best one that made his tattoos that much sexier. "And don't worry about it," she assured him with an evil smile, remembering sliding that black credit card. "Lucca wanted me to marry you, so I made him pay for it."

Dom shook his head at her, realizing how much trouble he put himself in by marrying her. "Maria, I love you, and I love the matching shoes you bought me, but you do know you're a bit spoiled, right?"

"Like I said, you don't call me princess for nothing." She placed a light kiss on his lips. "Would you want me to change?"

"Hell no." He kissed her back. "All I want to do is spoil you."

"I noticed." Maria smiled, reminded of the gift. "The shoes would have also been a great way to get me to marry you sooner."

"Well, I can't wait to see them up close later tonight," he said hotly, leaning down in her ear once again.

"Why wait?" she groaned as her stomach somersaulted. "We can go right now."

"Sorry, princess, but you're going to have to wait a bit longer." Dominic pulled her closer to him. "You can only get Jordan James to sing at your wedding once."

He has a point. Maria turned to look at their family and motioned for the couples to come up and share their first dance.

The girls had never dragged their men out of their seats faster, each couple coming up to slow dance together. However, the girls weren't looking up at their men; their eyes were focused on Jordan James.

Maria had never seen Chloe look at another man in her life, but she was glancing over at the singer, starstruck. Both she and Elle were girly girls at heart and had been in love with the singer since he exploded onto the music scene. Lake and Adalyn being in love with him went without saying.

Hearing the song beginning to end, she looked back at her husband, seeing the pure love in his hazel depths, as he stared at her.

"I have never been so happy in my life, Maria," he whispered to her with such honestly, as he placed his forehead against hers. "I just want you to know that."

"I don't think I have either," she admitted, closing her eyes, Maria didn't have many feelings, but she felt many things as their first and most perfect dance came to an end.

All clapping as the song ended, the girls' much more enthusiastically, Jordan exited off the stage and headed straight for the married couple.

"You're looking as beautiful as ever, Maria," Jordan complimented with a sly smile as he gave her a nod before he looked at them both. "Your father wanted me to tell you that he was sorry he couldn't make it, and he wanted me to congratulate you both, but I think you're the one to congratulate." He held out a hand to Dom.

Maria couldn't help but smile at Dominic, who had a look of shock on his face as he looked at her.

"That is true." Dom then smiled, taking the singer's hand. "Thank you for singing for us."

"No problem." Jordan's eyes slightly sparkled, clearly thinking about how he planned to spend the rest of the night. "Well, I hope you all have a lovely rest of your ni—"

"Actually." Maria stopped him from leaving, watching the men drag their women back to their seats to keep them away from the singer. "Do you think you can sing a few more of your best hits for me?"

"I don't actually sing a lot of my songs anymore," Jordan told her, not wanting to sing the songs that had made him famous at fifteen.

"Listen, I would tell you that I'd make sure you were taken care of for the rest of your stay," Maria just cut to the chase, giving him the blunt and honest truth, "but my friends are all in love with you, and I'm really just trying to piss my brothers and their boyfriends off."

"Well, in that case"—Jordan smiled a million-dollar smile as he looked at the uncomfortable men in the room—"I will."

Appreciating her honesty, Jordan headed back to the stage and began singing the song that made him famous as the girls started screaming and rushing the stage to dance together, leaving their men behind.

I knew he would understand. She mentally smiled to herself, knowing Jordan liked pissing people off as much as she did.

Knowing exactly where his wife wanted to go, they headed toward the table of men.

"So, you're telling me I got to marry probably the only woman in the world who turned down Jordan James?" Dom said to Maria.

Matthias, who had been taking a sip of his champagne, spit it out. "You turned down *him*?" He was one of the only ones unbothered by Jordan's presence, since he didn't have a woman. "I thought I might have lost my touch when I met you."

Taking a seat on Dominic's lap, she smiled, as it was clear he didn't feel anything toward her now, but it had apparently worried him that his playboy antics might have been wearing off.

"Oh, please," Vincent snarled at her, watching Lake lose her shit, knowing Maria was the reason Jordan was still singing. "Maria's turned down every man in the city because she's a frigid bitch. It's not a compliment." He nodded a furious head toward Dominic. "God only knows why she lets you touch her."

"Watch it," Maria hissed at him in warning before Dom could say anything, and he quickly realized he didn't need to stick up for her at all.

"What are you gonna do?" He tried to look through them to where they suddenly blocked his view of the girls freaking out. "Poke me with your little heel?"

Lucca's attention, that had been on his fiancée, went to Vincent's face, waiting for it, as did Dom's. Nero gave his friend a sympathetic look.

Vincent stupidly continued, his eyes not on Maria. "Oh, I'm so fucking scare— *What the fuck!*"

If they hadn't been watching Vincent, then their eyes would have been drawn by the flash of the object whizzing by. The only one who missed it was Leo, not looking at Vincent until he yelled.

Vincent grabbed the side of his face that hadn't been black and blue from her husband. *"What the hell was that? A fucking hammer?"*

"My little heel," Maria said, proud that she had hit her target perfectly.

"*Jesus Christ!*" Vincent wiped the blood that was beginning to form on his cheekbone. "What is it fucking made of? Cement?"

Both Lucca and Dominic knew what it was like to have blood drawn by the woman, and they looked awfully pleased.

"No … crystals."

Cassius was the one to pick up the shoe. He gave the slightest hint of a smile when he gave it gave it back to her.

"You better not have hurt my wife's shoe, or I'll break the other side of your face and make you pay for a new pair."

"*Me?*" Vincent looked at Dom like he was crazy. "I'm the fucking victim! She threw it at me!"

Maria gave the shoe a once-over, seeing they still looked brand new. "I like Louboutin for a reason. They're fine."

"Good, 'cause I think she already broke the rest of my face." Vincent held the throbbing pain on his face, feeling like the shoe from hell broke something.

"I don't know why you're surprised after yesterday," Amo spat at him like he was an idiot.

"What happened yesterday?" Dom asked.

All the men looked at him. Clearly, the girls had folded once they were alone with their men.

Maria gave her shoe a little twirl, daring one of them to speak. Not one uttered a word as she slipped it back on ….

"*Ahh!*"

The girls screeching behind them had all their heads turning as Jordan took off his suit jacket and rolled up the sleeves of his button-up white shirt that was hardly buttoned to reveal the black and white tattoos.

Matthias proudly raised his glass to the pussy legend on stage as he addressed the guys around him. "Men, this is why you invest in tattoos."

"He has a point," Angel bit out, watching Adalyn lose her shit.

Drago looked to be the most furious as his voice came out guttural. "I thought Kat was raised with a bunch of brothers?"

"She was, but I encouraged her love of girly things because it was cute." Dominic took the champagne from his brother-in-law's hand. "You're welcome."

Maria couldn't help but laugh, enjoying Drago's pain. It was obvious her husband had had fun raising a girl out of a bunch of boys.

"Man, Elle wouldn't even kiss me last night, and now this." Nero looked frustrated. "She ain't gonna want nothing to do with me for a week."

"Yeah, because these two couldn't even manage to date for five fucking seconds," Vincent threw at them. "I told you this would happen. They all expect us to get down on one knee now."

The only reason Dominic wasn't jumping over the table was because Maria sat in his lap. "Will someone please tell me who the fuck invited this prick? Because I specifically remember never inviting you."

"I'm Lake's plus one." Vincent looked at him stupidly. "Duh."

"It's okay." Maria patted Dom's chest, keeping him down. "If you knock him out a second time, he won't wake up and he'll miss this."

"In that case, thanks for coming." Settling back, Dom agreed that him having to watch Jordan serenade his girl was better.

Vincent gave him a silent *fuck you* with his eyes.

Maria thought Lucca sat awfully quiet as he watched Chloe. She knew her brother, but even she couldn't tell his dark thoughts behind his blue-green eyes.

"Y'all really must not know women." Matthias tossed back his drink. "Because this means they are going to leave here horny as fuck, and yes, they might be imagining Jordan as they're fucking you, but they will put out *a lot.*"

She could see the men were torn between loving and hating that fact, while one of them just hated it ...

"Thanks for that," Dominic gritted out, downing the rest of the contents of his glass as he sat beside Drago.

Drago the tank scooted his chair a bit to the side, unsure if their second fight would end in a tie.

Running her hands over his chest, she soothed him, instantly calming him and silently reminding him that his sister was married and happy and nothing else mattered.

"So, what exactly did the girls do yesterday?" he asked, smiling as he raised a brow.

Maria gave them all a daring look, but the one she would never hurt spoke. "They broke into some guy's car and dumped a bunch of glitter in it," Leo told him.

"That's some serious fucked up shit," Matthias spat at her,

unable to imagine the thought in his precious baby.

"No, it was just," she stated, making herself clear. "He cheated on a girl with her own sister."

"We heard." Lucca shot her a look but didn't look too mad.

"I wonder"—Dominic took her chin with his fingers that now displayed a glistening ring—"whose idea it was."

"Definitely Kat's," Maria obviously lied, smiling as she brought her lips to his.

"Ew, please get a room." Nero shivered in disgust.

"Okay"—Dominic scooped her up in his arms as he stood— "we will."

"Finally," she gasped out, wrapping her arms around his neck as he quickly went for the door and she started laughing at his sudden urgency.

Seeing Jordan James wave as he sang, the girls turned around to see Dom rushing Maria out. They gave her a quick wave for good luck, knowing exactly why she was leaving.

Maria couldn't help herself as she yelled out over the music, "Sign their tits for me, Jordan!"

FUCK ME OUT OF YOUR BLOODSTREAM

Dominic didn't let Maria's feet hit the floor until they were in the apartment. He didn't seem to trust himself to carry her up the stairs to her bedroom after bringing her all the way here.

Maria could feel it in him. It wasn't nerves; it was more like … anxiousness. *Maybe?* She wasn't really sure, but she did know she felt more relaxed than he seemed to, and he wasn't the one that was about to lose his virginity.

"Do you want a drink?" she offered.

Dominic shook his head, his hazel eyes unwavering from her and looked darker than usual, making her desperately wish she could read his thoughts.

"Okay ..." Maria put her fingers to her waist, revealing her little secret, as the long skirt flitted to the ground.

She watched his Adam's apple bob at the sight of her in the high-cut bodysuit that bared the curve of her hip and the length of her thighs.

Slowly, she turned, heading up the stairs while giving him a view of the thong suit riding up her ass. Maria made her way up in the stairs in her heels, aware of Dominic blindly following behind her.

Maria's goal was to have a lot of nuptial bliss in her near future. Namely, in the next five minutes. As they entered her bedroom, she was scared that he still wouldn't touch her by the look on his face, that for some reason, he was still afraid his sins would transfer to her, even after he protected her in the only way he knew how by marrying her.

Helping him out and scared he wouldn't initiate, she slipped one strap down off her shoulder, then the other, revealing her perfect C-cup breasts before slowly shimmying out of the bodysuit, until it was laying at her feet.

Standing unclothed before her husband for the very first time, Dominic's hazel eyes slid from her face down her body, making Maria swear she could feel the heat of his touch just from his eyes alone.

"You have your belly button pierced?" he asked as he stopped from looking any further.

Maria nodded, feeling butterflies fluttering in her stomach as her husband stared at her in the same possessive manner he did when he saw her walk down the aisle.

Taking a step closer to her until he was close enough to reach her, Dominic swallowed hard as he outstretched his shaky tatted hands. It wasn't from weakness, but from power, as he tried to keep himself in control.

Instinctively, Maria knew why he was holding back. His fears of hurting her and her soul were still ruling him, but the moment his hands touched her belly … he lost the battle.

Giving in, Dominic's palms went over her flat abdomen, going over her belly button ring before sliding up to her breasts.

The second she felt the pad of his thumb roam over her pointy, hard nipple, Maria brought her hands to his jacket to rip it off him.

Dom let her take the suit jacket off, and then his tie, but as soon as she went for the button on his shirt, he lifted her chin with his finger. Craning her neck upward, as he loved to do, his hazel eyes glowed as they took her in and stopped her from continuing. "I'll let you have your turn next."

In an instant, Maria found herself flipped around, the light hand on her hair telling her what he wanted as he pushed her toward the bed. Sliding on her silk sheets, she arched her back as she crawled on top.

"I have dreamed of this moment every second of every day, Maria," he said as he slid his hand from her head that he'd guided to the bed before he brought it all the way down her back in one, long line. "You will let me have my dream, and then I will give you yours."

Maria moaned into the sheets from his deep voice and words alone. Whatever part of himself he'd held back—the side of him he found sinful—had come out to play.

When his hand touched her uplifted ass, he placed his other hand on her, then took two handfuls of her pretty ass cheeks before he spread them apart. "Ah, Maria, I have the prettiest view of your gorgeous pink pussy." She knew she was already wet, he leaned his head down and licked the swollen bud before traveling all the way through the folds of her pussy and then her ass in one entire lick.

"Please ..." Maria's moan finally escaped. All she wanted was for him to relieve the constant ache she had felt every time he kissed her, and left her unsatisfied. And she loved everything he was doing to her, but it wasn't relieving the ache; it was just making it worse ... "Please just fuck me!"

"I could have made you come three times for me already." He let her know he was sure of those words—Maria didn't doubt it— as he brought his mouth to her ass cheek, taking a playful bite that stung before he soothed it with a kiss. "But you're not going to be able to fuck me out of your bloodstream, princess."

Maria's body screamed out as he flipped to her back now, letting only the smallest shriek escape her lips. Her eyes went to the face of the man who was controlling her body like it was nothing, that it would do his bidding and whatever he so pleased.

"No matter how many times we fuck, Maria, or how many times I make you come for me"—Dominic continued his puppetry, still standing at the edge of the bed while he raised her legs in the air—"you will never get over the feeling of needing to fuck me, because I fucking won't allow it."

Holy fuck. If the ring on her finger wasn't indication enough that she felt something for this man, then that was. The things that she would never allow any other man to say or do to her only made her that much wetter than she already was.

She darted her tongue out to lick her lips. "How about you fuck me already and let me find out."

"Don't worry." He smiled as he placed one of her heeled feet on his shoulder, then showed special care to the other, taking in the way her foot looked in the heels that he'd bought and obviously dreamed about fucking her in. "I'll give you what you want as soon as I'm done, princess."

Watching him kiss the exposed top of her feet, she was somehow turned on even more. She loved the way he looked at them, adored them, and the shoes she wore.

Breathing heavily, her chest rose and fell as she said, "You know ... I think you have a foot fetish."

Holding both ankles, he clicked her heels back together in front of his face, high in the air, then slowly spread her straight, long legs apart. "I'm aware."

She lay there, doing his bidding, as his eyes took in the exposed sight of her. She had never felt so self-conscious or vulnerable in her existence, but it all was quickly pushed to the side at his touch.

Taking his middle finger, he let her juices wet his finger before he slipped it deep into her pussy and pulled it out in the next. "Heaven," he groaned when he put his finger into his mouth to taste her elixir.

"Please!" she cried, reaching the end of her rope, not knowing how much more teasing she could take. He could fucking do that *after* he fucked her. "Dominic, you have to fucking give me something."

"My dream, not yours," he reminded her, now putting two fingers back in.

While what he was doing to her insides felt like bliss, they were very careful movements, meant to coax her for what was to come and not release the pressure. Instead, each stroke only built her pleasure higher.

Feeling him slowly remove the digits, Maria slightly rose up to quickly grab his wrist. She brought his fingers to her lips for her to taste the "heaven" as she slid them to the back of her throat and sucked.

Looking up at him when she slid the tips past her pouty lips, Maria said the magic words ... "Fuck me."

Immediately, Dominic placed his hand at the bottom of her throat, the action making her crane her pretty, long neck up to him as he crashed his lips down onto hers hard. Forcing his tongue into her waiting, open mouth, he stole back the piece of heaven she had taken from him.

Whispering into her ear, he asked, "You want me to fuck you, princess?"

"*Yes* ..." she ground out, thinking, *Finally!*

The whisper in her ear this time was a command. "Then lay back down ... and let me fucking finish."

Maria fell back onto the bed in a daze, obeying his order, hoping it would give her some points.

When her tits swayed to the side, the motion alone had Dom unbuckling his belt.

That seems to have fucking worked all right.

Her gaze went to his hands. Biting down on her bottom lip, she waited in anticipation, but she had only seen a flash of his skin before she felt the tip of his dick at her entrance.

Even though she was on cold, silk sheets, Maria felt her temperature rise as he slickly stroked his dick between her lips to coat it in her juices.

"You are the hottest fucking thing I've ever seen," he said, like it took all his strength not to come on her now.

Loving the sensation of what felt like a very large cock on her, she couldn't help but pout, wanting to see more of him as he stood there, still clothed. "I wish you would let me see yo—"

Maria gave a start of surprise when she felt the tip of his cock enter her. The slight pain had her head falling back against the bed as pure pleasure rocked her world, her nails digging deeper into the sheets she was about to pierce through.

"Am I hurting you?" Dom asked, the fear in him slightly returning.

Quickly, Maria answered, "No," greedily making sure her word held no hint of anything but satisfaction. The last thing she wanted was his conscience stopping this. It might feel a bit uncomfortable, but it would hurt a hell of a lot more if he stopped.

"Good." Dom's voice was pure seduction. The slow movement of his dick slid higher inside of her when he bent her knees to her chest, pushing on the back of her thighs until he folded her, only her heels in the air.

Seeing the sweat that beaded his brow, she knew he was still trying to hold back from hurting her. His movements were slow and precise while his eyes told her he wanted more.

Maria tried to coax him, as if it was his first time and not hers. "I don't break. Fuck me harder."

"Maria …" he hissed. "I don't need instructions." He began rocking against her, barely increasing his speed.

"Are you trying to drive me insane?"

"Yes, it's the best part of my dream." His voice slightly softened as he continued his motions inside of her. "You falling apart in my arms, wanting more and more, a night with Maria Caruso screaming my name; what man could ask for more?"

Maybe a man couldn't, but a woman could.

Maria started to plead, "Faster."

He moved against her faster. "Like this?"

"Yes!" *Damn*, him going faster just made the ache worse. "Slow down."

"No, princess." He showed her pussy no remorse. "There's no going back now."

His thrusts became harder, faster, searing flames of desire coursing through her body as Dom's hips slammed against hers.

If he expected a limp noodle in his bed, he was about to get educated.

Forcing her legs from his grasp, she crossed them behind his back, lifting herself into his thrusts.

Excitement built higher as they moved together, battling each other in an erotic skirmish of wills to bring the other to surrender. Maria was no submissive and would never be. Dominic was willing to give in to Maria's demands, but in bed, he wanted to exert his dominance.

Maria writhed under him, arching into him to drive him deeper. Smiling, he showed his dimples as he leaned down, branding her nipple with his tongue, twirling the bud before biting down.

For the first time, Maria gave in as she screamed his name. It felt too fucking good. In reward, she felt the ache burst into an explosion that had her clinging to him. Feeling his cock jerk inside of her only set Maria off on another round of explosions.

Damn. From his confident smile as he kissed her, there was no way Dom didn't know she had come twice. Fine, he might have won the first battle, but he had promised her the next turn. There was plenty of time for war.

"My turn." She smiled as she rose up and made him stand back, fully erect. Now she wasn't going to take no for an answer. "I want your clothes off."

Maria went to the buttons of his shirt, slowly unbuttoning them one by one from where she sat on the edge of the bed. Dom stood there, letting her have her turn as she made him slip the shirt off his shoulders.

Her throat constricted, tightening as she looked up at his body. Every fucking muscle was fully formed. He had a goddamn six pack that had to be sculpted by God Himself. Under his coat, Dominic had hid the fact he was ripped beyond belief, and even her dreams couldn't compare to the body she had imagined.

"I thought you would have more tattoos?" At least that was how she had dreamed him.

He shook his head. "Only the ones on my fingers. A tattoo has to have meaning for me to get."

What she didn't understand was why he had tried so hard to keep her from seeing his body, denying her request each time. Until now, as the city lights caught the imperfections in his tanned skin. The little scars that riddled his body, Maria didn't have to ask who or what they'd come from. It was why that eight letter word rested on his fingers had meaning.

If he expected her to hate them, then he was dead fucking wrong.

Forcing his pants down farther, she focused on his already rising cock that looked even better than she imagined when it slid inside of her just minutes ago.

Leaning forward, she licked the white leftover liquid off the tip of his dick. Then, as soon as she saw it become engorged again, Maria had him in her mouth within seconds.

"Fuck …" His head fell back in bliss for a moment before his hot, hazel depths returned to the pretty face that was sucking his cock. "You're not supposed to be that good at it for your first time, princess. *Jesus.*"

Maria looked up at him through her full lashes while she took him to the back of her throat.

"You better stop now"—he took a handful of her gold hair in warning—"before I come in your pretty mouth and your turn will be up."

Letting the tip fall from her mouth, Maria stood, heeding his warning. Then she forced him out of his pants the rest of the way before his back hit the bed.

All Maria knew, as she crawled on top of him where he now lay in the middle of the bed, was she wasn't going to be able to keep her hands off him. She didn't know bodies like this even existed, and she planned to appreciate every inch. Starting on his abs, Maria licked between the vertical line that separated the muscles. With her hands, she roamed over each peak and valley all the way up to his chest. Seeing the big bruise on his abdomen from his fight the night before, Maria placed a kiss on the discoloration before she pressed her lips into a scar that glittered. Going to another, she kissed more of them, letting him know how attractive she found his body, despite the blemishes.

Moving up, Maria finally let herself kiss the indentation on one cheek, letting her tongue fill the precious hole, then went to the other, showing the same attention to those two dents she couldn't get enough of. And finally, she kissed his lips as she straddled his hips. His dick was in the perfect position to impale herself on.

Breaking their kiss, Maria grinned down at Dom, rotating her hips to sink him farther onto him. "I plan to win this war."

Dominic's brows drew together. "What war?"

"The war of who can fuck each other better … You won last time"—her breasts began to bounce in his face—"but I plan to win this time."

"You think this is a war …?" He trailed off. His eyes had traveled down, getting an eyeful. "And who fucks better is the winner?"

"Yes." Maria started bouncing on his dick when she grew slicker. "Don't you?"

Instead of answering, Dom's eyes went to the ceiling, thanking God Himself under his breath. Maria was too focused on her movements and feelings that she hadn't paid too much attention.

Reaching out, he played with her belly ring, as he grabbed her inner thigh with his other hand. His touch on the sensitive flesh sent flames to her pussy, which was already beginning to doubt her ability to remain in control as long as Dominic had it. When she felt his fingers move higher toward her clit, she knew she was in trouble. She would tell him to keep his hands to himself, but she didn't want to alert him that she was having trouble stopping herself from coming again so quickly. How was she was supposed to know she would enjoy this position so much? She could control the speed and depth. Plus, she had him right where she wanted him.

"Looks like you're having a little trouble, princess."

Maria bit her lip when Dominic started thrusting his hips upward and she slammed down on him.

Shaking her head, she denied it, biting her lip harder as the fire began to rise.

"How about we call this a draw, princess?" Dom hooked a hand around her neck, bringing her head down to kiss him. "We can live to fuck another day."

Maria knew she was beat when the tingles started where their bodies were fused together.

"Fine." She already started giving up her body for him to take yet again. "As long as you remember this doesn't really count. I'll get better the more I practice."

Maria came crashing on his dick as Dominic thanked God for her again.

IN HER DREAMS

Smiling, *Dominic packed his strong-willed* yet limp woman into the bathroom and into the waiting shower.

If she hadn't just ate her words, Maria would tell him to wipe that smile off his face, but luckily, it was cute.

As Dom washed his princess, Maria washed him, both of them caring for the other and enjoying the bodies of whom they just married.

By the time he had taken his time washing her, she already felt the desire he had promised would happen. Dominic had been right; *I am never going to fuck him out of my bloodstream, am I?*

Reaching for his dick, he had to snatch her wrist, stopping her.

"You just had your turn, princess," he reminded her that she was going to have to wait as he shut the water off.

He dried her off quickly before running the towel over himself, not letting his sneaky bride do it, knowing she wouldn't wait her turn.

Lovingly placing Maria on her back on the middle of her bed, he laid down beside her, then began to rub the pad of his thumb over her pretty, pink nipple until it came to a hard point. He leaned down to take her breast into his mouth, and her eyes rolled to the back of her head when he teasingly lapped at the point.

Fuck, how did she already want him so badly? How many more times did she need to come before that feeling wore off? Right now, she had come three times.

He moved his hand and mouth to the flat of her belly where he played with her piercing. "I still can't believe your belly button is pierced."

"Do you like it?" she asked, already knowing the answer, but she couldn't help asking.

"Yes." He placed a kiss on the middle of her belly. "It'll be a shame when you take it off once you're pregnant."

Maria laughed, raising up on her elbows. She looked at him as he traveled lower down her waist. "We've been married five minutes and you're already talking about that?"

"Mmhmm." He spread her legs apart as he went even lower. "I'm thinking ... four."

"*Fou*—"

Maria's head fell back when he lapped at her clit.

"Four is a good number." He spread her folds apart farther. "I know I can handle four."

"*Four!*"

Again, Maria's thoughts left her body when his tongue entered her. Trying to gather her thoughts, she spoke through gritted teeth, "You expect me to pop four babies out of me when you haven't even asked if I want children or not?"

Dom looked up at her from what he was doing. "Do you?"

"I haven't really thought about it," she told him honestly.

"You will," he said confidently, returning his mouth to her pussy. "And you'll give me four."

As much as Maria wanted to be offended right now, the magic he was working on her had her biting back her sarcasm. "What makes you so sure?"

"Because"——he went deeper than before——"you'll like making them."

"Mmm ..." Maria moaned, her body betraying her as to how easily he could get her to give in. "If we do——and I'm not saying we will——I only want a girl," she warned.

Dom pulled back momentarily and smiled. "I don't think you get to choose, princess."

"My body wouldn't betray me like that," she announced while it was doing that very thing. "I'll *will* my body into having a girl."

"I like girls," Dom told her softly, having no problem with that. "But you will have girl*s.*"

She was about to fight him on that when he sucked her tender bud into his mouth, knocking her senseless for a moment. She figured she would let it rest for now before she let herself begin to fall deeper, denying herself that she was to the unyielding man.

When he hadn't even flinched at the thought of only fathering daughters and not sons, it had made Maria's stomach flutter into a knot. She wished he didn't have to be so fucking perfect, especially right now as he continued to lap at her. The motions he did with that tongue were only meant to soothe. Having fucked her twice on her first night, she knew it was his way of massaging out the ache.

She moved her hands to his hair, rubbing her fingers through the thick, dark strands, while he continued his lazy motions. As much as she wanted her release, he denied it … until he had his fill of his "heaven," and he was certain she was done for the night.

Make that four times.

Nothing in his existence had come close to today, and no day ever would, as Maria lay there, sleeping in his arms. Their wedding had been everything he could never have dreamed of, and marrying her was everything he had.

Maria Caruso was everything he thought she would be and then some. But the best part was …

She was finally his.

"*I love you,*" he whispered the words he could see hurt when he said them while she was awake, because she wasn't capable of saying them back *yet*. Maybe there in her dreams … she could.

THE THRONE

Maria's heels clicked as she entered the room. Taking a seat in front of the desk, she smiled at the man behind it. "Well …"

Reclining back in his chair, the corner of his lips lifted as he brought the cigarette to his lips. "I wondered how long you would be married before you came here," he said as he raised his arm to check his watch. "Not even twenty-four hours."

"I know there's a reason why you wanted me to marry him, Lucca," she hinted, knowing full well he didn't do things out of the kindness of his black heart. Everything he did, every move the boogieman made, was for a reason.

His blue-green eyes glowed. "Do you remember what I told you?"

"You've told me many things, brother. You might need to be specific."

"I told you two people could take this city from me—" Lucca drew hard on his cigarette, the orange glow on the end turning a bright red as the smoke escaped his lips with his words. "—you and Dominic."

Maria hadn't forgotten. She just hadn't entertained the idea. Luckily for him, she had been born a woman and, at the time he had told her that, there was no relationship between her and Dom. However, it still didn't make sense ....

"If you truly believe that, why would you want us together?"

"I made Dominic a deal." Flicking his long ashes that were about to fall into the glass ashtray, he continued, "When I take Dante's place, I will restore the balance between the two families and give him fifty percent of the city."

She could see the truth in his eyes, while he saw the shock in hers.

Lucca smiled. "He didn't tell you?"

She shook her head. She had known they were working together and had made some deal, but she hadn't expected the underboss, who had dreamed of his crowning moment since birth, to give up half of what was already his—

"Chloe," she said the name of the sole reason he had done it. The last thing Lucca would want was a war that could end with his scarred beauty in the crosshairs.

Nodding slowly, he confirmed her exact thoughts.

"And this is supposed to excite me because I'm his wife?" She raised a non-impressed brow.

Lucca stood, walking over to the floor to ceiling window that were behind him.

Knowing what he wanted, she got up and followed him to the window.

"The first time I went to Blue Park … I liked it," Lucca admitted. "I kept going, and each time I went, the more addicted I got. It wasn't until I saw Dominic murder a man on the street and watched the body get picked up a moment later—as if nothing even happened—did I know what I was going to do." His cold voice somehow went darker. "I planned to take it."

Maria didn't doubt it. Each time she had gone, she found herself going back for more, whether it was to see Dominic or not.

She enjoyed being there. Blue Park had a raw, rough quality that made it addicting to their dark natures.

"Just the littlest taste of power will make you crave more, Maria," he told her the truth of basic human nature. "I know because that's exactly what happened to me and what I know will happen to him. A man like Dominic may be satiated for a bit with half, but he would never fully be satisfied. One day, he would come for more."

Turning from the view of the city, Maria's cold heart revealed itself. "Maybe I'd want him to …."

"I wouldn't doubt it." Lucca didn't seem surprised. "But I know you're not changing your last name for a reason, Maria. You love this family and this city just as much as me, and even when it turned against you"—he mentioned not only his heinous act of murdering Kayne, but her father and the mafia for not accepting her because of what was not between her legs—"you still didn't give it up."

Maria's gut told her something big was coming, that all of

Lucca's chess moves were about to come to fruition.

"And now"—turning from the window, Lucca faced her—"I'd like to reward you."

"You're going to let me become made ..." she whispered as her breath hitched in her throat.

The boogieman's haunting eyes glowed. "How does consigliere sound to you?"

"You want to make me your equal?" Maria couldn't believe it. As if having a woman become made wasn't ridiculous enough for his men to get behind, placing her beside him would cause an uproar. Her brain couldn't even begin to comprehend it ... until it did.

Sitting beside Lucca would ensure one thing—Dominic would never, ever have the taste for more.

Maria couldn't help but smile. "You're smart, brother, but even I didn't expect that."

Not trying to deny it, he raised a brow. "Do you blame me?"

"No," she simply said, going back to looking at the city. "I can understand."

Everything he did was for Chloe, and this was the smartest move he could make. It solidified Dominic and Lucca's reign together as one. Even the smallest threat was gone. Dom would never go after the Carusos if she was consigliere, nor would any other Luciano, while Lucca wouldn't risk it for Chloe, but his consigliere would also be married to the Luciano boss.

"What do you say, Maria?" Lucca whispered to her dark soul as he outstretched a hand. "Do we have a deal?"

She looked away from the city and over to his hand. She had just been offered everything her little black heart desired. All she had to do was shake on it ....

Turning back to face him, her pointy heels directed toward him, she stood strongly before the underboss. "I want two things before I do."

Lucca took back his hand, but he didn't shoot her down, waiting to hear her ask.

"No guards, but I will take a *driver* of my choosing to watch my back." It was a compromise. She didn't want a suit watching her every move or telling her where to go, but she did understand that her being the consigliere would come with more risks than she was already under.

He waited to hear the second stipulation before deciding.

"And"—Maria smiled—"I want you to buy me a car."

He raised an amused brow. "What kind?"

"Whatever one I want," she told him, not revealing what she had planned.

Lucca held his hand back out for her to take. "Deal."

Making her own deal with the boogieman, she shook his hand. "Deal."

It was decided. The three would share the throne.

Clicking her heels as she headed out of his office, she had almost forgotten.

"Oh, and Lucca"—Maria looked back at him from over her shoulder—"I know you've been secretly helping Cassius."

The underboss smiled, not denying it.

"Unfortunately, in the process, you taught him to smoke." Going for the door, she didn't have to look back as she walked through to know Lucca had no idea Cassius picked up that habit. "Now fucking undo it."

Dominic sat in the cold warehouse on his old, tufted leather chair. His tatted hands gripping the arms, he stared at his three brothers who stood before him on the other side of his desk.

Angel's, Matthias's, and Cassius's gazes were unwavering, staring down at him not as a brother but as the boss. Every one of them knew why they all were here—Dominic had yet to choose the titles of consigliere, underboss, and enforcer.

This was a decision he hadn't come to lightly. It was one that could break their family and bonds apart if he chose wrong or one brother felt slighted by another. The only reason Katarina wasn't here was because Lucca had noticed her talents and employed her as the Caruso bookkeeper. That Caruso job excluded her from holding any power in the Luciano family, as it did his wife Maria. Those two actions alone caused Dominic to give his full trust over to the underboss and future Caruso boss once and for all.

"I have come to a decision," he told them, meeting the eye of each man before moving to the next. "We run this family—"

Each brother waited on bated breath as Dominic said his final word."—together."

YOUR SOUL TO TAKE

"Do *I get to see* you finally shoot now or what?" she asked, standing in his backyard. She had been married to this man for a week, and while they had fucked their way through most of it, she needed to see the legendary Glock in actio—

"*What the fuck!*" she yelled when the gunshot went off beside her. He had been standing perfectly still one moment, and the next, his Glock was in his hand and had already fired.

Dominic laughed. "Sorry, princess, but you asked for it."

There is no fucking wa—

Maria's mouth dropped seeing the can yards away with a bullet hole right through the middle. How was something like that even possible? *But fuck me, that is so hot.*

Looking back from the can to him, she raised a brow and

smiled. "Can I try?"

"Have you ever shot a gun before?" he asked, slightly unsure or slightly scared.

She wanted to lie but didn't. "No." She had someone following her twenty-four seven; she didn't need to have a gun in her hand.

Releasing the mag, he put it in his jacket pocket before he racked it, clearing the chamber of the little bullet before it was safe.

"Okay, come here," he said, pulling her waist until he planted her right in front of him and the target. Handing her the gun, he showed her the correct stance that his father had taught him many years ago.

"Now, this finger"—he removed her pointer finger to where she had instinctively placed it on the trigger to let it rest under the barrel—"goes here. Your finger only touches the trigger when you're certain you want to pull it." He began to stress this fact even more. "The only reason I didn't shoot you that morning when you surprised me is because I kept my finger here. You must be completely certain who is on the other side before you do, because"—he placed her finger back on the trigger and lightly pulled … *click*—"once you do, it can't be undone."

"Okay." Maria tried to swallow through her suddenly tight throat from his grave words. "Dom … can I ask you a question?" She stopped the lesson for a moment.

He nodded.

Maria turned to face him. "That morning, when you and Kayne fought and you pulled your gun on him … " She remembered the words he had spoken to her: *I had the gun in my hand, Maria. I might not have been the one to take his life, but I can't promise you I wouldn't have done the same as Lucca five seconds later.* "Was your finger on the trigger?"

Even though a part of her, deep down, already knew the answer, she wanted Dominic to realize just how wrong she was to ever call him monstrous like his father. She wanted him to know, once and for all, that he was everything Lucifer and she were not.

Dominic Luciano was good.

"No." Shaking his head, his brows drew together, almost disbelieving it himself. "No, it wasn't."

"I know." Maria kissed his lips hard. "I know you wouldn't have done it." She kissed his lips over and over, trying to make him see that he was pure, that he wouldn't have ever done something that would have hurt her.

Maria made Dominic kiss her until he began to get it through his head, and by the time she was done, he had taken the gun from her and they snuck back inside to quietly go up the steps.

She placed one last tender kiss on his lips before he pushed her hard down onto his bed. Staring up at him, even though she knew he was good on the inside, on the outside, he looked like a mean motherfucker who was about to fuck her senseless yet again.

Dom went to throw his leather jacket off, but Maria stopped him,

"No ... Keep it on."

"What are you doing?" Maria sleepily came into the living area to see Dominic at the table. "It's late."

"Go on back to bed, princess. I'll be up when I'm done," he assured her, not taking his eyes away from his task.

Seeing his guns laid out on the table, Maria had watched him clean those things every night since she'd been here. Yes, they had only been married for a week, but it was weird. At least when she spent those first two days together in her penthouse, he hadn't, and her place didn't give her the creeps. She was going to have to do something about their living situation because, while yes, Maria was spoiled rotten, it wasn't the house that bothered her; it was the remaining presence of a certain someone.

"I don't think this is something you need to do every day, Dominic." Taking his hand, she tried to pull him back to bed. "Come on, It'll be here in the mornin—"

"No," he ordered harshly, removing his hand.

What the . . .?

Maria had never even seen him like this. She hadn't been with him long, but either way, this wasn't her Dominic who treated her the way every girl dreamed to be treated.

Ever since earlier today, when she had asked that question about Kayne, he had acted slightly different, like there was a war going on his head, as he refused to believe that he wouldn't have killed Kayne because it would have hurt her.

Dom grabbed her hand, pulling her back to him and down onto his lap so he could rest his head on her forehead. "I'm sorry."

"What's wrong?" she asked, touching his beautiful face.

It took him a moment before he told her, "Every night I sat here with my father and cleaned these guns. I couldn't eat dinner or go to sleep until it was done. It's a habit I've yet to break, and I'm sorry."

"It's okay," she whispered, giving him a kiss. Maria could see he was nowhere near ready to break that habit. It was something they would have to work on a little bit at a time. "I'll let you finish. Come back to bed whenever you're ready."

Giving her one last kiss, he let her go, and then he continued cleaning them.

Maria had to hide the boiling emotions that began to rock through her body. Walking up the stairs and into the room that was Dominic's but wasn't at all, it only added fuel to the fire as pure rage soared through her.

Looking through the little window, she stared at the pathetic man on the other side. "Can I go in?"

Lucca contemplated for a second before he nodded. "I'll give you a minute."

Maria waited until Lucca was out of sight before she slid the metal door open with all her might, stomping her stilettos inside.

The sight of the man did not scare her as she growled at the devil himself, "*You.*"

The chain at his ankle didn't even so much as rattle when he saw her. The grotesque man that was only kept alive by an inch of his life had spread his hands out into a cross as he looked up in the sky, welcoming her with open arms when Maria's hands went to his neck.

Her emerald eyes were in a death haze as she squeezed Lucifer's neck. No words needed to be spoken—the devil knew his fucking sins. She had watched Lucifer die in her mind a million times on her way over here. Having heard *enough*.

In the little time she already spent with Dominic, she heard enough of the things the devil did to his own children for a lifetime. This man needed to pay with his life, and she wanted it *now*. Lucca was never going to let this man die.

Seeing the life force almost leave him, she was so close …

"*Maria!*" Lucca entered the room in a rush, going to her hands and trying to pry them off his neck. "*What the fuck are you doing?*"

"*He needs to die!*" Maria shrilled out as she spit on the dead man who was catching his breath while Lucca held her back.

"He is not for you. Do you understand me?" Lucca threw her out of the room, trying to calm her down. "That is not your soul to take."

"Then get Dom in here!" she cried, hitting him. "Why the fuck haven't you brought him here yet?"

"Maria …" He tried to calm her as he shook her to force her eyes to his. "Dominic has already been here …"

THE NIGHT BEFORE
THEIR WEDDING...

"**H**ello, Father." *The words slid* from his lips, arching in an eerie smile. He had waited here quietly for his father to wake from his nightmares, only to be greeted by another. "You've never looked better."

Startled, Lucifer jumped back, the rattling chain wound around his ankle that had been tightened several times over from his weakening echoed throughout the room.

Dominic's head fell back in laughter. "I see you have finally met your match."

Seeing who it was, a bony Lucifer started to ease. "What took you so long?" he hissed.

"I knew the day Lucca took you that you wouldn't be dead anytime soon," Dom revealed.

"Then why come now?" His haggard voice was on the brink of giving up. The only reason he was alive was because Lucca had willed it so.

"Tomorrow is a special day for me, Father, and I've come to tell you the news."

Lucifer's ears perked up. It was the most alive he had looked.

Dom knew that his successes were going to be his father's, Lucifer would take the credit that he had raised him, and it would give him a happy death. Only one thing would make Lucifer roll in his grave.

"Tomorrow"—Dominic's hazel eyes glowed—"I marry Maria Caruso."

Any bit of sanity Lucifer had broke as he crawled across the floor, the chains rattling as he went for his son.

Dominic threw him on his back in an instant, digging his shoe into his father's neck while Lucifer looked like a zombie that'd been brought back to life as he tried to scratch and beat at his legs.

And he thought Maria's father had handled it badly.

"Lucca has given me permission to kill you," Dominic whispered the words of his final sweet release that had Lucifer stopping from pathetically trying to kill him. Dom could see the prayers in his soulless black eyes that he thought were about to be answered. Stepping onto his neck harder, he smiled evilly, one last time.

"I love her."

"I'm going to marry her.

"We will have children.

"And this Luciano blood that sits in my veins will be mixed with those you hate most.

"Sleep well tonight, Father"—suddenly, Dominic released the pressure at his neck—"because you have twenty-seven fucking more years to go."

MY TURN

Maria's heels sharply tapped on the porch as she entered the dark monastery of Lucifer's home. There wasn't a time she had come that she hadn't felt the scope of his vileness that had been hidden from sight.

The television was playing, and Dominic was on the couch, watching. Maria went to him, ignoring the free space on the couch to sit on his lap. His arms surrounded her in a loving circle.

How this man could feel an ounce of love in his body after being raised by Lucifer was a testament to his strength.

"I hate this fucking house."

Dom took his eyes off the television. "Then find a house you want, princess."

Dominic knew who she was talking about. "You went to see him?"

"Why didn't you kill him?" she asked, trying to understand how he could possibly walk away. "I tried, but Lucca stopped me. He's saving him for yo—"

"I'm not ready to put him out of his misery," Dom told her the truth.

"Put me out of my misery."

"What misery?" He hadn't missed what she mumbled under her breath.

She placed a kiss on his cheek where his dimple was. "I want you to wipe him out of my mind."

Dominic stood, lifting her into his arms. She started unbuttoning his shirt as they went up the steps. By the time he laid her down on the bed, both of them were in too much of a hurry to remove the other's clothes, seeing who could get themselves naked faster.

Taking her ankles, Dominic lifted both of her heels to his shoulder before taking her hips to pull her pussy to his dick.

Any thought of Lucifer went out of her head like a nuclear invasion when he slid inside of her. Leaning over her forced her legs to go higher.

"Dom ... we're never going to get a divorce, are we?" was the sighing moan she gave as he thrust inside of her.

A surrender? Probably. But damn, if the only time she gave control over was when he fucked her, was that really losing? *Or is it a win ...?* It felt like a fucking victory as she grew slick around his dick, and he started nibbling on her neck.

"No, we won't."

He was right; he was never leaving her bloodstream. Fucking Dominic was more addictive than the most expensive drug sold on the streets.

"I would kill you before I let you leave me," she said the harsh words in a sweet tone as she grabbed his hair to lift his head to show him she was joking … *kind of*. She would kill him before she would let another woman have this.

Maria had kept each and every expensive shoe and purse that she had owned because they were hers, and she didn't want to go out and see what was hers on someone else.

"Why would I leave you, princess, when I have everything I could ever want with you."

"Me, too," she breathed the words out.

Dom stopped moving inside of her. "You do?'

"What else could I want? You have a big dick and know how to use it."

"Oh." Dom laughed as he started moving again, but Maria could see the hurt in his eyes.

"You promised never to tell me no when I want something," she continued, despite wanting to come, but she was determined to hold out this time.

His dimples were nowhere in sight as she went on.

"Promised me only girls …"

He pumped inside her faster. "No, I didn't."

"Quit interrupting and go slower."

"Maria, are we fucking or are you trying to bust my nuts?"

"We're not fucking." She searched for his hand that held the thick ring she placed on his finger. "We're making love."

Dominic suddenly stopped moving to search her eyes. "You have to be in love to make love, princess."

"You told me you love me … don't you?" she asked.

"Yes."

"Then what's the problem?" she grumbled, wanting him to start back inside of her.

"Maria …" Dominic's brows drew together. "Are you telling me you love me?"

"Isn't that what I've been saying?"

He shook his head at her as he went back to thrusting deep inside of her. "I must have missed the L-word."

"I L-O-V-E you, Dominic." Maria bore her emerald eyes into his as he fucked her. "Did that spell it out for you?"

Damn, the dimples did it. Unable to hold out any longer, Maria arched on his dick and let Dominic chalk up another win. *Well … hell.*

"I love you, Maria," he whispered into her ear as he let himself go when he felt her surrender.

Maria just held him to her as his ragged breath beat her skin. "I love you … and it's my turn."

GHOSTS

"**W**hat the hell are we doing here?" Matthias asked, getting out of his car, followed by Cassius, who had come with him.

"I don't know. She won't tell me," Dominic said, sitting on the hood of his Mustang next to Maria.

Angel pulled up and got out of the car with Katarina, both wondering the same thing.

Maria got off the hood of the car, taking a step toward the ivy gate. She looked past it and right at Blue Manor. Turning back around, she looked at Dominic. "What would you say if I told you I wanted to buy that house?"

Matthias whispered, "Oh no."

Her eyes then went to all of the Luciano siblings. "For all of us?"

"I'd say you were fucking crazier than I thought, princess,"

Dominic said before smiling. "But I wouldn't expect anything less."

"My father set up a trust fund the day I was born. The agreement was, I'd have to be married to receive it." She took a step toward him. "And, well, I kinda already bought it."

"Jesus," Matthias muttered, walking off.

"*Cool*," Cassius and Kat said in unison as they went up to the gate, already dying to get inside.

Angel smiled. Unlike his twin who he went after, he wasn't scared of ghosts.

The truth was the Luciano family was about the only family who could live in that house unafraid. Their real ghosts walked the home they already lived in.

"Is that okay?" She nervously looked up at him.

Grabbing her hips, Dom brought her closer to him where he sat on his car. "It's an awfully big, haunted house, princess." Leaning closer to her lips, his dimples were on display. "You plan on giving me children to fill it up?"

Maria nodded her head. "One."

Dominic stopped his lips from coming any closer.

Okay ... "Two."

His lips went slightly closer but not close enough.

Final answer ... "Three."

Again, just a little bit closer, but his lips hadn't yet touched hers.

"Fine!" she grumbled, giving in. "Four."

Winning, Dominic's lips finally fell on hers in a kiss that had Maria's breath disappear, despite having fucked the man all night.

"Sorry to interrupt." Matthias came back over, breaking up their kiss rather rudely. "But what happens when we fucking find out there really are damn ghosts in there and that Blue Manor actually is fucking haunted?"

"Well"—Maria turned back around to look at the manor that her gut had told her to buy ever since she had first seen it—"we're not going in to find the money; we're going in to make a home."

THE CALL
EPILOGUE

T he cherry blossoms were at the height of their beauty. Sitting on a bench, a blossom fell onto her lap, already beginning to die.

Taking out her cell phone, Maria dialed a number that she was never going to dial again ….

"This is Kayne Evans. Leave a message, and I'll get back to you as soon as I can."

Beep.

Listening to her ghost for the final time, it no longer brought any feelings of missed chances, regret, rage, or grief.

Nothing was there anymore.

"It's been a while," Maria began. "I came to see the cherry blossoms. It's beautiful, Kayne. I remembered the day I came here with you one year ago, and you told me there was a lot about you I didn't know. Not only did you deceive me …

"You deceived Leo.

"You deceived Nero, Elle, Chloe … every student you had into believing you were a good person.

"I put my heart on the line and thought you were worth giving everything for …

"When you went out for that jog, I fell back asleep, planning a future with you. It was a future that would have lasted as long as the cherry blossoms do, because none of the time I spent with you was real. Even if you hadn't been a cop and just been a teacher, it wouldn't have lasted.

"You told me you loved me. There wasn't any more truth to that than any other lie you told me. I was a coldhearted bitch, yet I believed you. At least I wasn't the only woman who'd been taken in by that lie. Bristol believed you, too, didn't she? How many others were there who believed in your lies? At least you won't be around to spread your lies any longer. At least your son will never be hurt by you or your lies.

"Your love was as fragile as the cherry blossoms and lasted just as long. What I have with Dominic will last years, growing through the seasons and, year by year, grow stronger. That's real love, Kayne … and not what I had with you.

"When I hang up, I'm deleting your number. I don't need to call anymore. I don't even have the regret of thinking I loved you. That's how little I care about you and how much I love Dom."

Taking a breath, she finally said the last words as she let her ghost go. "Good-bye, Kayne."

Dominic stood under a cherry blossom tree far behind his wife. He watched her sitting on the bench.

Hearing the *ding*, he pulled the cracked phone out of his jacket pocket, seeing the call and voicemail.

He brought it because he knew Maria would call, knowing she and Kayne had visited here one year ago. She hadn't called Kayne's phone in so long, and he feared what she might say.

Holding the phone in his hand, he finally let it go ….

As the phone fell in the trash can, he walked to his wife and sat down beside her.

"It's beautiful, isn't it?" Maria said as the blossoms showered down on them.

He placed his hand on her … "It is."

"I love you … *so much*," she whispered, placing her hands over his tatted one that rested on her expectant belly, tears brimming her emerald eyes as she stared at her name written in beautiful cursive letters on his neck.

Dominic didn't need to listen to the message, because the wind that carried the cherry blossoms had whispered it to his soul.

"I love you, too, princess."

DADDY
EPILOGUE

Dominic held the little hand in his as they entered the school and pretended to be strong.

"Daddy …."

Feeling his hand tugged down when they grew nearer to the classroom that he once sent Katarina off to, he bent down to look in his daughter's eyes.

"Do I have to go?"

As badly as he didn't want her to go to kindergarten, he had to. "Yes, you do, my angel."

She looked at the classroom with her little dimpled cheeks. It was full of kids, already running around.

Dominic turned her cheek with a soft finger. "What is it?"

"What happens if they don't like me?"

"At first, they might not," he told her truth of what bearing the last name Luciano was like. "But I know, once they get to know you, they will come to love you, Angelica Luciano."

Looking down at his firstborn, he smiled when she finally nodded. She was a mixture of both him and his wife, which had shaken him to his core.

Hugging her to him, he wasn't sure if he was going to be able to let go. "I'll be waiting right here when school is over, okay?"

"I love you, Daddy." She tightly squeezed his neck.

It was everything Dom could do to keep the tears back on his daughter's first day of school.

The man no longer deserved to wear the leather coat he still wore every day of his life ... because he'd been turned into a puddle of mush by a single little girl.

Maria squeezed the hand in hers for dear life. "I can't believe I let you do this to me again!" she screamed out in pain.

"You're doing so good. Just a few more pushes, princess." He smiled, giving her his dimples as he swept her gold hair off her face. "I told you four, and it's the last one I'll ever make you give me."

"I swear to God, Dominic, I'm tying my tubes after th—ahhhh!!" she screamed, trying to shove the head out of her. She wanted to strangle her husband's neck when all she had was his tatted hand to murder.

"She's almost out … just one more push," he told her, looking down as his final child was being born.

For the very last time, Maria did the last big push she would ever fucking do.

Dominic's silence when the baby came out frightened Maria. "What is it? What's wrong?"

She felt her worse fears come to life.

"It's a," He practically croaked out the word, "boy."

"A boy?" Maria's eyes went wide, wondering how in the hell her doctor had missed that little fact. All three of their children were girls, and they were supposed to be adding another.

She didn't even know how she was supposed to feel, unprepared for this moment. What if she couldn't love a son like her daughters? But then the doctor laid her newborn son down on her chest.

Three children before this, and while she teared up with each one, none of them had her tears falling in streams down her cheeks.

Softly, she ran her hand through his blond, fuzzy hair as more tears fell. Her son reminded her of what used to be … as he was the spitting image of her once sweet baby brother …

Leo.

THE STORY OF THE BLUE MANOR

"What are you doing?"* *Maria* asked, stopping the worker before he took off the big letter B from the gate. The remodel had just begun, and they had a hell of a long way to go, considering the company that agreed to do it wasn't from Blue Park and came at a high price. They had said they would not be working any time after the sun started to go down.

"You don't want to remove it? We can replace it with the letter L—"

"No." Maria shook her head. "I want to keep it the way it is."….

"It will be more cost effective to replace the flooring, Ms.

Caruso," the contractor informed her.

"No." Maria shook her head. "I want the original hardwood restored."….

"The crack in the water fountain is unfortunately apart of the foundation. It will need to be repl—"

"No." Maria shook her head. "I want it fixed."….

"Mommy! Daddy!"

Maria ran into the good-sized room that had been transformed into a playroom. "Where are you?"

Dominic ran into the room a moment later as she called out again, "Come here! Come here!"

Hearing her youngest daughter, they followed her voice to inside a closet.

"What is it—"

Maria's mouth dropped open.

"Look, Mommy!"

Seeing a little door cracked open, they watched their daughter push it back into the wall.

"Why don't you go find your uncle Matthias, sweetie," she told her.

Waiting for her to run off, Dominic and Maria stepped inside the closet. Kneeling down, they stared at the obvious crack in the wall.

"Do you remember this being here?" Maria asked. They had lived in this house for many years now and had checked every inch of it as it was remodeled, but Maria did not ever remember seeing this.

His brows furrowed as he pushed it back to crack it open. "No."

Slowly opening the tiny door, they both looked at each other again when they saw the old, heavy brown trunk that wasn't much bigger than the hidden room.

Dominic grabbed the handle and slid it out of the crawlspace. "Should we open it?"

Maria nodded. She had always felt the energy of places and homes and knew this one wanted her to open it.

Flipping the latch on one side, he then flipped the latch of the other and slowly lifted the top of the trunk.

"Holy shit ..." Dominic whispered.

Maria's eyes went wide at the sight. The amount of cash that rested inside was probably enough to pay back every cent she had spent on bringing the manor back to its former glory. It was as if the house itself was thanking her ... or the ...

A scream had them turning their heads to see a man who had been tatted hundreds of times over jump back ten feet. Matthias looked as if he had seen a ghost ... "*Aw, hell no!*"

MADE

The weight reminds me of …
what rests on my shoulders.

The warmth reminds me …
to Hell, I have been.

I was told the coat makes the man …

But what is it …
that Made you?

Sarah Brianne

Please, if you or someone you know ever needs help,
follow this link to get more information and help.
YOU ARE NOT ALONE.

www.victimsofcrime.org

www.ingramcontent.com/pod-product-compliance
Lightning Source LLC
Chambersburg PA
CBHW070306040726
47501CB00018B/53

* 9 7 8 1 9 4 6 0 6 7 1 7 3 *